5/09

O9-BTI-710

SEIZURE

A KURTZ AND BARENT MYSTERY

ALSO BY ROBERT I. KATZ

Edward Maret
Surgical Risk
The Anatomy Lesson

SEIZURE

A KURTZ AND BARENT MYSTERY

by

Robert I. Katz

Willowgate Press
East Setauket, NY

Seizure

A Kurtz and Barent Mystery

Copyright © 2009 by Robert I. Katz

Cover design by Steven A. Katz
Willowgate Logo © 2000 by Willowgate Press
All images not proprietary to Willowgate Press
Copyright © 2009 Clipart.com

This is a work of fiction. Any resemblance to any person, living or dead, is strictly coincidental.

All rights reserved, including the right to reproduce this book, or portions thereof, in any form, without written permission except in the case of brief quotations embodied in critical articles or reviews.

Willowgate Press
PMB# 86
248 Route 25A
East Setauket, NY 11733
http://www.willowgatepress.com

Printed in the United States of America
ISBN: 978-1-930008-12-0

To Lynn

Chapter 1

It had been raining steadily for most of the day, turning into an intermittent gusting drizzle around sunset, but those inside the operating room were barely aware of it. The operating room, as always, was cool, dry and brightly lit, a perfect artificial environment.

"Give me a tie," Kurtz said.

The nurse handed him a strand of double-0 chromic and Kurtz wrapped it around the serosa at the base of the clamp, knotted it three times and cinched the knot down tight. Adler released the clamp and the two men stared at the wound for a second. No blood.

Kurtz was in a bad mood. He had woken up in the morning feeling groggy, having gone to a boring but obligatory hospital fund-raiser the night before. Now it was almost midnight and he had been operating on and off since eight in the morning. You had days like this, days when disaster followed disaster and you barely had time to think or even catch your breath before you were cutting into the next bleeding victim. Not many, thank God.

The first had been a kid hit by a car, a nameless John Doe, eleven years old and basically dead before they even got him on the table. They had barely begun to operate before the kid went into slow V-tach from lack of blood to the heart. Kurtz had opened him up and tied off the blood supply to his ruptured left kidney but there hadn't been much he could do about the shattered liver except pack the wound and close. It hadn't helped. The kid was dead.

The next one was a jumper. She had a long medical history, most of it centered around trauma inflicted by her abusive boyfriend. Amazing that she had never left him, Kurtz thought. This time she had jumped out of a fifth story window because her boyfriend had gone off to California for the weekend with another woman. Her name was Kimberley Morgan and she was young, pretty and twenty-four, a pretty young woman with her whole life ahead of her. Except that as it turned out, her whole life was behind her because she, too, never got off the table. What happened exactly was uncertain. She had two broken femurs and a ruptured spleen. After Kurtz finished with the spleen, the orthopods were supposed to come in and pin the legs. Unfortunately, while Kurtz and the residents were closing the abdomen, the patient's oxygen saturation fell to zero and she promptly arrested. Again, they ran a code and again, the patient died. Probably a fatty embolus. It wasn't uncommon with broken femurs.

Kurtz had never before lost two patients in a single day.

By now, Kurtz was working on auto-pilot, too tired to think straight but thankfully barely needing to. The latest operation—a sub-total gastrectomy for a bleeding stomach ulcer—was one he had performed a hundred times before and this patient wasn't even dying. Hooray.

Even Adler, the Chief Resident, usually irrepressible, seemed wilted. The only one who seemed to be enjoying himself was the intern, Rodriguez. Rodriguez had just returned from a week's vacation and was comparatively well-rested. Kurtz tied off another bleeder and Rodriguez clipped the ends of the chromic.

Adler sighed and Kurtz grinned tiredly beneath his mask.

Adler's beeper went off. They all stared at it. The beeper was sitting on a small shelf beneath the clock on the opposite side of the OR.

Wordlessly, the scrub nurse went over and pressed a button on the top of the beeper, then squinted down at the number displayed in the tiny screen. "It's the ER," she said.

Adler sighed again.

Not another one, Kurtz thought, and glanced at the clock. "Rodriguez and I can finish closing," he said. "Why don't you go and see what they want."

"Sure," Adler said, and began to take off his gloves.

From the main desk of the Emergency Room, Adler could clearly see the remnants of the storm outside. He could even hear it. Rain pelted against the thick glass doors and the wind made them vibrate. Sheets of old newspaper, empty plastic bags and other bits of garbage too small to make out flew by, briefly lit by the lights in the parking lot, and then vanished.

An ambulance stood backed up against the curb, a ramp leading down from the opened interior to the sidewalk. The ambulance was empty but the paramedics had evidently been in too much of a hurry to close the doors.

A lot of noise was coming from Room 1. Adler walked down the hall and peered in. A crowd of people dressed in scrubs milled about the table. From somewhere inside the crowd, a voice was counting, "One and two and three and four and five. One and two and three and four and five…"

Adler knew what that meant. Whoever was speaking was also pumping on somebody's chest. After each five, somebody else was breathing for the patient.

Adler went up to the head of the table. A respiratory therapist was squeezing an Ambu bag, the clear plastic mask covering the mouth and nose of a little old lady. The lady was obviously dead but since they were doing CPR, perhaps not irreversibly dead. An ER doc named Carrie Owens, small, blond and good looking, was running the code.

"What can I do for you?" Adler asked.

"We can't get a tube in," Carrie said. "She needs a trach."

The code had evidently been going on for quite some time. The patient's stomach was swollen with air. This always happened with mask ventilation. You could squeeze air into the lungs through the nose and mouth but some of it went into the stomach as well. The stomach blew up like a balloon and put pressure on the contents of the chest, making it harder and harder to ventilate. And sooner or later, the pressure got too high and the air surged back up the esophagus, usually bringing stomach contents with it, the main component of which (aside from whatever the patient might have eaten lately) was hydrochloric acid. At least a portion of this would always go down the trachea. If the patient didn't then drown outright, she would wind up with aspiration pneumonia and probably die a few days later as her lungs rotted away.

"Has Anesthesia tried?"

A tall young man dressed in green scrubs and wearing a blue bouffant OR cap said, "I tried. She's got a receding chin and bad arthritis. I can barely open her mouth."

"Okay," Adler said. "Let me get up there."

A permanent tracheostomy required an incision in the neck below the cricoid cartilage. Sometimes you had to peel back a portion of the thyroid gland, which was highly vascular and would bleed if you accidentally cut it. You then cut through the tracheal rings, inserted the trach tube and sutured it down; but with the patient bouncing up and down on the table from all the pumping on her chest and with the respiratory therapist's hands in the way, a formal trach, in Adler's opinion, was not the wisest choice.

A nurse had opened a trach set on a stand and brought it up by the patient's head. The patient was a skinny little thing. You could practically see the anatomy. A cricothyroidotomy was not as stable as a formal trach. The structures were more delicate; sooner or later the tube would erode through the larynx but if the patient lived they could always revise it later and in an emergency, a cricothyroidotomy was the quickest, easiest way to get a secure airway. Adler picked up a number fifteen scalpel and slit the cricothyroid membrane, inserted a pair of clamps between the cricoid and the thyroid cartilage, spread the incision, picked up a 6.0 trach tube from the tray and popped it in. Instead of suturing it, he picked up some umbilical tape (Adler had always wondered why they called it 'tape.' The stuff looked like a pair of shoelaces.), inserted it through the openings in the flange around the trach tube and tied it around the patient's neck. The respiratory therapist took the mask off the Ambu bag, connected the bag to the trach tube and continued to ventilate the patient. "Thanks," he said.

Adler absently nodded. The patient seemed to have an intermittent rhythm but was wandering in and out of v-fib. Probably secondary to an MI. That was how most heart attack victims died—an irreversible arrhythmia.

At that moment, the patient's body grew rigid and began to tremble, then shake. Her shoulders jerked back and forth, her neck arched and her fingers clenched into claws. Adler shook his head. "She's seizing," he said. Lack of oxygen to the brain often did that.

"Give me five of midazolam," Carrie Owens said.

A nurse handed Carrie a syringe. Carrie inserted the needle into the IV line, injected the liquid and turned the flow up high. A few moments later, the patient gave a final shudder and grew limp.

The monitor screen still showed v-fib.

"Get back," Carrie Owens said loudly. The man who was pumping stopped and moved away from the metal table. The crowd hastily moved off a discreet two inches. Only the respiratory therapist stayed where he was, since the Ambu bag was made out of plastic and rubber and would not conduct. Carrie put two paddles on the patient's chest and pressed a button. There was a snapping sound and the patient bounced about six inches into the air.

For a moment the EKG screen showed only a flat line. Then a lone heartbeat wandered through, then another. "Give her some more lidocaine," Carrie said. "A hundred milligrams. And a milligram of atropine." A nurse injected two syringes full of clear fluid into the patient's IV line. The heart rate picked up. The guy who had been pumping on the chest, presumably a resident, looked at Carrie uncertainly.

"Is there a pulse?" Carrie asked.

One of the nurses had her hand on the patient's groin, where the femoral artery could be palpated. "I think so," she said.

The patient's heart rate seemed to have stabilized at around eighty. "You think so," Carrie said.

"She's got a pulse," the nurse said.

Carrie put her own gloved hand on the patient's neck and pressed down lightly on the carotid. Slowly, she nodded. "Okay," she said. "Let's get her up to CCU."

A save, Adler thought. For now. Maybe. If she wasn't brain dead and she didn't decide to fibrillate again and if what was left of her heart muscle didn't poop out completely in the next few days.

"See you later," Adler said.

Carrie briefly glanced at him. "Thanks," she said.

She had read about things like this but she had never dreamed that it would happen to her. She knew that she was dying, her body flaccid and unresponsive on the cold, metal table but she was totally aware of her surroundings. There was no pain. She floated, serene and invisible, above the chaos and viewed it all, in stark, minute detail, as if some stranger were dying on the metal table, not herself.

Terrible, she thought, just terrible. All this effort. In a way, she was grateful. She had been feeling poorly ever since the dinner party last night. She didn't get out too often. It should have been exciting but something about it…so many things seemed to disturb her these days. Little things, usually. The faces of people she had never met seemed to contain hints of memory, clues to a past that was seventy years behind her and long since forgotten. It was absurd, but then, growing old was always absurd. There had been one young lady in particular, a pretty young woman with light brown hair. She had come up to them at the party. Her name had been Regina Cole. "I'm the Associate Director of Human Resources," Regina Cole had said. "I wanted to meet you." She had looked back and forth between Vincent and herself, smiling. "I wanted to thank you for your donation to the children's wing. It was very generous."

She had been perfectly polite but something about Regina Cole disturbed her—frightened her, even—something in the smile, in the level, intent gaze. Vincent had found the young woman charming but she had been unable to get that disturbing smile out of her mind. She had difficulty sleeping and once she had finally drifted off, her sleep had been troubled by restless dreams. Then, when it was almost dawn, she had awakened with a pain in her chest, a pain which she foolishly had tried to ignore, a pain which had grown steadily worse throughout the day. And now here she was.

All this effort. Ridiculous.

After a little while, she began to lose interest in what they were doing to the decrepit old body. Why, this is fun, she thought. Her awareness floated above the table and the people milling about the room. It was just like flying. She smiled to herself. Seventy years ago, when she was just a little girl, she had once jumped off the roof of her house, flapping her arms, willing herself into the air. She had been so sure it would work, but of course it hadn't. She had fallen to the gravel and broken a leg and the servants had been very cross with her.

But now she could fly. She really could. All it took was the thought. The cabinets around the room were filled with all sorts of exotic things, syringes and medications and tapes and clamps and scalpels and others she couldn't recognize. She peered inside and examined them all but soon lost interest.

If she listened, she could hear voices coming from outside the room. Was it possible? Why not? She concentrated and found herself floating down the hallway, past the old-fashioned windows, past a wooden door that led out to the street. Wonderful! She came to a stairwell and floated up. There were patients here, and nurses and orderlies and a few doctors talking together in hushed voices.

The young man who had put the tube in her throat, the young surgeon, was walking near the end of the hallway. Curious, she followed him, floating invisibly above his head. The young man came to a doorway and knocked. He listened for a moment but heard no answer. He nodded slowly to himself and gave a little smile, then he walked on down the hall, his hands in his pockets, soundlessly whistling.

Curious, she floated inside. It was a bedroom. A woman was lying on the bed. The woman was naked. Her body was young and slim and firm, her face mottled and red. Her eyes were bloodshot and staring. Her mouth was open, the tongue swollen and protruding to the side. Blue and purple bruises circled her neck.

She recognized her at once, without surprise, as if she had somehow known what she would find in this room. The young woman lying dead and naked on the bed was Regina Cole.

Chapter 2

"It seems, Doctor Adler, that you have become involved in a homicide."

"I have?" Adler reached up a hand and scratched his head. "Whose homicide?"

Brody looked at him, gave a knowing smile and nodded his head. "For the moment, I prefer not to say. Why don't you sit down and tell us about it?"

Adler scratched his head again. Sean Brody was the Chairman of the Department of Surgery. He was a good surgeon, a good administrator and a good teacher but he was known to have a morbid sense of humor. He sat on the other side of his desk with a thin smile on his face. Richard Kurtz sat across from the desk, looking at Brody with glum disapproval. "I don't think you should be joking about this," Kurtz said.

Brody raised an eyebrow and gave Kurtz a wolfish grin. "I've asked Doctor Kurtz to be here today because I wanted a witness. This is a very serious business, very serious indeed. You have the makings of a talented surgeon but talent in the OR is no excuse for criminal behavior. No excuse at all. We can't have murder. Murder is bad for the profession, bad for the image, bad for everyone concerned. Why did you do it? You might as well confess."

"I really have no idea," Adler said. He sat down in a chair and glanced at Kurtz. "My mind is a blank."

"A random killing?" Brody made a regretful clucking sound. "Let me warn you, young man, the insanity defense rarely works these days. Juries have grown more cynical. I suggest you save all of us a lot of trouble and simply admit to your crimes. I doubt this was the first. Then we can kick you out of the program, quietly commit you to an institution upstate, sweep the whole thing under the rug and get on with the serious business of saving lives."

"Cut it out, Sean, huh?" Kurtz said.

"You," Brody said, "have no sense of humor."

"It's not that funny."

"What are you talking about, anyway?" asked Adler.

Brody sighed and turned to Kurtz. "Why don't you tell him?"

Kurtz cleared his throat and looked briefly embarrassed. "The lady that you trached last night, the one who was arresting in the ER?"

Adler just looked at him.

"She's doing quite well. Her name is Eleanor Herbert. Her brother is on the Board of Trustees of the hospital. Her family have been benefactors of the place for almost a century. It seems that while she was arresting, she had an out-of-body experience. She claims that she followed you up the stairs where you knocked on a door. You received no answer. You continued down the hallway. Eleanor Herbert then entered the room and found a young woman lying on a bed, strangled."

"I did?" Adler blinked back and forth between Kurtz' face and Brody's.

"So she says."

"Which young woman?"

Kurtz glanced at Brody. "The Associate Director of Human Resources. Her name is Regina Cole."

"Damn." A meditative look crept across Adler's face. "I thought I detected a faint spectral presence hovering over me." He shook his head regretfully. "I should have realized. What a fool I've been."

"Then you admit it?" Brody asked.

"You've got me," Adler said. He held out his hands, the wrists close together. "Put on the cuffs. I'll go quietly."

"Doctor Adler," Brody said with relish, "despite my attempts at levity,"—he eyed Kurtz—"misguided though they might be, I'm afraid that this is not a joke. Accusations of murder are to be taken seriously, particularly when they are made by major contributors and members of the Board of Trustees."

"Okay," Adler said. "I'm serious. What do you want me to do?"

Kurtz shook his head and sighed.

"Nothing," Brody said, his face suddenly tired. "We're just telling you. The woman is obviously a lunatic, but she's a lunatic who's making some serious accusations. If she persists in her delusion, we're going to have to call in the police, if only to satisfy her family."

"In which case," Adler said, "I'll probably sue all of you for slander, discrimination, and everything else my lawyer can think of."

Brody puffed out his cheeks and grimaced faintly. "Hopefully, it won't come to that."

"Don't let it." Adler said. He looked annoyed. He frowned, first at Brody, then at Kurtz. "Jeez, we're talking about my career here. Has anybody turned up missing?"

"Yes," Brody said. "One person has. The Associate Director of Human Resources." He grinned wanly. "She missed her shift and didn't call in."

"No shit," Adler said.

"So tell me about Adler."

Lew Barent was a cop. He was also a good friend of Kurtz. The two men were sitting in a restaurant not far from Easton. Kurtz had given Barent a call and invited him to lunch.

"Not much to tell. He's a chief resident in surgery, good hands, nice guy, conceited—but then, most of them are."

Barent took a bite out of his hamburger and chewed. "Family?" he asked.

Kurtz poured himself a glass of Coke from a small pitcher while he thought about the question. Kurtz was annoyed at himself. The last thing he wanted to do was stir up a hornet's nest but Regina Cole was still missing. "His parents live in Summit, New Jersey. His father owns a car dealership. His mother's a housewife."

"An obvious criminal background."

Kurtz grunted.

"The old lady, she says she saw him knock on the door. She didn't actually see him do it?"

"No. she says that he nodded his head and smiled, like he knew what was in there."

Barent looked skeptical. "Most of the time, you've got a body, your problem is finding a witness. This time, you've got a witness but no body."

"Some witness. The whole thing is nutty. She admits that she was nowhere near the murder that she claims to have seen and all the objective evidence says she was unconscious the whole time."

"Any history of irregular behavior?"

"I don't know."

"So maybe she's always been a nut and maybe what she's been through has driven her over the deep end."

"It's a nutty story. We're supposed to convict a man of murder because of some old lady's mystical adventure?"

"Don't jump to conclusions. You said she claimed to see a body. She didn't see anybody kill her. The old lady might believe what she's saying but that doesn't mean we have to. And it certainly doesn't mean that she actually saw what she thinks she saw. What can you tell me about out-of-body experiences? Is there anything to them? Medically?"

Kurtz sipped his Coke and ate a couple of fries before answering. "They're fairly common among people who've had close escapes from death. About ten per-cent of CPR survivors report having had them. The same with serious car-crash victims, people who've fallen from tall buildings and survived…you get the picture."

Barent nodded.

"The stories are quite similar. There's almost always the feeling of floating, as if they're looking down on their own body. They can see everything that's going on around them. Some have accurately reported on the contents of cabinets that they couldn't possibly have seen from where their body was lying. Sometimes they've even been aware of things going on in other rooms. Almost always they report a sort of hovering light which they feel they have to go to. Many of them claim a feeling of disappointment when their resuscitation is successful. They feel as if they're being pulled back into their bodies and they don't want to go back. They're drawn by the light. That's the name of a popular book on the subject, by the way, *Drawn by the Light*."

"It sounds as if you think there's something to it."

"Do I?" It was another gloomy day, Kurtz noted. A thin drizzle splattered against the window, typical for this time of year. March was lurching creakily toward springtime and Kurtz, like most New Yorkers, was sick of it already. He wanted some sunshine. "Most of the stories have turned out to be untrue. They saw somebody next to their stretcher or walking down the street and they just weren't there. They saw something in the room, maybe a chair, a coat rack, a pair of scissors, anything at all—and there was no such thing. We're talking about people who are dying. Their brains aren't getting a lot of oxygen and they don't function the way they're supposed to. These are not stories that can be regarded as reliable."

"But sometimes they turn out to be true."

"Yes."

"Not a lot of evidence," said Barent.

"I agree."

"And Regina Cole is still missing."

"Yup."

"What's happened with Adler?"

"Nothing. But if Regina Cole doesn't turn up soon, the administration is going to have to go to the police, officially. None of this is going to do Adler's reputation any good."

"Has anybody contacted the girl's family?"

"Somebody in administration put in a discreet phone call. Her mother is dead. Her father lives on Long Island. He hasn't seen her or heard from her in a couple of weeks, which apparently isn't unusual."

"Boyfriends?"

"Nobody knows."

"That's unusual. In this day and age, your co-workers almost always know more about you than your family does. You spend more time with them."

"She kept to herself, apparently."

"And if Eleanor Herbert persists in her delusion, the Board might insist on putting young Doctor Adler on suspension."

"That's what Brody is afraid of."

"I wish I had some advice for you." Barent chewed stolidly on his hamburger. "As you say, there's not much evidence for anything. Regina Cole will probably turn up. If she doesn't, then we'll have to be called in but even then, nobody is going to arrest Adler, not on the basis of a story like this. In my opinion, the whole thing is going to blow over."

"I hope so," Kurtz said.

"Well, we'll soon know." Barent rose to his feet and began to put on his coat. "Thanks for the lunch."

Kurtz nodded gloomily. "Sure," he said.

Chapter 3

Kurtz had his own reasons to be down on the legal system. They say a surgeon hasn't really arrived until he's been sued at least once. Kurtz, after seven years in practice, had finally arrived. The lawyer appointed by the insurance company was named Sallie Wilson. She was a small redhead, perky and not at all reassuring. She sat in the chair across from Kurtz' desk with her legs folded primly beneath her.

"Now, Doctor Kurtz," she said with a smile, "I can understand what you're feeling, but we're just going to have to deal with the situation as it develops."

"They're crazy," Kurtz declared.

"I know they are," she said sympathetically. "That's frequently the case."

"Then why do I have to go through with this?"

Ricardo Gomez had been a postal worker. He had come into the Emergency Room one night complaining of abdominal pain centered in the right lower quadrant. Kurtz had suspected appendicitis and recommended surgery. Gomez had refused Kurtz' advice and gone home. He came back three nights later, semi-conscious and septic, his blood pressure barely perceptible. They had rushed him into surgery and found necrotic bowel from a strangulated omental hernia. Two days later, despite antibiotics, massive transfusions and life-support, Gomez had died of irreversible sepsis and disseminated intravascular coagulation. Kurtz was now being sued for having missed the diagnosis.

"It's a principle of the American legal system," Sallie Wilson said, "that anybody can sue anybody for anything at any time."

"But I didn't do anything wrong."

"I understand that, which is why the case is not likely to go anywhere."

The case had already gone further than most such cases. Seventy per-cent of professional liability suits were dropped before trial. This case had already gone through deposition, a humiliating process where the opposing lawyer, a fat slug named Strub, had done his best to impugn Kurtz' education, morals, judgment and professional qualifications. Kurtz had had to restrain himself from punching the little fuck. So far, despite Sally Wilson's lukewarm reassurances, the family of Ricardo Gomez had refused to give up.

"Not *likely* to go anywhere?"

Again, the sympathetic smile. "I have every hope that the case will still be dropped, or at least settled for a nominal sum."

Of course, Kurtz had missed the diagnosis, but that was irrelevant. The patient's symptoms had been most consistent with appendicitis and Kurtz had recommended surgery. If the idiot had consented to be operated upon when he should have, then the correct diagnosis would have been discovered as soon as they opened him up—as it had been three days later. His bowel wouldn't have infarcted, he wouldn't have gotten septic and he wouldn't have died. It was his own stupid fault.

Kurtz stared at her. "It won't be settled, not for any sum at all."

Sallie Wilson looked worried but she had the grace to remain silent.

"Do you understand?" Kurtz said.

Sallie Wilson gave a disapproving sigh. "If that's the way you want it, you do have the right to refuse a settlement."

"That is definitely the way that I want it."

"In any case, the trial is scheduled to begin next Wednesday."

"Don't worry," Kurtz said. "I'll be there."

"Eleanor, *please.*"

Vincent Herbert looked tired. He also looked harried, which did not surprise Eleanor Herbert but did annoy her. "You're not taking me seriously," she complained.

"I am taking you seriously," he said. "Your story is another matter."

"I saw what I saw."

"Late at night when we're dreaming, we also see what we see, but our dreams are not real."

"This wasn't a dream," Eleanor insisted. She was not in a good mood. Eleanor Herbert had a lot of money. People with a lot of money are not used to having their opinions ignored. Eleanor Herbert had reluctantly become accustomed to feeling physically helpless as age and infirmity had stolen her former abilities. She resented being ignored, even by (especially by) her older brother, who despite his years, was active, vigorous and healthy. Also, she was still weak. Probably drugged, she thought grumpily, and her throat hurt. They had pulled the trach tube the day before and stitched up the hole in her neck but the ache was a constant reminder.

"No?" Vincent grinned wanly and allowed his eyes to drift around the room.

Eleanor felt her heart give a little lurch in her chest. Above her head, the ECG monitor showed an aberrant beat and then a pause. Calm down, she told herself. She drew a deep breath. "Have they searched the place?" she asked.

Her brother's eyes drifted back to her face. "Who? Searched what place?"

She almost gritted her teeth in frustration. Calm…stay calm. "Hospital security. The police. Anybody. Have they searched the hospital?"

"For the missing woman?"

This time, she did grit her teeth. "Of course, for the missing woman." On the ECG, there was another aberrant beat and another pause. She ignored it.

Vincent sighed. "Yes, actually. They have searched the place. I felt like a fool but I insisted. They discovered nothing."

"But the woman is still missing."

Vincent sighed again. "Yes. The woman is still missing."

Eleanor nodded triumphantly and settled back into her pillows. "Have them search again," she said. She spread the blanket across her lap and smoothed it down with her fingers. "Have them search until they find her."

"*Yaaaaah!*"

Kurtz hated it when they did that. The scream was expected and strictly by the book but it sounded so corny. Yell, scream, distract the opponent. Well, it *didn't* distract them, not unless they were rank beginners. It was Friday night. Kurtz had had a tough week and didn't feel like listening to any screams at the moment.

His opponent was a kid about ten years younger than Kurtz. The kid had a reputation for being tough. The reputation, Kurtz knew, was deserved. The kid was also cocky, which he would grow out of or get his head beat in until his brains turned to mush, because at this level of competition, everybody was good and nobody was impressed by a hot-dog. The kid turned, a beautifully fluid motion except that he seemed to be paying more attention to the audience than to Kurtz. Kurtz moved his head back a fraction. The kid's foot whizzed by his nose. Kurtz stepped in, kicked the kid's supporting leg out from beneath him and stepped back as the kid fell heavily to the mat.

"Point," the referee said.

The kid got up slowly, giving Kurtz a hurt look, as if what had just happened was somehow not in the script.

Kurtz sighed.

The sigh seemed to annoy the kid. His face turned bright red. He gave another scream and came in, his arms cartwheeling and his body wide-open. Jerk. Kurtz spun. His lead foot connected with the kid's belly. The kick had all of Kurtz' weight behind it and the kid dropped to the floor, clutching his abdomen and groaning.

"Point and match," the referee said.

The kid's breath whistled in and out. Kurtz was momentarily concerned for him but after a few moments he managed to climb back to his feet. He kept his head down as he and Kurtz bowed to each other, then staggered out of the ring into the waiting arms of a bewildered looking blonde.

Kurtz' own blonde looked amused. She was sitting in the bleachers, next to David Chao and Carrie Owens. "You're not going to get a swelled head, are you?" Lenore said. "I worry about that. You surgeons are a pretty self-satisfied bunch."

Kurtz had not fought competitively in over five years but he had recently been assaulted by a steroid freak with a black belt. Something about the experience had gotten him interested again.

"No," Kurtz said with a smug grin. "I'm not going to get a swelled head. A true master of the martial arts is always humble."

He sat down next to her. Lenore put her hands on either side of his chin, tilted his head back and forth and inspected his face. "Did he get you with that kick? I couldn't see. It was all too fast."

"No. The kid's a jerk. Maybe next time, he'll pay more attention to what he's doing."

"Hmmm…"

"You did good," David Chao said.

David was Kurtz' partner. He was also his sparring partner. One of the reasons Kurtz had picked him was David's interest in the martial arts.

"Well, I'm impressed," Carrie Owens said.

Kurtz gave a modest shrug. "Any of you want to stay? Or should we go get something to eat?"

Lenore glanced at her watch. It was almost eight o'clock. "I could eat," she said.

"It's over soon, anyway," David said. "The next bout is the last."

"I haven't had dinner," said Carrie.

"That sounds like a consensus." Kurtz rose to his feet. "Let me go change."

Forty minutes later, they were sitting at a table at Spark's Steakhouse, still famous many years later for being the place where Paul Castellano was gunned down by the Gotti mob.

The food and the wine were both good and Kurtz felt himself beginning to unwind. It had been a ridiculous week. First the lawsuit and then the thing with Adler. The whole hospital knew about Regina Cole and Adler and Eleanor Herbert. Adler had done his best to ignore the situation and go on with his work but he was starting to look haggard. Of course, there was no reason for Kurtz to take any of this personally but he couldn't help it. Neither could anybody else. A hospital is like a little world and Adler and Kurtz were both a part of it. The world had been thrown out of kilter and everybody was grumpy.

Kurtz was on his second cup of coffee when his beeper went off. He frowned at it. "Shit," he said.

"Ignore it," Lenore said. "You're not on call."

The number on the tiny screen was one that Kurtz recognized. A deep feeling of apprehension settled into him. Wordlessly, he unclipped his cell phone. Lenore shrugged and gave a little sigh.

He dialed. Lew Barent answered after the second ring. "Lew? It's Richard."

"Richard. Sorry to interrupt your evening but I thought you might like to know. We've found Regina Cole. She's dead. She's been strangled."

Chapter 4

"Where?" Kurtz asked.

It was Saturday afternoon. Lenore had gone to visit her parents up in the Bronx and Kurtz and Barent were alone in the apartment. Barent sat on the couch with a cup of coffee in his hand and a plate with two oatmeal cookies on the table in front of him. "Hidden in some woods next to a Seven-Eleven. New Hyde Park. She'd been dumped there."

"New Hyde Park is on Long Island."

Barent nodded. "She wasn't killed there. No sign of a struggle at the site. She was lying on her right side but the blood had pooled in the left side of the body and she'd been dead for at least a day."

"Who found her?"

"Some kids. Teenagers."

"What were they doing there?"

"They claim they were taking a short-cut home."

"Any reason to doubt them?"

Barent sipped his coffee, drew a handkerchief out of his pocket, gave a liquid cough and spat into the handkerchief. He moodily inspected what he'd deposited before folding the handkerchief and putting it back into his pocket.

"You really should stop smoking," Kurtz observed.

Barent looked at him stolidly. "For thirty years, everybody I know has been telling me to stop smoking. You know something? I don't want to stop smoking. I enjoy smoking."

Kurtz shrugged. "It's your funeral."

"Thanks. I appreciate that." Barent took another sip of coffee and nibbled on a cookie. "No," he said, "there's no reason to doubt their story. They're two ordinary kids. They live in the development behind the woods, get decent grades in school and have never been in trouble."

"Still…"

Barent smiled faintly and allowed his eyes to drift to the Hudson River clearly visible outside the window. He stared down at the water for a moment, then turned back to Kurtz. "We're investigating them. And their families, and the guy who owns the Seven-Eleven, and everybody who works there. We're not expecting much but we have to do it."

"If the body was dumped there, somebody may have seen something."

"This is true. What interests me more is the question of where she was for the past two days."

Kurtz nodded.

"She was last seen alive on Tuesday night, at a dinner for the hospital benefactors at the Waldorf."

"Really?" Kurtz frowned. "Lenore and I were there."

Barent gave him an evil grin. "So was Eleanor Herbert, with her brother. They met Regina Cole there, too."

"How did that happen?"

"She came up and introduced herself."

"Why?"

"She was one of the ones who organized the dinner. She was making the rounds, said she wanted to thank them personally for their support of the hospital."

"Sounds routine enough."

"It was, except for Eleanor Herbert's reaction. She said that Regina Cole disturbed her. She can't say why."

Kurtz puffed up his cheeks and gave a little snort. "A premonition, I suppose."

"You believe in premonitions?" Barent asked.

"Do you?"

Barent grunted and bit a corner off one cookie. His jaws worked as he chewed it.

"Who was Regina Cole with?" Kurtz asked.

"She went with a guy who works in finance at the hospital, name of Bill Jackson."

"Anything there?"

"I doubt it. Jackson is married but his wife had to go out of town unexpectedly to see a sick aunt. Seems Regina Cole had been planning on going with a boyfriend but they recently broke up. Jackson's wife knew about it."

"Does Jackson have an alibi for the next two days?"

"He does. His mother just turned sixty. The family was having a party for her Wednesday evening. They live in Chicago. Jackson caught a late flight out. His wife met him there."

"Maybe he strangled Regina Cole before catching his flight."

"No. Her roommate reports that she arrived home safe and sound."

"When did the roommate last see her?"

"That same evening. The roommate is a nurse at New York Hospital. She had to work the early shift Wednesday morning. Regina Cole's door was closed when she left in the morning. She never saw her again."

"How about Wednesday? Nobody noticed her missing?"

"She had a personal day. She'd arranged it the week before. Nobody thought anything of it. It was Thursday that she came up missing."

"But nobody saw her on Wednesday."

"Nobody that we know of."

"And Adler? How about him?"

Barent gave a little shrug. "We're taking him in for questioning."

"You've got no evidence."

"No," Barent said sourly, "what we've got is a sensation. The media will have a circus. We can't make anything stick against Adler, not on the basis of Eleanor Herbert's testimony, but we can't ignore it either. The press would crucify us."

"Poor Adler," Kurtz murmured.

Barent nodded. "You bet."

Adler was grim-faced and as silent as the situation would allow him. He glanced frequently at his lawyer. The lawyer was named Albert Raft, a tall, thin guy with a dignified pot-belly, a three piece suit and a tanned face. Raft was smiling, a relaxed, lawyerly smile, the smile of a man who was doing his job and doing it well but also the smile of a man who would be going home and sleeping soundly tonight no matter how things went with his client.

"So let's go over this again," said Barent. "You got beeped from the ER and then what?"

Adler glanced once again at Raft. The corner of his mouth twitched. He seemed about to say something, then thought better of it. "My client has been through this before," Raft said smoothly.

"I understand that," Barent said. "And now we're going to go through it again."

"What's the point?" Raft asked, and glanced at his watch.

The point was frustration, which Raft knew very well, frustration and inconsistency. You took a story and you tried to poke holes in it. You made the suspect go over it so many times he could recite it in his sleep and then you pounced on the parts that seemed just a little off (there were always parts that seemed just a little off). You delved and you poked and you prodded and maybe you would come up with something that truly didn't make sense and if you were able to do that, then maybe you had him. The problem with this approach was that anybody and everybody could be made to look guilty by it.

"Justice, Counselor," Barent said. "The point is justice." He gave Raft a toothy grin.

Raft audibly sniffed.

"So…" Barent said to Adler, "your beeper went off. Then what?"

"Richard told me to go answer it."

"Richard Kurtz?"

"Yes."

"Go on."

"I answered it. I walked out of the OR, took off my mask and cap, put on a white coat and went down to the ER."

"Why the white coat?"

"Hospital rules. You're allowed to wear surgical scrubs outside the OR but only if they're covered."

"How did you go?"

"You mean what route did I take?"

"Yes."

"The ER is on the ground floor. An ER has to be on the ground floor so that ambulances can drive up to it. The operating room at Easton is one floor above the ER. I took the stairway down. The stairway opens onto a main hallway which is about fifty feet from the ER entrance. I walked over to the ER, saw a commotion in the room near the back and went in."

"Who beeped you?"

"You mean who specifically made the call?"

"Yes."

"I have no idea."

The whole thing was bullshit. Adler did not kill Regina Cole. Eleanor Herbert was a lunatic with too much money and an overactive imagination. Unless, Barent reminded himself, Adler *had* killed Regina Cole, in which case Eleanor Herbert's psychic journey was either a miracle or a hell of a coincidence. Whatever it was, it wasn't evidence. On the other hand, Barent had no real suspects and so on the basis of simple arithmetic, Adler had as much of a chance of being the murderer as any of the other eighteen million people in the Metropolitan area. "So you walked in and saw the commotion…" Barent squinted his eyes at his notebook. "Who asked you to trach the patient?"

"Carrie Owens."

There were plenty of witnesses and no substantial disagreement about this part. "And after you trached the patient, then what?"

"I took the elevator up to the Fourth Floor."

"Why?"

"There's an automat on the Fourth Floor. I was hungry."

The cafeteria at Easton closed at 8:00 PM. "What did you get there?"

"A Kraft coffee cake, a container of milk and a package of M & M's."

"Regular or Peanut?"

"Almond," Adler said.

"Almond?"

Adler gave him a contemptuous look. "They make them with almonds now."

"I didn't know that."

Adler gave a little sniff and Barent barely suppressed a smile. "And then what?" he asked.

"I took the elevator back down to the OR."

"Did anybody see you?"

Adler shrugged. "I don't know. I wasn't exactly thinking about my alibi."

Albert Raft frowned. "My client doesn't mean that."

Adler gave a faint snort.

"I'll ask it again," Barent said. "Did you see anybody, and did anybody see you?"

"I don't know. I don't remember."

"Who is the first person that you do remember seeing?"

"Irene Rivera. She's one of the recovery room nurses."

"I thought you said you went to the OR."

"I poked my nose in to see if the case was still going on. It wasn't, so I went over to Recovery."

"And then what?"

"The patient was doing fine. It was Anesthesia's responsibility to watch him in Recovery. I went to bed."

"Was anybody else in the Recovery Room at that time?"

"No."

"Where was Doctor Kurtz and"—he glanced at the notebook—"Doctor Rodriguez?"

"I don't know. You'd have to ask them."

Barent already had. Rodriguez had gone up to the call rooms on the Eighteenth Floor and fallen asleep. He wasn't bothered for the remainder of the night. Kurtz had already left.

Barent gave Adler a long look and then shifted his gaze to Albert Raft. Raft smiled at him thinly.

"Go home," Barent said. "Don't leave town."

Chapter 5

"Notice the discrepancies?"

Harry Moran wore a high collar with a thin striped tie, a crisply starched white shirt and suspenders. His black shoes were polished and gleaming. He leaned back in his chair, put his feet up on the desk and stretched, at which the chair gave a protesting creak. "Sure," he said.

Barent blew a smoke ring up to the ceiling, where it slowly dispersed before drifting away. Moran sipped his coffee.

According to published statistics, crime in New York City was down. The number of murders was likely to fall below six hundred for the first time in twenty years. You couldn't tell it by Barent. He glanced at the newspaper scattered loosely across the desk. Page three documented a case of child abuse, an all too typical case. A woman had held her daughter in a tub of scalding water, ignoring the little girl's screams, for reasons that were not clear but centered around a cocaine addiction and a boyfriend who was fucking the woman's niece. The little girl was dead from third degree burns.

Page seven contained a luscious story about a woman named Astrid Fisher, a housewife from Queens, found naked in Central Park with tape across her mouth and about a hundred tiny knife wounds scattered all across her body. What had killed her was apparently a bullet to the lower abdomen. Her husband had been questioned but apparently was sincerely distraught and had a perfect alibi, having been at work during the time when the crime had taken place.

Page nine talked about an advertising executive named Paul Williams, who had had the bad luck to be strolling by as a couple of teenage gang members got into a gun fight over twenty bucks that they had just lifted from a little old lady. The teenagers had gotten away but Paul Williams was dead from a stray bullet to the head.

Oh, well. Just another day in the big city. Barent kept up with such incidents as a matter of professional interest but was glad that none of these crimes had taken place in his own precinct.

"Eleanor Herbert said there were old-fashioned windows, the pull-up kind with wooden slats. Easton's windows are triple pane and don't open at all. She also said there was a wooden door down the hallway from the ER. There isn't. She said Adler went up one flight of stairs to a patient unit. The only thing above the ER at Easton is the operating room. Eleanor Herbert is full of shit."

"So she's full of shit." Moran lit up a cigarette of his own and puffed the smoke out through his nose. "You're not surprised, are you?"

Regina Cole had, however, been strangled, just as Eleanor Herbert had said. There were distinct finger marks on Regina Cole's neck. It took strong hands to leave marks like that. The body was fully dressed in a blue business suit except that one shoe was missing and had not been discovered at the site. Autopsy had revealed small bruises around both nipples. Her stomach had contained the remains of a meal and some semen. There was no bruising around the mouth, which tended to indicate that the blow-job had been a friendly one, and there was no sperm in the vagina. Apparently, the guy had saved his load for the blow-job, unless he had used a condom. "Shit," Barent murmured.

Moran looked at him, curious.

"I hate coincidence," Barent said. "I don't believe in coincidence. Eleanor Herbert dreams she sees a woman being murdered and wouldn't you know it, the woman turns up murdered. Cutting through all the bullshit, what does that tell you?"

Moran blew a smoke ring of his own and happily watched it drift across the room. "Eleanor Herbert knows more than she's letting on." He sipped his coffee and took a bite out of a jelly donut and grinned at Barent. "Unless it's just coincidence."

"Yeah," Barent said morosely.

The Herbert mansion was in Rye, on a hill overlooking Long Island Sound. The building itself was brick, with five chimneys and a gabled roof. A neatly mowed lawn surrounded the house and a sandy beach sloped gently down to the water. Beyond the lawn stood a row of neatly pruned trees, oak and a few pines. A small dock with a thirty-five foot wooden Chris-Craft completed the picture.

"Nice," Moran said.

"The very rich are different from you and me, Harry."

"You bet they are. They have more money."

The door opened. An old guy dressed in a tuxedo, obviously a butler, with a scrawny neck and a bald head, stood looking at them impassively.

"Lew Barent and Harry Moran. We're here to see Mr. Herbert."

"Come in, please," the butler said. Barent had trouble repressing his grin. The butler looked like a caricature of Jeeves, the faithful family retainer. "Mr. Herbert is expecting you."

The foyer was covered in alternating black and white marble tile. A chandelier big enough and bright enough to light Carnegie Hall was hanging from the ceiling. The lobby opened onto an enormous living room furnished in Danish modern. The living room floor was oak, covered in rugs that Barent would have sworn were hand weaved and had to be worth a fortune. "Please follow me, sir," the butler said. He glanced at them from the corner of his eye. "You may call me Charles."

Not much better than Jeeves, Barent thought.

The house, from what they could see of it, did not look ancient. Apparently it had been renovated, perhaps more than once, sometime in the past. The ceilings were high, the walls painted in pastel blue and salmon pink and almond. There were skylights and sliding glass doors and windows opening onto the beach and the woods. Vincent Herbert must like color, Barent mused. A Miro hung under the chandelier, a Lee Krasner over the mantel in the living room.

Charles opened a door and beckoned to them with a nod of his head. They followed him and found themselves in a hallway containing a sculpture of a woman in flowing robes that appeared to be ancient Greek and about a dozen paintings, all portraits, at least three of which Barent thought he recognized. One was a man dressed in an old-fashioned frock coat and two were women in ball gowns. "I thought those were in museums," Barent said.

Charles barely smiled. "They're by John Singer Sargent. Mr. Herbert loaned them to the Met a few years ago."

The other paintings were members of the family, dating back for almost a century. None were recent. They were all young men, handsome and posed in pretty much the same way, standing against a dark background, wearing a suit, a tie and a wide smile. "This one is Mister Vincent," Charles said. He indicated a picture of a young man with glasses.

Next to the portrait of Vincent Herbert was a painting of another man dressed in almost identical clothes. This young man had a rakish smile and amused blue eyes. Barent thought that he looked somehow familiar. "Who is this?" he asked.

"That is Mister Vincent's brother, Joseph P. Herbert, Junior. He passed away many years ago."

The hallway gave a very different impression than the atrium foyer and the living room, which were full of air and light. This corridor was older, darker, sterner. The paintings hung over thick, flock wallpaper. The molding was cherry wood, dark and dully glowing in the pale light. Barent found the entire effect unpleasant. He felt as if the eyes of ancient Herberts were judging him and resenting his presence. "And this one?" Barent asked. He pointed to a man dressed in a business suit that looked almost modern, a man with tight lips and small, suspicious eyes.

"Garrison Herbert," Charles said. "Mister Vincent's oldest son."

Barent stared for a moment at Garrison Herbert. He had the impression that Garrison Herbert didn't like him. He chuckled. "Let's go on," he said.

Charles nodded and they continued to the end of the hallway, where Charles opened a polished wooden door, stood at attention and said, "Detectives Barent and Moran, sir."

Vincent Herbert looked up at them, smiling. "Thank you Charles. Come in, gentlemen. Please sit down."

Vincent Herbert's hair was thick and white, his fingers slender, his face wrinkled. His eyes were curious. He was sitting on a low, leather couch. A glass coffee table with polished steel legs sat in front of the couch, surrounded by three reclining chairs. The room was carpeted in off-white shag. Three of the walls were covered by sleek oak bookcases and cabinets. The remaining wall had a marble and granite fireplace and a painting above the mantel that looked like a Jackson Pollack. A gigantic HD-TV and two enormous speakers were set into one of the cabinets. Sunlight streamed in through skylights and casement windows. What appeared to be a martini sat at Vincent Herbert's side. "Would you care for something to drink?" he asked.

"No, thanks," Barent said. He sat down in one of the recliners and felt himself sinking into the cushion. He glanced at Moran, who was smiling sleepily at the decor. The very rich were different, Barent thought grumpily.

"Then what can I do for you?" Vincent Herbert asked.

"We have a few questions to ask that might help to clear things up."

"Things?"

"Regina Cole. The woman who was murdered...."

Vincent Herbert gave a tiny frown. "I wouldn't know anything about Regina Cole."

"Then you didn't know Regina Cole?"

Herbert shook his head. "No. We met her briefly the night before my sister had her heart attack. I had never seen her before that night."

"Did your sister know her?"

Herbert looked momentarily bewildered. "I don't see how. You'd have to ask her."

Barent stared at him. He said slowly, "You and your sister met Regina Cole at a party, and then the next day she had a vision where she thinks she sees Regina Cole's dead body, and then Regina Cole turns up murdered."

Vincent Herbert cleared his throat. His face was grim. He said nothing.

"Tell us about your sister," Barent said.

"Certainly." Herbert nodded abruptly and settled back into the couch. "What did you wish to know."

"This 'vision' that she had..."

"Yes. Of course."

"Was this the first time anything like that has happened?"

"Visions?" Herbert took a sip out of his martini. "Not visions, exactly." The corner of his mouth barely twitched. "My sister, however, has a long history of psychiatric..." His face grew thoughtful. He frowned at his drink and then gave a wry smile as if the truth were simply too ill-bred to bear. "Illness, I suppose would be too strong a word. Perhaps disturbance..." He smiled. "Yes," he said. "Psychiatric disturbance would describe it."

Barent glanced at Moran, who appeared to be almost asleep. "I'm afraid that the word 'disturbance' doesn't mean very much to me."

Herbert sipped his martini and settled himself more comfortably into the cushions. "It began many years ago, when my sister was a child, and continued, I suppose, until she was almost into her teens. Eleanor threw tantrums. She was subject to sudden and unexplainable rages. At the best of times, she was mulish, sullen and uncooperative." He shrugged.

Barent glanced at Moran. Moran was looking at Vincent Herbert, a soft, speculative look on his face.

"Why?" Barent asked.

"Why what?"

"Why was your sister 'sullen, mulish and uncooperative'? What caused her to throw these tantrums?"

"It wasn't only tantrums." Vincent Herbert smiled coolly. "Indeed no. She threw anything she could get her hands on. The household staff were scandalized. Eleanor's own maid was replaced on a regular basis. Not a one of them lasted more than a few months." .

"And how do you explain these tantrums?" Barent asked.

"I'm not a professional. As I said, 'mental disturbance' is the only way I can describe it."

"Did you ever seek professional help for her?"

"I? I was a young man myself at the time. I was not in a position to seek professional anything. My parents, however, did seek the advice of a number of psychiatrists—at least so far as I recall."

"And what did these psychiatrists say?"

Herbert shrugged and downed half of his martini. "I don't know. As I told you, I was young and rarely at home. I went to Milton, and then to Yale. My sister was considerably younger than I when these events took place. So far as I recall, my parents seemed to feel that I should be protected from unpleasant, possibly scandalous, realities. They rarely talked about Eleanor's problems in my presence."

"And so what happened?"

"Ultimately, Eleanor grew more tractable. I don't know why. Perhaps she simply grew up and grew out of it. Or perhaps one of the psychiatrists was able to help her." He shrugged.

"Do you think any of these psychiatrists would still be around?"

Herbert seemed surprised at the question. "Oh, I doubt it," he said. "It was fifty years ago." He looked momentarily thoughtful. "More than fifty, as a matter of fact, more than sixty." Herbert sighed. "Sixty years..." He looked at Barent and gave a sad smile. "Sixty years is a long time. A long time."

Sixty years was a very long time. Strange to think of Eleanor Herbert, the dignified little lady in the CCU as a tantrum throwing toddler. "Would you happen to remember the name of any of these psychiatrists?"

Herbert shrugged. "Sorry."

"And she never did it again?" Barent asked.

"Throw a tantrum?" Herbert smiled wryly and downed the last few drops of his martini. The olive was at the bottom of the glass, covered by a half melted ice cube.

Herbert frowned and swirled the glass. The ice cube tinkled to the side. Herbert gave a satisfied smile, tilted back the glass and ate the olive. He looked at Barent. "Oh, she always had a temper, but nothing like that." He gave a tiny shudder. "I still remember her screaming."

"What exactly was she screaming about?"

Vincent Herbert shrugged. "That I don't remember."

People didn't scream about nothing. "Would any of the servants that you had at that time still be alive?"

"Servants?" Vincent Herbert looked momentarily bewildered. "I don't really know. And what could you possibly hope to find out that would be relevant to Regina Cole's murder?"

A good question, Barent thought. "Probably nothing," he answered. "Still…"

Herbert shrugged his shoulders, drew a deep sigh and yawned. "I'm not a young man. I take a nap every afternoon about this time."

Barent rose to his feet. Moran followed. "Thank you," Barent said. "I hope you won't mind if we drop by again. We may have more questions for you later."

Herbert smiled slightly. "And if I do mind…?"

Barent said nothing and Herbert's smile widened. "Talk to Charles," he said. "He's been with me for forty years. He might have some information regarding the household staff, things that I wouldn't know."

"Thanks," Barent said.

Chapter 6

Barent spent the evening with a book and his own thoughts. Betty, who knew his moods well, puttered around the kitchen and let him alone. Absently, Barent appreciated that.

Charles had worked as a domestic since the age of twelve, first as a houseboy to the Crawleys, an old, established family on Long Island's Gold Coast. Charles' father had been a mechanic, servicing the Crawleys' fleet of automobiles, his mother, a maid. Charles had followed in the family footsteps, a gentleman's gentleman being the one goal he had always aspired to, but then when Charles was thirty-two, the Crawleys had fallen on hard times.

"They were kind enough to recommend me to their friends, the Herberts, whose own head man was preparing to retire. Mister Vincent offered me the position and I've been here ever since."

Charles, it turned out, was the garrulous sort once off duty. Moran and Barent sat around a table in the kitchen, sipping tea from cracked ceramic mugs, while Charles talked. The old guy must not get too much company, Barent thought.

"You must have seen *Upstairs, Downstairs*. A fabulous show, simply fabulous. A bit melodramatic, I suppose, but still, it captured the essence of the life perfectly."

The life. Some life. Barent must have let his doubts show on his face because Charles smiled. "Tell me," he said, "do you think that my work is unfulfilling?"

"To each his own, I guess," Barent said.

Charles looked at him from over the rim of his mug and wiggled a wise finger. "Oh, but you're wrong. It was a wonderful life. I married one of the maids, you see. Her name was Mary, an Irish girl. We had three children. My daughter is a congressional aide in Washington. My sons are both doctors." Charles suddenly sighed. "My wife passed away five years ago. Perhaps I should have retired but I wasn't ready to face a life of nothing to do. But don't delude yourself. Living in a place like this, the parties, the glamour, the elegance of it all. It was wonderful. I wouldn't have traded it for anything."

"But it wasn't your life," Barent said. "The Herberts are the one ones with the money, not you."

"Well…" Charles stifled a cough behind his fist and looked momentarily smug. "A position like mine carries very few expenses. Room and board were always included and the salary is really quite generous. I had the use of one of the cars whenever I needed it and when the family went away on vacation, most of the staff went along. The majority of my income went into the stock market. I think you'd find that I'm quite well off."

"I hadn't thought of that," Barent admitted.

"A gentleman's gentleman has an obligation to be a gentleman. I've done well. Looking back on my life, I wouldn't have done a thing differently. Not a thing." He looked like he meant it. Looking back on his own life, Barent thought there were quite a few things he might have done differently. Obviously, the life of a butler held possibilities he had not considered.

"Mr. Herbert told us that you had been with him for over forty years."

"That's correct."

"Then you must know the Herberts pretty well."

Charles smiled thinly. "I hope you're not going to ask me to betray the confidence of my employers. I couldn't do that."

Barent looked at him. "Mr. Herbert suggested that I speak with you. He didn't specify any topics that might be off-limits." None that the law would recognize, anyway. Butler-employer privilege was not a relationship protected by legal statute.

Charles looked doubtful. "You can ask your questions. I don't know that I'm going to answer them."

"Fine." Barent pulled out his notebook and opened it to a fresh page. "How old was Miss Herbert when you first arrived here?"

"Miss Eleanor would have been, oh, just about twenty-five or twenty-six, I think."

"What was she like, then?"

"Like?" The old man raised his brows.

"Mr. Herbert said that she was a difficult child. She was moody. She threw tantrums."

"That may have been true when she was very young," Charles said. "I do remember hearing something of the sort. It wasn't true by the time I arrived here. Miss Herbert was a lady, very proper, very dignified."

"Did she ever mistreat the staff?"

"Mistreat the staff? Never. What could have given you such an idea?"

"Mr. Herbert said that she went through maids like they were going out of style."

"He said that?" Charles pursed his lips and looked like a disapproving gnome. "I suppose he must have been referring to her early childhood. I saw no such behavior."

Barent looked down at his notebook. So far, the pages were blank. He sipped his tea, which was rapidly cooling. Barent usually drank coffee, but this stuff was pretty good. It had a rich, smoky taste. "What is this?"

"The tea?"

Barent nodded.

"Lapsang Souchong. I believe it's from India or Ceylon. It has a high creosote content, which gives it its flavor."

Creosote? Barent swirled it around the mug. "I don't drink a lot of tea," he said.

Charles shrugged.

"Did Miss Herbert ever marry?" Barent asked.

"Yes, she did." Charles paused, his cheeks puffed out. Barent let him think. "When she was twenty-six, she married a young man named William Renson. His family were major shareholders in Carnegie Steel."

"What happened?"

"She moved away. A few years later, her husband died; I believe in a boating accident. Miss Eleanor moved back here. I understand that she was not too fond of the Rensons."

"She never married again?"

"No."

"No children?"

"From what I recall, she had one miscarriage. There were no children."

"So her legal name is not Herbert, it's Renson?"

"I believe that's correct."

"How does she spend her time?"

"She gardens. Miss Herbert is a past president of the garden club. Her roses are famous. During the winter, she mostly reads."

"Does she see the family much?"

"Oh, yes. Miss Eleanor is extremely devoted to her family. They have a family dinner at least once a month. All the nieces and nephews come, with all their children, and sometimes there are guests."

"What sort of guests?"

"Oh, friends of the family. Anyone that they feel like bringing. The Herberts are generous. The Mayor was here quite often, the Governor more than once."

A normal enough life, Barent thought, for a billionaire. A little boring, maybe, but normal. "Did you ever see any erratic behavior on Miss Herbert's part?"

Charles looked at him suspiciously. "I don't know what you would characterize as erratic."

"Unstable. Violent. Suicidal. Irrational. Out of the ordinary."

"How many of us are really so ordinary?" Charles gave him a faint, sad smile. "After her husband died, Miss Herbert seemed depressed. She rarely came out of her rooms. She never smiled. This lasted for, oh…almost a year, I think."

"And then what?"

"Time passes. People change. She got over it."

"Did she ever see a psychiatrist during this time?"

Charles frowned. "I seem to recall that she saw a therapist. I don't remember the man's exact status, psychiatrist, psychologist, whatever." He shrugged. "He came here perhaps once a week for a period of a few months."

"Remember anything about him? His name? Where he lived?"

"No. I'm sorry."

"What did he look like?"

Charles squinted, his cheeks puffed up in thought. "He was a large man," he said. "I believe he had a beard."

Barent wrote *Large* and *Beard* in his notebook. "And when was this, so far as you remember?

"It must have been about 1965, maybe '66."

"Tell me about the rest of the family," Barent said.

"Mr. Herbert has two sons and a daughter. His daughter's name is Allison. She's married to a man named Gordon Donaldson, a lawyer. They live in Stamford, Connecticut. His older boy (though of course he's hardly a boy) is Garrison Herbert. You saw his portrait in the hallway. Garrison is in the business, Chief Executive Officer, now that Mister Vincent is retired. Mister Vincent's younger son, Ronnie, entered the priesthood. He's a missionary in South America."

The business...the Herbert business was real estate development, like Donald Trump and Harry Helmsley. "Are the Herberts Catholic?"

"No. They're Episcopalian." Charles raised both eyebrows and stared into his teacup. "Ronald converted to Catholicism. The family was not pleased."

"I see. How often does he get home?"

"Once or twice a year. The last time was before Christmas but I understand he'll be in town in a few days."

"Mister Herbert is a widower?"

"Yes. His wife died ten years ago."

"How about grandchildren?"

"Allison has four children and Gary has five."

"Any of them in the business?"

"They're mostly too young for that, but Gary's oldest son, Jerome, is in-house counsel."

"Who lives here, besides Vincent and Eleanor?"

"Only myself and one maid and a gardener named Bryant." Charles looked sad for a moment. "The house is very quiet these days. It didn't used to be that way."

"Barent looked at his notebook. Besides the names of the various Herberts, there wasn't much there. "Mister Herbert said that you might remember some of the staff who worked here when his sister was a young girl."

Charles looked surprised. "That was a long time ago."

Barent nodded.

"Well..." Charles tapped a finger thoughtfully on his mug. "There was Mrs. Winter, the chief maid. She was old when I first arrived here. She retired a few years later but I'm sure she's passed away by now. She would be well over a hundred."

"That won't help me. I need people I can talk to."

"Well, there was John Morris, one of the gardeners; he was a young man when I arrived. He retired in the seventies, so far as I recall. Sara Hemings...Jason Lester...

Vivian Moore…there was one more….” He snapped his fingers. “Caroline Niles, that's it, one of the maids. All of them were in their twenties or early thirties when I first came here. They may still be alive, somewhere.”

“You've no idea where?”

“I'm afraid not. I haven't heard from any of them in years.”

That had been it, so far as Charles was concerned. Barent and Moran had stayed and chatted for a few more minutes and then excused themselves.

The next day had been spent making phone calls and following up leads. They had put in a computer search for all the people Charles had mentioned but all of them had moved out of New York after leaving the Herberts’ employ and so far, nothing much had come up.

Regina Cole had lived in an apartment on the West Side, in the Seventies. The apartment was expensive. She shared the costs with a roommate, a young woman named Barbara Wood. When Barent and Moran had first knocked on the door, Barbara Wood had demanded that they hold their badges up to the peephole before admitting them to the apartment. “Just a minute,” she said. It was more like five minutes. Then the door unlocked and Barbara Wood motioned them inside, looking dubious. “I called the Station House,” she said. “They vouched for you.”

Barent nodded, unsurprised. “Thanks for letting us in,” he said.

“So what's up?” Barbara Wood asked.

Barent drew a deep breath, steeling himself. Now comes the hard part, the part that he hated. But Barbara Wood knew without having to be told. Her face grew abruptly pale. “Something's happened, hasn't it? Is it Gina?” Her right hand crept up in front of her throat, as if shielding herself from the bad news.

“Why would you think so?” asked Barent.

“She hasn't been home in two days. I didn't know what to do. I was thinking of calling you, myself.”

“I'm afraid you're right. She's dead.”

Quietly, Barbara sat down on a couch and began to cry. Barent gave her a minute before saying, “I'm sorry to intrude on you at this time, Miss Wood, but we have some questions we have to ask you.”

“I'm sorry,” she said, dabbing at her eyes. “I understand.”

Barbara Wood answered everything without hesitation. In Barent's estimation, she was telling the truth. “We got along fine,” she said. “Gina was a good roommate. She washed her dishes and did her part of the chores and she didn't play loud music. She was okay.”

“Did she have any enemies that you knew of?”

“Enemies?” Barbara Wood looked bewildered. “What sort of enemies?”

“Anybody who didn't like her, I mean.”

“No, not at all.” Barbara shook her head decisively. “Who would dislike Gina?”

“That's what I'm trying to find out,” Barent said patiently.

"No," Barbara Wood said again. "She didn't have any enemies."

Well, somebody killed her, Barent thought, but he didn't say it. "Was she seeing anybody? Any men?"

"She had a boyfriend but she dumped him." Barbara Wood shrugged. "His name was Mark Woodson."

"Why did she dump him?"

"I don't know, exactly. She wouldn't talk about it. I wasn't too surprised, though. I didn't like the guy much." She shrugged again. "These things happen."

"Why didn't you like him?"

"The usual reason. He was good-looking and smart and he knew it, one of these guys who thinks the world revolves around him." She looked at Moran and puffed up her cheeks. "Like most men," she said.

Barent moodily looked at her. These things did happen, and sometimes people got killed over them. "What does Mark Woodson do?" he asked.

"I think he's a banker."

"You're not sure?"

"They spent most of their time by themselves."

"Do you have an address for Mark Woodson?"

She frowned. "Just a second." She rose to her feet, went into a bedroom and came back a few seconds later with a business card, which she handed to Barent. "It was in her desk," Barbara Wood said.

Barent looked at the card, holding it gingerly by the edges. It read, *Mark Woodson, Investment Advisor, Gordon and Hill*. Probably a euphemism for stockbroker, Barent thought. The address was in mid-town. He slipped the card into a white envelope and sealed the envelope.

"Anybody more recent than Mark Woodson?" Barent asked.

She shrugged. "I don't know."

"If there had been, wouldn't she have told you?"

Barbara Wood looked doubtful. "You want to get along with a roommate, you don't pry into their business. Probably she would have talked about it, sooner or later."

"You've been calling her Gina," Barent said.

"She thought Regina was too formal. Most of her friends called her Gina."

Barent looked toward the open door of the bedroom. "That's her bedroom?" he asked.

"Yes."

"I'll have to ask you not to go in there again, for a little while. We'll come by later with some of the lab people."

Barbara Wood smiled wanly. "Looking for clues?"

Barent nodded. "Yes."

"Sure," she said.

Mitchell Cole had driven in from Long Island to claim his daughter's body. Cole's wife had died almost ten years previous and Gina was an only child. Cole brought with him a list of relatives and friends, none of whom, so far as he was aware, had seen Gina since she had last visited home. Cole was typical for parents in this situation (Barent had seen more of them than he cared to think about), visibly distraught, his voice trembling, his eyes tearing. He answered his questions as best he could but he wasn't a lot of help.

"First my wife, now Gina. You didn't know Gina…" He looked at Barent, his jaw thrust out, something challenging in the way he said it.

"No," Barent said. "Of course not."

"She was a beautiful little girl. Beautiful. She liked to read. She liked to play with her dolls. She never gave us a moment's trouble. Not a moment." Cole shook his head. "I never thought I'd be alone again, not at my age. I figured a family… kids, grandkids. You know?"

"I know," Barent said gently. "I'm sorry, Mister Cole."

"I'm going down to Florida. I've planned it for a long time. I'm retired. No work, no family. That's what people do when they've got nothing left, move someplace else, sit around in the sun and try to convince themselves that they've got a brand new life." Cole shrugged. Then he said bitterly, "Gina finished college five years ago and moved to the city. I asked her not to go. Why would anyone want to live in a sewer like this?"

Barent decided to let this comment pass. "Did she keep in touch with any of her friends, would you know, Mr. Cole?"

"I have no idea."

"When did you see her last?"

"Christmas. She came out for the holiday."

"Did she see any of her friends at that time?

"Marci Howe, maybe." Cole shrugged. "Maybe Jennifer Linden." Both names were on the list, Barent noted.

"Do you know if she had a boyfriend?"

"I don't know. I think so. When I asked her she only smiled and wouldn't say anything. That worried me. Why wouldn't she want to talk about something like that?"

Offhand, Barent could think of a number of reasons, some of them good, some not so good. "She never mentioned a name?"

"No."

Barent nodded. There was no evidence that a boyfriend had done it, of course, but considering that the majority of murders were committed by acquaintances—usually close acquaintances—a boyfriend was a pretty good place to start.

"I'm sorry to have had to bother you," Barent said. He handed Cole a card. "If you think of anything else that might help, please give me a call."

Regina Cole's father took the card, turning it back and forth between his fingers as if it were some alien object. Then he shrugged and put it in his pocket. "Sure," he said, and after a few routine condolences, had taken his leave.

Not a lot of help, Barent thought. He sighed. The trouble was, he had plenty of names but no leads. Any of the names could turn into leads, but right now, the investigation was both tedious and frustrating. Tomorrow, he would spend most of the day on the phone, which was better than walking a beat but was likely to be time completely wasted. He sighed again and behind his back, Betty smiled.

Chapter 7

"How's the VIP?" Kurtz asked.

Monroe Forman was a cardiologist. As such, he was even more supercilious than the average internist, which was pretty damned supercilious. Internists took great pride in the fact that their specialty was cerebral, rather than merely technical (like surgery). Internists diagnosed. They read books and ordered tests and doled out medications and thought deep thoughts about the root causes of obscure disease. They didn't have to get their hands dirty (well, the occasional rectal exam, but you got used to that). Cardiologists regarded themselves as the most elite of internal medicine's subspecialists. They not only prescribed and diagnosed, they had their own list of technical procedures, ranging from the insertion of pulmonary artery catheters to stenting the coronary arteries to putting in pacemakers. Procedures being inherently more lucrative than reading and prescribing, cardiologists were an exceedingly self-satisfied bunch.

"She's doing well," Forman said. Forman was tall and thin and had a large, egg-shaped, almost bald skull, which he tried to hide by combing a few long strands of hair from the side of his head up and over the top. He looked at Kurtz over the edge of his glasses. "She'll be transferred to the floor later today."

"Has she had any more visions?"

"Visions?" Forman gave him a frigid smile. "Not that I'm aware of. If she has, she's keeping them to herself."

"Just as well," Kurtz said.

Forman nodded.

"Tell me, what is she like?"

Forman shrugged. "Peremptory."

Forman was pretty peremptory himself. Eleanor Herbert must be a real firebrand. "Mind if I stop in and talk to her?"

Forman looked at him suspiciously. "Don't get her upset."

"I'll try not to."

"Don't just try. If she has another heart attack, her brother and the Board will not be pleased."

"I understand."

Forman glanced at his watch, frowned and seemed to lose interest. "I have to be going," he announced. "I have a meeting."

"Nice talking to you," Kurtz said.

Forman nodded and walked off without a backward glance. Kurtz looked at the clock on the wall. It was twelve thirty five. At one fifteen, he had a hernia scheduled in the OR.

A tall man with broad shoulders and a barrel chest stood in the hallway outside the cardiac care unit. His light brown hair was touched with gray at the temples and pulled back in a pony tail. He was dressed in a blue suit. He looked at Kurtz with blank eyes as he walked past, then seemed to dismiss him from consideration.

Kurtz pressed a button on the wall and the doors of the cardiac care unit slid open. The hallway inside was lined with small rooms, individual but not private. The walls were glass, the patients and the monitors both visible from the nursing station in the center of the hallway. When a patient had to use the bedpan or otherwise needed a private moment, they drew a curtain across the wall but never, under any circumstances, was the monitor disconnected. People in the cardiac care unit tended to drop dead with sudden and alarming frequency.

"Miss Herbert?"

She was a small woman, evidently frail, with snow white hair and wrinkled skin. Her eyes, however, were sharp, bright and suspicious. Two men were with her, sitting to the left of the bed. One appeared to be in his mid-fifties, the other about twenty-five. Both wore conservative gray suits and they both looked up at Kurtz as he walked in.

"Yes?" Eleanor Herbert said.

"I'm Richard Kurtz. I'm one of the surgeons on staff."

The older of the two men rose to his feet and held out his hand. "Garrison Herbert," he said. He smiled slightly. "Eleanor's nephew. This is my son, Jerome."

Jerome Herbert nodded his head at Kurtz but stayed in his seat and said nothing.

Garrison Herbert had a bald, bullet-shaped head and a brush moustache. His son was slim, with blonde hair and arched brows over clear blue eyes. They both wore their suits as if they had been born in them.

"Nice to meet you," Kurtz said.

Garrison Herbert smiled tightly. Jerome crossed his legs, glanced at the clock on the wall and frowned.

"I'll come back later," Kurtz said hastily.

Jerome raised an eyebrow and gave a soft, languid smile. "Don't bother," Garrison said. He bent down to kiss Eleanor Herbert on the cheek. "We were just going."

Jerome stifled a yawn behind his palm and rose to his feet.

"Is that fellow outside with you?" Kurtz asked.

"Marty Burnett," Garrison said. "My Security Chief."

"I see," Kurtz said. The guy had looked like a Security Chief. Or a mobster.

Both men nodded once more to Eleanor Herbert and then took their leave. Eleanor waited until they were gone and then said, "Well?"

"I'm sorry," Kurtz said. "I didn't mean to interrupt."

"You already have." She frowned down at a magazine that was open on her lap. *Modern Homes and Gardens*. They were pretty careful about reading material up here. It wouldn't do to get the heart racing. *Penthouse* and *Hustler* were definitely forbidden, *Field and Stream*, borderline. "Sit down," Eleanor Herbert said.

Kurtz did so.

"Now," she said. "What did you wish to speak about?"

Good question. "I wanted to see how you were doing."

"Why? You're not one of my doctors. I don't know you."

"That's not exactly true." Kurtz shifted uncomfortably. "I was in surgery on the night you came in. When the call came to the operating room that a patient in the ER needed help, I sent Doctor Adler."

"Ah…I hope you won't be sending me a bill."

"No," Kurtz said.

"Can I infer then, that your interest here is Doctor Adler, rather than myself?"

"In essence, that is correct."

She looked at him coldly but didn't order him out. Maybe she was bored. "I saw what I saw," she said.

"Please, Miss Herbert." Kurtz held up a hand in a gesture that was meant to be placating. "I'm not saying that you didn't. I'm sure the police have told you, however, that some of the things you described—the windows, the location of the patient units, the wooden doorway at the end of the hall—they don't exist."

"How do you know about that?"

"One of the policemen is my friend."

"Really?" She gave a minute shrug. "They have told me, yes." She closed the magazine. Her hands, Kurtz noted, were bent by arthritis.

"And what do you think of that?" Kurtz persisted.

"I don't know what to think." Her eyes roved around the room, unseeing. "I know what I saw. It was real. It was vivid. My brother and the policemen, they've suggested that I was dreaming but I've never had a dream like that. Never. So exact, so detailed. And I still remember it. That's the strangest thing. It wasn't like an ordinary dream, where it all begins to fade away as soon as you wake up. It's more like a moving picture on the inside of my brain. Fixed, permanent, unalterable." Her voice grew thin and began to tremble. "I can close my eyes now and see it again. The whole thing." The monitor skipped a beat.

"Please don't," Kurtz said.

She grinned faintly and opened her eyes. Her heart rate slowed. "I realize that one's brain can play tricks. I understand that I was dying. But I also know what I saw. And then of course there is the fact that what I saw turned out to be true."

"Regina Cole."

"Regina Cole. Yes. I met her only the night before but something about her immediately disturbed me. I can't say what it was." She smiled without warmth.

"Perhaps it was an omen."

An omen. Barent had also suggested an omen, or was it a premonition? Whatever, Kurtz didn't believe in omens.

"Miss Herbert, have you ever been hospitalized before?"

She looked at him. "Why do you ask that?"

"As you said, the mind has a tendency to play tricks. Wouldn't it be possible that, deprived of oxygen, your mind confused an earlier experience in your life with the one you were living at the time? Or an even simpler explanation—you said that when you saw Regina Cole's dead body, it looked just like a movie. Maybe it really was a movie. Perhaps you saw something—maybe it was years ago—which you subconsciously remembered and which chose that exact moment to pop back up."

"You're a surgeon, not a psychiatrist."

Kurtz grinned sheepishly. "I am."

"I don't claim to be an expert on the subconscious or the paranormal, but neither—allow me to point out—are you. I do know what I saw. And as for your question, I had my appendix removed in 1973 at New York Hospital. That's the only time I've ever been hospitalized. And I don't remember seeing any movies in which a young doctor strangled a young woman."

Kurtz' beeper went off. He glanced at the phone number on the top and then at his watch. "I have a case in the operating room," he said. "I'll have to be going. Thank you for talking with me."

Eleanor Herbert shrugged. "Not a lot to do up here. It's a good thing you didn't upset me."

"Yes. So I've been told."

Eleanor Herbert sniffed.

Movies, Kurtz thought. Talk it over with Barent.

Chapter 8

On Monday morning, Kurtz received a call from Sally Wilson. She sounded pleased. "They've offered to settle for a hundred and fifty thousand," she said. "I think we should take it."

The original suit had been for five million, Kurtz mused, alleging, among other things, failure to correctly diagnose, failure to obtain informed consent and negligent infliction of emotional harm. The latter point had already been thrown out in preliminary hearings. A hundred and fifty thousand was quite a comedown, all things considered.

Still…"No," Kurtz said.

"That's not very smart of you." Sally Wilson sounded annoyed.

"It's not my money. And I'm not settling. I didn't do anything wrong."

"Unfortunately for all of us, that is for the jury to decide."

"They're just going to have to decide it, then."

"I hope you're not making a mistake."

"In terms of points on my license, as well as the requirement to report to the National Physician's Data Bank, any settlement of any amount adds up to pretty much the same thing. Isn't that so?" The National Physician's Data Bank, in the opinion of every physician in the United States, was an abomination beyond words.

"Right," Sally Wilson sighed.

"Then I'll see you in court."

"What was that old movie with George C. Scott? The one about a hospital where a murderer is running around loose?"

"It was called *Hospital*," Lenore said.

Barent looked at her. "Yeah, that's right."

"I saw it on TV once. Dianna Rigg played a flower child sort who wanted to have George C. Scott's baby. I forget who his character was exactly, the Chief of Staff or something. Some honcho."

"I saw it too," Kurtz said. "There weren't any residents strangling young women, I remember that much. I'm pretty sure they were stabbed to death."

"Cookie?" Lenore held a plate with an assortment of bakery cookies out to Barent.

"No thanks, I have to get home for dinner."

"And then there's *The Fugitive*. Doctor Richard Kimball and the one-armed man."

"No residents," said Barent. "No strangled women. Of course, there's Kimball's wife. I think she was stabbed, too."

"Maybe it wasn't a movie," Lenore said. "Maybe it was a book that she read, somewhere."

"A book? Which book?" Barent asked.

"Of course," Lenore mused. "If we're talking about the imagination playing tricks, then a book might just be the answer."

"Do you have a particular book in mind?"

"Maybe. There's a series of books by Jonathon Kellerman about a clinical psychologist named Alex Delaware. His patients are always getting involved in crimes and he has to solve them."

"I never heard of him," Barent said doubtfully. "I bet the police just love the guy."

"His best friend is a gay police detective. They solve most of their cases together."

"How very PC."

"The author, Jonathon Kellerman, is a clinical psychologist, so he knows what he's talking about. He also happens to be married to Faye Kellerman, who writes the Peter Decker and Rina Lazarus mystery series. Peter Decker is a WASP detective and Rina Lazarus is his wife, an Orthodox Jew."

"A common arrangement," Barent said.

"It is in the mysteries. An intrepid detective and a Jewish female lead are definitely in. Look at Matthew Scudder and Elaine Mardell, or Spenser and Susan Silverman."

"I've read some of the Spenser books," Kurtz said. "I don't know what the big deal is with Susan Silverman. She spends most of her time dieting and buying clothes."

Lenore gave Kurtz an arch look. Evidently, Lenore found the peccadilloes of Susan Silverman sufficiently interesting. "But now that you mention it," Kurtz said, "Susan Silverman is a clinical psychologist, too. Think that might mean anything?"

"How about Elaine Mardell?" Barent asked, "another clinical psychologist?"

"No. She's a former prostitute who runs an art gallery."

"Oh." Barent smiled. "But then I suppose she has great insight into the criminal mentality."

"You don't read much, do you?" Lenore said.

"I don't read mysteries—they remind me too much of the job. And I doubt very much that the adventures of Alex Delaware or Susan Silverman, or even Elaine Mardell, are going to shed much light on Eleanor Herbert's twisted mind."

"What is?" Kurtz asked.

Barent grunted. "Leg work, most likely. I've asked the police in Gina Cole's home town to interview her friends. They'll send me the transcripts. Maybe then we'll know more. Tomorrow, I'm going to talk to the people she worked with."

"Gina Cole is from Long Island?"

"Greenport. It's a small town out in Suffolk County."

"You're not dropping the Eleanor Herbert angle, are you?" Lenore asked.

"No. Harry is going to follow up on that. He's trying to track down the old servants, the ones who worked there when she was a girl."

"When is Mark Woodson due back in town?"

"According to the bank, another two days."

"And then we'll see," Lenore said.

Barent gave her a morose look. "Maybe," he said.

Sara Hemings had died more than fifteen years ago from an aneurysm in the brain. Caroline Niles had been killed in a car crash in 1982. Jason Lester was in a nursing home in Montclair, New Jersey. The old man had suffered a number of strokes over the years. He lay in bed with his mouth open, staring off into space, ignoring (or oblivious to) everything that went on around him.

His nurse, a horse-faced young woman with nice legs, named Polly, told Moran that Jason Lester hadn't said a word in over two years. "They get like this near the end, some of them. It's sad."

"What do you mean, the end?" Moran said. "What's to stop him from lasting another two years, or even ten?" A distinctly horrible prospect.

"Well, he might but it's not very likely. Old people are fragile. They catch a cold. The cold turns into pneumonia and then they die. Probably by next winter."

So much for Jason Lester.

Vivian Moore was also in a nursing home, this one in Westchester County. She was in better shape than Jason Lester, but not much better. A tiny, shriveled bundle with thin, white hair, she lay in bed wrapped in a heavy, terry cloth dressing gown. "Eleanor Herbert?" She blinked at Moran through thick glasses. Her eyes were milky with cataracts. "I work for the Herberts. They're very nice people, the Herberts. They treat me very well."

"I'm sure they do," Moran said. "Is Eleanor Herbert a nice lady?"

"Miss Eleanor?" Vivian Moore blinked uncertainly. "Miss Eleanor screams quite a lot. She's only seven, you know." Vivian Moore blinked again. Her hands fluttered over the front of her robe. "Or is it eight?"

Moran perked up. Vivian Moore might be senile but her mental regression had carried her to the right era. "I don't know how old she is. Is she a nice little girl?"

"She throws things," Vivian Moore said confidingly. "If she were my daughter, I'd give her a good swat on the behind. That would settle her down."

"Her parents are much too lenient, aren't they?"

Vivian Moore nodded decisively. "Spare the rod, spoil the child, that's what I always say."

Not exactly an original idea. Moran scratched his head. "I bet they send her to a psychiatrist, don't they?"

"Dr. Van Gelden. Harold Van Gelden. He treats all the Gold Coast families."

Van Gelden…Moran stared at her. "And what is Dr. Van Gelden like?" he asked.

"A large man," Vivian Moore said, "with a black beard. A psychiatrist should always wear a beard, don't you think? It makes them look very professional."

"The Sigmund Freud look," Moran said.

Vivian Moore looked at him and blinked in sudden bewilderment. "Who?" she asked.

"Never mind," Moran said. "It's beside the point. Can you tell me more about Dr. Van Gelden?"

"Ah…" She looked vaguely around the room and closed her eyes. The breath began to whistle in and out of her mouth in a faint snore.

"Van Gelden," Moran said, and wrote the name in his notebook.

Bill Werth had black, frizzy hair and a pale face. He wore horn-rimmed glasses, behind which his eyes tended to blink uncertainly. He was a psychiatrist, also a good friend of Richard Kurtz.

"You ever hear of a Harold Van Gelden?" Moran asked.

Bill Werth glanced at Kurtz, who was sitting in one of the two chairs across from his desk.

"Van Gelden?" Werth said.

Moran waited.

"Sure. Harold Van Gelden. I never met him but he used to be well-known. I think he retired, maybe twenty-five, thirty years ago. He used to have admitting privileges here."

"Where is he now?"

"He's probably dead. It's been years since I've heard his name mentioned."

"Oh." Moran glanced at Kurtz, who shrugged. "That's too bad." Not surprising, however. Eleanor Herbert was close to eighty. Harold Van Gelden, if he was still alive, must be way past the century mark.

"Then again, maybe he's not dead," Werth said. "Maybe he's just retired and living in Florida. I wouldn't know."

"Wasn't there some scandal about Harold Van Gelden?" Kurtz put in. "I seem to recall hearing something."

Barent looked at him. "Why would you hear something about a guy who'd been retired for thirty years?"

"It was in medical school, on my psych rotation. They used to talk about the old-timers, supposedly quite a group of characters they had here." Kurtz grinned. "It wasn't just Van Gelden, and it's not just psychiatry. A lot of legends in this business, great names from the illustrious past."

Werth smiled. "We stand on the shoulders of giants."

"Yeah," Kurtz said. "God knows what they'll say about us in forty years."

Werth shrugged. "So far as I recall, the family of one of Van Gelden's patients sued him for supplying the patient with drugs."

"Drugs?" Moran said.

Werth frowned. "The patient was a psychotic and the medications were routine psychotropics. The family was crazy."

"Maybe he should have treated the family, instead."

"He wasn't paid to treat the family. I'm pretty sure the case was dropped."

"Justice triumphs," Kurtz said.

Werth said, "This job would be pretty good if it weren't for the patients."

"Yeah, I agree with you. Patients are a real pain. Not to mention one's medical colleagues."

"So you don't know anything else about Van Gelden?" Moran persisted.

"Nope," Werth said.

"I seem to recall there was more to the story than a nutty patient with a nutty family," Kurtz said.

Werth shrugged. "I don't know."

"Can you think of anyone who would know what happened to him?" Barent asked.

"Try the Departmental offices. They keep files on all the faculty, even the voluntaries. If he's still alive, they might have an address on him."

"Thanks," Moran said.

Regina Cole, at least according to her friends (and her High School records confirmed it) had been outgoing, popular, pretty and bright. Her activities had included the cheerleading squad and Vice President of the Honor Society. She had gone to Vassar, where she had majored in something called "Public Policy."

"What is "Public Policy?" Moran asked.

"Probably the study of how and in what ways politicians sell their votes," Barent said.

"Ah," Moran said.

"Good background for a job in Personnel," Barent said.

"Did she have any boyfriends?"

"A few." Moran opened the file and scanned it. "Bill Jordan is a car salesman, married, two kids. Wallace Stacey went to law school at University of Virginia. His family moved away. No reason to think he might have anything to do with Gina Cole once he left town."

"But he might have."

"Right."

Barent grunted. "Go on."

"Jason Glass went out with her for about two years. Nobody knows why they broke up. He's a pharmacist."

"Married?"

Moran skimmed through the report. "Divorced."

"Still living out on the Island?"

"Yes."

"Think he might still be carrying the torch?"

"They asked him. He said, 'No.'"

Moran shrugged. "Any reason to think he might be lying?"

"No reason to think so. No reason not to."

"What do the girlfriends say?"

"Jennifer Linden and Marci Howe both saw her last Christmas. Both of them say she had a new boyfriend. Neither of them got a name. Marci Howe thinks he might have been a banker. Jennifer Linden seems to recall that he was a stockbroker."

"That's it?"

"Yup."

Barent sipped his coffee and blew a smoke ring at the ceiling. "I'm looking forward to interviewing Mark Woodson," he said. "Two more days."

Chapter 9

Adler had lost weight and his formerly good humored disposition had turned sour. He rarely smiled. The police, so far as Kurtz knew, had not questioned him again but everybody who worked at Easton, including Adler, figured that it was only a matter of time. Not that any of them really thought Adler had done it but wasn't he the only real suspect? Sooner or later, the cops would get tired of pursuing leads that went nowhere and start pursuing Adler. And anyway, maybe Eleanor Herbert knew something that nobody else did. Stranger things had happened.

Luckily, the strain had so far not interfered with his work.

The patient this morning was named Julius Potter, a middle-aged man who worked for an importing firm. Julius Potter had what appeared to be a retroperitoneal sarcoma. The cancer had already squashed one kidney and, according to the CAT scan, was threatening to erode through the patient's aorta. Glumly, Kurtz looked down at it. The growth was huge, vascular and ugly, a tangled mass of ropy blood vessels, throbbing with every heart beat, extending beneath the peritoneum for a length that was impossible to fully estimate.

"Oh, boy," Adler muttered.

Kurtz nodded. Gingerly, he snipped off a small piece of the tumor, blotted the wound with a lap pad and then buzzed a tiny bleeder. The nurse held out a small glass jar filled with clear formalin and Kurtz dropped the specimen into it. "Send that for frozen section," he said.

The mood in the OR was grim. Adler and the nurses all knew what this tumor meant. The more Kurtz looked at it, the more dismayed he became. With most cancers, even the ones that had obviously spread beyond their site of origin, you could at least make a stab at it, remove the primary, zap all the metastases that could be seen with the naked eye and send the patient off for chemo. Maybe you could give him another year, maybe even more. But this thing…Kurtz repressed a shudder. He had seen inoperable cancers before and they hadn't filled him with this skin-crawling sense of revulsion. This didn't even look like a cancer; it looked like an evil alien entity, eating the patient alive from the inside out.

"Have you ever done a hemi-corporectomy?" Adler asked.

"No," Kurtz said, "and I'm not going to start now."

Adler shrugged.

He might actually have considered it if the cancer had been a little lower. In a hemi-corporectomy, you took off both legs, removed the bladder and the pelvis, basically cut the patient in half and threw away the bottom half. It was only done with highly invasive tumors confined to the lower portion of the body.

"It's too high," Kurtz said.

Adler reluctantly nodded.

"Maybe it'll respond to radiation."

"Sure." Adler looked disgusted but he was young. A few years ago, Kurtz himself might have tried it. A lot of surgeons might have. The problem was that the chance of success was one in a million and even if you succeeded, the patient was not going to have much of what physicians sometimes euphemistically referred to as 'quality of life.' Then again, they didn't give courses on quality of life in medical school. When you actually had to look the Grim Reaper in the eye, life—any sort of life—tended to look sweeter.

Maybe if he cut along this angle here…

Forget it. Kurtz shook his head. "It's too high," he said again.

The intercom buzzed and the circulating nurse flipped it on.

"Doctor Kurtz?"

"Yes?"

"This is Bill White, from pathology."

"Go on."

"The specimen you sent me is an invasive teratoma, poorly differentiated."

That meant that the type of cells composing the tumor were so primitive that no particular origin could be determined. The very worst kind.

"Thanks," Kurtz said.

"Sorry for the bad news."

"It's not your fault."

"No." The disembodied voice sounded momentarily embarrassed. "Good luck with it."

Kurtz grunted. The nurse flipped off the intercom. Maybe it would respond to radiation, at least for a little while. Grimly, Kurtz started to close.

The rest of the day was not much better. Kurtz' first patient in the office that afternoon was a taxi driver, an immigrant from India named Sanjay Patel. He had a gastric ulcer that was refusing to heal with medical therapy. Kurtz did an office gastroscopy. The ulcer was purple and inflamed, looking like a giant, purple crater beneath the scope. He grabbed a piece of it with a biopsy forceps and then withdrew the scope. He wouldn't know for sure until the path report came back, but it looked like cancer. The five year survival for stomach cancer was pretty close to zero.

The next patient was a woman named Lillian Gentry. According to the scale in the office, she weighed three hundred forty six pounds. Mrs. Gentry had a fat, round face, suspicious, tiny eyes almost hidden in folds of redundant flesh and an abdomen that rose quivering into the air like a billowing hill.

"It hurts," she said. She indicated an area just below the ribcage, on the right upper side. Kurtz gently palpated the area she had indicated and Mrs. Gentry gasped.

"There," Kurtz said.

"Yes," Mrs. Gentry said.

"How long has this been going on?"

"A few days."

"Any fever?"

Reluctantly, Mrs. Gentry nodded.

"On and off?"

Mrs. Gentry nodded again.

"It sounds like your gallbladder. You're probably passing stones. You're going to need surgery."

"I don't want surgery," Mrs. Gentry said. "I'm afraid of surgery."

She should be afraid of surgery. With her weight, she was a setup for thrombophlebitis, pulmonary emboli and pneumonia. Unfortunately, she needed surgery. "It's your decision," Kurtz said. "We can't make you have surgery, but if a gallstone gets trapped in there, you could die."

Mrs. Gentry set her lips in a stubborn line and didn't answer. After a moment, Kurtz shrugged. "It's your decision," he said again. "Come back to us if you change your mind."

An hour later, he was removing a small nodule that appeared to be a sebaceous cyst from the leg of a young woman when the patient's eyes suddenly rolled back, she gave a tiny moan and collapsed to the floor. "Shit," Kurtz groaned. The patient was breathing shallowly and her lips were blue. He grabbed an Ambu bag from its slot on the wall and began to squeeze air into the patient's lungs. "Take her blood pressure," he said to the nurse. "I think she fainted."

The woman's blood pressure was normal. She soon revived but seemed not to know where she was. It was possible, though not likely, that she had had a heart attack or a stroke. They called for an ambulance, which arrived within a few minutes. The paramedics trundled the patient onto a stretcher and off to the ER, where she would be worked up and admitted.

Kurtz went back to his office, his nerves jangling. Sitting behind the desk, he took a few deep breaths.

It was quiet here. The surgery texts neatly lined up against the wall were solid and reassuring. A bad day. Sometimes you had bad days. Sometimes you wondered just exactly why you had gone into medicine in the first place. He could have been a lawyer. He could have been a businessman. He could have gone back home to West Virginia and worked the family farm with his father, make the old man happy. He could have gotten a Ph.D in any one of innumerable subjects and not have had to deal with cancer and dying patients.

The intercom on his desk pinged. He looked at it with resignation. "Yes?" he said.

Mrs. Schapiro's voice came on. "There's someone here to see you, Doctor."

"A patient?"

"I don't think so."

Mrs. Schapiro knew he had office hours. Mrs. Schapiro knew he was booked solid for the rest of the afternoon. "Is this urgent?"

"He says so."

Mentally, Kurtz threw up his hands. "Fine," he said. "Send him in."

A small man with greasy blond hair and a face as thin and sharp as a hatchet walked into the office. His clothes hung off his limbs in ragged, dirty folds. His voice, however, was clear and precise. "Doctor Kurtz?" he said politely.

He looked like a street person, like he had been sleeping in a cardboard box under an overpass somewhere.

"Yes?" Kurtz said warily.

"I wanted to tell you. That young woman from the medical center. Regina Cole?" He smiled tentatively and gave an encouraging nod.

"Yes?"

The small man smiled. "I killed her."

"Oh," Kurtz said. A really bad day.

Chapter 10

"His name is Walter Stang. We've seen him many times before. He confesses," Barent said. "He confesses to every crime in the book. It's what he does."

"You're saying that he's a wacko."

"Absolutely. This man is definitely a wacko."

"So why did he tell me?" Kurtz asked. "Why didn't he tell you?"

"You heard him. He was afraid of us."

Walter Stang had been quite specific on this point. He had stated that the police were trying to kill him and so he was coming to Kurtz for protection. Exactly how Kurtz was supposed to protect him, Walter Stang had never clearly said.

"Has he ever been afraid of you before?"

"Nope."

"So why is he afraid of you now?"

"Because this time, there's a chance he may actually have done it. His story sounds plausible."

Barent did not look pleased. Barent should have looked pleased. "Then what's bothering you?"

"It's plausible but it's not plausible enough. There are, to put it mildly, holes in it. He knows the time and the place. He knows the scene where the body was dumped. He knows that she was strangled." Barent hesitated. "He claims that she had a dime sized birthmark on the left cheek of her ass."

"Did she?"

"She had a birthmark on the right cheek of her ass, a lot smaller than a dime."

"Sounds borderline to me," Kurtz said.

"Yeah, me too. But plausible. It's going to be enough to make Ted Weiss sit up and take notice." Ted Weiss was the Assistant DA assigned to the case. Barent had occasionally referred to Ted Weiss, with grudging respect, as a decent lawyer. He was less willing to plea-bargain than most. "But aside from the birthmark, he doesn't know a thing that wasn't in the papers. When you ask him how she got there, he gets vague. When you ask him exactly how he did it, he says he strangled her with his bare hands. Does that strike you as plausible?"

"I don't know. He's a puny little guy."

"Yeah, and Regina Cole was not a puny little girl. She probably could have strangled him."

"Anything else?"

"Yeah. How did he dump her? He says he rented a car from Avis. Avis has no record of the transaction."

"Maybe he used a phony name."

"You need to show a credit card. Walter Stang doesn't have one. They also check your driver's license. Walter Stang doesn't have a driver's license. And he says he used his real name."

"So then he's lying," Kurtz said.

"Why would he lie? He's supposed to be confessing."

"I don't know. These people who come in and confess all the time, why do they do it?"

"Every one of them is a nut. Some are psychotic with outright delusions. Some of them really believe they did it." Barent frowned. "Some of them aren't quite *that* nuts. Some just want a little notoriety. Get their name in the papers, become a celebrity."

"So maybe he wants the publicity but he doesn't want to go to jail. Maybe he's deliberately giving you a story that doesn't add up."

"Which would imply that he really did do it."

Kurtz shrugged. "I suppose so."

Barent shook his head. "I know this guy. Walter Stang is really nuts. Walter Stang, to my certain knowledge, has been on thorazine for the past twenty years. He says that he did it and I think he even believes that he did it. I don't think he's lying to us, not deliberately. He's just crazy."

"Lucky me," Kurtz said.

Walter Stang seemed perfectly content to sit in jail. He sat and read magazines and smiled and confessed his supposed crime to anyone who would listen. The other criminals—the real ones—stayed away from him. This guy was definitely not right in the head. Nobody wanted to take a chance that it might be contagious.

He was cooperative. He told them everything he knew or could remember. Most of it, Barent was sourly convinced, completely delusional. The little guy's story grew more baroque by the hour. Soon, Gina Cole had been in love with him. Soon, they had spent weeks together in Pago-Pago and Bali, lying nude on the beach and making passionate love as the sun set over the ocean and tiny, gentle waves softly caressed their bodies.

Sure.

"So how did he know about the birthmark?" Ted Weiss asked.

Barent grimaced. "It was the wrong size and the wrong cheek."

"All the more reason to believe him. He's psychotic. So he doesn't remember how or when he killed her or where he kept the body or how he got it to New Hyde Park, Long Island. This guy barely remembers his own real name."

"You have," Barent pointed out reasonably, "not a shred of evidence. The only thing you have is his own confession, which any good defense attorney would get thrown out in about twenty seconds."

Ted Weiss sniffed in disdain. "Defense attorneys. They used to be heroes. Now, you say you're a defense attorney, you can't get seated in a restaurant. The only good thing to come out of the O.J. trial is that the public finally recognizes defense attorneys for what they really are; defense attorneys are scum. Poetic, isn't it?"

"Could we stick to the point?"

"Okay, we'll stick to the point. The point is, you're probably right but he's the only lead we've got, so we're going to sit on him as long as we can."

"He's not the only lead. There is also Harold Van Gelden."

"Excuse me?" Ted Weiss made a rude noise. "Harold Van Gelden? Sixty odd years ago, a psychiatrist named Harold Van Gelden treated a seven year old kid named Eleanor Herbert for depression. I'm sure he'll be a tremendous help."

"He's a lead. Some leads pan out, some leads don't. There is also Regina Cole's ex-boyfriend."

"Who is conveniently out of town."

Barent sipped his coffee and gave a tiny shrug. "We're working on it."

Eleanor Herbert awoke suddenly, clutching at the sheets, panting hoarsely. Her heart was racing, thumping like a lead weight in her chest. She looked around, momentarily panicked by the unfamiliar surroundings, and then, realizing where she was, drew a slow, deep breath. The clock on the wall said three AM. The lights were dim. She had been transferred out of the CCU two days before, to a private room in the telemetry unit. A nurse poked her head in the door, glanced at the monitor over Eleanor's head, then looked at Eleanor. Eleanor gave her a tentative smile. The heart rate on the monitor slowed. The nurse smiled back, nodded her head and returned to the nursing station.

Eleanor sighed and sank back into the pillows. She had been dreaming. It was an old, old dream, a dream that she had dreamed many times as a child and a young woman. She was drowning, lost helplessly under cold, dark water, unable to see the surface, her lungs burning, her chest compressed by the pressure of the water, gasping for air. And then, somehow, she struggled upward. She took a long, grateful breath, savoring the cool air, and pulled herself wearily to the side of the pool and then again, for some strange, unaccountable reason, dove back in, and again found herself trapped under the water, gasping for air, drowning.

It had been years since she had dreamed that dream, so many years that she had almost forgotten it.

She put a hand up and rubbed at the stitches in her neck. Her throat hurt. Tomorrow, she was due to be released. It couldn't come too soon. She wanted to go home. She was profoundly grateful to the nurses and physicians who had helped her. She knew that she had almost died. But this fact did not make the hospital a pleasant place to be. No, she wanted to go home, to her own room, her own bed.

She drew another sigh, feeling the air move unimpeded into her lungs and closed her eyes.

Tomorrow…

Why him?

Walter Stang was not a patient at Easton. Kurtz had never treated him and Kurtz' connection to the case (not that there was one, exactly) had not been publicized. Unlike Sharon Lee, who was an old girlfriend or even Rod Mahoney, who was just a friend, this time, Kurtz didn't even know the victim.

"Let me get this straight," Bill Werth said. "This guy who you don't know walks in off the street and tells you he killed Regina Cole."

"Yep."

"Because he thinks you can protect him from the police."

"That's what he said."

"But when you immediately picked up the phone and called the police, he made no objection."

"Nope."

"And how does he think that you can protect him?"

"He said that my special position with the NYPD was well known."

"It's good to have connections. Can you fix parking tickets?"

"I'm not that connected, but I did get to go to the Benevolent Association ball this year."

"Wow. Can I have your autograph?"

Bill Werth and his wife Dina lived in an apartment on the Lower East Side, near NYU, where Dina taught English. It was a bright, sunny spring day, one of the first. Bill Werth and Kurtz were sitting out on the balcony, looking down at the street and sipping beer.

"Did you hear that Kathy Roselli is engaged?" Werth asked.

Kathy Roselli was Kurtz' former love interest, a close friend of Dina Werth. Kurtz and Kathy Roselli had been an item for almost a year, before Kathy had dumped him for not being sufficiently sensitive. About a month later, she decided that maybe Kurtz was okay after all but by then, Kurtz was on the verge of getting together with Lenore and was no longer interested. "No," Kurtz said, and took a long sip of his beer.

"A sociology professor. They make a nice-looking couple."

"I'm happy for her," Kurtz said.

Werth grinned. "I think Barent is right about Walter Stang. The guy sounds like a pretty typical schizophrenic."

"Do you know Henry Ross?" Henry Ross was Walter Stang's psychiatrist. He had an office down in the Village and admitted his patients to St. Vincent's.

"A little. I never heard anything bad about him."

"Do you know him well enough to give him a call?"

"What about? He wouldn't discuss one of his patients, not even with me."

Kurtz frowned down at the street. "I suppose not."

"So forget about it."

"I hate sitting around," Kurtz said, "doing nothing."

Werth gave him a bemused look. "Why don't you go take out a few gallbladders? Nothing like taking out a nice swollen gallbladder to make a surgeon feel happy. You'll forget about your boredom and do humanity some good at the same time."

Kurtz grunted and took another sip of his beer.

"I mean it," Werth persisted. "Regina Cole is not your responsibility. You are not the police."

"Now where," Kurtz said, "have I heard that line before?"

"Probably from everyone you know. It's good advice. You should mind your own business and take it."

Chapter 11

Kurtz had left his schedule free through Friday. He had hopes that the whole sorry business would be wrapped up by then but he knew it was just as likely that the trial would drag on into the next week. "Just play it as it goes," Sally Wilson had said. "We'll have to see."

He met her at the courthouse at a quarter to nine in the morning. They were the first ones to arrive. The room looked just like the movies: a high seat where the judge would sit, with a lower, boxed off area for witnesses, a wooden railing, rows of chairs for the plaintiff and defense teams and benches for any spectators who might show up. "We sit here," Sally Wilson said. She opened her briefcase, put on a pair of wire-rimmed glasses and proceeded to study a sheaf of papers.

The room quickly filled. Ricardo Gomez' son and daughter came in and sat down, accompanied by Jonathan Strub, their fat lawyer. The son glared at Kurtz, who tried to ignore him. The daughter sat with her head bowed, looking on the verge of tears. A scattering of spectators, none of whom Kurtz recognized, came in one-by-one and sat on the benches. At ten minutes past nine, the judge, a middle-aged man with a smooth, plump face and short brown hair, arrived and the trial officially began.

Strub had asked for a jury trial, which was the plaintiff's right. A jury, Sally Wilson had explained to Kurtz, was more likely to be sympathetic to the bereaved family than a judge, whose presumed fidelity was strictly to the law and the facts of the case. Jury selection took most of the morning and, all-in-all, Sally Wilson seemed pleased. Five potential jurors were dismissed because they had relatives who worked in hospitals, another six for expressing opinions disdainful of physicians and seven for feelings evidently judged by Mr. Strub as being either excessively sympathetic to the medical profession or anti-Hispanic in nature.

"Why do I have to be here?" Kurtz asked after the tenth dismissal.

"It helps," Sally Wilson said. "Believe me. You can learn a lot from the way they look at you."

All Kurtz had learned so far was that he hated lawyers. Since he already knew this, for him, the morning was a total waste. "Like what?" he asked.

"Well, for instance, that one…" She surreptitiously pointed to a black lady with a flowered hat. "She likes you. When she looks at you, she smiles."

"She does?"

"Don't look at her," Sally Wilson said. "It might make her nervous. That would turn her off. Right now, she's on your side."

"She hasn't heard a word of testimony. How can she be on my side?"

"Trust me."

Sourly, Kurtz reflected that he didn't have much choice. "Sure," he said.

At ten o'clock, Lenore arrived and took a seat on the bench. She smiled at Kurtz, which made him feel a bit better. By noon, they had a jury, seven women and five men, six Blacks, three Whites, one Asian and two Hispanics.

"We'll adjourn for lunch," the judge said, and banged his gavel. "Be back at one thirty."

"Come on." Kurtz took Lenore by the elbow. "Let's go."

The next hour and a half was a drag. They grabbed a burger at a corner diner but Kurtz was in a surly mood and Lenore did not try to jolly him out of it. "I hate this," Kurtz said.

Lenore nodded. "That's only natural."

"We have a jury of twelve people who know nothing about medicine. Not one of them is competent to evaluate the issues. It's ridiculous."

Lenore nodded and silently chewed an onion ring.

"They've got some supposed 'expert witness' who'll claim that I totally screwed up the case and we've got one who'll swear that my care and judgment were superb and how the hell is the jury supposed to know the difference? The fact is that if you ask a hundred surgeons to look at what happened here, at least ninety-eight of them will say that I did everything right but I guarantee you that particular fact will never come out. The whole thing makes as much sense as trial by combat, which it is. It's their hired gun against my hired gun, and may the best man win. Jesus, what a system…"

"It's the only one we've got," Lenore said.

Morosely, Kurtz nodded.

They were back in their seats by one twenty-five and the trial began in earnest. The first witness was the son of the deceased. Though Kurtz remembered him as a hood in a bandanna and a motorcycle jacket, today he wore a conservative blue suit. Strub led him carefully through his testimony. "I first saw Dr. Kurtz at the emergency room, when I brought my father in. He was complaining of pain in his stomach."

"And what did Doctor Kurtz do for him?"

"Objection," Sally Wilson said. "The question is excessively broad."

The judge looked at Strub over the tops of his glasses. "Try to be more specific, Mr. Strub," he said.

"Yes, your Honor," Strub said. He turned back to Gomez. "Now, Mister Gomez, at what time did Doctor Kurtz first see your father?"

"At about eight fifteen at night."

"This would be the evening of March 12th?"

"That's correct."

"And how long had you been at the emergency room by that point?"

"Almost five hours." Gomez gave Kurtz a wounded look. The jury nodded in apparent sympathy. Kurtz tried not to look guilty.

"Had anyone seen your father prior to Doctor Kurtz' arrival?"

"One of the nurses came and asked him some questions. A woman doctor also came by and examined him."

Strub looked down at folder that was open on the table in front of him. "Was that Doctor Carrie Owens?"

"Yes."

"After she finished examining your father, what did Doctor Owens tell you?"

"She said he needed to be seen by a surgeon."

"And how much longer did you wait until Doctor Kurtz arrived?"

"Another two hours. My father could have been dying. What did he care?"

"Objection," Sally Wilson said.

The judge looked at Gomez. "Confine your testimony to the facts, please, Mister Gomez."

"Sorry, your Honor," Gomez said. He gave Kurtz a wounded look.

Kurtz was seething. He had been on call that night and was in surgery with a perforated diverticulum when the call came from the ER. He had gotten there as soon as he could. In the meantime, on his orders, they had sent the guy for a CAT scan of the abdomen and drawn blood for routine labs. Even if Kurtz had been there hanging on his bedside, the workup wouldn't have gone any faster.

"And when Doctor Kurtz arrived, what did he tell you?"

"Nothing," Gomez said.

Strub turned to Kurtz and gave him a disbelieving look. "Nothing?" he repeated.

"He said the workup was negative." Gomez turned to the jury and looked aggrieved. "My father was lying there, moaning in pain, this guy says the workup is negative."

The workup had been negative, Kurtz thought. The workup often is negative.

"And what did Doctor Kurtz say then?"

"He said my father could have surgery or he could wait and see what happened."

This, Kurtz reflected, was absolutely true.

"And which of these options did he recommend?"

"He said if it was him, he would go on home and forget about it. It was most likely just a stomach ache."

This was a bare-faced lie. Kurtz had recommended surgery. He had indeed said that it could be just a stomach ache but he had told the patient and his family in no uncertain terms that the smart thing to do in this circumstance was to operate.

"I see," Strub said. He turned to the jury and sadly shook his head, then he sighed, spread his hands out and let them fall to his sides side. "Your witness," he said to Sally Wilson.

Sally Wilson rose to her feet. "Mister Gomez," she said, "isn't it true that after you left the hospital, you waited for three more days to bring your father back."

Gomez nodded reluctantly.

"Speak up, please, Mister Gomez."

"Yes," Gomez said.

"And isn't it also true that when your father left the hospital, he signed out against medical advice?"

"No," Gomez said.

Unfortunately, while the elder Gomez had left against medical advice, he had not, strictly speaking, signed out. He had refused to sign the form. The only documentation to this fact were the notes put in the chart by Carrie Owens, Kurtz and the nurse in charge.

"Isn't it also true that it was your father who refused to have surgery, after Doctor Kurtz recommended that he do so?"

"No," Gomez said again. "He told us to go home."

"And isn't it also true," Sally Wilson said, "that after your father refused to have surgery, Doctor Kurtz urged him to stay in the hospital under observation?"

"No," Gomez said. "That's a lie."

A number of the jury were frowning, Kurtz noted, including the black lady who Sally Wilson had said was on Kurtz' side.

"While your father was home, during the three days before he came back to the hospital, did he get better or did he get worse?"

"He got worse. He was hurting so bad he could barely get out of bed. He started to throw up and he had a fever."

"How do you know that he had a fever? Did you actually take his temperature?"

Gomez gave her an annoyed look. "Of course we took his temperature. We took it with a thermometer."

"And how high was his fever?"

"It went up to a hundred and four."

Sally Wilson, along with at least three members of the jury, shook their heads. "And when was this?" she asked.

"The next day," Gomez said.

"The next day," Sally Wilson repeated. She looked at the jury, then back to Gomez. "His temperature went up to a hundred and four the very next day. He was throwing up, and nevertheless you waited for two more days to bring him back to the hospital?"

Gomez shifted in his seat and didn't answer.

Sally Wilson smiled tightly. "Thank you, Mister Gomez," she said. "You may step down."

Gomez opened his mouth. He seemed about to say something. "Thank you,

Mister Gomez," Sally Wilson repeated. "That will be all."

At eight o'clock in the morning, Barent called Mark Woodson's apartment. He had already checked with the airlines and verified the fact that Woodson's flight should have arrived from Aruba at nine the previous evening. There was no answer on the phone. He called again at nine and again at ten with the same results. At ten fifteen, he called the airline.

"No," he was told. "Nobody named Mark Woodson was on that flight. The reservation was cancelled the day before."

"Did he reschedule?" Barent asked.

"No, sir. Not according to our records."

"Thank you," Barent said, and hung up. He waited a moment, gathering his thoughts, and then called the bank. The manager, whose name was Leonard Bailey, soon came on. He sounded glum. "You haven't heard?" Bailey said. Then he said, "No, of course you wouldn't have heard. Why should you? Mark Woodson is dead. He died two days ago, in a scuba diving accident."

Chapter 12

Aruba was a popular destination for scuba divers, having blue skies, crystal clear water, schools of tropical fish and extensive coral reefs. There were also numerous wrecks to explore, some of them dating back to the 1500's, old Spanish galleons that had been caught in hurricanes and tropical storms or sometimes even sunk by pirates.

On Monday morning, Mark Woodson had taken a diving tour of one of the more spectacular wrecks, a freighter from the 1930's that had gone down in a summer squall with all hands aboard. Somehow, Mark Woodson had become separated from his diving buddy. He had not returned to the surface. His body had so far gone undiscovered.

"So he's only presumed dead," Moran said.

"It's a pretty good presumption. You get lost in the middle of the ocean, there's not much to do except drown."

"I don't like the fact that there's no body."

Barent shrugged. "I don't like it either but we're stuck with it."

Mark Woodson had been born and grew up in Katonah, a suburb in Westchester County. Barent and Harry Moran had driven out to see the Woodson family on Wednesday afternoon. Mark Woodson's father was a tall, slim man with a sad, tired face. His mother had straight brown hair and puffy blue eyes. She had obviously been crying.

Barent and Moran identified themselves and Mark Woodson's father nodded and held the door open. "Come in," he said. "Please sit down."

The living room contained a set of mismatched brown chairs and an old green sofa. There was a Persian rug on the floor, a wooden coffee table and a desk with a series of family photographs. The oldest of these was a black and white photo showing a young woman who bore Mrs. Woodson a strong resemblance, standing in front of the Tower of London and holding a little girl in her arms. Most of the rest were in color. Some were obviously Mr. and Mrs. Woodson at various stages of their lives. Others showed two girls and a boy, ranging in age from childhood up to adulthood. One of the most striking was a picture of the boy, now grown into a young man, his hair wet, his head outlined against a deep blue sky. He had black, curly hair and blue eyes. He was very handsome.

"This one's Mark," Mister Woodson said. The corner of his mouth twitched. "My son."

"Please accept our condolences," Barent said.

"Thank you." Woodson shrugged, a sad, tired lift of his shoulders. "Can I offer you a cup of coffee?"

"No. We won't take any more of your time than we have to." Barent and Moran both sat down in the chairs. Woodson and his wife took opposite ends of the sofa. "Now," Barent said. "Could you tell us whether or not your son ever mentioned a young woman named Regina Cole?"

"Why, yes," Woodson said, "of course. Mark and Gina were going out." He glanced at his wife, who nodded silently.

"I see." Barent glanced at Moran, who had a look of sleepy interest on his face.

"For how long were they going out?"

"I'm not sure." Woodson looked again at his wife. "Quite a while, I think."

Mrs. Woodson cleared her throat. When she spoke, her voice sounded hoarse. "I think about six months," she said.

"Was their relationship serious?"

"These days, that's hard to tell." Mrs. Woodson smiled faintly. "Mark never mentioned marriage, at least not to us. He may have to Gina. I doubt it, though. Gina wasn't the only girl he went out with." Her eyes screwed up in thought and she focused on Barent's face. "Why are you asking us these things? I thought you were here to talk about Mark."

"Not exactly," Barent said, "or rather, we are, but there's more to it than that." He hesitated. "How well did you know Gina Cole?" These people were already grieving. Barent had no desire to add to their burdens but he saw no way to avoid it.

Mr. Woodson raised his eyebrows. "We met her a few times. She seemed like a nice girl. Why?"

"Mrs. Woodson? Do you agree with that estimate?"

"That she was nice?" Mrs. Woodson gave a slight shrug. "She was okay, I suppose, but she seemed just a little too nice to me, if you know what I mean."

Barent didn't. "What do you mean by that?" he asked.

"Oh, she was nice enough. That's just the point. She was too nice, always smiling, always cheerful, always looking on the bright side of things. She seemed too good to be true. I couldn't stand her, frankly."

Mister Woodson looked at his wife, looked at Barent, shrugged. Barent shrugged back.

Mrs. Woodson, who was looking sadly down at the floor, did not notice these shared, manly shrugs. "Why are you asking us this?" she said.

"Did you know that your son had recently broken up with her?" Barent asked.

"No." Woodson looked inquiringly at his wife, who shook her head.

"And did you also know that Regina Cole is dead?"

Woodson stared at him. Mrs. Woodson breathed a sigh and bit her lip.

"Regina Cole was murdered—strangled, her body left by the side of a road in New Hyde Park, Long Island."

Woodson continued to stare while a slow, tight smile spread across his face. He nodded. "We knew that, of course," he finally said. "It was in the papers. You think Mark had something to do with it."

"I don't know," Barent said. "When somebody is murdered, the odds are that the murderer is either a member of the family or a friend." Barent grinned wanly. "A supposed friend. I have no reason to suspect your son other than that."

"I think you'd better leave," Woodson said.

"Please, Mr. Woodson. I'm sorry about this. I really am. I have no desire to make things more difficult for you. Try to understand that I'm investigating a murder."

"My son was not a murderer," Woodson said tightly.

"And I haven't said that he was. Still, Gina Cole is dead and I need to ask you some questions. The sooner we get it over with, the sooner we'll be able to leave. Please."

Woodson frowned. "Ask your questions."

"When did Mark see her last, so far as you know?"

"Mark was twenty-eight years old," Mrs. Woodson said. "He didn't tell us every time he had a date."

"When was the last time he mentioned her, then?"

The Woodsons looked at each other. Some wordless communication seemed to take place. Mister Woodson turned back to Barent. "It must have been about four weeks ago. They went to the opera."

"No mention of any difficulty with their relationship?"

"No, but I doubt he would have told us if there had been."

"Mrs. Woodson? You mentioned that Mark was going out with someone else. Who was that?"

"A young woman he met at the bank. Her name is Lynn Baker."

"Have you ever met Lynn Baker?"

"No. Mark hadn't been involved with her for very long." She shrugged. "If involved is the word."

Jealousy was a motive, Barent thought. A very fine and solid motive. Plenty of people had been killed for love gone bad, thousands, down through history, even millions.

"Lynn Baker..." Barent said.

At last, Kurtz against the bad guys. The forces of justice versus the unscrupulous shyster. "Isn't it true, Doctor Kurtz," said Jonathan Strub, "that your diagnosis of appendicitis in this case was incorrect?"

"Yes," Kurtz said. And fuck you.

Jonathan Strub gave the jury a little smile. "And isn't it also true that Mr. Gomez had no chance whatsoever of survival without immediate surgery?"

"Objection," Sally Wilson said. "That question calls for speculation on the part of my client."

The judge was scribbling something on a notepad. He didn't even look up. "Sustained," he said.

Strub barely frowned. "I'll re-phrase the question. Isn't it true that on the night of March 12th, when Mr. Gomez initially presented to the emergency room at Easton Medical Center, you told him to go home, rather than have surgery?"

"No," Kurtz said. "That is not true."

Strub pursed his lips thoughtfully, walked over to his table and picked up a photocopy of the deceased patient's medical records. Kurtz had a similar copy lying in his lap. "I'll ask you to turn to the notes you made on the night Mr. Gomez was initially admitted. Tab F."

Kurtz opened the record to the page Strub had indicated. "This is your note, is it not, Doctor Kurtz?" Strub asked.

"Yes."

"I'll ask you to read it for the jury."

"Alright," Kurtz said. "'Symptoms highly suspicious for acute appendicitis but laboratory data at this time non-confirmatory. Options explained to patient. He has chosen to sign out AMA.'"

"There's nothing in there about surgery, is there, Doctor?"

"Surgery is one of the options."

"What were the other options?"

Kurtz reluctantly said, "I told him that he could choose to wait until the picture became clearer."

"Thank you, Doctor Kurtz." Jonathon Strub smiled tightly. "No further questions."

Sally Wilson immediately rose to her feet. "Doctor Kurtz, in your note, what does AMA mean?"

"It means against medical advice," Kurtz said.

"What advice?"

"I told him that the laboratory data was often inconclusive but his symptoms were most suggestive of acute appendicitis. I recommended surgery but I also told him that waiting for the situation to become clearer was a viable option. I told him that if he decided to wait, he should stay in the hospital where he could be monitored closely."

"What is the treatment for acute appendicitis, Doctor?"

"Surgery."

"And what is the treatment for an incarcerated omental hernia?"

"Surgery." Kurtz glared at Strub. Take that, asshole. The problem with this whole process was that it wasn't a fight, more like a series of insinuations mixed with a little legal bullshit just to impress the jury. Kurtz was frustrated. You swore to tell the truth, the whole truth and nothing but the truth but you could only answer the questions the lawyers asked and neither of them had any concern whatsoever for the whole truth. They were only interested in the tiny segment of it that supported their own position.

"So the treatment for what you suspected Mr. Gomez had and what he actually did have should have been exactly the same, isn't that so?"

"Absolutely."

"Thank you, Doctor." Sally Wilson turned to the judge. "I have no further questions for this witness, your honor."

The judge hid a yawn behind his fist. "You may step down," he said to Kurtz.

Chapter 13

Lynn Baker was a pretty young woman with cold blue eyes and a hard, competent manner. A modern woman, Barent thought, a woman who knew how to operate in a man's world and had made that world into her own. She lived in a small one-bedroom in midtown, nicely furnished in solid wooden furniture with blue upholstery. The walls were an off white. The rug was the same bright blue as the upholstery. Lynn Baker wore a dark green business suit with a dress tastefully below her knees, an off-white blouse, a demure string of pearls around her neck and matching pearl earrings. Her hair was straight, dark blonde and hung just above her shoulders.

"I liked Mark," she said. "I'm sorry about what happened." She shrugged.

"But you're not devastated," said Barent.

"Devastated?" She shook her head. "I didn't know him well enough to be devastated. Upset would be more like it."

"How upset, Miss Baker?"

She raised her eyebrows and gave Barent a clinical look. "Moderately."

"Tell me, had you ever slept with Mark Woodson?"

"Sure," she said.

"But you didn't know him well enough to be devastated."

"What century do you live in? We must have gone out about six times. We slept together on the fourth date. That's one more than standard. Nice girls don't put out until the third date." She grinned faintly. "Unless there are extenuating circumstances like totally uncontrollable lust or he picks you up in a chauffeur driven limo and flies you to Paris for the weekend in his own private jet. Then you might ask yourself just how nice you feel tonight. No, Detective, I wasn't devastated, but I was pretty upset."

"I see," Barent said.

Lynn Baker shrugged as if she really didn't give a damn whether Barent saw or not.

"Did you know a woman named Regina Cole, Miss Baker?"

"No," she answered. Her face, Barent noted, became suddenly wary.

"Did Mark Woodson ever mention Regina, or Gina, Cole to you?"

"No."

"Do you know who Gina Cole was, Miss Baker?"

"No. I don't."

"Gina Cole was an administrator at Easton Medical Center. Six days ago, she was found dead by the side of a road. She had been strangled."

"So?" Lynn Baker said cautiously. "That's too bad, but why tell me?"

"For approximately six months, Gina Cole was 'going out,' if that's the correct term, with Mark Woodson."

"Oh," Lynn Baker said. She thought about that for a moment, then sighed and looked vaguely disgusted. "I didn't know that but I can't say that I'm surprised. Mark wasn't the only man I was seeing, either. Still…" She shook her head and suddenly looked on the verge of tears, which made Barent, suddenly and unaccountably, feel like shit.

"You think you know somebody," Lynn Baker said. "You start thinking that maybe this time it's going to work out. You start to hope and make plans, even when you know you shouldn't, even when you know that it's stupid." Lynn Baker's shoulders began to quiver and suddenly, her face was in her hands and she was sobbing.

"I'm sorry, Miss Baker."

"Oh, shut up," she whispered between sobs.

Barent rose to his feet and said as gently as he could. "I don't know yet where my investigation is going. We may have to talk to you again. If so, I'll give you a call." He hesitated. "I'm sorry," he said again.

She said nothing, nodded her head, and continued to cry.

Carrie Owens made a good witness. She was tiny, shy and unassuming, but she answered the questions without hesitation and seemed completely sincere. Clearly, Carrie Owens was the sort of girl any mother would be proud of and any father would love. The jury took to her immediately.

Jonathan Strub had failed to get anything out of Carrie that might help his cause. He sat now with an intent expression on his face as Sally Wilson examined the witness.

"What was your impression of Mr. Gomez' symptoms, Doctor Owens?"

"He had an acute abdomen. There are a lot of things that can cause an acute abdomen. The most likely one is appendicitis."

"Would you please define an acute abdomen, Doctor Owens?"

Carrie blinked modestly and looked like a little girl. "An acute abdomen is severe abdominal pain, usually—but not always—associated with nausea, vomiting, fever and diarrhea."

"I see. Now, could you tell us, please, what are the other things that can cause an acute abdomen?"

"Oh, an incarcerated hernia is one. Cholelithiasis, that's gallstones. Diverticulitis. An hepatic cyst. Acute pancreatitis. Mesenteric lymphadenitis can do it, so can a bad case of gastroenteritis."

"Is gastroenteritis like food poisoning?"

Carrie smiled apologetically. "Food poisoning can mean a number of different things. For instance, food that has spoiled can contain toxins, botulinum for instance, which can cause serious illness. Or food can be contaminated with salmonella or E. coli or hepatitis A or an enterovirus. The end result of any of these things is an acute abdomen."

"Thank you, Doctor Owens." Sally Wilson smiled at the jury. "That explanation was most enlightening. Now, after you had diagnosed an acute abdomen, what did you do for Mr. Gomez?"

"I had the ER secretary page the general surgeon on call."

"Was that Doctor Kurtz?"

"Yes, it was."

"And how long was it before Doctor Kurtz answered?"

"He called back in about five minutes."

"Did you talk with him on the phone?"

"Yes, I did."

"And what did he say to you?"

"Objection," Jonathan Strub said. "This is hearsay."

Sally Wilson reared her head back and looked offended. "It is not hearsay. I am asking for testimony of a conversation in which the defendant played a direct part. There is nothing hearsay about it."

The judge puffed up his cheeks and peered down at Jonathan Strub. "Overruled," he said.

Jonathan Strub shrugged and sank back into his seat.

"Now, Doctor Owens, what did Doctor Kurtz say to you?"

Carrie looked bewildered by all the controversy. "He said that he was tied up in the OR but he asked me to draw blood for routine labs and get a CAT scan and a flat plate of the abdomen."

"Which you did."

"Yes, of course."

"How long did these things take?"

"About two hours."

"And how long after Mr. Gomez' CAT scan was finished, did Doctor Kurtz arrive in the Emergency Room."

"About a half hour."

"After Doctor Kurtz had examined the patient, did you discuss the case with him."

"Yes, I did."

"And what did he say to you?"

"He agreed with me that it was an acute abdomen. He said that the labs and the CAT scan were non-conclusive. He said that it was most likely appendicitis." Carrie hesitated.

"Yes?" Sally Wilson prompted.

Carrie shrugged contritely. "He said the patient was not being very cooperative. He said that he was recommending surgery but the patient was refusing."

"Did you talk to Mr. Gomez yourself, Doctor Owens?"

"Oh, yes. Of course. He was still my patient."

"Did you also recommend surgery?"

"Absolutely."

"And he refused?"

"Yes, he did." Carrie frowned. "He said that no quack son-of-a-bitch was going to cut him open."

"Objection!" Jonathan Strub roared.

Carrie looked distraught and about ten years old. "I'm sorry, but that's exactly what he said."

The judge frowned at Jonathan Strub. "Sit down, Mr. Strub."

Jonathan Strub opened his mouth. He seemed about to say something, then evidently thought better of the idea, shrugged and sat back into his seat.

"Then what happened?" Sally Wilson asked.

"Then Doctor Kurtz told the patient that if he was going to refuse surgery, he should at least stay in the hospital where he could be observed."

"Were you present for this conversation, Doctor?"

"I was right there."

"What did Mr. Gomez say to this?"

Carrie hesitated. "I wouldn't want to repeat it," she said. "It was pretty unpleasant."

Sally Wilson looked over at the jury, grinned and shook her head sadly. Two of the jurors nodded back. "Give us the gist, Doctor Owens," she said. "In your own words."

"Well, he said he was leaving."

"Did you advise against his leaving?"

"Absolutely."

"Did Doctor Kurtz advise against his leaving?"

"Yes, he did."

"And Mr. Gomez left anyway."

"Yes."

"Tell me, was the patient's family present for these conversations?"

"Yes. They were right there."

"Did any of them say anything?"

"His daughter suggested to Mr. Gomez that it might be better if he were to stay in the hospital."

"What did Mr. Gomez' wife say?"

"Nothing."

"And his son?"

"He said that if his father wanted to go home, then his father was going to go home, and we could all go to hell."

Jonathan Strub opened his mouth, hesitated, then closed it. He shrugged. Sally

Wilson looked at him and waited for a second. She said to Carrie Owens, "Thank you, Doctor Owens. You may step down." She turned to the judge and said in a ringing voice, "The defense rests, your Honor."

The jury was out for over an hour. Kurtz was too nervous to leave while they deliberated. Sally Wilson looked exhausted. "You did great," he said to her.

She shook her head. "It's a good thing Strub didn't know about Carrie and your partner. He would have torn us apart."

"The fact that Carrie Owens is going out with David has nothing to do with this case," Kurtz said frigidly.

"It would if Strub knew about it, believe me."

Kurtz believed her. That was the thing about the law, trial by misdirection and innuendo and may the slickest bastard win. He shook his head. "What shit," he said.

"Sorry you didn't settle?" Sally Wilson asked.

"No," he said.

She smiled wanly. "Well, I am."

Ten minutes later the jury filed out.

"Have you reached a verdict," the judge asked.

The foreman of the jury said, "We have, your honor."

"And what is your verdict?"

"We find the defendant not liable, your honor."

"Alright…" Kurtz said.

Sally Wilson breathed a long sigh of relief and finally smiled as if she meant it. "Congratulations."

He grinned at her. "Still think I should have settled?"

"You won, so it doesn't matter." She grinned. "It could have gone either way, believe me. You can never tell with juries."

"Well, I did win, so that's that."

She nodded. "I'm glad."

The last thing Kurtz saw as he and Lenore left the courthouse was Gomez' wife, son and daughter, sitting at their table with Jonathan Strub. The son gave Kurtz a burning glance as he walked by. The wife sat silently at the table, her shoulders hunched. The daughter was clutching a handkerchief and crying.

Kurtz felt a pang of regret for the wife and daughter. The son could go to hell. "Suddenly," he said to Lenore. "I don't feel much like celebrating."

Lenore looked over at the plaintiffs. The son was waving his arms over his head, almost spitting as he snarled something unintelligible into Strub's impassive face. "The whole family would have taken you to the cleaners, if they could."

"I suppose," Kurtz said. Then he shrugged. "Ah, well, let's get something to eat."

Chapter 14

Kurtz woke up in the morning feeling better. Even though it had been an idiotic case, even though his own personal assets had never been at risk, such objectivity was impossible for him. His judgment, his reputation and his good name had all been attacked. It didn't matter to Kurtz whether the case had been for ten million or for ten cents. He wanted vindication.

Now he had it.

It was Friday. He briefly considered going into the office but decided instead to relax. He had previously arranged to have the day free, just in case the trial lasted this long. He found, however, after trying to read a book and then puttering around the apartment for an hour, that he could not relax. He had won a battle. His adrenaline was rushing.

He smiled to himself. Why not pay a little visit to his old buddy, Barent?

"You want to do what?" Barent said.

"Talk to him," Kurtz said. "Just talk to him."

"Why?"

"Maybe he'll tell me something that he wouldn't tell you."

"And why would he do a dumb thing like that?"

"He came to me for protection, remember? He trusts me. He doesn't trust the police."

Barent scratched his head and gave Kurtz a look that said he was wasting his time.

"What have you got to lose?" Kurtz protested. "Has he said anything useful to you?"

"No," Barent said, "not really."

"So?"

Barent shrugged and rose abruptly to his feet. "Come with me."

Barent conducted him to a small room that was divided in two with a sheet of thick glass. There were small holes drilled in the glass, too small to pass anything through but big enough to allow sound. A bench sat on both sides of the glass, with a chair on each side. "Sit down," Barent said. "I'll get him."

A few minutes later, a door opened and Walter Stang walked in, saw Kurtz on the other side of the glass, gave a crooked smile and sat down in the chair. "Officer Barent said you wanted to talk to me."

"That's right."

Stang said nothing but at least he looked interested.

"How have you been getting along?" Kurtz said. "I've been curious. Have they been treating you well?"

Stang blinked his eyes. "I don't think they take me very seriously."

"That's understandable, isn't it?"

"The police have a simplistic view of things," Stang said. "They just don't understand the big picture."

"Tell me about it. I'm concerned about you."

"Why?"

"You came to me for protection. Remember? I feel responsible."

Stang puffed his cheeks up and leaned back in his chair. "That's a very mature attitude," he said.

"Thank you."

"It's unusual in this day and age to meet a man who takes his responsibilities seriously." Stang's face grew pensive. "I believe it was Dostoevsky who said that we are all responsible." Walter Stang's eyes assumed a faraway look. "Yes," he said. "It was definitely Dostoevsky."

Walter Stang didn't look like someone who would be reading Dostoevsky. Comic books, maybe…"Dostoevsky was a smart man," Kurtz said.

Walter Stang's face positively beamed. "Now then, what would you like to know?"

"Well, for starters, why did you kill Gina Cole?"

"That's very difficult to say." Stang suddenly frowned, his cheeks bunching up into a mask of tiny wrinkles. "She annoyed me, I guess."

"But I thought you two loved each other."

"Love." Stang made a faint disparaging sound. "Love is fleeting. In the end, she was just using me. She was like all the others, when you come right down to it. She only cared about herself."

"Women are like that, aren't they?" Kurtz said.

Stang nodded sadly. "You bet."

"Where were you when you decided to do it? Kill her, I mean."

Stang's head began to bob up and down, as if he were listening to some secret music that only he could hear. For a long moment, Kurtz thought he wasn't going to answer. Then he said, "Sheridan's. We were at Sheridan's."

"When was this?"

"Oh," Stang said vaguely, "about a week ago."

"I see."

Stang was frowning, as if he didn't like the direction the conversation was taking him.

"Did you do it that same night?"

"No," Stang said reluctantly, "the next night."

"Where were you when you killed her?"

"My place, where else? We had just made love and were drinking a glass of champagne. It seemed like the right time."

SEIZURE   69

"And what did you do with the body?"

"I wrapped her in a sheet and brought her down the back steps."

"Did anyone see you?"

"No. I was careful."

"What made you come to me?"

"I knew about your relationship with the police."

Due strictly to bad luck, Kurtz had in the last year wound up in the middle of two murder investigations, during which he and Barent had gotten to be pretty good friends. This did not constitute a 'special relationship' with the assorted forces of law and order, not one at least, that the general public would likely to be informed of.

"And how exactly did you come to know about this relationship?"

"I saw your face in the papers."

This might actually have been true. During the course of the second murder investigation in which he had unfortunately gotten involved, Kurtz himself had been hit over the head with a lead pipe, abducted, and almost killed. The story had made the papers.

Walter Stang seemed to have gotten over whatever it was that had been bothering him. He smiled at Kurtz happily. "Anything else I can tell you?"

"Can you tell me who Gina Cole's friends might have been?"

A slow, bewildered look came over Walter Stang's face. He shook his head. "Strange," he said. "We never talked about other people. Never. It was like we lived in a little world of our own. What we had was so perfect, you see? So very perfect…" He sighed. His lips trembled and he suddenly seemed on the verge of tears.

Kurtz winced. Despite the fact that this was obvious and total bullshit, Stang's distress made him feel guilty. "One last thing," Kurtz said, "do you have any friends who might have known of your good fortune? I mean your relationship with Gina Cole."

Stang gave a tiny shrug. "I have so many friends."

"Anyone in particular?"

"Lenny, I suppose. Lenny is my best friend."

"And when did you see Lenny last?"

"I'm not certain. Probably that last night with Gina. I introduced them. Lenny was certainly impressed. She was a fine looking woman."

"Does Lenny have a last name?"

Walter Stang looked suddenly confused. "Everybody has a last name."

"This is true," Kurtz said. "What is Lenny's?"

Walter Stang shook his head in sad resignation. "My memory plays tricks on me sometimes. I'm on medication, you see."

"I understand," Kurtz said. "Thanks. Maybe we'll talk again."

Stang smiled tremulously. "I would like that. It does get a bit boring here."

"Did you get anything?" Barent asked.

"No," Kurtz said. "They were in love. It was too good to last, so he killed her."

"I told you."

"Where does Stang live?"

"He has an apartment on the lower East Side."

"How does he afford it?"

"His mother left him a trust fund. He's actually pretty well off."

"He can't manage his own money."

"No. An uncle is the conservator of the estate."

"Have you talked to the uncle?"

"Of course. The old boy signs the checks every month. Aside from that, they haven't seen each other in years."

"Any reason to doubt him?"

"Not a one."

"Oh, well," Kurtz said. "Nothing ventured, nothing gained."

Sheridan's…

Sheridan's was a bar not too far from Walter Stang's apartment. He really should have told Barent about it but what the heck, Kurtz thought, it couldn't hurt to give the place the once over all by himself. He knew, of course, that this was not exactly the most prudent course of action, but Kurtz was not feeling prudent. He felt like kicking back his heels. Whatever, it wouldn't hurt the investigation or anything else to wander in and have a drink.

And maybe he would run into Lenny.

From outside, the place looked like a dive. The neighborhood was seedy. An alley right next to the building contained nothing but an overflowing dumpster and a few straggly weeds. The street was full of potholes that the city had not yet gotten around to repairing. A couple of well-used Harleys were tied up outside.

From inside, the place looked a little better. The lights were dim and the chairs all matched. The long mirror behind the bar was clean and the bar itself was polished. A TV over a long row of bottles was tuned to a basketball game but no sound came from it. The bartender wore black pants and a white shirt opened at the neck. He was wiping a glass with a towel and whistling softly to himself. An old man, bald and skinny, sat at a corner table with a mug of beer in front of him, staring off into space. Every once in a while, his hand would reach out and bring the beer up to his lips. His eyes never wavered from infinity and the mug, when he put it down, seemed to contain just as much beer as it had before. A little man in a brown, polyester business suit sat at one end of the bar, his tie loosened at his neck, drinking what appeared to be whiskey. Small groups of men sat at three other tables. All the men were dressed in casual clothes, all talking quietly among themselves. Two big guys in denim jackets sat at the opposite end of the bar, their heads together, whispering. They were drinking tequila from shot glasses—straight, no salt, no lime. Kurtz winced and sat down in the middle of the bar, as far away as he could get from the characters in denim without crowding the guy in the suit. A few seconds later the bartender walked over. "What'll it be?" he asked.

"What do you have on tap?"

"Bud, Bud Lite, Sam Adams, Harp and Guinness."

Not a bad selection. "You get a lot of call for Guinness here?"

The bartender looked at him with flat, gray eyes. "Lot of Irish in the neighborhood. They drink Guinness."

"I'll have a Sam Adams," Kurtz said.

Wordlessly, the bartender poured the beer into a mug and set it in front of Kurtz.

"Thanks."

The bartender grunted and moved back to the other end of the bar.

Kurtz sipped his beer. Kurtz was good at sipping beer. Kurtz had grown up in a time when one beer was distinguished from another solely by its temperature. It wasn't until he went to Munich with the army that Kurtz learned what good beer was supposed to taste like, but about fifteen, maybe twenty years ago, America had re-discovered quality beer. Now there was Anchor Steam and Sierra Nevada and Catamount Porter and Brooklyn Brewery and Sam Adams and a couple of hundred others. Kurtz smacked his lips and took a big swallow of his Sam Adams and sighed contentedly. It made one proud to be an American.

"You got any peanuts?" Kurtz said.

Wordlessly, the bartender reached under the bar and brought out a bowl of shelled peanuts. He placed them in front of Kurtz. "Thanks," Kurtz said. He ate a few peanuts. "Nice place you've got here."

The bartender glanced at him, then glanced away.

"Nice neighborhood place." Kurtz let his eyes wander over the room. The old man was still sitting with his mug of beer, the two bikers still whispering between themselves in between shots of tequila. The guy in the brown suit quietly blew his nose into a handkerchief, then picked up his glass of whiskey and stared into it. "I guess you know most of the people who come in here."

The bartender ignored him.

Kurtz reached into his wallet, pulled out a twenty dollar bill and placed in on the bar. "How about another beer?" Kurtz said.

Wordlessly, the bartender filled a new mug with Sam Adams and placed it in front of Kurtz, then looked at him from heavy-lidded eyes. "Thanks," Kurtz said. "A guy I know recommended this place. A little guy named Walter. You know him?"

The bartender frowned. He glanced at the twenty. "Walter?"

"Walter Stang."

"Walter Stang," the bartender repeated slowly. His mouth twitched. "Are you a cop? You don't look like a cop."

"I'm not a cop."

"Walter Stang is a lunatic. He comes in now and then, has a drink and bothers the other customers."

"How does he bother them?"

The bartender smiled slightly. "He tries to talk to people who'd rather be by themselves. This isn't a place to talk to people who would rather be by themselves."

Kurtz nodded. "But you're the bartender. People always talk to the bartender."

The bartender took out his rag and slowly wiped the bar in front of Kurtz. The twenty disappeared. "That depends," he said, "on what they want to talk about."

"You ever see a woman with Walter Stang, a pretty, young woman with brown hair?"

The bartender looked at him as if he were nuts. "No," he said.

Kurtz reached into a pocket, brought out a picture of Regina Cole that he had torn from a newspaper. "This woman," he said. "You ever see her in here?"

The bartender took it, stared at it for a few moments, shrugged. "Can't say that I have."

Kurtz grunted. "Thanks," he said. He looked out at the tables. "These guys all regulars?"

"Mostly." The bartender continued to wipe down the bar. "Will that be all?" he asked.

Kurtz sipped his beer. "You know a guy named Lenny?"

The bartender's rag stopped moving. He blinked at Kurtz. "Lenny," he said.

"You know him?"

The bartender wrinkled his nose, as if an unpleasant odor had just wafted past. "A lot of guys named Lenny."

"This is true," Kurtz said.

The bartender gave Kurtz a hard look. He smiled thinly. "In back," he said. "The left corner table. That's Lenny."

Kurtz turned slowly. In the dim light, he could barely see a man sitting at the left corner table. From this distance, Kurtz could not see what he looked like.

"Anything else?" the bartender asked again.

"Not for the moment."

The bartender shrugged. "You probably don't deserve it but I'm going to give you a little advice. You should stay away from Lenny."

Kurtz sipped his beer. "Thanks," he said.

So now what? The intrepid private detective was uncertain. Probably it would be better at this point to finish his beer and go give Barent a call. Barent no doubt would be annoyed with him but probably grateful to get the information. Kurtz could call it a job well done and be out of it without risking his neck.

Lenny…

Chapter 15

Arnie Figueroa said, "Harold Van Gelden had a record."

Barent looked up. The day before, he had followed Bill Werth's advice and consulted the secretary of the Department of Psychiatry at Easton. "Deceased," the secretary had said. "He died in 1987 of prostate cancer." The secretary was an old biddy with tied back hair and a thin, unsmiling mouth.

"Where was he at the time of his death?"

"You mean what hospital?"

"No. I mean where was he living up until he died?"

"The last address we have for him is in Ridgewood, New Jersey."

"Could I have the address?" he requested.

The secretary blinked at him as if searching for a reason to refuse. Finally she gave a minute shrug and told him.

"Thanks," Barent said.

She looked unhappy and barely nodded her head. Barent thought about arresting her for contributing to public depression but decided to let her go, just this once. He gave her a toothy smile and left.

Upon arriving back at the station house, Barent had asked Arnie Figueroa to look up Harold Van Gelden. All the records from the relevant period had long since been put on microfilm and removed to storage. It would take a day or so to retrieve them. Now, Arnie Figueroa stood over him in the office holding a sheaf of papers in his hand. "Yes?" Barent said, and blew a smoke ring at the ceiling.

"Quite a long record," Arnie added.

For some reason that he could not explain, Barent was not the slightest bit surprised. Maybe it was the name. Harold Van Gelden…if that wasn't phony, what was? Or the goatee. "Let me see," he said, and held out his hand.

"Enjoy," Arnie said. He closed the door.

Van Gelden did indeed have a record. Van Gelden, it seemed, in addition to his position at Easton, had run a small, private psychiatric clinic out in New Jersey. Three charges of dispensing narcotics without the proper documentation, two charges of Medicare fraud, all of them dismissed because of lack of evidence. The DA at the time must have really had it in for the guy. The more serious stuff was at the back. One charge of sexual assault on a patient and another of forcible restraint, which was just one step below kidnapping. Both of these charges had also been dropped. The complainants, it seemed, had been deemed unreliable.

The malpractice complaint that Bill Werth had mentioned, that of dispensing drugs incorrectly, was not mentioned in the criminal record. The charge of forcible restraint, had, however, gone on to result in a civil claim of professional liability—specifically that Harold Van Gelden had resorted to "deprivation therapy." Deprivation therapy, it seemed, was an invention of Dr. Van Gelden himself. He had written a number of papers on it. According to the theory, you could significantly ameliorate the symptoms of psychosis by treating the patients, not as victims of their disease, but as willful accomplices. The disease, in this light, was to be perceived as an outside force that had taken over the patient's brain. The patient was not to give in to it. A patient who did, had to be punished. This was where the "deprivation" came in. Since the patient had to some extent "chosen" his disease, the therapist would deprive him of his right to choose. The process had often involved either electroconvulsive therapy or insulin shock, which used to be an accepted alternative to electroconvulsive therapy but which today was considered barbaric.

The theory had not been widely accepted but Van Gelden did claim some notable successes. The malpractice suits, as Werth had said, had been thrown out.

Barent remembered reading somewhere that a psychiatrist's malpractice insurance was the lowest of any physician's. Psychiatrists were rarely sued successfully. In a situation where it was one man's word against another's, psychiatrists tended to have more credibility than their patients.

And the name had indeed been phony. Morton Schmidt was the name he had been born with. Definitely a name worth changing. Barent probably would have changed it, too.

The clinic, Barent noted, was still in operation. He would have to go out there, maybe tomorrow.

The back corner of the bar was dark. Lenny, whoever he was, could be seen as only a shadow. Kurtz smiled to himself, put his empty mug back down on the counter and threaded his way between the tables.

"Excuse me," Kurtz said.

Lenny looked up. From this distance, Lenny didn't look too impressive. He had black, curly hair and a pale face. He wore a blue blazer over a white shirt with no tie. He looked at Kurtz and said nothing. His eyes were peculiar—flat, expressionless, they looked at Kurtz as if he barely existed, as if Kurtz were swimming somewhere in space a million miles away.

"Lenny?" Kurtz said.

Lenny cocked his head to the side. His right hand raised a glass to his lips, then put the glass down. His face stayed expressionless.

"I was told that your name was Lenny," Kurtz said.

Lenny's lips barely smiled. "Get lost," he said.

"Gee," Kurtz said. "They didn't tell me you were a tough guy." Kurtz slid a chair out and sat down at the table.

For the first time, Lenny actually looked at him. It would be too much to say that he looked incredulous. Mildly interested was more like it. "They should have," Lenny said. "They usually do." He drank some more beer. The beer, Kurtz noted from the bottle, was Thomas Hardy's. His opinion of Lenny reluctantly rose a notch.

"You hang out here much?" Kurtz asked.

Lenny looked up at the ceiling and slowly shook his head. He didn't answer.

"Sort of a dive, isn't it? Though they do have a good selection of beer."

"What do you want?" Lenny asked.

"I was told that you know a man named Walter Stang."

"Stang?" Lenny's brows drew together. "Can't say that I do."

"A little guy, I was told he spends a lot of time here. He's nuts."

Lenny almost smiled. At least, Kurtz thought he almost smiled. "If he's the guy I think he is, he comes in for a drink now and then. Nobody pays him any attention. Like you said, he's nuts."

Kurtz reached into a pocket and unfolded the picture of Gina Cole. "You ever see this woman in here? With or without Walter Stang?"

Lenny's face grew abruptly serious. He looked at the picture for a long time. "You're not a cop," he finally said. "Who are you?"

"I'm a friend of Walter Stang."

"Walter Stang doesn't have friends. Whoever you are, you're an idiot." Lenny's eyes flicked to the side. He gave a tiny nod.

"This guy bothering you, boss?" a voice said.

Kurtz turned and looked up. Maybe six and a half feet tall, bald, red-faced, beefy, enormous shoulders and a belly that bulged over his belt. Not quite as strong as a bull, but very, very close.

"Yeah," Lenny said.

"Come along," the big guy said.

"But we weren't done with our conversation," Kurtz protested.

"Yeah," Lenny said. "We were."

The big man clapped a hand on Kurtz' shoulder. "Now," he said.

Kurtz sighed and rose to his feet. "What's your name?" he asked.

"Dominick."

Dominick. Kurtz gave a little whistle. "Don't tell me. It used to be Bob but you changed it to something more appropriate when you joined the mob."

"A joker," Lenny said. "The guy's a joker."

"This way," Dominick said. His hand was still on Kurtz' shoulder.

"It's really too bad that Luca Brassi was already taken."

Dominick smiled gently. "This way," he repeated. Kurtz let himself be pushed along while Dominick guided him toward the door. The patrons of the bar ignored them. The bartender looked at them regretfully and shook his head.

Unfortunately, once they reached the door, Dominick did not let go of Kurtz' shoulder. The sun had long since set. There was a faint drizzle in the air and the street was almost empty. A perfect setting for an anonymous beating—or worse.

"This way, Sport," Dominick said.

"Where are we going?" Kurtz asked.

"Around the back."

There was nothing around the back but an alley and a dumpster.

"Would you mind letting go of my shoulder?"

Dominick gave a tired sigh but did not otherwise answer. He also did not let go of Kurtz' shoulder.

Kurtz reached up, grasped Dominick's beefy index finger and broke it. Dominick screamed. He also let go of Kurtz' shoulder. Kurtz turned and kicked the big man in the kneecap. Dominick fell to the ground, looking up at Kurtz with naked disbelief. For a second, Kurtz almost felt sorry for the guy. Dominick suddenly seemed to recollect that Kurtz was not supposed to be the one doing the beating. He blinked his eyes and scrambled to his feet, roaring.

Kurtz spun. The edge of his foot took Dominick on the side of his fat, bald head. The head was as hard as a boulder. Dominick lurched, stopped for an instant, shook himself and kept on coming.

Kurtz blocked one awkward punch, stepped in and raised his knee into Dominick's groin. This worked a little better. Dominick let out a squeal and once again dropped to the ground, where he folded up into a ball. Without looking at Kurtz, he began to scrabble at the inside of his jacket with his good hand.

"If you go for your gun," Kurtz said, "I'll make you eat it." Duncan Macleod, the Highlander. Kurtz had been flipping through the channels once and would always remember this as one of the great ridiculous lines.

Dominick stopped. He looked up at Kurtz, looming over him and smiling. His hand dropped away from his jacket.

"That's better," Kurtz said. "Get up."

Dominick did so, wheezing. Delicately, Kurtz reached into his jacket. It wasn't a gun. It was a set of brass knuckles. Kurtz brought them out and inspected them. Not brass, actually. They were made out of iron, heavy, solid and hard. They gleamed in the dim light. Kurtz slipped them over his fingers. They fit snugly. He flexed his hand and smiled at Dominick. The big man turned pale.

"I don't think we'll be needing these," Kurtz said. He took them off and tossed them into a corner of the alley. "Turn around." Dominick swallowed. He turned around, his bullet head hunching into his shoulders.

Delicately, Kurtz reached up his right hand and put it on Dominick's shoulder. Dominick flinched. "Start walking," Kurtz said. "I'll be right behind you."

"Where are we going?"

"Back inside," Kurtz said. "I haven't finished my conversation with Lenny."

Chapter 16

Physicians all had their little stereotypes. Internists, according to popular legend, were arrogant but hostile. They regarded themselves as the physicianly elite but they didn't make as much money as they thought they should and so they resented the World. Psychiatrists were unbalanced. The reason they went into psychiatry was to try to figure themselves out, an endeavor at which they rarely succeeded. Anesthesiologists were meek but resentful. They had to deal with surgeons, after all, which was enough to try anybody's patience. Surgeons were macho, aggressive, smug and arrogant, even (or especially) the female ones.

There was at least a little truth to the stereotypes, Kurtz thought, just enough so that nobody was surprised when a surgeon acted like a surgeon. A surgeon's arrogance, however, rarely expressed itself physically. They yelled at the nurses and bullied the residents but most of the time they kept their hands to themselves. All doctors studied hard and spent many years with their books. A surgeon's work demanded a cool head and quick, decisive action but most of them were flabby and had never thrown a punch in anger.

Kurtz was the exception. Kurtz had grown up on a farm, played football in High School, spent three years with the army, was an ardent practitioner of the martial arts and worked out four times a week. In the little world of the hospital, Kurtz was regarded with something close to awe. By physicians' standards (Kurtz realized that this wasn't much of a standard), Kurtz was a real tough guy.

Not that he acted like one. Kurtz prided himself on his humility and hated looking like a jerk.

Still, as he walked up to Lenny, his hand on Dominick's shoulder, he felt himself to be truly alive. His blood raced through his veins and his heart sang. Kurtz was enjoying himself.

As they neared the table, Lenny looked up. All he saw at first was Dominick, looming in front of him. Then he saw Kurtz. His brow furrowed. He opened his mouth to say something.

Kurtz didn't give him the chance.

Dominick must have weighed three hundred pounds. A kick behind the knee and a little shove sent Dominick's three hundred pounds flying. He crashed onto the table and the table crumbled. Beer splashed into the air and made a pattern of dark drips on the wall. Lenny's chair split open beneath him and he sprawled to the ground, his arms flailing, his legs trapped beneath the splintered table.

Dominick groaned. He rolled over and sat up, looking dazed.

"Get off me, you goddamn idiot!" Lenny smacked Dominick, who was sitting partly on the table and partly on Lenny's chest, on the back of the head. Lenny seemed, for the moment, to have forgotten Kurtz.

Kurtz cleared his throat. "Ahem," he said.

Lenny looked up. He focused on Kurtz. His eyes grew wide and his hand darted for his jacket.

Kurtz stepped on the hand. "Don't," Kurtz said.

Lenny grunted. He strained his hand. His fingers wriggled and began to turn blue.

Kurtz reached inside Lenny's jacket and came out with a pistol. A Ruger nine-millimeter, he noted, the weapon of choice for the well-equipped hit man. "You made a mistake," Kurtz said. "Everybody makes mistakes. No hard feelings. Life is like that. You'll be a better man for the experience. Now tell me about Gina Cole."

"Go to hell," Lenny said.

Kurtz kicked him in the side. Lenny groaned. "Wrong answer," Kurtz said.

"Fuck you."

The guy looked like he meant it. A little kick in the ribs wouldn't do him any permanent damage but Kurtz had gone just about as far as he was willing to go. Lenny wouldn't necessarily know that, however. Kurtz squatted down next to Lenny's face. Without turning his head, he said, "Get lost, Dominick."

Dominick swallowed. He rolled over, scrambled to his knees and staggered to a seat at the next table.

Kurtz pointed the gun at him. "I said, 'Get lost, Dominick.'"

Dominick looked helplessly at Lenny. "Boss?" he said.

Lenny said nothing. His eyes burned into Kurtz.

"I'll count to three," Kurtz said pleasantly.

Dominick's shoulders slumped. He shook his head sadly, rose to his feet and stumbled out the door.

The other patrons of the bar sat silently, paying rapt attention to this little tableau. The bartender, in particular, looked as if some freak of nature had just entered his establishment. Nobody, including the bartender, seemed inclined to interfere.

Kurtz pursed his lips and touched the barrel of the gun to the spot between Lenny's eyes. "Nobody can hear us," Kurtz said. "Now, tell me about Gina Cole."

Lenny drew a deep breath. "Nobody mentioned any names, you understand? I was playing cards with a couple of guys who sometimes hang out here. They got talkative." Lenny's lips curled. A respectable mobster did not get talkative.

"Minor league guys? Bit players?" It occurred to Kurtz that Lenny was something of a bit player himself. Big time mobsters had more than one ape to watch over them and spent their time in better joints than this one.

Lenny nodded. "Yeah."

"And what exactly did they say, these minor league guys?"

"They said they knew who killed the girl."

"They didn't do it themselves?"

"No."

"Who did?"

Lenny shrugged.

"Why was it done?"

"I don't know. They didn't say that."

"And what was their involvement?"

"Transport. They dumped the body."

"And who are these talkative guys?"

"I don't know their last names. One of them is named Joey. The other one is Don."

"Joey and Don," Kurtz said.

Lenny nodded.

"What do Joey and Don look like?"

"Don is a big, beefy guy. Joey is short and skinny and he's got a red face."

"Have they been in here lately?"

"Not in a few days."

"Where was Walter Stang while this card game was going on?"

"I don't know. He might have been around."

"Okay." Kurtz rose to his feet. He thought about it for a few moments, shrugged. He popped the magazine out of the Ruger and tossed the gun onto Lenny's chest. Lenny looked up at Kurtz from the floor. The table still lay across his legs and half of his chest. Kurtz smiled. "Have a nice night," he said.

The next morning, Kurtz was examining a patient named Jerry Schnider, a truck driver with a hernia. "You do much lifting?" Kurtz asked.

"Yeah."

It figured. The canal where the vas deferens came through the abdominal wall was subject to rupture. Men who did a lot of physical labor were particularly prone. Jerry Schnider's hernia was a large one. It bulged with intestines beneath Kurtz' fingers. "Relax," Kurtz said.

Schnider relaxed. The hernia was freely movable. Kurtz pressed it back into the abdomen and the bulge where it had been disappeared. The defect, however, still remained and the hernia was apt to pop back out at any time. The next time, it might become incarcerated in the canal, which could cut off the blood supply to the bowel. The trapped bowel would then strangulate. Hernias by themselves were annoying but not dangerous. Dead bowel was.

"You need surgery," Kurtz said.

"I figured." Schnider's voice was resigned. "When can you do it?"

"Next Thursday?"

"Okay. Can you give me a note? I'll have to take sick time."

"Sure." Kurtz scribbled a note on a prescription pad. "The hernia will probably pop out again in a day or so. That's okay, but if it begins to hurt, don't wait. Go right to the Emergency Room and have them page me. You understand?"

Schnider nodded.

"The nurses from pre-admission testing and ambulatory surgery will call you. You'll need a complete blood count and an EKG. You can arrange to have that done by yourself or you can have it done here but if you have it done yourself, make sure they fax the results to the ASU. Otherwise, don't eat or drink anything after midnight on Wednesday and show up at the OR when the nurses tell you to. Okay?"

"How long will I be in the hospital?"

"Unless I run into something unexpected, you'll go home the same day."

Schnider looked startled.

"Managed care," Kurtz said. "Thank your insurance company."

Schnider shook his head, put his clothes back on and left. Kurtz washed his hands and walked back into the waiting room. Harry Moran sat on a chair, reading a copy of *Sports Illustrated*. Kurtz glanced at Mrs. Schapiro.

"I told him you were busy," she said. "He insisted on waiting."

Moran gave him a smile. Kurtz smiled gingerly back. "Hi, Harry," he said.

Moran continued to smile. Something about the smile made Kurtz nervous. "Can I help you with something, Harry?"

"Yeah," Moran said. "You can. Where were you last night, around eight o'clock?"

"Last night? Around eight o'clock?" Kurtz had the unpleasant sensation that his voice was squeaking.

"Must be an echo in here," Moran observed. "Yeah. Last night, around eight o'clock."

"I don't know," Kurtz said. "I suppose I was home."

"You suppose."

Kurtz had not yet told Barent and Moran about Joey and Don. In the clear light of morning, Kurtz was coming to have second thoughts about last night's little escapade. So okay, he hadn't gotten hurt. He had found out some information that might be useful. He had also interfered with an ongoing police investigation and withheld other information that people more qualified than himself might be able to use. And now what? The intrepid private detective had patients to see and not a lot of time to follow up on clues, even if he had some idea where to find skinny little Joey and big beefy Don.

"Come on back," Kurtz said.

Moran grinned. He unfolded his long length from the chair and followed Kurtz into his private office. "Sit down."

Moran sat in a chair across from the desk. He continued to grin. Kurtz found the grin to be unaccountably annoying. "Eight o'clock, you say?"

"Yup."

"Well, actually, I stopped off for a drink last night, it was about eight." He really wished Moran would stop grinning.

"Go on," Moran said.

"A place downtown. Sheridan's."

"Irish bar? Seedy?"

"Yeah," Kurtz said. He paused. "Why do you ask?"

Moran's smile grew even wider. "We had some information that a guy fitting your description went in there and roughed up a couple of the customers."

Kurtz frowned. "From where did you receive this information?"

"From ourselves. A couple of our guys were there undercover. They think you're crazy as a loon."

"I deny everything," Kurtz said. "I admit nothing. What were the cops doing at a place like Sheridan's, anyway?"

"I could ask you the same thing, except that we taped your conversation with Walter Stang."

Kurtz stared at him.

Moran raised a brow. "Don't give me the aggrieved look. You're not Stang's lawyer and you're not his priest. You're not even his physician. There was nothing confidential about the conversation."

"Okay," Kurtz said. He sighed. "You've got me. Which ones were they? The cops, I mean."

"I believe they were masquerading as bikers."

"The big guys at the bar? Drinking tequila?"

Moran frowned. "They're not supposed to drink while on duty."

Kurtz grinned faintly. "Straight tequila, no salt, no limes. Quite a lot of tequila. I suppose you could say all that tequila would make them unreliable witnesses."

"I suppose you could say you're full of shit." Moran said it amiably. "So, Lenny and Dominick. What did they tell you?"

"You know Lenny and Dominick?"

"You might say that Lenny and Dominick have a passing acquaintance with the forces of law and order."

Kurtz leaned back in his chair, thinking it over. "Dominick didn't say a thing. Lenny claimed that two guys named Joey and Don transported the body. They were supposedly bragging about it."

"Joey and Don."

"Joey is a skinny little guy. Don is big."

"Is that all?"

"Yes. Lenny himself had no other involvement, or so he claims."

"Lenny," Moran said, "is not a character that most of us would choose to fool around with. He's an enforcer. He breaks people's kneecaps with baseball bats."

"I'm sure you exaggerate. I found him to be perfectly pleasant once we got over our initial difficulties."

"I'm not kidding. Lenny is an Irish wise guy. They're the worst kind."

"Irish?" For some reason, Kurtz had figured Lenny for the mafia. Italian. "I thought he was mob connected."

"He is mob connected. The Irish mob. You never heard of Hell's Kitchen? The Westies?"

"Can't say that I have."

Moran sadly shook his head. "They're not people you want to cross."

"Now you tell me."

"I would have told you before if you had bothered to ask."

"How about Dominick? Is he Irish too?"

"Leonard Flanagan and Dominick O'Brien. He's as Irish as they come."

"My mother was Irish," Kurtz said. "I've always had a soft spot in my heart for the Irish."

"Well, you better hope that Lenny feels the same way."

Chapter 17

"How's Denise?" Moran asked.

"She's good. No problems with the baby."

"Paul?"

"Hanging in."

"He better enjoy it before the shit hits the fan." Moran's wife was about two months along. This was their third, so Moran at least knew what to expect. Barent's daughter was pregnant for the first time. Not quite eight months, a brief hiatus of calm before the main event. Morning sickness was pretty much over and Denise wasn't yet looking like a total balloon. Barent clearly remembered the last month or so of Betty's pregnancies. She had been, to put it mildly, a little grouchy.

"I've told him," Barent said.

The sky was mostly gray and a cold wind made the car shudder but at least it wasn't raining. Moran was driving, which gave Barent plenty of time to think. Unfortunately, he didn't have a lot to think about at the moment. The case was going in at least three different directions and Joey and Don were the only solid leads. He was going through the motions with the Van Gelden connection but he didn't expect much to come of it. Gina Cole's friends and colleagues had so far contributed nothing. The death of Mark Woodson, if he was dead, worried him, but aside from the fact that the whole thing smelled, he had no real reason to suspect a connection.

Kurtz was another problem. Barent liked Richard Kurtz. Despite the difference in their professions, the two men had a similar outlook on life. In the past, however, Kurtz had managed to restrain himself, confining his involvement in Barent's cases (Barent was aware that Kurtz might not regard them in quite the same way) to providing sympathy and some well thought advice. Oh, Kurtz had been shot at once or twice but that was sheer bad luck. This latest move was something else. Kurtz shouldn't have done it. No doubt Kurtz knew it. No doubt he had known it before he did it.

"I'll have to have a little talk with Richard," Barent said.

Moran shook his head. "The guy's a loaded gun."

"Yeah," Barent said morosely.

"Ted Weiss is right about him."

"Kurtz didn't ask Walter Stang to walk into his office."

"And you didn't ask him to track down Joey and Don but he did it anyway."

A lot of cops were Irish—Moran, for instance. In the middle of the last century, a wave of young men who had spent most of their lives plotting war against the

British (and seeing their families slowly die from starvation after the potato famine) had taken a long, hard look at their situation and decided that America offered better odds. The wave of Irish immigrants had continued almost unabated for over seventy years. A few had become crooks and some had become cops and almost all, one way or another, had put their talents and ambition to work and bought in to the American Dream.

Joey and Don, if they were Irish, should not be hard to trace. The cops had plenty of connections in the neighborhood.

"Isn't old Klein about to retire?" Moran asked.

"Klein? What about him?" Klein was a police surgeon. The city kept a number of them on the payroll, just in case they were needed, which they too often were.

"Isn't it obvious? Recommend Kurtz for the spot. Maybe it'll keep him out of trouble."

"Kurtz?"

Moran just smiled. A stray drizzle misted the windshield and Harry turned on the wipers. Another twenty minutes and they should be there. Barent stretched out his legs and scratched behind the ear. Kurtz? A police surgeon? "It's an interesting idea," Barent said.

"Think about it."

"I am thinking about it."

Lucky Lenore was understanding. Lenore knew when to give a man space. Lenore did not exactly approve of violence and mayhem but she seemed to instinctively know that a man had to do what a man had to do. She also knew that boys would be boys.

"Lucky you didn't get killed," Lenore said.

Kurtz bit his lip and tried hard to look sheepish.

"I mean it."

Kurtz tried on a tentative smile. Lenore was not smiling back but neither was she frowning. "I didn't realize you were such a macho lunatic when I met you in Cancun."

"Now you know," Kurtz said.

"Why did you do it?"

Why, indeed? "I suppose you could say that I wanted to."

She shook her head sadly. "Too late to throw you back. Just try not to get in over your head, okay?"

"I'll try." He meant it. Kurtz had no intention at all of getting in over his head. Life was too good.

Lenore put down her wine glass and snuggled into his shoulder. "We won't tell my mother. She's just getting acquainted with the real you."

Kurtz grunted. He didn't want to talk about Lenore's mother. Esther Brinkman could be disregarded but she couldn't be ignored. She had always reminded Kurtz of a predatory bird, an owl maybe—a little, Jewish one. "I think we should tell her," he said. Now that he thought about it, he would really enjoy the look on Esther Brinkman's face. He felt a smile spreading across his own face. "We shouldn't keep secrets from your mother."

Lenore silently whistled. Then she giggled. "Sure," she said. "Why not? Maybe it'll do her some good." She laughed out loud. "How about Saturday night? We're going over to talk about the wedding. The perfect time."

Lenore reminded him of her mother sometimes. Just a little. She had the same sharp gleam in the eye. "What shall we do between now and then?" Kurtz asked.

Lenore's hand trailed delicately up Kurtz' thigh and she grinned. "We'll think of something."

The Van Gelden Institute looked like a cross between a rich man's estate and an exclusive hotel. The main building was red brick, three stories high, with towers on all four sides. Three smaller houses clustered around the big house. A spacious lawn dotted with woods surrounded the buildings and a brick wall surrounded the lawn. The wall, Barent noted, was too smooth to climb and too high to jump over.

The foyer had a white tile floor and an enormous crystal chandelier hanging from the ceiling. The foyer reminded him of the Herbert estate. Considering the relationship between Harold Van Gelden and Eleanor Herbert, the resemblance may well have been deliberate. The Van Gelden Institute was evidently a place where a rich neurotic would feel perfectly at home. A curved desk crouched against the wall beneath the stairwell and a pretty, dark-haired woman in a green dress sat at the desk. "Can I help you?" she asked.

"Detectives Barent and Moran to see Doctor Shields."

"Oh, yes." She picked up a phone, said something into it and smiled widely at Barent. "Go right in. He's expecting you. The first door on your right."

The first door on the right was made of solid cherry wood. A small plaque in the center said, "Francis Shields, MD—Medical Director." Barent knocked. A voice from inside said, "Come in," and Barent pushed it open. The office was lined with bookcases. There was a salmon colored carpet, a couch, a coffee table, two easy chairs and a wooden desk with an intercom in the corner. Behind the desk sat a man in a vest and a gray business suit. "Doctor Shields?" Barent said.

"Yes. Detective Barent?"

Barent nodded. "This is Harry Moran."

Shields was smiling. He was plump. He wore wire-rimmed glasses. His hair was curly. He looked much too young to be director of anything. "Sit down. Would you like a cup of coffee?"

"Coffee would be nice." Barent glanced at Moran. "Harry?"

Moran expressed assent. Shields pressed a button on the intercom and ordered the coffee, then leaned back, rubbed his hands together and said, "Now, what can I do for you?"

"Have you ever heard of Eleanor and Vincent Herbert?"

Shields looked thoughtful. "I don't think so."

Barent told him an abbreviated version of the story, leaving out the parts regarding Harold Van Gelden's police record. Shields listened intently. When Barent had finished, Shields looked doubtful. "It sounds as if you want me to confirm Miss Herbert's psychiatric history."

"I would appreciate it."

"You know I can't do that. The information is privileged."

"But you weren't her psychiatrist. There is no relationship to protect."

"I'm a member of the staff. The privileged relationship extends to the entire institution. If Miss Herbert was a patient here, then nobody who is or ever was associated with the place can reveal anything about her, not without her permission. In any case, the records might no longer exist. Harold Van Gelden is dead. When a psychiatrist retires, his office records are destroyed. It's the only way to ensure confidentiality."

"What about hospital records? Would they be destroyed?"

"Probably not," Shields conceded.

"How about financial records? Are they privileged?"

Shields frowned. "What financial records?"

"Bills. Receipts. That sort of thing."

Shields opened his mouth to say something but just then there came a knock at the door and the pretty receptionist walked in with their coffee. Shields waited until she had left before speaking. "If the patient's name is on them, any such records would still be privileged."

"How about if somebody else's name is on them? Eleanor Herbert was just a kid. She wouldn't be paying her own bills. Presumably her parents would have paid."

"I could check," Shields said. "I sort of doubt we keep records going back that far. And anyway, how could this information help you? It seems pretty far removed from the murder of Regina Cole."

Good question. Moran, who had been sipping his coffee, barely nodded. "I don't know that it can," Barent conceded. "You never do, in this business."

The look on Shield's face expressed doubt but he was too polite to voice it. "I'll look," he said. "Is there anything else?"

"As a matter of fact," Barent said, "there is."

Shields sighed. He glanced at his watch. "And that would be?"

"Harold Van Gelden. What sort of man was he?"

Shields gave a tentative smile. "I never met him. Some of the older workers tell stories about him, though. Supposedly, he was quite a character."

"Is that a psychiatric diagnosis?"

"Sometimes there's not a lot of difference between a diagnosis and a categorization. Psychiatrists don't use the word 'normal' very much. Normal means average and very few people, strictly speaking, are average. We don't encourage normality. We strive for functionality."

"Which means what?"

"At its simplest, if you can get up in the morning, get dressed, go to work and hold down a job, you're probably doing alright. You're functional. Most of what a psychiatrist does is deal with mental or emotional processes that interfere with the ability of the patient to function."

"Not to belabor the point, but are you saying that Harold Van Gelden wasn't normal?"

"No," Shields said. "I'm saying that he had a reputation for sleeping with every woman he could get his hands on. Also, he was supposedly a real tyrant. Anybody who annoyed him got fired instantly. And his treatment methods were pretty bizarre."

"Deprivation therapy."

Shields looked surprised. "Exactly. It's not an idea that ever gained much acceptance."

"You don't use it, then?"

"I don't know anybody who uses it."

"How about electroconvulsive therapy?"

"Electroconvulsive therapy has been proven time after time to be an effective treatment for depression. Very few reputable psychiatrists don't use electroconvulsive therapy."

"How about insulin shock?"

"Ah." Shields sat back in his chair, a thoughtful look on his face. "Insulin shock used to be considered an alternative to electroconvulsive therapy. It was pretty horrible. You injected the patient with insulin, their blood sugar would fall so low that their brains began to starve. It induced seizures. If used to excess, it also resulted in brain damage."

"And Harold Van Gelden used it."

"A lot of people used it, back then. This was before the benefits of anesthesia had been thought of. ECT was just as bad."

"But Van Gelden didn't use it to treat depression. He used it as punishment."

"Like I said, his theories are no longer held in great esteem."

"Yet you keep his name on the door."

"What can you do? He was the founder. And aside from his more unusual theories, he had a reputation as a great clinician. Things were different back then."

A brief silence fell. Moran seemed content to sip his coffee. Barent wasn't sure what he had gotten from this conversation but he had nothing left to ask. Shields glanced again at his watch. Finally, Barent sighed. He drained the remainder of his coffee and rose to his feet. "Thank you," he said. "You've been very helpful."

"Any time," Shields replied. "I'll give you a call when I've located those records."

Barent nodded. "I'd appreciate it."

Chapter 18

John Tweed had a round, ruddy face, twinkling blue eyes and curly black hair. Barent hadn't seen him for a few years but he hadn't changed much. Tweed had been a cop for fifteen years. Unlike most cops, John Tweed had always enjoyed walking a beat. He had no interest in driving a patrol car and even less interest in working at a desk. Tweed had a conviction that real police work was done in the community, showing up at odd times and unexpected places, making the police presence known, even taken for granted. Drug dealers were less likely to make a deal if John Tweed's smiling face might saunter around the corner. Hitmen were less likely to hit the local grocer if John Tweed might be walking on by. John Tweed had been born and raised in the old neighborhood and for the past ten years, he had made it his territory. Many citizens did not love him but they all knew him and they all respected him.

"It sounds like Joey Cork and Don Lonigan," John Tweed said. "They're hoods. They work for Mickey Nolan."

Mickey Nolan was a known and feared name in the criminal universe of the city. According to rumor, Mickey Nolan had been responsible, either personally or by proxy, for the deaths of over fifty men. He had ruled what was left of the Irish mob in New York for nearly thirty years. "Nolan's in jail," Barent said.

Tweed shrugged. "It doesn't matter. He's still the boss. And there are always plenty of opportunities for enterprising boys who are willing to work."

"Could you find out?"

"I'll try," Tweed said, and he did try. Joey Cork and Don Lonigan, however, seemed to have vanished. They had last been seen three days before, in Sheridan's. None of their family or friends knew where they had gone, or if they knew, they were not telling.

"They don't seem very concerned, though," Tweed remarked.

"Maybe," Barent said, "that's because their friends don't like them."

Tweed barely smiled. "Boys like these have a tendency to vanish and then reappear. They're probably off somewhere, working."

"I don't know that I'd call it work."

Tweed shrugged.

"Keep your eye out," Barent said. "Hopefully, they'll show up."

Esther Brinkman had gotten to the point where she was no longer actively obnoxious after Lenore, smiling sweetly, had informed her mother that she did not have a choice. She simply had to be nice if she wanted to associate either with her or with any future grandchildren.

"How can you treat your own flesh and blood this way?" Esther had complained. "I'm your mother. For this sort of ingratitude, I've got to live with stretch marks and an inverted uterus?"

Lenore, who had over the years been told many times about her mother's inverted uterus, only yawned. "Maybe you should think about that hysterectomy," she said.

"I'm not going to have a hysterectomy," her mother protested. "There are risks involved. There could be nerve damage. You could live the rest of your life in a diaper. You could die."

Lenore had been through this discussion before. She said calmly, "You're not going to die. Nobody dies from a hysterectomy."

Esther set her lips. "So? There are worse things than dying. You want to take care of me in my old age when I'm in a diaper, wetting the furniture?"

"Certainly not," Lenore said. "I'm going to let Daddy take care of you."

"What? With his bad heart and his angina and the way he takes nitroglycerin?" Esther glanced at her husband, who was sitting in an armchair determinedly reading a newspaper. "How could your father take care of me? I have to take care of your father. Besides, by that time, he may not be here. I know this is not a pleasant thing to think about but we have to be realistic."

Lenore had never seen her father actually take a nitroglycerin. He fumbled with the bottle now and then. It was like a little play between her mother and father. Stanley reached for the nitro; Esther shut her mouth, at least for a while. "True," Lenore said. "I guess you'll have to go into a nursing home. I understand they have some nice ones up in Riverdale."

Esther drew herself up to her whole five feet. "You would put your own mother in a nursing home?"

Lenore tried not to laugh out loud but she couldn't restrain a brief giggle, at which her mother's face turned red. Regretfully, Lenore thought that a little appeasement might be in order. "Now, Mom," she said, "you know we'll always do what's best for you." It occurred to Lenore fleetingly that was best for her mother would probably be a prescription for lithium and a very large enema. Lenore couldn't help it. She began to laugh and once she started, she found that she couldn't stop. She could barely catch her breath. Her mother simply stared, her lips compressed into a thin, disapproving line.

Finally, Lenore's laughter ground to a halt. "Oh, my," she said. "I didn't mean to laugh."

Esther Brinkman continued to stare at her daughter's face, saying nothing, determinedly unamused.

Oh, well, spilled milk…"Anyway," Lenore said. "Richard and I will be over for dinner on Wednesday. Remember—be nice."

Esther Brinkman merely sniffed.

She was, however, nice. Esther Brinkman, Lenore had frequently told Kurtz, wasn't really a bad sort. She was loyal. She was intelligent. She was hard-working. She meddled in her daughters' lives because she desperately wanted them to be more than she herself was. Also, she was bored and depressed and had nothing better to do.

Kurtz was willing to give the old bat the benefit of the doubt but he wasn't going to put up with any shit.

He found himself somewhat embarrassed, however, as he recounted the tale of his recent exploits. Heroes in novels rarely had any sense of irony, Kurtz reflected. They got into impossible situations and beat tremendous odds by the strength of their arms and the sweat of their brow and they never felt ridiculous. Now, sitting in Esther Brinkman's living room, telling the tale of Lenny and Dominick, Kurtz felt ridiculous.

But to his surprise, Esther Brinkman did not seem at all horrified by his story, or even disapproving. She listened to Kurtz' recitation silently, her brow furrowed. When he had finished, a slow smile spread across her face. "Let me get this straight. You walked into this place, this den of thieves, and you beat up two gangsters, just like that?" She shook her head in amazement and looked at her husband, as if wondering why Stanley Brinkman had never beaten up gangsters. Stanley, bewildered, scratched his bald head.

"I didn't intend to beat up anybody," Kurtz said. "They're the ones who started it."

"The Nazis are always the ones who start it. On *Krystallnacht*, when the Nazis came to rob all the Jews and break their arms and their heads and run them out of their homes, if someone had beaten them up, or even shot them between the eyes like the animals they were, it would have been a *mitzvah*."

Kurtz looked at Lenore questioningly. "A *mitzvah*," she said, "is Hebrew. It means, 'a good thing' or 'a blessing.'"

Esther Brinkman smiled at Kurtz. The smile was ferocious. "You want to beat up Nazis? You should enjoy yourself. Just don't get in over your head."

Kurtz glanced at Lenore. "Yes," he said. "I've been told that before."

The next day, Barent received a call from Francis Shields, MD. "Detective Barent?" Shields' voice sounded strangely tentative.

"Yes?"

"I've managed to locate those records you asked for. I'm surprised we still had them. They were in a crate in the basement."

"Great," Barent said.

"There are invoices for a series of bills charged over a span of nearly three years. They were paid by a man named Joseph P. Herbert."

"Eleanor's father."

"I suppose so. Eleanor Herbert is not mentioned." Shields' voice hesitated.

"If she had been mentioned, I wouldn't have admitted it. The name of another patient is mentioned, however. I'm telling you this because the patient is deceased. There is some controversy over the ethics of revealing the medical history of a dead patient. A few years ago, the psychiatrist of Anne Sexton released audiotapes of her treatment. Do you know Anne Sexton?"

"A poet," Barent said. "She committed suicide."

"That's correct. There was quite an uproar…"

Barent waited with some impatience. Obviously, the guy was going to tell him but he needed to make his excuses first.

"The patient's name on the invoices is not Eleanor Herbert," Shields finally said. "The name is Joseph P. Herbert, Junior."

Chapter 19

Two large, hard-eyed young men stood on either side of the door as Barent drove up to the mansion, got out of his car and pressed the buzzer. The two men looked at him but said nothing. Barent looked back. After a moment, the door opened. Charles stood on the other side.

"Hello, Charles. Remember me?"

The old butler gave him a quizzical look. "Detective Barent," he said. "Of course."

The men immediately looked away. Barent smiled, first at one, then at the other. They both ignored the smile.

"Might I come in?" Barent asked.

"Mister Herbert is busy."

Which suited Barent just fine. "And Miss Herbert? How is she?"

Eleanor Herbert had been released from the hospital three days before. Her injured heart was healing nicely.

"Miss Herbert is resting. She is not to be disturbed."

"I have no intention of disturbing her. Actually, I was hoping to speak to you."

Charles seemed doubtful. He glanced at the two men. They pretended they were statues. Charles made no move to get out of Barent's way. "Mister Herbert did say you were to cooperate with us," Barent said.

"That is true." Charles frowned but stepped to the side. "Please come in."

A few minutes later they were seated together in the kitchen, sipping tea. "Who's the muscle?" Barent asked.

"Garrison is in the den with his father. He goes nowhere without security."

Barent frowned. Kurtz had mentioned the name Martin Burnett. Barent had put in a search and discovered that the Herberts' Security Chief had served in the Marines, then had worked as a cop in Seattle for five years before going into private security. The only thing of interest in Martin Burnett's résumé was an arrest for drunken assault at the age of nineteen. Since this had taken place on the eve of the Panama invasion, the judge had taken his alleged state of mind into consideration and shown leniency.

Rich men were sometimes paranoid. And sometimes paranoia was justified. A man in Garrison Herbert's position might receive the occasional threat. Still...

"Why is that?" Barent asked.

Charles shrugged. "The Herberts are in a highly competitive business," he said. "They've always had security."

"Have there ever been any incidents that might justify that?"

"Not to my knowledge, but I have never been involved in the family business. I would not necessarily know."

And if there had been incidents, the police wouldn't necessarily know, either. Not if they had been handled privately. The drawbacks of living in a democracy.

"What can you tell me," Barent asked, "about Joseph P. Herbert, Junior?"

Charles gave him a quizzical look. "I believe you saw his portrait, the first time that you came here."

"I remember," Barent said.

"I never met him. He died before I arrived. It must have been sixty years ago."

"Tell me about it."

Barent kept quiet while Charles sipped his tea, thinking. Finally the old man said, "I know very little, I'm afraid." Charles hesitated. "Does this question really have something to do with your investigation?"

"It might."

"I don't see how."

"Neither do I, at this point." The time spent on following up leads that led nowhere outweighed the time that actually produced useful information by at least twenty to one. "But I don't know that yet."

Francis Shields, MD had done more than merely look up the old financial records. Curious, he had looked up the medical records as well. Joseph P. Herbert, Junior had been the eldest son of Joseph P. and Mary Herbert. Junior, it seemed, had been something of a ne'er-do-well. Tall, dashing, good-looking and rich, he had spent most of his evenings drinking and dancing in New York's clubs and speakeasies. And then one night in 1931, there had been a gas explosion in a building on the Lower West Side. Nobody seemed to know what Joseph P. Herbert, Junior had been doing there but he had lain in collapsed rubble for nearly two days before his semi-conscious body was discovered. He had a broken arm and two broken legs and had suffered a fractured skull. His physical injuries ultimately healed but the psychological scars went deeper. He had stayed in the hospital, recovering from his wounds, for almost two months and was then sent home to his family, where he proceeded to lie in bed for most of the day, staring silently into space. After a few months of this, Joseph P. Herbert, Senior had shipped his eldest son off to the Van Gelden Institute.

Junior had stayed at the Institute for nearly five years. He never entirely recovered. He ate little and soon grew thin. He would walk around the grounds and gardens of the Institute and even talk occasionally to the staff. His conversation, when he deigned to speak, had been rational. Loud noises sent him into a funk, however. He would scream and huddle himself into a ball or dive under a table. He rarely slept and when he did sleep, would awake crying from troubled dreams. Van Gelden's diagnosis had been shell-shock, what they called today post traumatic stress disorder.

During his last six months, Joseph P. Herbert, Junior seemed to be making a little progress. He would sometimes smile, even laugh. The staff was encouraged. And then one morning he was found hanging from a shower fixture, an apparent suicide.

Charles said, "From what the other servants told me, it must have been a relief to the family. They went to visit him twice monthly and almost always, they would come back gloomy and depressed—except near the end. By the end, they had begun to hope again, at least a little. And so his suicide was an even greater shock to them."

"To what did they attribute this suicide?"

Charles raised an eyebrow and sipped his tea. "He was mentally ill. The mentally ill do strange things."

"But why then, at that particular time? He was supposedly doing better."

Charles gave a minute shrug. "You should ask a psychiatrist."

Barent already had. Shields had claimed that suicides in such circumstances were common, that any apparent improvement was apt to be illusory and temporary.

"And Eleanor? How did she take all this?"

"It's strange," Charles said, "I haven't thought of these things in years." He frowned in concentration. "That's a very good question but I don't really know. It was years before I came here."

"At the time of her brother's death, Miss Herbert must have been seven or eight. That would make Vincent about twenty-two and Joseph Herbert over thirty when he died."

"True. Mary Herbert died shortly after giving birth to Vincent, possibly as a complication of pregnancy. Mister Herbert waited more than ten years to re-marry. Eleanor is the child of Mister Herbert's second wife, Alice Herbert."

"And so Eleanor Herbert's psychological troubles must have begun shortly after her brother's suicide."

Charles shrugged. "I suppose that's true," he said. "But it was more than sixty years ago. How can it matter now?"

Barent just looked at him, wondering the same thing.

Adler sneezed. He turned his face away from the open abdomen on the table and sneezed twice more. There was a wet spot in the middle of his mask and his eyes were red.

"You," Kurtz said, "are disgusting."

"I have the flu," Adler said, miserably.

"Maybe you should take some time off," Kurtz suggested. "You'll infect the whole hospital."

"I can't. I'm on call tomorrow."

Kurtz just looked at him. The physicians' creed was a strict one. If a patient came down with the flu, none of them would hesitate for an instant in ordering him to bed but they held themselves to a different standard. You came to work unless you were ready to drop.

There was no question that people who were stressed out were more susceptible to minor ailments. A surgery residency was tough enough but Adler had other problems.

Kurtz thought for a moment of telling Adler about Joey and Don. In essence, Adler was off the hook, if he had ever really been on it. But Joey and Don were tidbits whose existence should not at this point be revealed, not until they were safely in police custody and their role, if any, clarified. No, best to let Adler wriggle a little longer.

"Cheer up," Kurtz temporized. "They have no evidence. You're not a serious suspect."

Adler shrugged and gave him a wan smile. "I know that. You know that. But this whole thing is ruining my sex life. Everyone I'm interested in is worried that I'll strangle them."

It was more than that, of course. The Board of Trustees, for a wonder, had insisted on doing the right thing, the more rational among them probably more worried about a lawsuit on Adler's part than the miniscule chance that he was guilty. Adler was not on probation, not even on leave without pay. Until there was some real evidence linking him to Regina Cole's murder, Adler was going to be treated just like any other young resident. Except that he wasn't treated just like any other young resident. When he came onto a floor, the nurses tended to vanish, or they gathered together into little groups and pretended not to stare at him. The patients, so far, seemed unaware of these undercurrents.

Kurtz just hoped that it stayed that way. He tried to grin. "A little abstinence will be good for you. You can concentrate on your work."

Adler shrugged, evidently not cheered up.

The case was a simple appendix on a healthy young woman. Kurtz let Adler close the skin and went to the locker room. While he was dressing, his beeper went off. The number on the screen was one he knew well.

Barent picked up the phone on the second ring. "Richard," he said, "I need to talk to you and your friend, Bill Werth. Can you arrange it for this afternoon?"

Kurtz had office hours until three. "I can manage it later on, maybe around four, four-thirty. I'll have to check with Bill."

"That would be fine. Please get back to me."

"Sure," Kurtz said.

Bill Werth had the same thick glasses, frizzy hair and enthusiastic look that Barent remembered. He sat in his chair behind a mahogany desk and smiled eagerly. "What's up?" he asked. "Did you get the goods on Van Gelden?"

"Doctor Van Gelden is dead," Barent said. "I have no reason to suspect him of any involvement in the death of Regina Cole."

Werth looked disappointed. "Oh. Then what do you want with me?" He glanced at Kurtz, who was sitting quietly to the side. Werth was evidently wondering as well what Barent wanted with Kurtz. The answer to this unspoken question was that when it came to medical issues, even ones outside Kurtz' specific area of expertise, Barent valued Kurtz' advice. Also, Kurtz was involved with the case whether Barent liked it or not and he wanted Kurtz where he could keep an eye on him.

"What can you tell me about post traumatic stress disorder?" Barent asked.

Barent had already asked this question of Francis Shields, but it never hurt to check on such things. Shields, considering his place of employment, might not be as unbiased as he seemed.

Werth looked quizzical. "The name describes a group of ailments which are probably not otherwise related. Occasionally it comes about as a result of physical trauma to the brain but more often it's a purely psychological reaction to experiences that are too horrible for the victim to bear. Sometimes it can take the form of severe, morbid depression. What these patients have gone through, what they've suffered, destroys their confidence in a sane, stable world. Other times, it can be a form of induced psychosis. It can be devastating. Their perception of reality is completely warped. They hear voices, perform repetitive actions, hallucinate. There's a theory that it only happens to people who are predisposed to it, that these patients are already borderline schizophrenics and the precipitating events are only the final insult but since we don't really understand schizophrenia, the theory doesn't help us much."

"Does anyone ever get over it?"

"Quite often. Time is a great healer. It helps if they can forget."

"Have you ever heard of such a patient committing suicide years after the event?"

"Absolutely. They commit suicide frequently. The mortality rate from morbid depression is over thirty per-cent. They kill themselves."

"Is electroconvulsive therapy ever used?"

"For the depressive form, certainly. ECT rarely helps in psychosis, though it is sometimes tried."

"What will help psychosis?"

Werth shrugged. "Phenothiazines. Haldol." He smiled wanly. "Maybe."

Barent pursed his lips and sat back in his chair. So far, what Werth said agreed entirely with what Shields had told him. Junior, apparently, had suffered from the depressive form of post traumatic stress disorder. According to his medical record, there had been no evidence of voices or visions or hallucinations. His perception of reality had not been significantly impaired. "Are there any cases where such patients seem to be getting better, and then kill themselves?"

"Certainly. It's actually classic. They reach that final decision to go through with it and it eases their minds, at least for a little while. They can relax. It's all over. That's when you have to watch a depressed patient most closely, when they suddenly seem happy and there's no apparent reason for it."

Again, pretty much what Shields had said. So what did he have? Eleanor Herbert had been a disturbed child, probably from trauma over her brother's death, her older brother whom she had presumably looked up to and admired. She had been treated by the eminent Doctor Van Gelden, who had also treated her brother. She got over it. She lived her life. Then, in her twenties, Eleanor Herbert's husband had died and Doctor Van Gelden again provided counseling. Half a century later, Eleanor Herbert had a heart attack which led to a cardiac arrest, was successfully revived, and dreamed she witnessed a murder. At approximately the same time, a real murder was taking place, under entirely different circumstances from those Eleanor Herbert described.

Thank you, Eleanor Herbert, and good night.

Only one more thing to try, and then he could write off the Herberts from serious consideration. Joey and Don were much better bets.

"Hello, hello," Barent said.

The voice on the other end of the phone belonged to John Costas, a reporter for a great metropolitan newspaper and a sometimes acquaintance of Barent's. Costas' voice sounded aggravated. It always did, when it didn't sound sly and wheedling. "I'm busy, Barent. What do you want?"

"Information."

Costas snickered. "My stock in trade. What will you give me for it?"

"An exclusive."

The voice hesitated. "On what?"

"Murder. What else?"

"Whose murder?"

"Regina Cole's."

"The woman who was strangled? Not exactly front page news."

No. Gina Cole wasn't the latest Mrs. Trump or Christie Brinkley or Madonna. She wasn't famous. She had lived an ordinary life until she suffered an extraordinary death. "Page three, maybe?"

"It's been over a week. The public's interest is short. More like page seven."

It occurred to Barent that the public's interest was anything the media said it was but the purpose of this phone call was not to argue with John Costas. "So how about it?"

"What do you want?"

"I want you to go into the dead files and tell me if there's anything at all on Joseph P. Herbert, Joseph P. Herbert, Junior, Doctor Harold Van Gelden or the Van Gelden Institute. I'm particularly interested in the decades of the twenties and thirties, give or take a few years."

Costas, when he spoke, sounded doubtful. "How does any of this tie in to Regina Cole?"

"I don't know that it does."

"And what if I can't help you?"

"You get the exclusive anyway."

"If you ever solve the case, which is not too certain."

"That's right."

"What have I got to lose?" Costas said. "Done."

Chapter 20

She sat up in bed, her heart pounding, her breath coming in rapid, shallow gasps. Frantically, she looked around, then relaxed. "Home," she whispered. With a sigh, she sank back into the pillows. Another nightmare, another visitation out of the past. She was running down endless, dark corridors, trying to escape from something huge and nameless, some obscene, unspoken horror. But even as she ran, she knew it was no use. She was too small and too slow and her pursuers were omnipotent and relentless. It was only a matter of time, and then...

A dream. Only a dream, a dream that she had dreamed many before times as a little girl, and then again as a young woman after her husband had died. "Calm down," she muttered.

Her hands were trembling, her gnarled, arthritic fingers trembling where they lay on the blankets. Helplessly, she clenched them, pulled the blankets up to her chin and closed her eyes. "It was only a dream," she whispered. "Dreams can't hurt me." She had told herself this before but she didn't believe it.

She never had.

"What exactly is it that a police surgeon does?" Kurtz asked.

"Mostly oversee the treatment of wounded cops. When somebody gets shot, for instance, you go to the hospital, review what's being done and make sure everything is on the up and up."

The physicians in charge must really love that, having an outsider looking over their shoulders, critiquing their every move. "Why is this necessary?"

"It's PR, mostly. Public relations and a little psychotherapy." Barent shrugged. "Cops get shot at. They like the idea that one of their own, someone they trust, is looking out for them."

"And what exactly is the deal?"

"The deal is you carry a beeper for twenty-four hours a couple of times a month. If anything happens during your shift, a police car will pick you up and drive you to the scene. For this, you get a badge and a stipend of sixty thousand a year."

"A badge?"

"I believe the rank is Inspector," Barent said sourly. Evidently, this grated on Barent. Inspector was an exalted rank, two grades higher than a Captain. Kurtz didn't hesitate for an instant. "I'll do it."

Barent gave him a morose look. "I figured you would," he said.

Schizophrenics tended to be creatures of habit. Walter Stang was released from jail and immediately returned to his old haunts. He spent much of the day wandering in Central Park and much of the evening in either Sheridan's or the Brendan Inn, another Irish Pub in the old neighborhood. A surreptitious tail was kept on him but it proved fruitless. Nobody approached him. Everybody, in fact, kept a careful distance. Walter Stang, with his vacant gaze and unwashed clothes, was obviously not normal. Lenny, it was noted, gave him a hard look the first time he walked into Sheridan's Bar but made no attempt to bother him. Stang, for his part, seemed to have forgotten that Lenny was his 'friend.' He sat with his pint of Guinness at a corner table, sipping slowly until it was gone, mumbling all the while to himself, and then left.

A day later, two bodies floated up from the East River and were discovered by a couple of kids looking for empty cans and bottles to turn in for the deposit. The bodies' hands and feet had been tied together and they had each been shot twice in the head, once in the temple and once again under the chin.

Joey and Don had finally returned home.

"I wish I could blame you for this," Barent said. "But they've both been dead for over a week."

Kurtz only grunted. It was ridiculous to take the murder of two hoodlums personally but Kurtz could not help being annoyed. So much for his marvelous clues.

"It was a professional hit," Barent said, "two bullets each, nice and neat."

"Wouldn't a professional have dumped the bodies in the ocean? They should never have been found."

"Sure he would. Or buried them in the Jersey swamps or ground them up for dog food. That's what he would have done if he wanted them to disappear."

"You're saying that they were meant to be found."

"Absolutely."

Lenore sat on the couch, listening intently and sipping a brandy. "I should invite my mother over," she said. "She would really get a kick out of this."

Barent looked at her. "Two men have been murdered, in addition to Regina Cole. Your mother would find that entertaining?"

"My mother has a simple outlook on life. She saves her sympathy for the good guys."

Barent barely shrugged. "Presumably Joey and Don got it because they had big mouths. The way they were found was meant to send a message."

"Don't talk," Kurtz said.

"Exactly."

"So who else did they talk to?"

"Nobody who would talk to us, you can bet on that."

Kurtz reached over to the bottle and poured himself another brandy. "Isn't that what informants are for?"

"My," Barent said, "you are getting so good at this."

Kurtz raised an eyebrow. "Just trying to be helpful," he said.

"Yeah," Barent said. "That is what informants are for."

Costas called the next day. "There's quite a file on these guys," he said. "What's the story, anyway?"

Barent's ears pricked up. "Tell me."

"Joseph P. Herbert's grandfather, Joseph Madison Herbert, was an early investor in Standard Oil. He was rich."

"I knew that."

"Alright, then did you know that Joseph M. Herbert's son, Paul Joseph Herbert, liked to gamble? He liked to gamble so much that by Nineteen Twenty, the family was just about broke."

"No," Barent said. "I didn't know that."

"It seems that Paul Herbert was quite a character. Gambling wasn't his only expensive habit. He also fancied himself a connoisseur of race horses. He bought a stud farm in Kentucky and spent fifteen years trying to breed himself a Derby winner. No luck. He also drank quite a lot and would periodically hole himself up in his suite of rooms with a couple of cases of liquor and a favorite mistress or two and not come out for weeks at a time."

"Ah, the old days, when men lived life to the fullest."

Costas snorted. "Yeah, a real role model. Anyway, by the time the old boy finally died, the family fortune had pretty much disappeared. Joseph P. Herbert, Paul Herbert's son, took what was left and put it into bootleg liquor. Prohibition saved their bacon."

Well, well. Put a different spin on the mansion up in Westchester. So much for old family money.

"Joseph P. was quite a story, himself. He trusted nobody, especially lawyers. He kept all the company records in his head, which actually makes some sense when you consider that his real business could easily have gotten him locked up in the federal pen. Supposedly, Herbert was a close associate of Owney Madden."

Owney Madden had been dead for over fifty years but the name lived on in gangland legend. Owney "The Killer" Madden, boss of the Irish mob, close associate of Dutch Schultz and Vito Genovese and Charles "Lucky" Luciano. Nice friends, Barent thought.

"Any of this confirmed?"

"No. It was all rumor. The old boy was investigated by three different DA's and at least once by the FBI. Nothing ever came of it."

He should have been surprised, Barent reflected. He really should have. Why wasn't he?

"How about Vincent Herbert?"

Costas' voice hesitated. "Rumors. Rumors of ties to organized crime but nothing ever mentioned publicly. Ostensibly, the guy is a pillar of the community.

He donates to half the charities in town."

"And his brother, Joseph P. Herbert, Junior?"

"A sad story. The kid got caught in a bombing and wound up a fruitcake. He spent three years at Van Gelden's place in Westchester and then hung himself."

"A bombing? I thought it was a gas explosion."

"The official story was a gas explosion but the unofficial word was that the building was bombed out. It was an illicit distillery owned by Vito Genovese. This was around the time that Arthur Flegenheimer was making his moves. You know the name, Arthur Flegenheimer?"

"Dutch Schultz," Barent said.

"That's right, Dutch Schultz."

"Dutch Schultz was murdered in a mob hit. His organization was taken over by Genovese and Luciano."

"And Owney Madden."

"So what was Junior doing in the building?"

"Nobody knows. Probably buying liquor for his old man."

"What else do you have on him?"

"He was well-connected and he had a violent temper. He got thrown out of three different prep schools, mostly for not bothering to study but once for beating up another kid and also taking a swing at one of the teachers, and then when he was a little older he almost killed a guy who was making eyes at a girl he was interested in. There were two charges of statutory rape and one suit for breach of promise. Seems Junior liked the ladies and the ladies liked him back. Why not? He was young, he was good-looking and he was rich. None of the charges stuck."

"Anything else on Junior?"

"Afraid not," Costas said. "Isn't that enough?"

"Then tell me about Van Gelden."

"Another strange one. During his career, at least three different patients accused him of sexual abuse and one accused him of physical assault in the form of repeated and enforced electrical shocks to the brain. All of the cases were either dropped or thrown out of court."

"A prophet is without honor in his own country," said Barent. "You got any more?"

"You don't sound surprised."

"I'm not. I've already had occasion to look into Van Gelden."

"Okay, then how about this: three weeks before Joseph P. Herbert, Junior hung himself, a nurse at the Van Gelden Institute, named Claire Reisberg, was raped and strangled. A patient was accused of the crime but was found innocent by reason of insanity. Rumor had it that Van Gelden was doing the nasty with her but of course that was never confirmed. The autopsy did confirm that the girl was pregnant."

Chapter 21

"Owney Madden," Moran said thoughtfully. "Amazing."

"The kingpin of the Irish mob in the nineteen-twenties and thirties," Barent said, "friend and associate of Al Capone, Meyer Lansky and Lucky Luciano. Isn't that special?"

Moran squinted at him and then smiled. "Puts a new light on Lenny and Dominick, that's for sure."

"It does lead one to suspect that the Herberts have kept up the old school tie, as it were."

"But why would they need guys like Lenny and Dominick? They've got Marty Burnett and their own security team."

"Who knows? Maybe Burnett is straight-laced." Barent thought about the two men standing outside the door of the Herbert mansion. "Legitimate security doesn't go around killing people and then dumping the bodies in the river, not even Joey and Don."

"Unless they're not legitimate security."

"There's no reason to think that."

"There's no reason not to."

Barent grinned. "True."

Moran slowly sucked in on his cigarette and let the smoke dribble out of his nose. "The Irish mob is not what it used to be. Mickey Nolan is in jail."

For a period of nearly seventy years from the late eighteen-eighties, the Irish mob had owned the West Side of Manhattan, hence the name "Westies." Unlike their Italian counterparts, the Westies had not initially possessed either a hierarchy or an organization. Composed almost entirely of young men fleeing from famine and British rule, they were a true mob, a mob ruled by the iron fist of the strongest and the most violent. By the time of Owney Madden, however, the era of the small time hood had given way to a more sophisticated—and more successful—veneer. And then over the next fifty years, the children of the mob grew up and went to American schools and learned professions and joined the middle class and largely drifted away from the old neighborhood. Most of them.

"Owney Madden spent some time in jail, too," Barent said. "That didn't stop him from running the organization."

"Even if Mickey Nolan still has his hand in, which is probably true, and even if he's in business somehow with Vincent Herbert, a tie-in to Gina Cole seems pretty far-fetched."

"There are other Herberts than Victor. Why assume it's the old man?"

"This is also true." Barent smiled and blew a smoke ring at the ceiling. "Love or money, isn't that the saying? That's why people commit murder; it's one or the other, every time. We haven't done so good with love, so let's follow the money."

Anticipating the returning stream of service men at the end of World War II, the Herberts had invested heavily in real estate on Long Island, Westchester, New Jersey and Southern Connecticut. Their money went into housing developments, parking lots, and shopping malls. Their fortunes had taken a brief dip during the real estate crash of the late nineteen-eighties but their investments had never been highly leveraged and the family fortunes soon recovered, or so went the stories. The truth was harder to ascertain. Ownership of stock accounting for more than five per-cent of a public corporation was on file with the SEC and could not be kept secret. The Herberts' holdings were not public. No stock had ever been issued and their partners, if any, were strictly anonymous.

A talk with their adversaries proved illuminating, however, more for what was kept silent than for what was said.

Jacob King was a short, fat man who wore a business suit and smoked a cigar. Except for two tufts of black hair sticking out over both ears, his head was bald and seemed much too large for his body.

"Herbert?" King peered quizzically at his cigar. The look on his face was pained. "The old man hasn't touched the business himself in over ten years. He's retired. Gary runs the corporation now. Garrison Herbert. You have to respect him, in a way, but I wouldn't want to live like him. Twelve hours a day at the office, every day. They say he hasn't taken a vacation in ten years. Most guys, you sit down at the table, you start with a little small talk, maybe a cup of coffee, even a drink or two, just to break the ice, show you're both human. Not Gary. Gary doesn't joke. He barely even smiles. Gary underbid me on a development near the Meadowlands, a couple of years back. I don't like Gary Herbert. Nobody does."

Barent nodded. By this time, he had heard the story before. Nobody underbid the Herberts. Their suppliers were able to deliver goods at prices consistently lower than anybody else's. Their workers were all union but, somehow, they never went on strike.

"And how was he able to do that?" Barent asked.

Ostensibly, the Herberts' advantage over their competitors was the simple but overwhelming advantage of capital and size. Herbert Development could do what it did because the corporation had no necessity for outside financing. Goods and services were both cheaper when interest payments were not a consideration.

King sniffed and gave him a sly look. "A guy named Richie Adams tried to underbid Herbert, a few years ago this was. After a couple of days negotiating, Adams sold out his company to Herbert, went to Mexico and hasn't been seen since."

"And why would he do that?"

King peered sadly at the end of his cigar and said, "I guess Herbert made him an offer he couldn't refuse."

"I see," Barent said.

"I'm sure you do," said Jacob King. "I'm sure you do."

"It's gone beyond us," Barent said. "We're out of our jurisdiction, also out of our league. Vincent Herbert lives in Rye. He has business interests throughout the Tri-State area. I don't have the resources for a full-scale investigation into organized crime."

Kurtz gave him a long look, then shrugged and took a bite out of his burger. "You don't have to go after the organization. You just have to go after whoever murdered Regina Cole."

"Yeah," Barent said. "That's so." He nodded glumly.

The two men were sharing a lunch near Easton. Kurtz had finished with his morning cases and had nothing scheduled for the afternoon. Barent seemed depressed. He wanted to talk.

"Of course, there's not a whole lot to tie any of the Herberts to Gina Cole," Kurtz said.

"Just Walter Stang's idiot story and a couple of dead hoods."

Kurtz was uncomfortably aware that he himself was the source of the idiot story. From Walter Stang to Lenny and Dominick to Joey and Don, from there to Owney Madden and Joseph P. Herbert to Vincent Herbert and God knew who. "Don't forget Eleanor Herbert," Kurtz said.

"What about her?"

"Without Eleanor Herbert, there would have been nothing whatsoever to link anybody that we know of to Gina Cole."

"So?"

Barent must really be down, Kurtz reflected. He was usually swifter on the uptake than this. "So Eleanor Herbert herself is either innocent or she's got a death wish, unless you're willing to believe in astral projection, which means that she knows more than she's said. She may not even know that she knows it, but she knows it. She has to."

"That's the assumption we started with, way back when."

"So maybe you should return to it. Eleanor Herbert is the only real lead that you have."

Barent gave a crooked smile, cut a piece of apple pie with a fork and stolidly chewed it. "Let's not forget Lynn Baker and Mark Woodson."

"Do you really think Lynn Baker could have had anything to do with murdering Regina Cole?"

"It doesn't matter what I think."

"Bullshit," Kurtz said pleasantly.

Barent shrugged. "She's being investigated. Sarah Lawrence College and

Columbia Business School, no criminal record. No, I don't believe Lynn Baker had anything to do with it."

"So who did?"

"Someone who had something to gain."

"Woodson?"

"Mark Woodson is dead."

"But he didn't used to be dead. And anyway, his body hasn't been discovered."

"So you figure he faked his own death so he could get away with the loot? What loot? Where's the loot?"

"If the Herberts are involved, then there's money in there somewhere."

"So now we're postulating some sort of connection between Mark Woodson and the Herberts?"

"Maybe there is one," Kurtz said.

"Like what?"

"Try the obvious. The Herberts are rich and Woodson worked for a bank."

Barent stared at him. He sniffed and said coldly. "Mark Woodson worked in the loan division of Gordon and Hill, a medium sized investment bank. Gordon and Hill has never done any business with Herbert Development. Leonard Bailey, Woodson's supervisor, seemed a little wistful when he told me this. They would like to do business with Herbert Development. Herbert Development would be a major plum." Barent wiped his lips daintily with a snowy white napkin and gave Kurtz a thin smile. "But I would like to assure you, just because I know you're so concerned, that we will continue to pursue every possible connection, just like we're continuing to pursue the connection to Joey and Don." Barent's smile grew wider. "You haven't forgotten Joey and Don, have you?"

In point of fact, Kurtz had been trying to. The subject of Joey and Don was still an embarrassment. "No," he said sullenly. "I haven't forgotten Joey and Don."

"Good." Barent nodded firmly. "See that you don't."

Five minutes later, they had paid their bill and were out on the sidewalk. Barent stopped for a moment next to his car. "Give you a lift?"

"No, thanks. It's only a couple of blocks. I'll walk."

"Alright, then, I'll see you."

Barent's car shuddered as half-a-dozen bullets thudded into its opposite door. The windshield exploded. Barent cried out and clutched at the side of his head as something high pitched whizzed by Kurtz' ear. "Get down!" Kurtz yelled. Both men dropped. The street, crowded an instant before, rapidly emptied as pedestrians ducked into open doorways.

"Shit," Barent said. He was peering at an alley across the street. His gun was in his fist.

"Are you alright?" Kurtz said.

"I think so." A thin red line creased Barent's temple. It dribbled blood but didn't look too deep.

It was lunch time in Manhattan. Every parking meter had a car by it. "I can crawl to the end of the street," Kurtz said, "and circle around the block. Maybe come at him from the back end of the alley."

Barent gave a gentle snort and blinked his eyes as blood dripped down the side of his face. "Forget about it. You don't have a gun. And you're an amateur." Three more shots rang out and the side window of Barent's car shattered. Both men ducked their heads. "We're going to sit nice and tight. We're protected here."

Unless a lucky shot went under the car and ricocheted off the curb. Not likely, though.

"There may be more than one of them," Kurtz said. "They could be circling around us right now."

"They'd have to cross a street full of traffic, then come at us down an empty sidewalk. I'd like to see them try it. They'd be easy targets."

Not necessarily, Kurtz thought. Whoever it was could go around the block, duck into a back entrance, maybe climb through a window, and pop out of any one of the dozen or so doors that fronted onto the street.

The windshield of the car next to them suddenly shattered, a shower of glass cascading to the ground. Distantly, the sound of police sirens came to their ears. Whoever was shooting at them must have also heard the sirens because at least six more shots rang out, thudding into Barent's car. The car shook and vibrated and then there was silence. After a long moment, Kurtz asked, "Think they've gone?"

"Probably." Barent shook his head. He was looking a little green. "I feel dizzy," he said.

The wound in Barent's head was shallow but still bleeding. There was a pretty good chance that Barent had suffered a concussion, a smaller chance that the temporal artery beneath the bone was ruptured, in which case Barent's dizziness was only the first sign of an accumulating epidural hematoma, an injury which would probably kill him unless he got into surgery fast. Barent squinted down the street and blinked his eyes.

"If you're seeing double," Kurtz said, "you better give me the gun."

Barent frowned at him, then reached down and removed a snub-nose .38 from an ankle holster. "Take it," he said. "I'll keep this one."

A Charter Arms police special. Kurtz hefted its weight, released the safety and smiled grimly.

Nothing else happened, however. Within five minutes, six police cars roared up. Two of them cordoned off each side of the street, one double parked opposite the car that Kurtz and Barent were hiding under and one drove up the opposite curb into the mouth of the alley. A few seconds later, a uniformed cop waved his arm. "All clear," he yelled.

They could hear a car door slam. "Come out with your hands up," a clear voice said. "If you have weapons, drop them."

"They think we're the bad guys," Kurtz said, offended.

"Do it," Barent said. He put his gun down on the curb and slowly got to his feet, his arms raised. Kurtz reluctantly followed. Above the roof of the car, four uniformed cops and a plainclothesman could be plainly seen. They were standing in the road and pointing guns at Barent and Kurtz. The plainclothesman was Harry Moran.

Kurtz smiled at him. "Hi, Harry," he said.

Moran stared at Kurtz, then at Barent. "Jesus," he said in disgust. "Let's get you to the hospital."

Chapter 22

"It's just a mild concussion," Kurtz said to Betty. "He'll be alright."

Betty looked at him and slowly, tentatively smiled. She was standing. She had been on her feet, alternately staring moodily out the window, and then pacing back and forth ever since she had arrived in the Emergency Room a little over an hour ago. Now she breathed a deep sigh and sank down in a chair. "Thank you," she said.

"We'll keep him overnight for observation. Assuming nothing else turns up, he can go home in the morning."

She nodded her head, her face still pale. At that moment, a tall young man and a pretty young woman, very pregnant, entered the room. "We got here as fast as we could," the woman said. "How is he?"

"He's got a concussion," Betty said, glancing at Kurtz, "but it's not too bad."

"Oh, thank God." The pregnant woman was Denise Janus, Barent's daughter. The young man was Paul Janus, her husband. Kurtz hadn't seen them since the wedding, almost a year ago.

"What happened?" Denise asked Kurtz.

"We were coming out of a diner after lunch and somebody tried to shoot us," Kurtz said.

"Who was it?" Paul asked. "Why?"

"We don't know," Kurtz said. "They got away."

Betty sniffed and gave Kurtz an angry look. "Who were they shooting at? You or him?"

"Me?" Kurtz scratched his head. "Why would anybody shoot at me?" Despite the disclaimer, he could think of a few people who might have a reason…Lenny, for instance, or Dominick, but no reason to mention either of them.

"Because they don't like you?" Denise said.

"Denise," Betty said, "stop it."

Denise opened her mouth to say something, then gave a startled little jump and grimaced. "I'm sorry. The baby's been kicking me. I'm not getting much sleep." She smiled wanly at her husband. "I've been irritable."

They did get irritable as they approached the ninth month. Paul Janus blinked at his wife and suppressed a smile. Betty grinned at him.

Denise jumped again. A surprised look crossed her face. "Uh-oh," she said. A spreading stain, tinged pink with blood, abruptly ran down her legs and puddled on the floor at her feet. Betty and Paul stared at it.

"When is this baby due?" Kurtz asked.

"Apparently, right now," Denise said.

"A boy…" Barent had a stupid smile on his face. He had awakened only a few minutes before and was sitting up against the pillows, his head wrapped in a white bandage.

"Congratulations," Kurtz said.

"Too bad you're not allowed to smoke in here. We should have a cigar. We should have a couple of cigars."

Denise's labor had been short, only two hours. The baby, though a month premature, was apparently healthy. Denise was now sleeping and Paul had gone home, dazed but happy.

"No cigars," Betty said.

Barent looked at her absently. Then he looked at Kurtz. "So," he said, "who shot me?"

Harry Moran stepped forward. "The alley led all the way back onto the next street. By the time we got there, they were long gone."

"They?"

Moran shrugged. "Whoever."

"So what have you got? Anything?"

"A couple of shells left in the alleyway. The gun was a nine-millimeter. A Glock. You can tell by the imprint of the firing pin. That's it."

"Nothing else?"

"Nothing."

"Too bad," Barent observed.

Moran nodded. Barent closed his eyes and slumped back against the pillows. "I'm a little tired," he said.

"Go back to sleep," Moran said hastily. "We shouldn't be bothering you."

"Sure," Barent said. Then he smiled. "A boy, huh?"

Outside the room, Betty gave both Kurtz and Moran a kiss. "I'll see you tomorrow."

"Congratulations, again," Kurtz said.

"Sleep tight," Moran added.

Both men watched her walk off. When she had gone, Moran gave Kurtz a tight, appraising smile and said, "Where can we talk?"

Kurtz sighed. He had known it was coming. Harry was a cop. Cops take it personally when their partners get shot. "My office?"

"Fine."

They stopped off in the cafeteria for coffee and a couple of donuts and five minutes later, they were sitting in Kurtz' office. "Lenny and Dominick I know about," Moran said. "Who don't I know about?"

"Hey," Kurtz protested. "Why assume this had anything to do with me?"

"I'm not assuming anything. But I know you. You attract trouble."

A dignified silence seemed like the best response. After a few moments, Moran grinned. "Okay," he said. "Let's put it this way; assuming for the moment that the shots were intended for you, rather than for Lew—just assuming, mind you—who can you think of who might have had a motive?"

"There is one other person," Kurtz admitted.

Moran smiled smugly. "Yes?"

"A patient ignored my advice. He died. The family sued me for malpractice. I won the case but the patient's son seemed pretty upset." Kurtz hadn't liked the way the younger Gomez had stared at him as he left the courtroom, now that he thought about it. He hadn't liked it one little bit.

"What's his name?"

"Carlos Gomez."

"Anybody else?"

"Not that I can think of."

"We'll look into it," Moran said.

Amazingly, it was only five o'clock by the time Kurtz arrived home. He heard sounds coming from the kitchen, walked in and found Lenore leaning over the stove, stirring a pot with a slotted spoon. He wrapped his arms around her from behind and kissed the back of her neck.

"Who is that?" Lenore asked. "No," she added quickly, "don't tell me. It's more exciting if I don't know who you are. Just keep kissing me."

"I'm going to do more than that," Kurtz said, nibbling at the top of her ear.

Lenore gave a tiny shudder and pressed back against him, rubbing her firm little butt into Kurtz' groin. "We can't right now," she said reluctantly. Lenore put down the spoon and turned around, snuggling into his arms. "I'm making spaghetti." She kissed him hungrily. "If we take more than ten minutes, it'll get ruined."

"Ten minutes? We can do a lot in ten minutes."

"Men are always in a hurry. Women take a little longer to get going. Wait till after dinner."

"Why am I always frustrated? Why are my needs never met?"

"Hah!"

"Ten minutes?"

"Until dinner. You'll just have to wait for dessert."

There was something about getting shot at that stirred a man's juices. The birth rate, Kurtz had read somewhere, always went up during wartime. It was instinctual to propagate the species when danger threatened…and of course it helped a man to forget that only a few hours before someone had been shooting at him, that a bullet had flown so close to his head that he could hear it whizzing by. "Alright," he said reluctantly. "I'll wait for dessert."

"How are you tonight, Danny?" John Tweed asked.

Danny's face grew pale. "Jesus, man, don't talk to me here. Okay?" He looked up and down the street to see if anybody could see them. Nobody could. The street was empty.

Tweed smiled at him. "Now, where shall I talk to you then, Danny boy?"

"Not here, okay?" Danny was sweating. He shifted his feet and grimaced. "Look, meet me at Riverside in an hour. Opposite 73rd."

Tweed pursed his lips and pretended to think this proposition over. "Alright, then," he said. "Riverside in an hour. Don't be late." And he sauntered off.

Riverside Park stretched for much of the length of Manhattan, a strip of wooded greenery between the Hudson River and the West Side Highway. There were innumerable places in the Park where you could not see a car or a bus or a wire passing overhead, where the only sounds you could hear were the chirping of birds, the soft hush of wind rustling leaves. There were benches and cobbled paths and shady trails where two people who wanted to talk without being seen could saunter off together into the woods.

An hour later, John Tweed was sitting on a bench, eating an ice cream cone, when Danny came walking down the path. His eyes passed over Tweed without apparent recognition but he sat down at the opposite end of the bench. "Nice day, isn't it?" Tweed said.

"Shit, man, don't play games with me. What do you want?"

Danny was an addict. Tweed had busted him not too long ago with a needle in his arm and a packet of heroin in his pocket. Tweed had confiscated the needle and the heroin but had otherwise only smiled at the little junkie, and let him go. Danny knew what this meant—it was a proposition. Danny could have refused the proposition by waiting until Tweed wanted something from him and simply saying "*No*," at which point Tweed, would give a sad, regretful sigh and arrest him for possession. Whether or not Danny managed to beat the rap was irrelevant because Danny would find himself being held in jail for the maximum twenty-four hours before being charged, during which time Tweed would most surely have a little talk with the judge. Danny would be labeled a flight risk and bail set beyond anything that he could afford to pay. Danny's court appointed attorney would protest. The judge would take the protest under advisement. Danny would probably be released, but not until at least three days had passed and that meant cold turkey. Danny was not willing to go through cold turkey and they both knew it.

"Well, for starters," Tweed said, "I want you to be polite."

Danny shifted awkwardly in his seat and scratched the back of his neck. He looked pained. "Okay, Officer Tweed, sir, I'm sorry. I apologize. What can I do for you? You like that better?"

Tweed grinned. "I'd like it better if you meant it. Now, tell me, Joey Cork and Don Lonigan—you know the names?"

Danny stared at him. "Oh, man, you have got to be kidding."

"And why would I be kidding?"

"Cork and Lonigan are dead," Danny declared. "Both of them."

"I know that," Tweed said. "And I would be very interested in knowing exactly how and why they became dead."

Danny gave him a hurt look. "The word is they had big mouths."

Tweed smiled happily. "One always has to watch what one says, eh, Danny?"

For only a moment, Danny's eyes flashed and a hard, cold look came over his face. Tweed moved his right hand a little closer to his gun. Finally, Danny blinked, frowned and scuffed at a dying clump of grass with a toe. Reluctantly, he said, "I hear they got involved in some heavy shit."

"Go on," Tweed said.

"The word is Mickey Nolan ordered it."

"And why would the venerable godfather do such a thing?"

Danny shrugged. "You'd have to ask him. I never even seen the guy."

"And who exactly carried out this order?"

"I don't know. I don't have any idea. Lotsa guys would of done it."

No need for the little junkie to add that he didn't want to know, either. "Alright, Danny," Tweed said. "I believe you." He didn't, really, not exactly. Danny might be telling the truth or he might not, no way at this point to tell. "You have anything else for me? Anything at all?"

"No," Danny said.

Tweed smiled at him. "Thank you, Danny." He rose to his feet. "I'll be seeing you."

"Yeah," Danny said sullenly. "Right."

Chapter 23

Not exactly subtle, Kurtz thought, but then subtlety had never been the point. The place looked more like a monument to conspicuous consumption than a family home. Nice, though—Kurtz had to admit it. Ivy curled up the brick in artfully arranged patterns. The grounds were neatly planted, the windows clean and sparkling. A gargoyle up on a balcony might have been fearsome except for the happy smile on its face. The boat tied up at the dock was ready for the sea. The whole place gave an impression of immaculate care…but quiet. Too quiet.

Eleanor Herbert had her own suite on the second floor. She received Kurtz in what he supposed could be called a drawing room (did they used to draw in them?), or maybe it was a sitting room. Whatever, Eleanor Herbert was sitting stiffly in a high backed old chair with wooden arms. "Dr. Kurtz, Madame," Charles announced.

Her eyes flicked to his face. "Thank you, Charles. That will be all."

Charles gave a little bow and shuffled off, closing the door silently behind him.

"Sit down, Doctor. May I pour you some tea?"

Kurtz sat. The chair, despite its stiff appearance, was comfortably padded. "Thank you," he said. "That would be very nice."

"Cream? Sugar?"

"Both, please."

The room was lined with bookshelves. The furniture was some dark wood, butternut maybe, or teak. Glass doors opened onto a balcony which gave a view of Long Island Sound. A persistent wind gusted, humming against the windows and foaming the water into white capped waves sparkling in the sunlight.

Barent didn't know that Kurtz was here, which fact bothered Kurtz only a little. After all, a physician was not required to seek police permission before paying a visit on his patient. This was a sacred relationship and none of the Department's business.

"So, Doctor," Eleanor Herbert said, "what brings you here?"

"I wanted to see how you were doing."

She raised a brow, took a sip of her tea and carefully replaced the cup in the saucer. "Is the tea to your liking?"

"Yes," Kurtz said, hastily trying it, "it's very good."

"I'm glad you like it. I myself, am doing just fine, thank you." She smiled wickedly. "Was there anything else you wanted to talk about?"

The old bird wasn't bad, Kurtz thought. At least she had a sense of humor.

"I'm afraid," Kurtz said carefully, "that there is."

"Afraid…an interesting choice of words."

"You know that Doctor Adler is a surgical resident at Easton."

"Of course."

"Then you can understand my interest in seeing that Doctor Adler's name is cleared."

"No," she said, "I cannot." Placidly, Eleanor Herbert sipped her tea. "We both realize that there is not a shred of material evidence linking your Doctor Adler to the death of Regina Cole. And whatever it was that I experienced on that unfortunate night, I have never claimed that Doctor Adler killed her."

"Only that he was on the scene, and seemed from the expression on his face to know what was behind the door."

"Which does not prove him to be a murderer. Furthermore, I cannot see that this is any of your business. If you have some romantic notion of investigating Regina Cole's death, then I suggest that you leave it to the police."

Ouch, Kurtz thought, Barent couldn't have said it any better.

"The matter has recently become somewhat personal."

"Why is that?"

"Because yesterday afternoon, somebody took a shot at me."

Eleanor Herbert's teacup halted midway to her lips. "I'm glad to see that they missed."

"They didn't, exactly. Whoever it was, hit Detective Barent, with whom I had just finished having lunch. Lew Barent is my friend. He should recover but the incident sort of ruined our afternoon."

"And you think that this shooting has something to do with Regina Cole? Why would you think that?"

Lenny and Dominick, not to mention sad, dead Joey and Don, might have been able to give reasons. Kurtz did not feel it prudent to mention any of these names to Eleanor Herbert. "Regina Cole's death is an open case that Lew is investigating. Regina Cole worked at Easton. I work at Easton. Aside from that, I don't know."

Eleanor Herbert raised a brow. "It seems to me more likely that Detective Barent was the target. After all, murder is his business. It isn't yours."

"That could be," Kurtz admitted.

"Then why don't you mind your own business and leave Detective Barent to his? I doubt that he will appreciate your interfering in his work." She said this without rancor and looked at him pleasantly over the top of her teacup.

"There's more to it than that," Kurtz said.

She waited, smiling politely.

"Have you ever heard of a man named Harold Van Gelden?" Kurtz watched her face closely. The reaction surprised him. Her smile grew wider. He had been expecting something else—horror, maybe, or at least distaste. The picture that Kurtz had formed of Harold Van Gelden, from everything Barent and Bill Werth had told him, was that of a sadist, a man who abused his position as a therapist in order to torment his helpless patients.

"Of course," she said. "He was my psychiatrist for many years."

"What was he like?"

She looked at him. "Why do you ask? Doctor Van Gelden is dead."

"You sound as if you were fond of him."

"Why wouldn't I be?" She looked out the window. A wide lawn sloped down to a sandy beach, where a willow tree bent with the wind. "He saved my life, or at least my sanity." She frowned, and then she sighed and sipped her tea and gave Kurtz a reluctant smile. "That was a long time ago."

"Could you tell me about it?"

"Why should I?" She said it almost absently, as if her mind were still elsewhere, then she gave a little shrug. "But then again, why not?" she said. "Why not?" She poured more tea into her cup and looked inquiringly at Kurtz. Kurtz shook his head. Eleanor Herbert stirred a spoonful of sugar into her tea, tasted it and then said, "I was not a happy little girl. My mother died shortly after I was born, from an aneurysm in the brain. My father had little time to spend with me. I had two brothers, both considerably older than myself. Vincent was pleasant enough, but he had no real interest in a baby sister. Joe, my older brother, was my idol. I adored him." Eleanor Herbert shook her head sadly. "Joe was caught in an accident, a building was bombed. The police never did discover who was responsible. Doctor Van Gelden owned a private psychiatric hospital. Joe was confined there for several years but he never recovered. Finally, one morning, he was found hanging from a doorframe, a suicide.

"For some reason, I blamed myself. Children are like that, you know. Children see the whole world as if it were an extension of themselves. They make associations. They see relationships that, frankly, contain no sense. Why should I have blamed myself for my brother's illness, and later, his death? Why did I feel such guilt?" She shrugged again. A pained look crossed her face. "I don't know. I don't remember. And really, it doesn't matter. I did blame myself. I felt guilty. I became depressed."

"And so your family turned once again to Doctor Van Gelden?"

Eleanor Herbert nodded her head. "He was very patient with me, very gentle. He made me see that my perception of these things was warped and incorrect. It took me years before I could bring myself to realize, to *believe*, that I had nothing to do with my brother's death."

"It sounds,"—Kurtz hesitated—"as if you must have been lonely."

"I suppose that I was." Eleanor Herbert nodded primly. "I never went to school, you see, not as a young girl. I had tutors. Occasionally, I was allowed to play with Caroline McFadden and her brother Michael, who were the children of our housemaid, but my father was not entirely approving of these relationships."

"Not exactly an egalitarian point of view," Kurtz said. Not surprising, though. What fun would it be to have all that money if you couldn't put down the help?

"They were not egalitarian times." Eleanor Herbert smiled wistfully. "Caroline and her brother were the children of servants and I was the little queen, the heiress. It just wouldn't do."

"And so what happened, with Doctor Van Gelden, I mean?"

"Nothing happened. He was my therapist. I saw him once or twice a week for many years. He would come here, usually. A few times, I was driven to his office at the Institute." She sipped her tea. "I don't really remember. And then later on, after my husband died, I saw him again for a little while."

"Were you on medication?"

She frowned. "I think so," she said.

"But you don't remember?"

"Why should I? It was many years ago."

"True," Kurtz said. "Tell me, have you ever heard of a woman named Claire Reisberg?"

She looked at him with faint interest. "No," she said. "Should I have?"

"I suppose not," Kurtz said. He sipped his tea. They chatted for another few minutes. Eleanor Herbert had a quick, lively wit. Despite her physical frailty, she had obviously kept up with current affairs. Finally, Kurtz glanced at his watch, and unable to think of anything else that might be helpful, he took his leave.

"Claire Reisberg," said Moran. "She was thirty. The police report says she was blonde, blue eyes, about five-seven, one-twenty. It even lists her measurements. 36-22-36."

"Sounds attractive," Barent said. Barent had a bandage wound around his head and a persistent headache. He had been told not to come to work for at least three days but Harry Moran had stopped by the house to give him an update. Betty, who knew her husband well, apparently realized that keeping in touch with the case would be better for his blood pressure than sitting around and stewing. She left the two men alone and went out to the supermarket for some dinner.

"She must have been. The investigating officer was a guy named Jason Quinn. Quinn's report doesn't exactly say so but apparently he always had some doubts regarding the official version of the story. At least one member of the staff expressed the opinion that Claire Reisberg was having an affair with Harold Van Gelden. It seems that she was seen getting into Van Gelden's limousine on at least three separate occasions."

"Was Van Gelden married?"

"Divorced."

"Before or after Claire Reisberg?"

"Before."

"Gives him less of a motive, doesn't it? And having an affair wasn't illegal, not even then."

"No," Moran said.

"And while it makes you wonder, it certainly doesn't constitute evidence that Van Gelden killed her."

Moran shrugged. "The patient who was accused, a guy named William Burke, apparently had a history of sexual abuse. He had been accused of the rape of two High School girls. The charges were apparently true, but Burke's family had money and so they cut a deal with the DA and incidentally made some pretty hefty contributions to his political campaign: confinement to the Van Gelden Institute rather than jail. It was reported that Burke made several advances on Claire Reisberg but of course she turned him down."

"Did Burke deny the charges?"

"No. He admitted doing it but his lawyer claimed insanity."

"Then what's the problem?"

"The problem is that they kept Burke pretty heavily hopped up. Also, his brain had been fried by insulin shock, an early victim of Van Gelden's theories. Supposedly, by the time of Claire Reisberg's murder, he was disoriented as to place and time, a complete psycho."

"Doesn't mean he didn't kill her," Barent remarked.

"The night nurse and an orderly both initially reported that Burke was asleep at the time of the strangling. Quinn is very clear about that. They later recanted the story. Claimed they must have been mistaken."

"Not good," Barent said.

"No. And there were traces of Claire Reisberg's blood on Burke's pajamas, so that was that."

Barent pulled a cigar out of his pocket and stuffed it in his mouth. Betty didn't let him actually light the things up inside the house but he liked to chew on them, get a little flavor of the tobacco. "Joseph P. Herbert, Junior also had a history of abusing women."

"Correct," Moran said.

"Makes you wonder."

"Yeah," Moran shook his head sadly. "But it all happened over sixty years ago. Not much chance of getting to the bottom of it now."

"Yeah," Barent said. "I know."

Chapter 24

"Dr. Kurtz, OR Six, *stat.*"

"What the hell…?" Kurtz glared at the overhead speaker in the surgeons' lounge but nevertheless put down the tuna on rye that he had barely begun eating, rose to his feet and trotted down the hall.

Nobody paid him any attention when he first walked into the OR. An infant wrapped in blankets placidly sucked its thumb in an isolette. Nobody was paying the infant any attention, either, because a woman, anesthetized and intubated, lay upon the OR table with a resident pumping rhythmically on her chest while an anesthesia team stuck her in the neck for a central line. Three men in masks and gowns were working over her open abdomen and blood was flying everywhere.

"Oh, Jesus," Kurtz muttered.

One of the men turned around: John Letterman, an obstetrician. Kurtz knew him from the OR but had never had much to do with him before. "Richard," Letterman said. Sweat dripped from Letterman's brow and his voice was ragged. "Could you give us a hand?"

"What's going on?"

"Caesarian hysterectomy. Placenta accreta. She's bleeding out." Sometimes a pregnant woman's placenta, instead of sitting nicely inside the uterus, eroded into the uterine wall, occasionally even through it. It was like a swiftly invasive cancer. Sometimes the patient started to bleed near the end of the pregnancy but sometimes there was no way to make the diagnosis prior to delivery. Since they were doing the case in the OR rather than up on obstetrics, they must have at least had some suspicions. Without drastic treatment, placenta accreta was almost always fatal unless the uterus was removed, along with any other tissues that had been invaded.

"Let me scrub," Kurtz said.

"Hurry up."

Kurtz stepped out of the room, hastily scrubbed his hands and forearms and stepped back in. A nurse held up a gown. He slipped his arms inside, then shoved his hands into rubber surgical gloves. A circulating nurse tied the gown around Kurtz' back and he stepped up to the table.

A steady pool of blood welled up from deep in the pelvis. A suction catheter continually drained the blood into a canister. The woman's uterus was boggy and swollen. Both broad ligaments, which contained the uterine blood supply, were clamped, which should have stopped any bleeding from the uterus itself. "Where's she bleeding from?" Kurtz asked.

"Lower down," Letterman said. "The placenta's eroded into the vaginal wall, maybe the bladder. I think it's got into a loop of bowel, as well."

Kurtz glanced up at the head of the table. The arterial line trace on the monitor read a blood pressure of forty over twenty-three. The EKG showed a slow, agonal rhythm. The patient's body shook every time the resident pumped on her chest. Kurtz looked down at the blood welling steadily up into the wound and asked, "Do you have a Satinsky clamp on the table?"

"No," the scrub nurse said. "This wasn't supposed to be a vascular case."

"Then give me a DeBakey."

The scrub nurse handed him a large, curved clamp. Kurtz reached into the opened abdomen and palpated the aorta. A pulse was barely detectable. He lifted up the aorta and squeezed the clamp around it. The bleeding from the pelvis perceptibly slowed. The blood pressure tracing rose to sixty over forty-two. The EKG picked up speed.

Letterman peered at the DeBakey. "You clamped the aorta," he said.

"You got any better ideas?" Kurtz replied.

"Not at the moment," Letterman said. He turned to the scrub nurse. "Give me a handful of lap pads."

"How many?"

"As many as you've got."

The nurse shrugged and handed him a mound of snowy white pads. Letterman began to pack them into the pelvis, putting pressure on the lower portion of the uterus and the bladder. "That won't hold it for long," he said. "But maybe we can catch up with the bleeding."

The anesthesiologist, Vinnie Steinberg, was squeezing rubber bulbs with both hands, inflating pressure bags which were wrapped around units of blood. "We're doing a little better," Steinberg said. "Stop pumping for a minute." The resident doing CPR looked at Letterman, who nodded. He stopped pumping. The blood pressure stayed steady at sixty-seven over forty. The heart rate picked up speed.

Better was hardly good. The patient was alive but it was a temporary gain. She couldn't bleed at the moment because most of the blood supply to the lower half of her body was cut off and most of the rest was held in by the packs. They had maybe an hour, two at the most, to finish up and get out or everything below the cross-clamp would begin to necrose.

Blood flowed in through the IV lines. The pressure steadily rose. "Alright," Letterman said, "let's get to it."

An hour later, the uterus was out and the oozing from the vaginal vault was again packed. If she lived, they would have to bring her back to the OR in a few days to take out the packing. Half the woman's bladder, where the invading placenta had eroded, plus a three inch portion of the left colon, had been removed and sent off to pathology. They transferred the patient, still intubated, to the ICU on dopamine and epinephrine drips, the blood still trickling in, hopefully faster than it was oozing out.

"All bleeding stops eventually," Letterman said. Not exactly a reassuring thought. Letterman smiled sheepishly at Kurtz and gave a tired shrug.

Maybe she would live, Kurtz thought. He hoped so.

Mickey Nolan's face looked like a slab of concrete. It was pale and hard and marbled with old acne scars. His eyes looked out at the world with placid curiosity, impassive, even serene, the expression of a man who knew that humanity could no longer touch him. Nolan and Moran both sat in padded chairs, separated from each other by a pane of plexiglass.

"My name is Harry Moran. I'm a cop."

Nolan smiled slightly.

"I'm investigating a murder in the city. I have some questions I'd like you to answer."

Nolan said nothing but his eyes were still curious.

"Have you ever heard of a woman named Regina Cole?"

For the first time, Nolan spoke. "Why should I talk to you? What have you got to offer me?"

Good question. Not much, and both of them knew it. "We have information that a couple of your boys were involved, Joey Cork and Don Lonigan."

Nolan yawned. "Never heard of them," he said.

"No? Then I guess it doesn't bother you that Cork and Lonigan are both dead."

"Not at all," Nolan said. "Why should it?"

Most big time crooks at least played the game of pretending to be fellow members of the human race. A little forced sympathy, a sad, regretful smile, maybe even a crocodile tear or two. These things might be protective coloration but they tended to put the listener at his ease. Not Mickey Nolan.

"Tell me," Moran said, "you have any money in real estate, maybe a development near the Meadowlands?"

A tiny frown creased Nolan's forehead. "I don't have to talk to you," he said.

"No, of course you don't, but why not give it a try? Things can't be too exciting in prison." At least, they weren't supposed to be. Prison was supposed to be boring. That's why it was prison. Crooks dealt with this fact in different ways. Some worked out, pumping iron like it was a drug, sedating themselves into a few hours of dreamless sleep. Some (not many) took advantage of the time and enforced isolation to read books and write memoirs. Some got the equivalent of high school or even college degrees. A few of these played little jokes, using their newly acquired knowledge to file motion after motion with the criminal courts, all of which, by law, had to be properly responded to.

Mickey Nolan was plump and flabby. He had never, to Moran's certain knowledge, checked a book out of the prison library. Nolan, despite his apparent circumstances, did not suffer from the usual boredom of prison. A string of visitors, old friends, family, lawyers, kept him entertained. No doubt bribes had been placed. No doubt the food that Nolan ate was just a bit better than the food that his fellow inmates had to live with. No doubt he had music in his cell and a television set of his own and probably access to a phone if he wanted one. Mickey Nolan was still the Godfather, even here.

Nolan shrugged. "I'm excited enough," he said.

Moran frowned and scratched at his cheek in exasperation. "Does the name Vincent Herbert ring any bells?"

Nolan rose to his feet, calmly walked over to the door on his side of the room and banged on the bars. A guard peeked in through the tiny window. "Get me out of here," Nolan said. "I'm bored."

The door opened. Nolan stepped through it without looking back and the door closed.

Moran sighed and rose tiredly to his feet. Win some, lose some. He glanced at his watch. At least two hours to get back to the city. He hoped Barent was having a restful day.

It was Barent's first day back at the office and it started off peacefully enough. Evidently, the boys had decided that he was not yet entirely a hundred percent, since they were making an unusual effort to keep the noise down and not disturb him. Barent found this touching and mildly amusing.

Nevertheless, sitting at his desk and listening to the silence, he had to admit that his head still ached. Tiredly, he picked up the file on the Cole case and went through it. He didn't really expect to see anything that he hadn't seen before and he didn't, but it was something to do.

There came a tentative knock on the door. He glanced at the clock. It was ten-fifteen. "Come in," he called out.

Arnie Figueroa stuck his head in the door. "Some people here to see you, Lew."

"People?"

Arnie shrugged.

"Send them in."

Arnie nodded. A few seconds later, the door opened wider and Garrison Herbert walked into the office, accompanied by a good looking woman about forty. The woman had long blonde hair arranged onto the top of her head, a thin, uptilted nose, a strong chin and cold blue eyes. She was dressed in a black leather coat and a black hat with a green feather on top. She looked around the office as she came in, frowned, and looked expectantly at Barent.

"Detective," Garrison Herbert said, "this is my sister, Allison."

Barent nodded brusquely. "Mrs. Donaldson."

"Yes," she said. She looked mildly surprised.

"Sit down," Barent said. They both sat.

"What can I do for you?" he asked.

Garrison looked at his sister, puffed up his cheeks. Some silent communication seemed to take place between them. Allison Donaldson frowned. Garrison gave a reluctant nod and turned to face Barent. "It's about Eleanor," he said.

"What about her?"

"We're very fond of Aunt Eleanor. We all are. She's had a difficult life. We wanted you to be aware of that. She's..." Garrison frowned at his sister. Allison only stared at Barent, a faint look of disapproval on her face. Garrison shrugged. "Eccentric, I suppose you could say."

"So?" Barent said.

Garrison set his lips in a stubborn line. Allison looked annoyed.

"Eleanor," Garrison said, "has a long history of psychiatric disturbance. This latest episode, her out of body experience, is only the latest."

"From what I've been told," Barent said, "she was depressed about the death of her husband. That was a long, long time ago. Nobody has mentioned any problems since then."

Garrison shrugged and looked at his sister. Allison nodded. She said, "Eleanor sits in her rooms, sips tea and reads. In the spring and summer, she tends her roses. She rarely sees visitors. She hardly ever goes out. Does that sound like a normal life to you?"

"Psychiatrists don't use the word normal very much," Barent said. He smiled. "One of them recently told me that. They strive for functionality, not normality. It sounds to me like your aunt is doing exactly what she wants to do."

Allison shook her head impatiently. "Sometimes, when you speak to her, you realize that she's not listening. She has a faraway look on her face. You stop speaking and she doesn't even seem to notice. Then she'll look at you and say something and you'll realize that she hasn't heard a word that you've said."

Maybe she was bored, thought Barent. He was getting a little bored himself. He stifled a yawn behind his palm, at which Allison gave a tiny frown. "Hardly evidence of an unbalanced mind," he said.

"We don't want to give the wrong impression," Garrison said quickly. He looked impatient, even annoyed.

Barent sighed. Maybe he should have taken a couple more days. "I have to admit that I'm having some difficulty with this conversation," he said. "What exactly is it that you want?"

Allison leaned forward over the desk and said, "We want our Aunt not to be disturbed."

"So who's disturbing her?"

Allison's lips thinned. Garrison frowned. "That surgeon friend of yours," he said.

"Kurtz?"

"Yes. He came out to the house yesterday to see Aunt Eleanor. Afterward, she seemed upset."

Kurtz. It would be Kurtz. "What was it exactly that they talked about?"

"I don't know," Allison said. "And I don't care. I don't want Eleanor bothered. She had a heart attack only a week ago. She almost died. I want you to tell Dr. Kurtz to mind his own business."

On the one hand, Barent didn't really give a shit what Allison Donaldson wanted. On the other hand, she had a point. "I'll talk to him," he said.

Garrison nodded. Allison glowered at him. "See that you do."

Fifteen minutes later, Barent had finished his cup of coffee and was again going through the Cole file (and again coming up with nothing). He was thinking about lighting up a cigarette when Richard Kurtz walked into the office. Barent looked up at him sourly and grunted. "Sit down," he said.

Kurtz looked tired. His eyes were puffy. He collapsed into the chair, the same chair that Allison Donaldson had sat in, put his head back, closed his eyes and sighed.

Looking at him, Barent frowned. He decided that what he had been about to say could wait a little while. "Bad day?" he asked instead.

"Bad case. I just got out."

"Something unusual?"

Kurtz shrugged. "These things happen. It's why they pay me."

"So what can I do for you?"

Kurtz barely smiled. "It's not what you can do for me, it's what I can do for you."

Barent rolled both eyes briefly in their sockets. "Sure," he said. After Garrison and Allison's little visit, he suspected that he was not about to be thrilled. "Tell me."

"You should try to find a woman named Caroline McFadden."

Chapter 25

Kurtz was jogging in Central Park the next afternoon when somebody snuck up behind him and shot him in the back with a taser gun. One instant, Kurtz was running serenely along, enjoying the fresh air of an early season warm spell, the next instant, forty thousand joules of electricity, enough to temporarily paralyze an elephant, was running up his back and out along his legs and arms. His mouth opened. His jaw shook. His head rattled and he fell to the ground, his hands tensed into claws, convulsing.

A man dressed in a Nike jogging outfit walked up to him. The man was young and good-looking, with short, brushcut dark brown hair. Kurtz had never seen him before. The man looked down at Kurtz with apparent satisfaction and kicked him calmly in the abdomen. The air rushed out of Kurtz' lungs. Since his diaphragm was as paralyzed by electricity as the rest of him, Kurtz was unable to draw more air back in. A haze swam in front of his eyes as he felt himself losing consciousness. The young man kicked him again, this time in the head. Before he blacked out, Kurtz heard the man say, in a deep, satisfied voice, "This is only a taste. I'll be back, you bastard."

Barent looked down at Kurtz' sleeping body with curiously mixed feelings. Barent was, as he almost always was at such times, struck by the perverse nature of mankind. Mankind in this instance meaning himself. Barent was honestly relieved that Kurtz was not seriously hurt but at the same time there was a certain nagging sense of guilty satisfaction. Kurtz could, on occasion, be a real pain in the ass.

He kept these thoughts to himself, however, and looked appropriately solemn. Lenore stood next to him, her face grim.

Kurtz groaned, stirred in the bed and opened his eyes. Lenore took his hand and gave it a squeeze. Kurtz squeezed back. His eyes, however, were not on Lenore. They were on Barent.

"Any clues?" Kurtz asked. His voice was hoarse. He cleared his throat. Kurtz had woken up for the first time some hours before, given Barent a brief description of what had happened to him and then drifted back to sleep. Barent was surprised that he remembered.

"Not yet," Barent said.

"How am I?"

"Just some bruises," Lenore quickly put in. She glanced at Barent. "You'll be fine."

"First you, then me," Kurtz said.

Barent shrugged. He had been thinking the very same thing. "I don't know."

"I never saw the guy before. He could have killed me."

"Good that he didn't," Barent said.

Kurtz slowly nodded. "He said he'd be back."

Kurtz didn't say it like a man dreading the prospect. He said it like he was looking forward to it. Lenore heard it too. She gave a wan smile and squeezed Kurtz' hand a little harder.

"Get some sleep," Barent said.

You didn't kill just one cop, not if you were a criminal engaged in serious criminal activity. There was no point to it. Cops were like bees. You killed one and a hundred others would swarm to the scent, alerted and enraged by the blood of one of their own. Cops died in the line of duty, alright. Gun battles, accidental car crashes during high speed chases, stoned out junkies armed with boxcutters and knives were all occupational hazards. But it was rarely a premeditated, cold-blooded killing, not on the part of organized crime. Something personal, maybe. Not business.

Therefore, if Mickey Nolan and Vincent Herbert (or his son, Garrison, don't forget about him and his Security Chief) had been behind Barent's shooting, then Barent could not have been the target. The target must have been Kurtz (unless the shooter had been some random sociopath, which theory Barent saw no current reason to accept). If Nolan and Herbert had been behind it, however, Kurtz would undoubtedly be dead by now. If the intent had been to kill him, which this latest episode made less likely. The guy with the taser and the brush haircut had said he'd be back, which made it definitely personal, a crime of passion (but a *premeditated* crime of passion, always the worst kind) committed by somebody who wanted Richard Kurtz to suffer, to twist slowly in the wind. No, it wasn't Nolan and it wasn't likely to be Vincent Herbert. It was somebody else. Which didn't mean that it wasn't at least related to Nolan and Vincent, because guys like Lenny and Dominick sometimes wanted a little revenge and guys like Nolan didn't mind their subordinates enjoying themselves so long as the bosses were not implicated.

Which left Barent exactly nowhere, a feeling he was uncomfortably used to.

Michael McFadden, as it turned out, had made a career out of the military, retiring after thirty years at the rank of Master Sergeant. He drew a pension from the army and had kept in touch with local veterans' organizations. He lived in Fort Lauderdale and was happy to speak to Moran on the phone. "Strange place to grow up, I suppose, though it didn't strike me that way at the time. It was like a big, extended family. If I fell down and skinned my knee and my own mother wasn't around, one of the other maids would pick me up and put a bandaid on it. In a way, I miss it." His voice grew wry. "I suppose that's why I did so well in the military. I liked the security, the idea that I was part of a community, an organization that would never let me down."

"How about the Herberts? Did you have much to do with them?"

"Not at all, really. Not after I was seven or eight or so. We lived in different parts of the house. We went to different schools. We had different friends. Mr. Herbert was like a general, you saw him now and then, and occasionally he would come by and inspect the troops, but he moved in a different world."

"And Eleanor Herbert? Did you have much to do with her?"

McFadden's voice hesitated. "My sister did. They played together, on and off, I suppose until she was ten or eleven. After that, a young lady was supposed to be a lady."

"Did your sister ever resent that?"

"I'm not sure resent is the right word. It made her sad but she accepted it. I resented it, though. I remember that to this day. It was probably the only time that I ever really felt that we weren't good enough for something. I didn't like seeing my sister so sad."

"What was she like as a child? Eleanor Herbert, I mean?"

"She was a nice little girl, at least until her brother died. That seemed to change her. She grew moody."

"Was she ever violent?"

"I seem to remember her throwing a few things, on occasion. But kids are like that, aren't they? My great-granddaughter is only three and she bangs her head against the floor every time she doesn't get her way, so I'm not sure Eleanor Herbert was really unusual."

"Did you ever see her therapist, Doctor Harold Van Gelden?"

"Big guy? With a goatee?"

"So I've been told."

"I saw him coming in and out of the house, going up the stairs. I never said anything to him."

"Were there any stories about him that you can remember?"

"No. Not that I know of." Again, McFadden's voice seemed to hesitate. "What's this all about, anyway?"

"Just a routine investigation."

"Hah," McFadden said, and for a moment he sounded like the old sergeant. "I've never heard of a *routine* investigation."

"I'm sorry, but that's all I can say about it."

"What else can I do for you, then?"

"Your sister, where is she now?"

"Caroline? She's still up North. She lives outside of Philadelphia."

"What does she do?"

"Plays with the grandkids, mostly. She used to teach kindergarten. She's retired now."

"Do you have her number?"

"Sure," McFadden said. "Give me a second. I'll go get it."

Caroline McFadden (Caroline Johnson, for the last forty six years) was happy to talk about her childhood. She echoed her brother's sentiments. The Herbert Estate had been a pleasant place on which to grow up. She had never seen herself as being "different" from other children. "Why should I? Some kids' parents were salesmen, some worked in a garage, some were plumbers or doctors or dentists. My mother was a maid. So what? At least she wasn't on welfare."

"But you were different from Eleanor Herbert," Moran said.

"But Eleanor Herbert was different. She was rich."

There was no clear reason for him to argue this point, Moran realized, except that the statement bothered him. The fault did not lie in Caroline McFadden. It lay in himself. Like Caroline's brother Michael, Moran found that he also resented the Herberts. The Herberts, who according to John Costas, were the children of drunks, thieves and bootleggers. Who the hell were the Herberts to think that they were better than anyone else?

"Maybe," Moran conceded, "but it's beside the point. What I need to know is the nature of the relationship between Harold Van Gelden and Eleanor Herbert."

Caroline McFadden was silent for a long moment. Then she said, "Why are you asking about this?"

"It's part of an investigation. I'm not at liberty to reveal any more." This was a lie. Moran could reveal anything he damn well pleased but information was like money. You tended to hoard it.

"Harold Van Gelden was a horrible man," Caroline McFadden said.

Considering the man's police record, Moran was not surprised to hear it. "Why makes you say that?"

Moran could hear her draw a deep breath over the phone. "I've never told this to anyone but my mother. That was over fifty years ago."

A tingle of anticipation crept up Moran's spine.

"Eleanor was a perfectly normal little girl." Caroline McFadden's voice grew small. "When we were little, I thought of her as my best friend. We played together almost every day. The difference in our status was never an issue between us. We spent almost all of our time together. We told each other our dreams, and our secrets.

"All of this changed after Eleanor's brother died."

"Joseph P. Herbert, Junior?"

"Yes."

"Did you ever meet him?"

"Probably. I don't remember. He was confined to an institution when I was very young."

"Go on," Moran said.

"After her brother died, Eleanor was inconsolable. It lasted for months. She would lie in bed and cry. She wouldn't play. She would barely eat. They drove her out to see Doctor Van Gelden, generally twice a week, and sometimes, he would come and see her. The doors were always locked. Nobody knew what went on behind those doors but after he left, Eleanor was always sleepy. She seemed dazed, sometimes incoherent. Van Gelden was giving her drugs, I'm certain of it."

Drugs…"Psychiatrists use a lot of drugs," Moran said.

Caroline McFadden laughed softly. "I happen to have done a bit of reading on this subject. I was curious, you understand. Psychiatrists use anti-depressants and anti-psychotics. So far as I know, chloral hydrate is not a usual aid to psychotherapy."

"Chloral hydrate…"

"Sometimes she had a strange smell after he'd gone. A sort of sweet smell, like flowers. It was on her breath. It was all around her."

Flowers…chloral hydrate did smell like flowers.

"It was definitely chloral hydrate," Caroline McFadden said. "I've smelled chloral hydrate. It was in a college course on chemistry. I recognized the smell instantly."

"And what did you do with this information, once you had smelled chloral hydrate?"

"Nothing." She gave a tiny sniff into the phone. "It was more than ten years later. What was I supposed to do?"

Chloral hydrate was a common hypnotic, used mostly to sedate children for minor surgical procedures. It was also used by criminals for various illicit purposes, such as robbery and rape. "So Harold Van Gelden gave Eleanor Herbert chloral hydrate. What did everyone else in the household think? Someone aside from you must have known."

"If they knew about it, they weren't talking. Even my mother. When I tried to ask her, she told me to mind my own business. Small children are easily intimidated. I never referred to it again."

"And Eleanor Herbert threw tantrums."

"That was later. In the beginning, she was dazed and sleepy. It was hard to catch her attention. She would drift off in the middle of a sentence. After the first few months, she seemed to come out of it. She was no longer tired all the time. Now she was angry. She would throw tantrums. She would throw anything she could get her hands on. She screamed at everybody, for any little slight or for nothing at all. She became impossible to be around, even for me."

"Did she continue to see Van Gelden?"

"Oh, yes."

"But you no longer smelled chloral hydrate."

"No."

"Did you ever talk to her? Did you ask her why she was acting the way she was?"

"Of course I did. She said that she was angry. She said she felt as if there were bars wrapped around her skull. I remember that phrase very well, bars wrapped around her skull. She said she didn't know why."

"And later, when you were both older? Did she still throw things?"

"It took a few years, but she grew out of it. By the time she was ten or eleven, her behavior was more rational. She no longer screamed at people and she stopped throwing things. By this time, of course, Eleanor and I had drifted apart. Eleanor was the little princess and I was the child of a servant. We no longer had very much to say to each other."

"No," Moran said. "I suppose you didn't."

Kurtz was released from the hospital at about noontime. An orderly took him down the elevator in a wheelchair, which made Kurtz feel like a fool, and rolled him up to the front ramp, where Lenore met him with the car.

"Have a nice day, Doctor," the orderly said.

"Thanks," Kurtz said. He got in beside Lenore and put his head back. He had to admit that every muscle in his body ached. Lenore drove. They didn't say much on the way home. Kurtz was just thankful to be alive. He was looking forward to nothing more than getting back into bed.

They pulled into the garage and got out of the car. Kurtz winced and Lenore looked at him, worried. "Do you want to lean on me?"

"No," Kurtz said, "I'll manage."

She gave a mild snort and smiled. "Sure," she said, and took his arm. They stopped in the lobby to pick up the mail and five minutes later, Lenore put the key in the lock and opened the door of the apartment. Lenore flipped rapidly through the mail while Kurtz hung up his jacket. Lenore looked startled, turned an envelope back and forth between her fingers, finally shrugged and handed it to Kurtz.

It was from Eleanor Herbert. Kurtz opened it and read the letter inside. He looked up. "It seems we've been invited to dinner," he said.

Chapter 26

Richard Kurtz was unhappy. Kurtz was old enough to know that the state of one's happiness, by and large, is something that comes from within. Some fortunate people are simply happy. Despite sickness or poverty or personal disaster, they stay happy. Other people are miserable. They may be rich and good-looking and talented and the idol of millions. None of this matters. They feel like shit.

Kurtz himself had always fallen somewhere in the middle (well, maybe just a little below the middle), like most people, he imagined. Happiness to Kurtz had depended on his circumstances. Sometimes he was up. Sometimes he was down.

Since he had gotten together with Lenore, Kurtz had rarely been unhappy.

Now he was unhappy.

In his rational moments, he supposed that the beating he had taken was responsible but he wondered if something more than that was at work. Life, suddenly, seemed pointless. Kurtz got up in the morning and went to the OR or the office. He treated the sick. Sometimes he saved lives. So what? Sooner or later, everybody died. If God was out there, Kurtz had seen no evidence of it. The Universe didn't care.

"Cheer up," Lenore said. She kissed him on top of his head, reached over and put a snifter of brandy on the table next to Kurtz' chair.

He smiled wanly. "Sorry. I've been brooding."

"I know." The fact that Kurtz was brooding did not appear to bother Lenore. Very little about people bothered Lenore. Lenore understood people, in some deep, visceral way. More than that, she seemed to understand herself. It was her family, he supposed. Lenore's family could very easily be described as dysfunctional—except that in its own screwy way, it functioned just fine. Lenore's mother, as nuts as she obviously was, must have done something right.

Kurtz had never known his own mother. He remembered her only as a shadow, a dim memory of warmth, of rain pattering against a window, of soft arms holding him in the night. She had died before Kurtz was two.

Kurtz had been thinking of his father lately, his silent, awkward father. Eleanor Herbert, for some reason, reminded him of his father. Maybe it was just that they were both old, two old people who time had passed by. Maybe it was that both of them had lost their spouse and had drifted ever since in a world of their own making, cut off from the rest of humanity. Kurtz' father had never remarried. After the death of his wife, he had turned into himself, tending the farm, having little to do with other people, rarely speaking. Though he had lived under the same roof with his father until he was eighteen, Kurtz could never remember saying more than two sentences at a time to the old man.

This bothered him. It had bothered him at the time and it bothered him now.

"What are you thinking?" Lenore asked.

Kurtz sighed and swirled his snifter of brandy. He held the snifter up to the light and watched the amber shadows within the glass.

"I'm depressed," Kurtz said.

"So I noticed. What about?"

"I'm not sure."

Lenore nodded wisely. For some reason, this annoyed Kurtz. "You think you can tell me?"

"What's bothering you?" Lenore looked at him with a clinical eye. "Nope."

"Oh." Surgeons, Kurtz had often noted, were a pathological bunch. The divorce rate among surgeons was well over seventy percent. More of them were alcoholics than any of them were willing to admit. The problem was that they had no goals. They had arrived at the place where they had struggled for so long to be and for many of them, the struggle had turned out to be more satisfying than the achievement. They had no more worlds left to conquer. This was only one way of looking at it, of course. The other was simply to acknowledge that the hours were inhuman, the work horrifying and the pressure almost unbearable.

"I'm frustrated," Kurtz said.

Lenore puffed out her cheeks and nodded. She did not appear to be surprised.

"Am I one of those people who always need something new to be going on? Why can't I be satisfied with the way that things are?"

"Are you bored with your work?" Lenore asked.

A lot of surgeons were. Kurtz had never before been among them. "I don't know," he admitted.

Lenore made a clicking sound between her teeth. "Have you ever wondered why you get into fights so often?"

Kurtz gave her a wounded look. One of the things he loved the most about Lenore was that she had never tried to change him. She accepted him, just the way he was. At least, he *thought* she accepted him just the way he was. "You too?" he asked.

She smiled. "I'm merely pointing out that most grown men don't get into fistfights very often. It happens to you on the average of what? Two or three times a year?"

"I wouldn't call them fights. Most of the time, I'm just reacting to circumstances. Things are happening. Somebody has to do something."

Lenore nodded. "You're trying to right what you perceive to be wrongs. But why are you so sensitive to those wrongs? Most people aren't."

Kurtz stared at her. "What are you saying?"

She smiled. "Maybe you have some unresolved conflicts left over from your childhood."

"Well, isn't that trendy of you?" Kurtz said. He had to admit, of course, that she was most likely correct. He glanced at the letter from Eleanor Herbert, sitting on his desk on the other side of the room like a silent rebuke. For his own purposes, Kurtz had presumed upon his relationship with Eleanor Herbert, the supposedly sacred relationship between physician and patient. Now she had called him on it.

He glanced at his watch. It said five minutes to four. Gratefully, Kurtz rose to his feet. At last, he thought, time for some action.

"Say hi to Lew for me," Lenore said.

"You bet."

"And Bill. Why don't you set up a date for dinner?"

"I'll do that."

She smiled at him. "See you later, then."

"Chloral hydrate?" Bill Werth frowned. "I've prescribed chloral hydrate once or twice as a sleeping medication. Aside from that, I know of no legitimate use for chloral hydrate in psychiatry. Certainly not as an aid to psychotherapy."

"Doesn't chloral hydrate loosen inhibitions?" Barent asked. Aside from the small bandage over his temple, he didn't seem any the worse for wear.

"About as much as a shot of whiskey." Werth shook his head. "Loosening inhibitions is not exactly what you're after in therapy. You're trying to make connections. That takes a sharp mind, not a dull one."

Barent scratched his head. Kurtz, watching the interplay between the two men, felt curiously divorced from what was going on. His mind kept swinging back to his own problems, foremost of which was that he couldn't figure out what was bothering him. "Whatever it was," he said, "Van Gelden wanted her asleep."

"Sexual abuse?" Barent said uncertainly.

"Could be," Werth said.

"Not likely." Kurtz shook his head. "The family, at least, must have known what was going on."

"Why do you say that?"

"Because they were paying for it."

"Maybe they didn't know what they were paying for."

"If a seven year old kid like Caroline McFadden knew that Eleanor Herbert was coming home drugged twice a week, then you can bet that the grownups knew it too. And all of them, including the servants, knew enough to keep their mouths shut, which would indicate that that's the way the family wanted it. I think that they knew exactly what they were paying for, and that they got it."

"This went on for years?" Werth asked.

"The chloral hydrate was only a few months. After that, she threw tantrums. That went on for years."

"She sounds like a seriously disturbed young lady."

"For this," Barent said, "we need a psychiatrist?"

A faint smile flit across Werth's face. "I'd like to see her."

"Why? What could you do?"

"Maybe nothing. I won't know until after I see her."

Barent glanced at Kurtz. "Think we could arrange that?"

"I think so. She wants to find out who killed Gina Cole, that's for sure."

"Then why," Werth asked reasonably, "are you concentrating on things that happened sixty years ago? None of this has anything to do with Gina Cole."

"I'm not certain of that," Barent said.

Werth looked doubtful. He shrugged. "Whatever," he said. "I'd be happy to take a look at her."

"I'll see if I can arrange it," Kurtz said. "I'll be seeing her tonight."

"Hello, is this Lew Barent?" The voice on the phone was gruff, also bored. The voice sounded, quite frankly, as if it couldn't have cared less if it had the wrong number.

"Yes?" he said. "Who is this?"

"Dave Jonas, Detective Third, Suffolk County."

"What can I do for you?"

Harry Moran looked up from the corner chair, alerted by the change in Barent's voice. Barent gave him a tight smile and shook his head.

"I thought you might like to know," Detective Dave Jonas said. "The Cole house, out in Greenport? It burned down last night. We're not certain yet but it was probably arson. I understand you're investigating what happened to the daughter."

A clue? Barent gave Moran a grin and shook his head again in disbelief. He said, "We'll be out as soon as we can get there."

Chapter 27

Moran and Barent arrived in Greenport, Long Island, a little more than three hours later. It looked like a nice, quiet town. Most of the houses appeared to be wood clapboard; only a few were brick. A tall ship was moored against a pier in the harbor. The streets were clean and lined with trees.

The Cole house had been a medium sized four bedroom on a third of an acre in the middle of a residential neighborhood. Portions of the back and one side wall were still standing. The front had collapsed. Nothing remained of the contents but a pile of smoking rubble.

The police suspected arson because of the speed of the blaze. Also the timing. Mitchell Cole had gone out for dinner. Ten minutes after he left, the center of the house had gone up in flames. The remains were still too hot to approach. It would be hours yet before they could test for hydrocarbon residue.

"No gasoline cans left on the lawn?" Barent asked.

Dave Jonas' mouth twitched. It might have been a smile. "No," he said.

Barent grunted. "No way to tell if anything was stolen."

Jonas shrugged.

"There wasn't anything worth stealing," Cole said. He stared at the remains of his home with a dazed look on his face, shaking his head now and then.

"Depends," Jonas said. "You had a TV, didn't you? A stereo? Maybe some silverware?"

"Yeah," Cole admitted.

"Motive enough for some people."

"I understood you were moving," Moran said.

"I'm going to Florida. But not for another couple of weeks."

"Was all your stuff still in the house?"

"I sold most of the furniture. The rest of it was still in there, mostly packed up."

Moran nodded and stared at the blackened timbers, his brow wrinkling.

"You get a lot of crimes like this around here?" Barent asked.

Jonas was a big, beefy guy with a moustache that used to be brown but now was mostly gray. He looked at Barent from sleepy looking eyes and smiled. "Not usually," he said.

"Any jewelry in the house?" Barent asked.

"No," Cole said. "We sold my wife's jewelry years ago."

Jonas and Moran looked at each other. Moran gave a tiny shrug. Jonas nodded.

"Documents?" Moran asked. "Bearer bonds? Stock certificates?"

Cole shook his head. "Nothing like that."

Moran said, "Maybe you pulled on some wires, shorted something out, while you were packing."

Cole held up his hands, dropped them to his side. Moran frowned, evidently realizing that this theory was unlikely.

Jonas said, "We'll know more in a day or so, as soon as it cools down."

Barent looked at Jonas. "How about the neighbors?"

"What about them?"

"Did anybody see or hear anything unusual?"

"We're checking. We don't know yet." Most such crimes, when they were solved at all, were solved because somebody, usually a neighbor, saw something. Unfortunately, most such crimes were not solved. "We'll assign a patrol car to keep a watch on the neighborhood, at least for the next few days. It's possible that whoever did it might come back."

Cole gave him a disgusted look. "Wonderful," he said, and gave an aggrieved sigh. Barent could see a tear glinting in the corner of his eye. "I guess I'd better check into a hotel."

"Good idea," Barent said. "You don't want to be here if they return." Barent smiled at Jonas. "Harry will stick around for a day or so, maybe give you a hand, if that's alright. I'm getting back to the city."

Jonas gave a tiny grunt and rolled his eyes. "Sure," he said. "Be my guest."

The dinner invitation had specified 'casual,' which Kurtz took to mean something less than a tuxedo but more than a tee shirt. He settled on a blue blazer and a tie. "You men have it easy," Lenore complained. "Anywhere you go, anything you do, a jacket, a tie and a nice pair of pants will fit the occasion. It's the all purpose costume for the modern era. Women aren't so lucky." She frowned at her closet and bit her lip. "What am I going to wear?"

"Wear a jacket and tie," Kurtz said. "You'll look daringly chic."

Lenore gave a mild snort and otherwise ignored him. Eventually, she settled on a cream colored blouse, a black skirt and a string of pearls.

The invitation had specified seven o'clock. They arrived at five minutes after. A Lincoln Town Car and a gold colored Mercedes 560 were already in the circle in front of the mansion. As they were parking, a Buick Electra drove down the driveway and pulled in behind them. A small man with thinning hair, wearing a priest's collar and a tweed blazer, got out of the car.

"Hello," he said, holding his hand out to Kurtz and giving Lenore a smile. "I'm Ronnie Herbert."

"Richard Kurtz, and this is Lenore Brinkman."

Ronnie Herbert looked like an elf. His eyes sparkled, his cheeks were rosy. "I've been looking forward to meeting you," he said. "Aunt Eleanor says that you're the curious sort. Always thinking, she says."

Was this a compliment? Kurtz wasn't certain. "Not at all," he said cautiously, "thinking gives me headaches."

Ronnie Herbert smiled even wider. "It's a sad commentary on the times we live in that people who make their living by using their brains get less public respect than a man who can hit a golf ball or put a basketball through a hoop. But don't mind me. Priests think they can say anything they want and get away with it." He pointed up. "They have diplomatic immunity, you know."

Reluctantly, Kurtz returned the smile.

"Very good," Herbert said, and nodded approvingly at Kurtz' smile. He gestured toward the door with both hands. "You are suitably armored. Shall we enter the lion's den?"

Two of Garrison Herbert's security men were stationed in the foyer. They looked at Kurtz and Lenore and nodded but didn't say anything. One of them made a check mark on a clipboard. Ronnie Herbert glanced at them once and otherwise ignored them.

Charles led the way to a large room with a tiled floor, three large couches and numerous small tables and chairs. Antique silver sconces that had probably once contained candles now held light bulbs. A bar stood against one wall and a set of floor-to-ceiling glass doors opened out onto a balcony which looked out over the sloping grounds and the water of Long Island Sound.

The place looked better with people in it, Kurtz thought. A small crowd was milling around. Eleanor Herbert sat on a high backed chair next to an elderly man who Kurtz assumed was her brother, Vincent.

Eleanor Herbert smiled up at them as they walked over. "Doctor," she said, "it was so nice of you to come. And this must be your young lady."

"Lenore Brinkman," Kurtz said.

Lenore and Eleanor exchanged smiles.

"My brother, Vincent," Eleanor said.

Kurtz and Lenore both shook hands and smiled at Vincent. Neither of the old people got up. Kurtz felt like they were being presented to royalty. He had to resist the urge to bow.

"I hope you enjoy yourselves this evening," Eleanor said. "We have a very nice menu planned. Afterward, we'll talk."

It was obviously a dismissal. "Come on," Ronnie said. "I'll introduce you." Kurtz recognized Garrison Herbert. He was holding a glass in one hand and talking to a tall, well-built man with thinning, sandy hair. A plump woman with a smiling face clung to Garrison's arm. Jerome Herbert sat on a couch next to a pretty brunette who was staring at the crowd with wide eyes. There seemed to be numerous children milling about. They kept coming and going through three opened doors so it was hard to get an accurate count.

Ronnie brought them first to a tall blonde woman in a blue dress. She looked to be in her early forties. She had a strong face and carried a few extra pounds, but she carried them well. "Doctor Richard Kurtz and Lenore Brinkman," he said. "My sister, Allison Donaldson."

Allison Donaldson held out her hand and gave Kurtz a grudging smile. "My aunt has mentioned you. I admit I was a little surprised when I found out you would be here. It seems that Aunt Eleanor likes you."

She did? It was news to Kurtz. "I like her, too."

"Still, I very much disapprove of you coming out here and bothering her with all this murder business. I complained to the police about you. I'm sure you know that." She looked him in the eye while she said this, not challenging exactly, just letting him know where she stood.

Barent had let him know and Kurtz could not have cared less. "I wasn't intending to bother her," Kurtz said. "I don't know if you know it, but somebody took a shot at me the other day. Detective Barent was hit in the head. We both could have been killed. It occurred to me that there might be a connection."

Allison looked briefly taken aback. "I don't see how."

Neither, frankly, did Kurtz, but that wasn't the point. "I've always noticed," he said, "that once people begin to reach a certain age, other people think they've got the right to make decisions for them. I've seen it a hundred times. Somebody is seventy, seventy-five, and he needs surgery, suddenly the whole family is talking at you over his head, telling you exactly what they imagine the patient wants, what he's thinking, what he's feeling. Half the time, the patient himself can't get a word in edgewise. It often comes as a shock when the family is finally done talking and you turn to the patient and ask him whether he has any questions and whether or not he's made up his mind about going through with the operation. Half the time, the oldest son or daughter thinks that they're the ones who are supposed to sign the consent form."

Amazingly, Allison smiled. Kurtz liked the smile. It made her look much less severe. "So you're telling me to mind my own business," she said.

"No. I'm telling you that your aunt is entitled to her opinion and I'm entitled to talk to her as long as she lets me."

"I guess I can't argue with that," Allison said, still with a smile. "Of course, we can always sue you if she has another heart attack."

"I suppose," Kurtz conceded.

"Anyway, nice meeting you." Allison nodded to Lenore, smiled at her brother and walked off.

"I do believe that you've tamed the dragon," Ronnie said.

"Brains and personality," Kurtz said. "Works every time."

Lenore gave a low whistle and rolled her eyes.

Kurtz patted her hand. "I've already met Garrison and Jerome. Anybody else here we should meet?"

Ronnie shrugged. "The man talking to Gary is Gordon Donaldson, Allison's husband. The woman with him is his wife, Jane. I don't know the young woman with Jerry but it probably doesn't matter. He'll most likely have a new one in a week or so. I really don't know how he does it."

"Brains and personality?" Lenore hazarded.

"Jerry?" The Priest looked doubtful.

"Quite a lot of kids," Kurtz said.

"Oh, yes. Allison has four and Gary has five. Jerry is the eldest."

"That's unusual these days."

Ronnie shrugged. "Eleanor and my father have encouraged them. We're a close family, though you might not realize it from looking at us bicker. The Herberts have always stood together when it counted. The more Herberts there are, the more Herberts you can count on. They weren't too happy when I chose to enter the priesthood." Ronnie smiled at them. "Well," he said, "I'm going to get myself a drink. Please ask if there's anything you need."

Ronnie walked off. As soon as he left them, Garrison caught their eye and smiled. Garrison didn't look like he smiled very often. Kurtz wondered if his face would crack. Lenore eyed Garrison and said to Kurtz, "I'm going to get a drink, too. You'll feel more free to butt heads without me."

"Huh?" Kurtz said.

She kissed him on the cheek and followed Ronnie to the bar. Kurtz walked over to Garrison, Jane Herbert and their brother-in-law. Gordon Donaldson had a pleasant smile and vague blue eyes. "Doctor," he said. "Nice to meet you."

Gordon, it seemed, had no other agenda, which Kurtz found refreshing. Gordon nodded at Garrison and Jane, smiled again at Kurtz, and walked over to his wife, who was sitting on the couch, talking to Jerome and his date. Jane Herbert looked at Kurtz and said, "I'll be back in a few minutes. I have to go powder my nose." She giggled.

Garrison watched her walk off, then turned to Kurtz and said, "Glad you could come."

"Glad I could make it."

Garrison nodded his head and looked thoughtful, more thoughtful than these obvious pleasantries warranted. "I understand," he finally said, "that you were not one of Eleanor's regular physicians."

"This is true."

"That young surgeon...Adler?"

Kurtz nodded.

"How is he doing?"

"He's depressed. Thankfully, he hasn't been arrested but everybody is treating him like he might suddenly start killing people at random. There's nothing to tie him to the murder except your aunt's vision, or dream, or whatever it was, and that doesn't count as evidence. Still..."

"No. Even she realizes it."

"Your aunt doesn't strike me as the sort to imagine things."

"Usually she's not."

"What do you think is going on?" Kurtz asked.

Garrison grinned faintly and sipped his martini. "I was going to ask you that."

"I wouldn't know," Kurtz said. He had theories, alright, but it didn't seem too smart to discuss them with Garrison. "Tell me, those security people who are always around. Are they just for show?"

Garrison looked surprised. "Hard to say. I've been sued three times by environmental groups convinced that building condo developments is going to pollute the groundwater, or cause mutations in frogs or something. Twice, I've received death threats."

"Recently?"

"No. The last was five years ago. Still...having security seems prudent. If Marty and his men weren't around, there might have been more than lawsuits and simple threats." Garrison cocked his head to the side and looked pensive, then he shrugged. "Would you like a drink?" he said. "We'll be sitting down soon."

"Sure," Kurtz said.

Garrison walked with him to the bar. The custom of the household, it seemed, was to mix your own. The bar was well stocked. Kurtz poured a glass three-quarters full of tomato juice over ice, added a couple of drops of tabasco and a squeeze of lime, then put in a jigger of vodka and mixed it with a swizzle stick. Garrison made himself another martini. "Cheers," he said. Kurtz raised his glass, nodded and sipped his Bloody Mary.

Charles appeared at the doorway and announced, "Dinner is served." Vincent and Eleanor both stood. Eleanor took Vincent's arm and all the adults moved into the dining room. The children, evidently, ate their dinner elsewhere.

Kurtz and Lenore were seated near Eleanor. Lenore chatted with her about gardening and modern art. Eleanor might not get out of the house much but she obviously knew what she was talking about. Kurtz just listened and concentrated on his food. The first course was shrimp in a creamy mustard sauce with fresh basil. Kurtz approved. Next came a salad of mixed fresh greens, followed by tournedos au poivre with asparagus and pan-fried new potatoes. The wine was *Chateau Lynch-Bages 1985*.

Kurtz noticed that Vincent was looking at him. "The food is great," Kurtz said.

"Thank you," Vincent said. "When the family comes over"—he smiled down the table—"we try to make it worth everybody's while."

Nobody seemed inhibited or tense. The conversation centered around current affairs and mayoral politics and gardening and sports. Business, it seemed, was avoided at the table.

What was it Tolstoy had said? All happy families are alike, unhappy families are each unhappy in their own way. The Herberts seemed like a happy family, even including the formidable Garrison. According to Barent, Garrison Herbert had a reputation as a workaholic, a ruthless business man. Here, with his family, Garrison seemed relaxed, even jovial. Kurtz didn't know why that surprised him. Stereotype, probably. On TV and in the movies, hard driving barons of business are almost obligated to be screwed up.

"A bit more, sir?" Charles was standing over him, holding a platter.

Kurtz quickly swallowed. "No, thanks. I'm saving some room for dessert."

Lenore was talking animatedly with Ronnie Herbert, something to do with Braque and Picasso. Ronnie had recently been in Barcelona, where he had visited the Picasso Museum. On Kurtz' other side, Jerome Herbert's young lady, whose name was Elizabeth Reed, leaned close to Kurtz and whispered. "Do you know the Herberts well?"

She had a serious look on her face. "Not really," he said. "I've never seen most of them before tonight. Why do you ask?"

"It's Jerry," she said. "I only met him a few weeks ago. I don't really understand him. He's very nice but he seems so moody most of the time."

Moody? Kurtz looked across the table at Jerome Herbert. He had a wide, vacant smile on his face and was holding a glass of wine up to his eyes, through which he peered around the room, amusing himself. Jerome, it seemed to Kurtz, was a young man who liked to amuse himself. Maybe it was the money. You have enough money, you can amuse yourself as much as you want.

"I'm sorry," Kurtz said. "I've only met him a couple of times."

"I see." Elizabeth Reed sipped her wine and looked at Jerome with a level, appraising gaze. Jerome gave her a wide smile back.

"Having fun, Doctor?" Jerome said.

"Yes," Kurtz said. "The food is good. The company is pleasant. What more could I ask?"

"What more, indeed?" Jerome puffed up his cheeks and gazed at Kurtz owlishly, then sighed. Kurtz and Elizabeth Reed looked at each other. Elizabeth Reed shrugged.

Dessert was an orange mousse. Soon after the excellent coffee, people began to wander away from the table. Eleanor Herbert rose to her feet, came around the table and leaned over Kurtz shoulder. "Come with me," she said. "I have something to ask you."

Nobody seemed to pay them any attention as they walked from the room, nobody except Ronnie Herbert, who stared at them with a quizzical smile, and Allison, who frowned and shook her head. Eleanor opened the glass doors and led Kurtz out onto the balcony. The night time air was cool. The moon was three quarters full. Kurtz could hear the rush of small waves on the beach.

"What do you think of the place, Doctor?" Eleanor asked.

"It's very nice," Kurtz said.

"You sound like you're being polite. Tell me the truth."

"Alright," Kurtz said. "Then truthfully, it makes me uncomfortable. There's nothing wrong with it exactly. It seems too ostentatious, too big. It seems like more than any one person, or any twenty people, would need."

"It is, of course. When you're rich, you can have what you want, and what we want is most often considerably more than we need. This makes you uncomfortable?"

Kurtz shrugged.

"Forgive me, Doctor, but I've known more than a few physicians in my time. Their politics are rarely so liberal."

"I grew up poor," Kurtz said.

"Ah," Eleanor said, and nodded wisely. "That explains it." She pointed to a spot by the water. "My eyes are not what they used to be. Can you see that far?" She was pointing to a slide, a swing set and a large wooden maze, set up near the beach, clearly visible to Kurtz in the moonlight.

"It's a playground," Kurtz said.

"Yes. It's not used very often, only when the family visits. I have always loved children." She said this wistfully. "And yet I have no children of my own. I suffered a miscarriage when I was very young and afterwards, the doctors said that I couldn't have children. And then my husband died. I am very fond of my nieces and nephews but I did want children of my own." She shrugged. "And so the old clichés turns out to be perfectly correct; you can't always get what you want, and money can't buy happiness."

"I understand," Kurtz said, "that you and your brother made a sizeable donation to the new pediatric wing."

"This is true." Eleanor grinned. "A very sizeable donation. It's why we were invited to the benefit dinner, where I met Regina Cole. In retrospect, I could have done without the honor." Eleanor looked down at the water below them in the moonlight. She shook her head sadly. "Ever since my heart attack, I've been having nightmares. Unpleasant nightmares. Sometimes I dream that I'm drowning, that I'm trapped underwater. Other times I dream that something is chasing me through a dark, deserted house, through endless dusty corridors. I'm running, but whatever it is that's following me is only toying with me, and I know that I cannot escape. When I was a child, I sometimes had dreams like these." She turned and looked Kurtz full in the face. "I don't like these dreams. I want them to stop."

Did she, now? "Funny coincidence," Kurtz said. "I have a friend; his name is Bill Werth…"

The next afternoon, Arnie Figueroa walked into Barent's office and sat down in the chair opposite the desk. "Carlos Gomez claims that he was drinking with some buddies at the time when you got shot."

"In the middle of the day?"

"Mister Gomez has a lot of time on his hands, being currently between jobs."

"Ah, I see."

Arnie wrinkled his nose and looked with disapproval at the cigarette in Barent's hand. Barent ignored him. "You've checked it out?"

"The alibi? Gomez' friends confirm it. They were playing cards and having a few beers."

Kurtz had not recognized the man who shot him with the taser but he had gotten a good look at him. Kurtz had never seen the man before but it had not been Carlos Gomez. The fact that he had used a taser was more than interesting. You can't buy stun guns in your average hardware store. Generally speaking, only the police, the military and licensed private security firms had access to them.

"Then I guess we'll have to wait," Barent said.

"For what?"

Barent blew a smoke-ring at the ceiling and frowned. "We'll have to wait for him to try again."

Chapter 28

Once the remains cooled down and they were able to sort through the rubble, a strong smell of gasoline became apparent. One of the neighbors, an elderly lady who lived across the street, claimed to have seen two men walking by the Cole property a few minutes before the fire began but it was already dark out and she could not describe them.

There were footprints in the caked dirt next to the house, one size twelve, one nine and a half, both Nikes. The firemen and police had been all over the place but firemen wore boots and policemen did not wear sneakers on the job.

They pulled a pair of brass candlesticks and some ivory chess pieces out of the debris. There was also a set of soot stained coins dating back to the eighteen-nineties that was probably worth some money. A few old photographs had been found out on the front lawn, black and white, yellowed with age. One of them showed a young girl, hardly more than a toddler, dressed in a leotard and tights, smiling at the camera. The back of the picture was labeled, Lena, 1938.

Mitchell Cole had looked at it without interest and shrugged. "It's my wife's mother. Her name was Lena Nye. The others are from my side of the family."

Moran looked at the pictures, looked over at Jonas, who raised an eyebrow.

"Where did they come from?" Moran asked Cole.

"I don't know. We had an old picture album in the living room. I think there were some other copies, maybe in the attic. My wife had a trunk full of old stuff up there."

Old stuff. Moran glanced at the photograph, stared at the still smoking rubble of the Cole household, and carefully placed the picture of Lena Nye in a white envelope.

And that was it. Nothing else that resembled a clue. There was no doubt that the fire was arson, but this fact left them exactly nowhere, so far as the murder of Gina Cole was concerned.

"You happy now?" Jonas asked.

It had begun to rain. The burned out remains were slowly congealing into a black, sodden mass. Moran listened to the patter of rain on the roof of the squad car and closed his eyes for a moment. "Not really," he said.

"Cerebellar ataxia. It's mild but unmistakable."

Kurtz nodded somberly, unsurprised. "Anything else?"

"Some facial asymmetry," Bill Werth said. "Slight. You could only see it if you do a full neurologic."

"What does that mean?" Barent asked. "*Cerebellar ataxia?*"

"A problem with balance. The cerebellum is the part of the brain that controls balance and coordination. Cerebellar ataxia can be an early sign of Parkinson's. It can also indicate brain damage. In this case, my money's on brain damage."

"From the cardiac arrest?" Kurtz asked.

"No." Werth smiled wolfishly, tossed a set of photographs onto the desk and leaned back. "Take a look."

Kurtz flipped through the photographs. He whistled. Barent, peering over his shoulder, looked bewildered. "This is a CAT scan," Kurtz said.

"A CAT scan is like an x-ray."

"It is an x-ray, a computerized series of x-rays." The photos showed sagittal sections of Eleanor Herbert's brain, each section a few centimeters distant from the next. Scattered throughout the cerebral cortex and cerebellum were small, white spots.

"Lacunar infarcts," Werth said.

"Oh?" Barent still looked bewildered.

Kurtz squinted down at the picture in his hands. "They're old," he said.

"Yeah. That's what's interesting."

"What are you talking about?" Barent asked.

Werth said, "Lacunar infarcts are most commonly seen as a consequence of disseminated vascular disease. A blood vessel thromboses, the area of the brain that's fed by the vessel dies, resulting in a small stroke. Individually, the damage caused by any one of them is minor. Put them all together, you've got organic brain syndrome: progressive loss of IQ, emotional lability, problems with short-term memory. Everybody's seen it. It's what happens to Grandma when she gets very old. The common term is senility."

"Eleanor Herbert is hardly senile."

"No," Werth said. "She's not, and that's exactly the point." He looked at Kurtz and smiled knowingly. Kurtz smiled back.

"These infarcts are all old," Kurtz said. "With organic brain syndrome, you get some old ones and some new ones and some that are in between. Not here." He lightly tapped one of the photographs with a fingernail. "These have all healed, leaving small scars in the brain."

"So what's the point?"

Werth said, "The point is that you never completely recover from trauma to the brain, but you can adapt. Particularly when an injury occurs in childhood, the undamaged areas of the brain can take on new functions. This has been experimentally verified many times."

"Childhood," Barent said.

"Considering her history? The tantrums? The behavioral changes? Doesn't it seem likely?"

"How could this happen?" Barent asked. "To a child?"

"Cerebral anoxia might do it. Maybe she was caught in a fire and breathed in too much smoke." Werth shrugged. "She's been dreaming about drowning. The dreams might be true." He held up his hands, let them drop to his sides. "I don't know."

Kurtz looked up from the photographs and stared off into space. "Maybe somebody tried to strangle her?"

There was a moment of silence while all three men considered this idea. Then Barent said, "How about deprivation therapy?"

Kurtz looked at him. "Now, there's a thought."

"Deprivation therapy was used to treat psychosis," Werth said. "Conceding—just for the sake of argument—that deprivation therapy might have been a legitimate therapeutic technique, Eleanor Herbert would not have been a legitimate candidate."

Barent gave him a pitying look. "Let's concede—just for the sake of argument—that Harold Van Gelden was not troubled by such scruples."

"But what would he gain?" Werth protested.

"How about money?" Barent said.

"If Caroline McFadden can be believed," Kurtz said, "Eleanor Herbert was drugged repeatedly over a period of months. The family must have known about it, and if they knew about it, then presumably they must have approved."

"Tell me again about deprivation therapy," Barent said.

"The idea," Werth said, "is that the psychotic patient is a sort of co-conspirator, that the disease can do its damage only if the patient allows it to do so. Deprivation therapy is a form of punishment, designed to convince the patient not to give in to his symptoms."

"Didn't you say that it worked?"

"I said that Van Gelden reported some successes. What was most likely happening is that the patients learned to pretend. Even psychotics do their best to avoid pain. They were hearing just as many voices as they were before but the fear of punishment led them to at least try to ignore them."

"Didn't you tell me that modern psychiatry concerns itself mostly with functionality? That if you could get up in the morning, hold down a job, function in a normal manner, that the rest of it was all minor?"

"I did?" Werth looked confused. "I don't think so."

No, Barent realized, it was Frances Shields who had told him that, not Bill Werth. "Well, what do you think of the theory?"

Werth shrugged. "To a certain extent, it's accurate. You have to realize, though, that people can learn to function pretty well and still be in pain. It doesn't mean they're not ill."

"So deprivation therapy treated only the symptoms."

"It didn't even treat the symptoms. At best, it convinced the poor patient that he would be better off if he ignored the symptoms."

"Insulin shock, I think you said."

"And electroconvulsive therapy. Without anesthesia." Werth grinned wanly. "An old professor of mine was present at one of the first demonstrations of succinylcholine use for ECT in the United States. Do you know about succinylcholine?"

"Never heard of it."

"ECT causes grand-mal seizures, seizures so strong that the patients used to tear muscles all over their bodies and damage vertebrae in their backs. And for the duration of the seizure and sometimes for a few minutes after, the patient wasn't breathing too well. Succinylcholine is a short acting paralytic. Today it's used routinely, but in the case I'm telling you about, they gave some poor patient a little pentothal to put him to sleep and then some succinylcholine. Then they zapped him. The EEG showed that he was seizing but no problem, he was paralyzed. He couldn't move. No trauma to the back, no torn muscles. This was a great advance. Everybody was excited, milling around, talking about the wonderful implications for therapy when somebody noticed that the patient was turning a little blue. It hadn't occurred to these distinguished idiots that if you add pentothal and succinylcholine to a grand-mal seizure, then you better be able to assist the patient's ventilation, which is why, today, we have anesthesiologists present. The anesthesia team gives the drugs and breathes for the patient while we shock them. But in the old days, they didn't use anesthesia, not routinely. They strapped you down to a table, sent electricity through your brain and watched while you went into convulsions. Pretty gruesome."

"And what would the point be of giving somebody chloral hydrate and then zapping their brain?"

"Chloral hydrate is a form of anesthesia. If Van Gelden was performing electroconvulsive therapy on Eleanor Herbert, even under chloral hydrate, she would have received both the benefits of the treatment as well as the drawbacks."

"Are you saying that electroconvulsive therapy with chloral hydrate could have caused cerebral anoxia?"

"Unless they ventilated the patient, yes, it's entirely possible." Werth sat back into his seat and puffed up his cheeks in thought. "And, of course, the most common side effect of ECT, even today, is memory loss."

"Memory loss…"

Werth nodded.

"Reversible memory loss?"

Werth made a see-saw motion with his hand. "ECT is usually used to treat morbid depression. Depression can also cause disturbances in memory. The studies are inconclusive."

"But in Eleanor Herbert's case, it wasn't done correctly." Barent pointed to the photographs on Werth's desk. "She has, what did you call them? Lacunar infarcts."

"This is true," Werth said morosely. "If that's what was done to her."

"Let's assume that it was—so what did Van Gelden want her to forget?"

"No," Kurtz said. "Not Van Gelden. If we're going to assume that Van Gelden was giving her electroconvulsive therapy, or maybe inducing seizures with insulin, then I think we can also assume that Van Gelden did just what he was paid to do. The question is, what did her family want her to forget?"

"Claire Reisberg was murdered," Kurtz said. "And her brother hung himself. Or did he?"

Barent steepled his hands together beneath his chin and nodded. "I think that we shall have to have another little talk with Caroline McFadden."

Chapter 29

"So as near as we can figure," Kurtz said, "they took this seven year old girl, drugged her so she wouldn't know what was happening to her and then either gave her insulin until her blood sugar went to zero and her neurons began to fry or else they subjected her to repeated electrical shocks to the brain. Maybe both."

"How awful." Lenore put her spoon down on the table and gave a tiny shudder. "Does she know?"

"Not yet. We told her that we were still going over the results. That doesn't bother her. She's lived with it, whatever it is, for over sixty years."

"Why wait?"

"Barent wants to see if he can find out more."

"From who? Caroline McFadden?"

"Or her brother."

Lenore spread a teaspoon of Hoisin sauce on a flat Chinese pancake, then placed a large piece of duck breast, a slice of cucumber and some flakes of scallion on the pancake before folding it into a roll and taking a big bite out of one end. Kurtz did the same. The restaurant was a hole in the wall but the food was super. Chinatown. Kurtz loved it.

It was a fine spring evening. The stars were shining overhead and the temperature had finally turned warm enough to walk around without a coat. The streets outside the restaurant were crowded. "Look at that," Kurtz said.

"Where?"

"That guy outside, with the girl on his arm. See him?"

Lenore looked where Kurtz was pointing. A young man dressed in a blue blazer and a tie had stopped at a street-corner, waiting for a light. A decorative young woman was hanging on his arm and laughing.

"It's Jerome Herbert," Lenore said, "and the girl from the party. I forget her name."

"Elizabeth Reed."

"That's right."

Jerome Herbert smiled happily down at the top of Elizabeth Reed's head. Then the light changed, they walked across the street and vanished around a corner.

"He looks rich," Lenore said.

"How so?"

"He looks like he hasn't a care in the world."

Kurtz fixed himself another pancake. At the moment, despite his compassion for Eleanor Herbert and his revulsion at what she had been subjected to, he felt the way Jerome Herbert looked, as if he hadn't a care in the world. They had discovered a major piece of the puzzle. What had been done to Eleanor Herbert sixty years before, if not why it had been done, was, he thought, becoming clear.

"What are you doing tomorrow?" Lenore asked.

"Two breast biopsies, a peritoneal dialysis catheter and a gall-bladder. Office hours in the afternoon."

"A regular routine day."

"Nothing wrong with that," Kurtz said.

She smiled. "No."

And yet only a few days before, the routine aspects of his life had seemed to stretch endlessly out in front of him, dull and pointless and gray. Amazing.

"Happy now?" Lenore asked.

"Yep. Good food, a beautiful woman and a nice, plump gall-bladder to take out. What could be better than that?"

Lenore looked thoughtful. "An abdomen full of pus?"

He looked at her skeptically. "An abdomen full of pus does not measure up to a nice, plump gall-bladder. Gall-bladders are my favorite."

Lenore took another bite of her Peking Duck. "I never knew this about you."

"Stick with me, kid," Kurtz said. "I'll show you the World."

Lenore wiped her mouth with a napkin. "I can hardly wait."

Caroline McFadden could add very little to what she had already told Barent. "You're asking for something scandalous," she said. "Some deep, dark secret that the Herbert family would want to keep hidden at any cost."

"Yes," Barent said. "That's exactly what I'm asking for."

"Don't you think that I've wondered about this, all these years? I don't know any secrets. I wish that I could help you."

In truth, Barent had expected nothing different, and so he was surprised to find that he was disappointed. "That's too bad," he said, "but it never hurts to ask."

"I was seven years old," Caroline McFadden said defensively. "What's a seven year old supposed to know?"

Barent reflected that Eleanor Herbert was seven years old, also, once upon a time, and what Eleanor Herbert had known must have come close to getting her killed.

Michael McFadden was no better. "Secrets?" His voice on the phone sounded bewildered. "I'm sorry. I never knew anything about Harold Van Gelden. And I certainly don't know anything about Eleanor Herbert or any scandal. Maybe my mother knew something but she's been dead for years."

That was the trouble with sixty year old crimes. Anybody who knew anything was long since in the grave.

"Thanks," Barent said. "It was worth a shot."

"Well, I'm sorry," McFadden said again, "but I just don't know."

"You know Jimmy Featherstone?" Danny asked.

They were sitting on a bench in Riverside Park. A seagull did lazy cartwheels over their heads while a squirrel sat in an oak tree a few feet away, nibbling on an acorn and gazing down at the two men with open suspicion. Aside from the seagull and the squirrel, they were alone.

"Of course," Tweed said. Everybody who was anybody in the conjoined worlds of crime and enforcement knew Jimmy Featherstone. Jimmy Featherstone was Mickey Nolan's number two man, now that Nolan was in jail, the man who actually ran the day to day operations of the organization. He was thirty seven years old, five foot five inches tall, with a freckled face, jug ears and an innocent, earnest smile. He had spent a total of nine of his thirty seven years in prison on a variety of charges ranging from rape to burglary to receiving stolen goods. The more serious charges of kidnapping and murder he had thus far managed to beat, usually because the witnesses had declined to appear or the plaintiffs had changed their stories.

"Word has it that Featherstone is your guy."

Tweed gazed down at him and raised a curious brow. "And which guy would that be, Danny boy?"

Danny gave Tweed a wounded look. "You wanted the guy who did it for Joey Cork and Don Lonigan. I'm telling you, I hear it was Featherstone."

"Featherstone..."

Danny nodded earnestly.

"How do you know this?"

Danny looked around. The squirrel was still nibbling on his acorn. The seagull had flown away. Danny lowered his voice. "Talk to Wanda."

"Wanda."

"Wanda is her trade name. Her real name is Sharon. Sharon Wilse."

"And exactly what trade is it that we're discussing?"

"Jesus, man, are you dense? She's a whore. Whores is Featherstone's main business. What else would she be?"

Offhand, Tweed could think of a number of occupations that a young woman might have called her own, despite any putative involvement with Jimmy Featherstone. "A whore," Tweed said.

Danny eagerly nodded.

"Thank you, Danny." Tweed smiled on him with benign good will. "We will pursue the subject with Wanda."

Acting on the tip given to them by John Tweed, Harry Moran and Arnie Figueroa paid a visit to the one bedroom apartment rented by Sharon Wilse, aka Wanda. The apartment was not what they had expected, being neat, clean and tastefully decorated. Wanda, too, did not conform to their stereotypes. She was small, blonde, brown eyed and dressed in a simple white blouse and denim skirt with a pink hair band on her head. She looked like the girl next door, the little girl next door, pretty but hardly garish. She did not look like a whore.

It quickly became apparent, however, that Sharon Wilse was well acquainted with the ways of the streets. "How did you get on to me?" she asked.

"We can't tell you that," Moran said.

She frowned. "It doesn't matter. If you know enough to come see me, then Featherstone knows it too. Which means that unless I can cut a deal, I'm going to end up at the bottom of a landfill somewhere. I want immunity, and I want witness protection."

"Witness protection is federal," Moran protested.

Sharon Wilse shrugged. "Work something out," she said. Then she smiled. "I can give you Jimmy Featherstone. Wouldn't that be worth it to you?"

Moran looked at her. Her smile contained no doubts. "Yeah," he said. "That would be worth it to us."

For the next hour, they took notes. Sharon Wilse was a smart and observant young woman, having completed two years of junior college and worked as a secretary before succumbing to the lure of what appeared to be quicker, easier cash. "A friend of mine in the office was doing it on the side. All sorts of girls did it, she said. It was like a secret economy of respectable prostitutes. Whores in their spare time. I thought about it. I like men, I like sex and I could certainly use the money. It seemed like an interesting idea." She shook her head. "What a joke. Turned out, the joke was on me."

"Not as lucrative as you were led to believe?"

"No. It might have been, if it wasn't for the overhead, but there's lots of overhead. And then the people you meet are definitely not the sort you could take home to Mom."

"This is true," Moran said.

She shook her head sadly. "What it comes down to is that they think they own you. They give you the keys to a hotel room or a little apartment, depending on the neighborhood you're working in, which you can use for the night, or the afternoon, or whatever.

"Then they provide 'protection,' which really means that nobody is allowed to beat you up but them.

"The worst is the free samples. Whenever one of the boys wants it, you have to put out, and sometimes they bring around their friends. Pretty soon, I stopped liking sex so much. When I started out, I figured the whole thing was just a goof, something to do in my spare time. Enjoy the attractive ones, go through the motions with the rest, fake a few orgasms, get paid. But it didn't work out that way."

"A nice business," Moran said. "So tell me about Jimmy Featherstone."

"Okay." They were sitting around the table in her kitchen. Sharon Wilse was sipping a diet coke with a slice of lemon in it. She hadn't offered any to Moran and

Figueroa. She lit up a cigarette, blew a cloud of smoke off into space, shook her head regretfully. "Nobody knows what Jimmy Featherstone does with most of his time but pimping is his first love. It's the part he takes a personal interest in. He makes the rounds every night, checking up on the girls, making sure that they're where they're supposed to be, pumping their little butts off, making their quotas. The organization gets seventy per-cent. Like I said, it's a high overhead business. Lots of costs in the oldest profession.

"It is well organized. If you're overweight or not so good-looking or you just act a little sleazy, it's the street corners. You attract a lower class of clientele on the street corners but the business is steady. If your hair is neat and you know how to wear makeup and you don't look like you're in the business, then you work the bars in the hotels. Always lots of horny, lonely guys in hotel bars.

"I did the hotels."

"I can see why," Moran said politely.

She gave a demure, cynical snort. "You're not coming on to me, are you?"

"Certainly not," Moran said. "I'm married."

"So?" She looked at him as if he were a side of beef. "I'm not too crazy about you big, Irish types, if you know what I mean." She grinned slyly at Figueroa. "You, on the other hand, are definitely cute."

"Thank you," Arnie said. "Many women have told me so."

"Well..." She sipped her coke, took a last puff of her cigarette and stubbed it out in an ashtray. "Where was I?"

"Featherstone," Moran said. "Did you ever personally give him any of the money you had earned?"

"No. Usually, I gave the money to Richie Coogan, sometimes Willie Blake. About half the time, though, Jimmy was there."

"Did he ever hit you?"

"No." She shook her head. "Not personally."

"Did anyone ever hit you?"

She gave a quick, unamused grin. "Once," she said. "They've got it down to a science. They don't want to leave bruises, at least not the first time. Bruises are bad for business. They might turn off the customers. They do it where it won't show, under the arms, the inside of the thighs. The second time is different. The second time, they put the bruises where they *will* show and then you've got to go out and make your quota anyway. That's harder. Some men are turned on by bruises but you generally want to stay away from those. If you can't make the quota, you owe them the money anyway."

"Why did they hit you?"

She shrugged. "They figured I was holding out on them. They were right. I was."

A knock came from the front door. Sharon Wilse pursed her lips thoughtfully and glanced at Figueroa. A slow smile crept across her face. "Looks like you boys got here right on time," she said.

Another knock, this one louder. Sharon Wilse stayed where she was, smiling.

"Maybe it's one of your neighbors," Figueroa said, "wanting to borrow a cup of sugar."

"Maybe," Sharon Wilse replied. "I doubt it.

Sighing, Moran pulled his gun and cradled it loosely in his fist. Figueroa followed suit. "Go over to the door," Moran said. "Ask them who they are." He added, "Stay to the side."

"If you say so." She rose to her feet, walked over to the door and called out loudly, "Yes?"

A male voice answered. "Open up, Wanda. We got things to discuss."

Sharon Wilse didn't wait for Moran's input. "Go away," she said.

"Don't make me ask again, Wanda," the voice said.

Moran picked an easy chair and crouched behind it, resting his gun hand on the arm. Arnie scrunched himself out of sight between the kitchen wall and the refrigerator. From here, he had a good view of the front door but was well hidden himself. "Open it up," Moran said. "And stay to the side."

Sharon Wilse turned the lock and opened the door. Two men dressed in suits walked in. One was tall and thin, with slicked back brown hair and a pale face. The other was even taller, fat and bald. The fat one saw Sharon. He smiled slowly, said nothing and reached into his jacket.

"Put your hands up," Moran said.

Both men froze.

"This is the police. Do it. Slowly. Now."

The fat one shook his head, gave a long, slow sigh and slowly raised his hands above his head. He turned, squinting his eyes, saw Moran behind the chair and sadly nodded.

The thin one stepped out from behind the fat man's sheltering bulk, gave a sudden shout, leaped forward, rolled and came up with a gun in his fist.

Two shots rang out. The thin man's body jerked and a gout of red sprayed into the air. The gunman stopped, looked with disbelief at the spreading red stain on his chest and then crumbled loosely to the floor. A droplet of blood bubbled up out of the corner of his mouth. He sighed once and stopped breathing.

Moran rose to his feet, keeping his gun centered on the fat man's chest. "Turn around," he said. "Assume the position." The fat man turned, spread his legs and placed both hands against the wall. "Arnie," Moran said. "Search him."

Arnie found a Colt nine-millimeter in a shoulder holster, a snub nose .38 around the fat man's ankle and a gravity knife with a five inch blade strapped to his thigh. "You got a permit for these?" Arnie asked.

The fat man didn't bother to answer.

"Put your hands behind your back," Moran said.

The fat man did so. Arnie cuffed him. "Sit down," he said. The fat man sat down in the easy chair while Moran picked up the phone and dialed.

"What are we waiting for?" Sharon Wilse asked. Her face was green.

Moran nudged the dead man with a toe. "Medical examiner. We can't leave here until the death has been officially certified."

"Oh."

Moran gave her a thin smile. "While we wait, suppose you tell us about Gina Cole?"

She looked at him. "Who's Gina Cole?" she said.

Chapter 30

"So here's the story: Astrid Fisher was a part time whore, just like Sharon Wilse. Only she wasn't quite as smart as Sharon Wilse. She thought she could hold out on these guys. She didn't do it just once or twice. Apparently, Astrid had a high tolerance for pain. She also held a grudge. The third time she tried to play fast and loose with the lunch money, she stuck a knife into a hood named Richie Buchanan, one of Jimmy Featherstone's boys. Jimmy decided to make an example of her. He carved her up, nice and slowly, then had two of his boys dump the body in Central Park." Barent shook his head sadly and took a bite out of a chocolate chip cookie. "I read about it in the paper. I remember being glad that it happened in another precinct so I wouldn't get the squeal."

"That's terrible," Lenore said. "Why did she do it? Did she need the money so badly?"

"Nope. She was a housewife. Her husband makes a decent salary."

"That's hard to believe," Lenore said.

Barent shrugged, then gave a cynical grin. "More common than you might think. Hubby works all day, the wife doesn't have a job, she gets lonely. Maybe she's bored. Maybe she drinks. It puts a little excitement into her life."

"Do you think her husband knew?"

"It's possible. Some of them don't mind. They enjoy the extra money. Some of them even get off on the idea. They like getting for free what other men have to pay for."

Lenore wrinkled her nose. "Yech," she said.

"I don't know," Kurtz said. "Call girls get to wear interesting outfits. You yourself would look pretty good in a garter belt and a black bustier."

For a moment, Lenore seemed annoyed. She opened her mouth to say something, then stopped. She smiled slowly. She looked at Kurtz and her smile widened.

Kurtz blinked, then began to grin.

Barent rolled his eyes and looked faintly nauseous. "Down, boy. Wait till I've gone. There's one more thing you might be interested in knowing: Astrid Fisher had a birthmark the size of a dime on the left cheek of her ass. You do know what this means, don't you? About Joey and Don?"

Kurtz' smile abruptly faded. "Oh, shit," he said.

"Yup. Joey and Don appear to have had nothing to do with the murder of Regina Cole."

"Then Walter Stang turns out to be just as nuts as you always thought." So much for his grand clue.

"You got it," Barent said.

That afternoon, Barent received a call from the Chief of police in Aruba. The man had a deep voice and spoke with a vaguely British accent. Barent liked the man's voice but wasn't too happy with what he had to say. The body of Mark Woodson had been discovered the day before, about three miles from where he had been reported diving, wedged beneath an outcropping of coral at a depth of seventy feet. His tanks were missing. There wasn't too much left of the body after all this time; the crabs and fish had polished off most of it. He had been identified by dental records shipped from New York. The cause of death, however, had not been difficult to determine. It was listed as a spear gun through the base of the skull.

The first time, Kurtz had been shot at. The second time it was a taser gun. Hard to figure that: why not just shoot him the second time and be done with it, if that was the intention? And if it wasn't, then why try to shoot him the first time? Unless the shooting had never been intended to do anything but put a scare in him. But that didn't make sense either. Barent had been hit. Kurtz could have been hit, too, unless the guy was a really lousy shot, or unless he got carried away with the excitement of the moment, or unless shooting Barent had been a matter of total indifference to him, which was possible.

What next?

He had promised that there would be a next time and Kurtz believed him. Kurtz was getting a little tired, truth to tell, of inspecting every alley that he passed. He was getting a little tired of always looking over his shoulder. He was tired of wearing the kevlar vest that Barent had loaned him. But that was part of the whole idea, wasn't it? Make him sweat a little, and then, when he least expected it, *pow!*

Except for the fact that the character, whoever he was, didn't know Richard Kurtz very well. Kurtz wasn't dreading the prospect in the slightest. He was almost looking forward to it.

"Oh, Jesus," Lenore said. Her eyes were closed and she was panting. Lenore, while willing and eager to try anything of an erotic nature that Kurtz could think of, when left to her own devices, had a fondness for the good old-fashioned missionary position, a fondness which Kurtz did not in the least mind satisfying.

Kurtz reached down, grabbed the cheeks of her ass in both of his fists and raised her up off the bed. Lenore's breath came short and she moaned, knocking her heels into his back. Kurtz loved it when she did that. A woman who squirmed and made a little noise in bed really let a man know he was appreciated.

Kurtz spasmed, groaned himself and then slowly collapsed on top of her.

Lenore ran a hand through his hair and whispered, "What are you thinking?"

He licked the side of her neck, then nibbled on the lobe of one perfect ear. She closed her eyes again, arched her neck and made a purring sound.

"I'm thinking that my life has gotten complicated, lately," he said.

She ran her long fingernails down both sides of his back and he groaned again, still inside of her, feeling himself once again growing hard. "The simple things are best," she said. "That's what I always say."

He smiled at her in the dark. "Did your mother teach you that?"

She opened one eye, peered at him suspiciously, then closed it again. "Leave my mother out of this."

Lena Nye, a pretty little girl smiling shyly into the camera, eight years old, a pretty little girl long since grown into a young woman, then a middle-aged woman. She had died, Bill Cole had told them, in 1979, of breast cancer.

The picture had proven to be just a picture. There were no fingerprints on it. The police had no real idea how it had gotten out onto the front lawn. Perhaps the arsonists had stolen the album and a few pictures had fallen out as they left the house. In the end, it made no difference. It was just a picture.

Strange, Barent thought, the way an old picture could stir a man's memory. You closed your eyes and suddenly, you were young again. In your memory, time had not faded things. The sun was just as bright, the air just as sweet, the breeze just as warm as today. What was it Faulkner had said once, about the South? *In the South, the past is not forgotten. It isn't even past.* That's the way it was with memory. Barent smiled. When he was eight years old, his mother had made him take dancing lessons. The experiment, thank God, had lasted less than a year.

He shook his head, took a drag on his cigarette and a bite out of a chocolate donut. His coffee had gone cold.

Barent had a box of old photos just like these, up in the attic. Betty did, too. He hadn't looked at them in years but somehow, he couldn't bear the thought of throwing them away. It would have been like throwing away a piece of his soul.

Carefully, he replaced the photograph in its white envelope and put it in his drawer.

Chapter 31

"A package for you, Doctor."

Mrs. Schapiro stood at the door to the office, holding a small box wrapped in light brown paper. Kurtz looked up. "Thanks," he said. "Just put it down."

Mrs. Schapiro placed the box on the corner of the desk and walked out. Kurtz finished dictating and picked up the box. It was addressed to him, in neat, handwritten block letters. There was no return address but the postmark said Brooklyn.

It was heavy for a box of its size, a couple of pounds maybe. He held it up to his ear and shook it. Nothing. It felt as if it were filled with something solid.

Kurtz was not in the habit of ordering merchandise through the mail. Lenore shopped through the mails quite a bit but she wouldn't have sent something to the office, and anyway, the package was addressed to him. Finally, he shrugged and tore away the paper. The box inside was cardboard, sealed with packing tape.

He stared at it. He didn't exactly know why, but something about this plain brown box disturbed him. Maybe it was the fact that the address was hand-written. A corporation would have used printed labels. Hand-written labels weren't professional. And aside from the label, the box said nothing. No L.L. Bean. No Cabela's. This wasn't business. It was personal.

Enough had gone on lately that Kurtz didn't feel like opening any strange boxes.

If he called Barent and the thing turned out to have ties or cufflinks or samples of surgical supplies in it, he would feel like a jerk. On the other hand, if he opened it up and it exploded in his face, he would feel like an even bigger jerk.

Shrugging his shoulders, he picked up the phone. Barent answered on the second ring. "Yeah?"

Kurtz explained the situation. Barent grunted. "Don't touch it. I'll send somebody down."

Twenty minutes later, two uniformed cops who Kurtz didn't know arrived at his office. One of them took a statement from Kurtz while the other immediately left with the box.

Kurtz saw a few patients, watched the clock out of the corner of his eye and tried not to think about it. Three hours later, Barent called. "Somebody doesn't like you," Barent said.

"We already know that. Tell me."

"It was a bomb. A very small bomb, not much stronger than a firecracker."

"Then what's the point?"

"The point is what else was in the package. There's this tiny bomb, and then sitting next to the bomb is a plastic bag filled with about two pounds of dog shit. It would have made quite a mess out of your office."

Kurtz looked at the clock on the wall and allowed himself to feel momentarily smug. "What have you done with it?" he asked.

"The bomb squad will detonate it."

"Lucky them."

"The postmark on the paper said Brooklyn. You noticed that?"

"Yeah," Kurtz said.

"You know anybody lives in Brooklyn?"

"I know a lot of people. I don't know where they all live."

"Carlos Gomez lives in Brooklyn," Barent said.

Kurtz smiled. "I didn't know that."

Barent's voice was momentarily silent. "Well, now that you know it, you're going to forget about it. You hear me? I shouldn't have told you."

"Sure," Kurtz said. "I hear you."

Barent sighed. "No," he said. "You don't. So let me make myself plain. You take the law into your own hands, I'll arrest you. You hear me now?"

"Oh, I hear you," Kurtz said. "I most definitely hear you. Don't worry about it. Don't worry about a thing."

"The plot sickens," Moran said.

"Not a nice joke," Barent said.

"Why'd you tell him about Gomez?"

Barent shrugged. "Kurtz isn't stupid. He would have figured it out for himself. This way, I've put him on notice."

"Good luck."

Barent gave him a beady-eyed look. "When I told him I'd arrest him, I meant it."

"Not my problem," Moran said.

"No."

Moran's problem, and Barent's problem too, was the murder of Regina Cole. First Regina Cole, then Mark Woodson, then the Cole household being burned to the ground. He stared down at the photograph of Lena Nye, Gina Cole's grandmother. It was barely possible that the heat of the fire might have simply lifted the photographs up and floated them outside onto the lawn, except that in that case, the paper should have suffered from the heat, at least been browned around the edges. It hadn't.

"Why would somebody steal a picture album?"

Moran shrugged.

"So somebody broke in, took an old album and burned the place down, presumably to cover their tracks. What else did they take?"

Moran shook his head. "Hydrocarbon residue isn't hard to find. They weren't trying to cover their tracks; they were trying to make it impossible to figure out what—if anything—had been stolen."

Barent nodded. "If we hadn't found these photos on the front lawn, we wouldn't know that anything was stolen."

"Exactly," Moran said, then smiled. "If anything was stolen, which we still don't know for certain."

Barent smiled thinly. "Let's assume it."

"Okay, let's assume it. How did they know?"

Barent looked at him.

"How did they know?" Moran said. "How did they know about the album?"

"Two people have been murdered, Gina Cole and Mark Woodson. You think Mark Woodson knew about the album?"

"Could be. Both of them were out there not too long ago, helping to pack the place up. You start going through the family heirlooms, trying to figure out what to throw out and what to take along, you get nostalgic. Maybe she showed him the pictures."

"And who knows what else?"

"Right."

"So let's assume that one of the other of them found something, something that involved the Herberts. What would they have done with it?"

"The album had been in the Cole house for years. Gina must have seen it, whatever it was, many times before, which means that Woodson is the one who made the connection."

Moran nodded. "Sounds right."

Barent reached into his pocket, pulled out a pack of cigarettes. He offered the pack to Moran. Moran shook his head. "Blackmail?" Barent said. "Presumably, something the Herberts would have paid to keep secret?"

Moran smiled. "Or would have killed to keep secret."

Barent took a drag on his cigarette, let the smoke dribble out through his nose. "If I were Mark Woodson," Barent said, "and I had found something, maybe a picture, that would be worth killing for, I would have made a copy of it, maybe a lot of copies."

"So let's say he did find something, and let's say he hid it," Moran said. "Where would it be?"

"His apartment was empty. He didn't have a safe-deposit box. His desk at work contained nothing suspicious. Somewhere in his parent's house?"

"Maybe," Moran said.

Barent reached for the phone. "Let's find out," he said.

The Woodsons were bewildered but cooperative. Barent brought a whole squad from the Homicide Unit and they went over the house from top to bottom. They looked behind paintings and under carpets and inside the crossbars in the showers. They looked beneath drawers and under mattresses. They spent most of the afternoon in the Woodsons' house and came up with nothing.

"Win some, lose some," Barent said.

Arnie Figueroa shrugged.

"I've been thinking," Moran said.

"Does your head hurt? I've got some Tylenol in my pocket."

Moran ignored him. "I've been thinking," he said again. "Where else could a guy like Woodson stash something that he didn't want to be found?"

Barent's brow wrinkled. "That is the question, isn't it?"

"Regina Cole wasn't the only woman that Mark Woodson was involved with. Remember?"

Barent looked at him. A slow smile crossed his face. "Yes," he said. "I remember."

The legal paperwork with which Kurtz had been served listed the address of all the plaintiffs in the case: Carlos Gomez, his mother and his sister. Brooklyn. Kurtz, not entirely unmindful of Barent's warning, told himself that he was not going to take the law into his own hands. This did not mean that he couldn't ask a few questions. And so he decided to take a little drive.

Carlos Gomez, or so Barent had informed him, was "between jobs at the moment," which meant that there was at least a chance that Gomez might be home in the middle of the afternoon on a beautiful spring day. Unfortunately, Carlos Gomez was not in his apartment, or if he was, he was choosing to ignore the buzzer. Nothing to do but wait, then. Kurtz parked his car across the street and pressed the automatic door lock attached to his key chain. The locks snicked closed.

Two hours later, Kurtz had worked his way through the stack of magazines that he had brought with him and was getting bored. The day had turned cloudy. It would be dark soon. He was considering giving the whole thing up when Carlos Gomez came walking down the street. Finally. He was alone. Good. Kurtz had a plan, a simple plan but one which should, Kurtz thought, tell him what he wanted to know. Kurtz got out of the car, stretched and crossed the street.

Gomez appeared to have been drinking. His face was red. He weaved a little from side to side as he walked. Once, he almost stumbled.

"Mr. Gomez?"

Gomez stopped. He peered at Kurtz uncertainly. "Who are you?" he said.

"Nobody in particular. Tell me, have you mailed any packages lately?"

Gomez frowned. "Mail?"

"Maybe a package like this?" Kurtz held out a box. It was a plain cardboard box covered with brown wrapping paper. It was, so far as Kurtz could make it, exactly the same size, shape and appearance as the box which had been sent to his office.

Gomez looked bewildered. He shook his head irritably. "Who are you, man? I don't know what you talking about."

"No? Maybe you would like to have this," Kurtz said. "Go on. Take it."

Gomez looked at him suspiciously. "What's in it?"

"I don't know. Maybe a million bucks." Kurtz grinned. "Maybe a pound of shit. Here." Kurtz held out the box. "Take it."

Slowly, glowering at Kurtz, Gomez took the box. He held it up to his ear and shook it, just as Kurtz had done. He looked at Kurtz and belched. "I don't know you," he said. "Why you giving me this?"

He didn't know him. He really didn't. That much was obvious. The guy sues him for a couple of million bucks but he doesn't recognize him when they pass on the street. "You know me," Kurtz said. "You know me just fine." He smiled. "My name is Kurtz."

"Kurtz…" Gomez' head reared back. His nostrils flared and his red face turned even redder. "You're the quack who killed my old man." He dropped the box at Kurtz' feet. "Whatever you got in there, I don't want it. I don't want nothing from you."

He didn't look guilty, that was for sure. And he sounded as if he meant it. For a brief, sweet moment, Kurtz thought that Gomez was about to take a swing at him. Kurtz hoped that he did. Carlos Gomez, Kurtz realized, really did not like him. This did not bother Kurtz in the slightest, since he did not like Carlos Gomez, either. But the moment passed. Gomez sneered at the box where it lay on the ground. He kicked it, then, without looking again at Kurtz, Gomez walked past him, put his key in the lock, opened the door and went inside—the picture of offended dignity.

Too bad, Kurtz thought. Unless the guy was one hell of a fine actor, strike one suspect.

Chapter 32

"Sorry to bother you again, Miss Baker. May we come in?"

It was seven o'clock at night. They had called before coming over and verified that she would be at home. Lynn Baker looked back and forth between Barent and Moran. "Sure." She stepped aside. "Come on in. Sit down."

"You've heard about Mark Woodson," Barent said when they were seated. "You know that his body was found." It wasn't a question.

Lynn Baker swallowed. "Yes. It was in the newspapers."

"We have reason to believe that Mark Woodson was murdered because he had discovered something. Exactly what that something might have been, we don't yet know, but we also have reason to suspect that Regina Cole was murdered for the same reason and by the same people."

"Regina Cole." Lynn Baker wrinkled her nose.

Barent said nothing. He only looked at her. After a moment, she seemed to grow uncomfortable. "Why are you telling me this? What can I do about it?"

"Did Mark Woodson leave anything with you before he left for Aruba? An envelope, maybe?"

She shook her head slowly. "No," she said. "Nothing at all."

"You're sure?"

"Of course I'm sure. He hasn't given me anything since my birthday. That was almost two months ago."

Barent and Moran looked at each other. Moran raised an eyebrow. "Your birthday," Barent said.

"Yes, my birthday."

"What did he give you?"

"Some cookbooks." She smiled—a sad, sheepish smile. "It was a joke. He knows that I don't cook. I can barely boil water. I don't have the time for it. Aside for a can of tuna fish or a salad now and then, I eat all my meals out."

"Cookbooks," Barent said.

"The Great Chefs series, to be exact."

Barent drew a deep breath. "Can we see these cookbooks, Miss Baker?"

Wordlessly, she rose to her feet, went into the kitchen and came back with four books, which she placed on the coffee table. "Be my guest," she said.

They found it almost immediately, a thin envelope stuffed into one of the books. "May we?" Barent asked.

Lynn Baker shrugged.

Smiling at Moran, Barent opened the envelope. Inside, he found a sheaf of papers, obviously xeroxed copies. Folded inside the paper was a single photograph. Barent looked at the photograph and felt the hair rise on the back of his neck. "Jesus," he whispered.

Moran, who had been looking through the papers, glanced up at him. "Something?"

Barent finally remembered that he had to breathe. He felt light-headed, almost dizzy. "Take a look," he said.

The photograph was an old black and white print, the edges yellowed and brittle with age. The picture showed three people, all young, all good looking. In the center was a man, dressed in a black tuxedo. Standing next to him were two young women. The women had dark, curly hair and wore dresses that exposed about half of their shapely breasts and were cut well above the knees. All three were grinning at the camera. Something about the man's grin made Barent wonder if he might be drunk.

Written on the back of the picture in fading, blue ink were the words: Joe, Ronnie and Claire, 1929.

Moran looked at the photograph for almost a minute. He gave a tiny, satisfied smile, carefully placed it down on Lynn Baker's coffee table and held out the sheaf of papers to Barent. "Get a load of these," he said.

The first piece of paper was a copy of an undated letter written on personalized stationary. The name at the top of the page was Joseph P. Herbert, Junior. It read:

> *Dear Ronnie,*
>
> *I'm glad to hear that you're feeling better.
> I have to admit that your decision comes as a
> surprise. I wouldn't have expected you to be the
> maternal type, all things considered. Let me
> know if you change your mind. I have certain
> connections who might be able to help.*
>
> *Joe*

"Good old Joe," Barent said, "always ready to help."

"Look at the rest."

"What is it?"

"Just look."

Barent quickly flipped through the pages. They were a single copy of a notarized document, prepared by the firm of Reagan and Wright, Attorneys at Law. The document outlined an agreement on the part of a corporation known as Stardust Realty to loan to the Herbert Development Corporation the sum of seventy million dollars, said moneys to be paid back within the span of ten years at a yearly interest rate of seven point four per-cent.

That was all.

"What are these things?" Lynn Baker asked.

Barent frowned at the papers in his hand. "I'm betting they're a motive," he said. "A motive for murder."

"That's ridiculous. What if I had found them? I could have thrown them out."

"Would you have thrown them out, Miss Baker?"

She shifted uncomfortably. "No," she said at last. "No. I guess not. I would have figured they were Mark's. I would have saved them for him."

"What motive?" Moran said. "I don't get it."

"I think I might." Barent rose to his feet and smiled at Lynn Baker. "Thank you, Miss Baker," he said, "you've been very helpful."

"Will you tell me how it turns out?" she asked.

He grinned at her. "You can count on it."

"Hello, Miss Moore. Remember me?"

Vivian Moore peered at Moran, a sad, bewildered expression on her face. "No," she said slowly. "I'm afraid that I don't. Are you my nephew?"

"No, Miss Moore," Moran said gently. "I'm not your nephew."

Vivian Moore was sitting in the hallway, tilted back in a lounge chair. She was dressed in white flannel pajamas with a blue cotton blanket across her lap.

"My nephew brings me candy. Do you have any candy?"

On the verge of saying no, Moran remembered suddenly that he did have a pack of lifesavers in his pocket. He fished them out. "Would you like one?" he asked.

She peered at the lifesavers. "That would be very nice, thank you."

"Take the whole pack," Moran said. "I have more at home."

Vivian Moore's eyes lit up. "Aren't you a sweet young man?" Her jaw moved stolidly back and forth as she sucked at a candy.

An auspicious beginning. Moran took a photograph out of his pocket and handed it to her. "I recently came across this picture," he said. "I was wondering if you could tell me anything about it."

She stared at the photo, her arthritic hands holding it loosely by the edges. "Oh, my," she said. "I haven't seen that face in many years."

"You recognize it?"

"Certainly." She tapped her finger on the picture. "It's young Joe. Who else would it be?"

"Joseph P. Herbert, Junior?"

Joe. Mitchell Cole had of course been shown the photograph. "Ronnie" turned out to be Veronica Nye, the mother of Lena Nye, which would make her Gina Cole's great-grandmother. A search of the city records had turned up a birth certificate for Lena Nye. The father was listed as unknown.

Mitchell Cole had frowned at the picture. "I'm pretty sure I've seen it before. It came from the old album."

Gina Cole's father had been unable to identify either the man or the other woman…Claire. A call to Frances Shields, MD, had resulted in nothing helpful. There were no personnel folders left from the nineteen-thirties, certainly no pictures of Claire Reisberg. The dead files of the *Times* had proven more helpful. There, on microfilm, they had found it. Claire Reisberg's smiling face, part of an article on Claire Reisberg's lurid and untimely death.

It was the same face of the young woman in the photograph, the photograph that Vivian Moore clutched in her bent, arthritic fingers. And what were they supposed to make out of that?

Vivian Moore nodded. "Yes," she said, "it's Joe, alright."

"Do you recognize either of the women?"

Slowly, she shook her head. "No. Young Joe was a great one for the ladies. He always had a young woman around him, sometimes two or three." She sighed. "Such a handsome young man. Such a sad thing."

"Do you know what happened to him?"

"He hanged himself. That's all I know."

"And you don't recognize either of the women."

She peered at him, frowning slightly. "I don't think so." She looked confused. "Did I already say that?"

"Yes, Miss Moore, you did." He took back the photograph and put it in his pocket. "I'm sorry to have troubled you. Have a nice day."

She nodded. Hands trembling, she put a lifesaver in her mouth and sucked on it. One down, Moran thought.

Talk about long shots, Jason Lester had about three brain cells left, and those three were on the verge of final disintegration. Jason Lester sat in his reclining chair, his head tilted back and to the side, his eyes fixed somewhere out into the distance, his tongue peeking out of one side of his mouth, the breath wheezing slowly into his chest.

"Mister Lester?" Moran asked.

The nurse, Penny, looked skeptical. "I think you're wasting your time. He hasn't said ten words in the last two years."

She was probably right. Moran reached out and placed his hand on Jason Lester's bony shoulder. He gave him a little shake. "Mister Lester?" he said again.

"Ehh?" Jason Lester blinked his eyes and turned his head slowly toward Moran. He frowned. "Ehh?" he said again.

"How are you today, Mister Lester?" Moran asked.

Jason Lester said nothing and continued to blink.

Already, Moran had gotten more of a response than he had really expected.

Not hoping for much, Moran reached into his pocket and pulled out the picture of Joseph P. Herbert, Junior and the two young women, one the great-grandmother of Gina Cole, one the victim of rape and murder. "Do you recognize any of the people in this picture, Mister Lester?"

Jason Lester stared at the photograph. Slowly, one trembling hand reached up. His head craned forward. His rheumy eyes blinked and his jaw shook. He glanced up at Moran, turned again toward the picture. His mouth stretched wide and a low, whining sound came from his throat.

The nurse looked suddenly concerned. "You're upsetting him," she said.

Moran held up a hand. "Shut up," he said. "Please."

Jason Lester's breath came faster. He opened his mouth, coughed, cleared his throat.

"Yes, Mister Lester? What are you trying to say?"

The old man's hand came up and rested on Moran's arm, as light as paper. "I…"

"Yes, Mister Lester?"

"I…only…drove," he whispered. "I…only…drove. I didn't…kill…" His hand dropped away. He swallowed and closed his eyes.

"You didn't kill who?" Moran asked.

Jason Lester's breath whistled slowly in and out. He appeared not to have heard. "Who didn't you kill?" Moran repeated.

"I think you've bothered him quite enough," Penny said. "More than enough."

The old man's head had returned to its original position. His mouth was opened, the tongue peeking out of the left corner. His eyes were half opened, focused on nothing. Moran passed a hand in front of his eyes. There was no response. "Right," Moran said. "You bet."

"According to Charles, Jason Lester was the Herbert's chauffeur."

"He only drove," Moran said. "He didn't kill."

"Who did kill?" Arnie Figueroa asked.

"Yeah," Barent said, "and who did he kill?"

"Claire Reisberg was strangled."

"Joe Junior hung himself," Moran said.

"Did he now? Did he really?" Barent squinted at him through the haze of smoke in the office. "Do we know that for sure? How well was Joseph P. Herbert's death investigated? His father was a rich man with ties to organized crime. I wouldn't doubt that he could have hushed things up if he wanted to, particularly since it's obvious that Harold Van Gelden was on his payroll."

Moran shrugged, his face expressionless.

"How does Gina Cole and Mark Woodson's murder tie in to Joseph P. Herbert, Junior? What did Eleanor Herbert, a seven year old girl, see or find out?"

"Murder?" Arnie asked.

"Whose murder? Claire Reisberg? Joseph P. Herbert, Junior? Somebody else?"

"Maybe Gina Cole knew," Moran said. "Maybe that's why she was killed."

There was silence while all three men pondered this suggestion. Arnie Figueroa sipped a cup of coffee. Barent idly blew a smoke ring at the ceiling. "I think it's time to have another talk with the only surviving victim," Barent finally said.

"Eleanor Herbert?"

"Yeah," Barent said. "Eleanor Herbert."

Chapter 33

They made a detour to Kurtz' apartment, where Barent, looking none too pleased about it, asked Kurtz to accompany them. Kurtz found himself unable to suppress a grin at Barent's sour expression. "You bet," he said.

Lenore glanced at Barent, then gave Kurtz a kiss on the cheek. "Don't you have surgery in the morning?"

"Not until ten," he said. "Don't worry, I'll get a good night's sleep."

"I don't think we'll be late," Barent said.

Lenore looked at Barent and gave a faint snort.

"Don't wait up," Kurtz said.

"Sure," Lenore said. She kissed him again. "Be careful."

Three minutes later, they were on the road. Kurtz appreciated the invitation, grudging though it might have been. He was with them, Barent explained, because Kurtz could present the medical facts better than Barent could, their theory regarding insulin shock and lacunar infarcts in the brain and Harold Van Gelden, sixty years in the past. "I don't know much about CAT scans. You tell her." Aside from this, the next few miles were almost silent. Moran shook his head now and then. Barent was glum.

After awhile, Kurtz asked, "So what else have you found out?"

Barent grinned faintly. "Wait till we get there. I don't want to have to explain it twice."

It was Barent's show. Kurtz shrugged. "Sure," he said.

Eleanor Herbert was awake when they arrived, as usual, drinking tea. Her great-nephew, Jerome Herbert, was sitting with her in the drawing room. "Gentlemen," he said, and raised his teacup. "How nice to see you again."

From the way he slurred his words, it seemed obvious that Jerome Herbert had until recently been drinking something stronger than tea.

Eleanor Herbert gave her nephew a tired smile, patted his hand and otherwise ignored him. She looked at Kurtz and Barent with sharp eyes. "I've been hoping you would come by," she said, "or at least call."

"I'm sorry," Barent said. "We wanted to know more before talking to you."

"And now you know more?"

He hesitated. "Yes."

She nodded primly. "Then sit down."

"A mystery?" Jerome Herbert said. "How exciting!" He settled back in his chair and pasted an intent expression on his face.

Barent looked at him. "I would prefer it if we spoke in private."

"Don't mind me," Jerome Herbert said. "I'll be as quiet as a mouse."

Barent said nothing. Eleanor Herbert frowned. "I'm sorry, Jerry," she said. "I think you had better leave."

Jerome Herbert drew a reproachful sigh and heaved himself tiredly to his feet. "Never around for the good parts. The story of my life." He swayed, shook his head once to clear it, then shuffled toward the door.

"Wait," Eleanor Herbert said. Jerome Herbert stopped, blinking his eyes at her. "You're in no condition to drive. Charles will find you a room."

He yawned. "Perhaps you're right. Gentlemen…" He smiled at Barent, Kurtz and Moran. "Goodnight."

Barent waited until the door had closed before saying to Eleanor Herbert, "Doctor Kurtz will speak to you first. After that, we'll tell you what else we've discovered."

"Very well, Doctor," Eleanor Herbert said. "Tell me your story."

Kurtz told her. He told her about a seven year old girl who screamed and threw things and broke out into tears. He told her about chloral hydrate and the side effects of insulin shock and electroconvulsive therapy and lacunar infarcts in the brain. He showed her the pictures of the CAT scan. Eleanor Herbert listened silently and intently and nodded at the pictures. When Kurtz had finished, her face was pale. The only sound that they could hear was the faint ticking of a clock across the room. Finally, she cleared her throat. "Caroline McFadden…" she said.

"You mentioned the name to me," Kurtz said.

Eleanor Herbert nodded. Her shoulders were slumped, her expression grave. "She never told me this."

"She was afraid," Barent said.

"Afraid of what? Afraid of me?"

"Afraid of your family. Afraid of looking like an idiot. She had no proof of anything, you see."

"No. I suppose she didn't." Eleanor Herbert sighed slowly. "Those years are a blur to me. Just a blur."

"If we're correct, they were supposed to be. That was the idea."

Eleanor Herbert raised her teacup to her lips, sipped, put it down. "Is that all?" she asked.

"No," Barent said.

She looked at him and gave a tired grin. "You have been busy. Tell me the rest of it."

Barent looked at her, concern evident on his face. Eleanor Herbert arched a brow. "I'm tougher than I look," she said. "Just tell me."

"Alright," Barent said. He drew a deep breath. "First of all, you said that you first saw Regina Cole at the annual dinner for the medical center benefactors. You said that something about her disturbed you. You had trouble sleeping that night and the next day, you suffered a heart attack. You almost died. During your resuscitation, you dreamed that you saw the dead body of Regina Cole lying on a bed."

"That's correct."

"And two days later, Regina Cole turned up dead. She had been strangled, just as you dreamed."

"So I have been told," Eleanor Herbert said. She gave a wintry smile. "I myself have not seen the body."

Barent ignored her comment. "The day after Regina Cole's body was found, I came here for the first time and talked to your brother. In the hallway leading to the den, I saw a series of paintings. One of them is a portrait of your older brother, Joseph P. Herbert, Junior. Do you know the portrait?"

She nodded. "Of course."

"It's an interesting portrait, quite life-like. When I first saw it, I thought that your brother looked vaguely familiar to me but I thought nothing more of it at that time. I remembered that feeling of familiarity only when I found this." Barent took out the picture of Joseph P. Herbert, Junior, Veronica Nye and Claire Reisberg and handed it to Eleanor Herbert.

She stared at it, turning it back and forth in her fingers. "I never saw this picture," she finally said. "Where did you get it?"

"It was in the possession of a young man named Mark Woodson. Mark Woodson was a former boyfriend of Regina Cole's. She broke up with him shortly before she was murdered. Mark Woodson went on a scuba diving vacation to the island of Aruba. He disappeared. His body was found a few weeks later with a spear gun through the head."

Eleanor Herbert grimaced. "And what do you make of all this?"

"Wait," Barent said. "There's more. Do you recognize either of the young women in the picture?"

She stared at it. Her hand began to tremble. Kurtz cleared his throat and started to rise from his chair. Barent held up a hand. Kurtz stopped. "I don't know," Eleanor Herbert said in a strangled whisper. "This one,"—she tapped the picture of Claire Reisberg—"she looks as if I should know her."

"That is a picture of Claire Reisberg. She was a nurse at the Van Gelden Institute."

Eleanor Herbert glanced at Kurtz. "You mentioned her to me."

Kurtz nodded. Barent looked annoyed. He shook his head and continued. "On the night of April 24, 1935, Claire Reisberg was strangled to death. One of the patients was accused of the crime. He admitted it. A few days later, your brother, Joseph P. Herbert, Junior, hung himself."

Eleanor Herbert closed her eyes tightly. She reached up her hands and rubbed at the sides of her face. "Is that all?" she asked.

"No. I'm afraid that it isn't."

A small scratching sound came from the doorway. Barent stopped and nodded his head at Moran. Soundlessly, Moran stepped forward and opened the door.

Vincent Herbert stood outside in the hallway.

"Come in, Mister Herbert," Barent said. "I think you should hear this."

Vincent Herbert's face was pale, his eyes wide. "Though it appears," said Barent, "as if you already have."

"Vincent?" Eleanor Herbert said.

Vincent Herbert blinked. He looked back and forth between Barent and Moran.

"Do you have anything to add to what I've said so far, Mister Herbert?" Barent asked.

"No," Vincent Herbert said.

"Vincent?" Eleanor Herbert said again.

"No." Vincent Herbert's voice was hoarse. "No. Nothing." He sat down heavily in a chair.

Barent gave him a faint smile. "Then I'll go on."

Vincent Herbert stared at the wall. He took no apparent notice of Barent's words.

"The other woman in the picture," Barent said, "the one who Joseph P. Herbert, Junior has his arm around, has been identified as Veronica Nye, the great-grandmother of Regina Cole."

Vincent Herbert continued to stare at the wall. Eleanor Herbert stared at him. Kurtz, who had heard none of this before but who thought he could see where it was all heading, suppressed a giddy urge to laugh.

"Gina Cole's grandmother, whose maiden name was Lena Nye, was born on August 15, 1931, at her mother's home in Manhattan. The birth certificate on record with the city lists the father as unknown. A letter, however, written by Joseph P. Herbert, Junior, to Veronica Nye prior to that date, discusses the pregnancy. The letter implies, though not in so many words, that if Veronica Nye wishes to seek an abortion, he would be willing to help her out."

Slowly, Eleanor Herbert's eyes rose to meet Barent's. "My brother has been dead for nearly seventy years," she said. "Why are you telling me this, now?"

Barent shrugged. "Gina Cole has been dead for only two weeks."

"Gina Cole…" Eleanor Herbert stared at her brother. "You're telling me that Gina Cole was my niece, aren't you? My niece. And I didn't even know she existed."

"When I first saw this picture," Barent said, "and read the letter from your brother, I realized why his portrait had seemed so familiar to me. His face was Regina Cole's face."

"Yes," Eleanor Herbert whispered. "I can see it now. I can see it. That's why her face disturbed me so." She hesitated. "Her face looked like death."

Barent said, "The laws of inheritance in New York state that if a man dies without leaving a will, then his property is divided among his wife and his 'natural heirs.' Joseph P. Herbert, Junior was unmarried. He had no legitimate children. The law states that paternity of illegitimate children must be acknowledged prior to death for them to inherit. The letter that we found is not exactly an acknowledgement of paternity. However, the Cole household was recently burned to the ground. We have reason to believe that it was burglarized. It could be that other evidence of paternity still exists." Barent shrugged. "Or existed. It could be argued that Regina Cole, and Regina Cole's mother, and Regina Cole's grandmother, if she were still alive, all have a claim on Joseph P. Herbert, Junior's estate."

"After seventy years?" Eleanor Herbert said.

"There is no statute of limitations on the right to inherit."

"Vincent?" Eleanor Herbert said.

Vincent Herbert shook his head slowly. "Except for the night of the party, I never met Gina Cole," he said.

"No?" Barent said. "Then how about Claire Reisberg? Did you ever meet Claire Reisberg?"

"I don't have to answer your questions," Vincent Herbert said.

Kurtz could see Barent hesitate. This was true. They had no leverage on Vincent Herbert. Whatever crimes had been committed so many years ago could not be proven today. "But it's so coincidental, isn't it?" Barent said. "Claire Reisberg knew your brother, and she also knew Veronica Nye. And later, when Joseph P. Herbert, Junior was a patient at the Van Gelden Institute, Claire Reisberg was his nurse. How did that come about? We know nothing at all about Joseph P. Herbert's relationship with Claire Reisberg but we do know that Claire Reisberg was pregnant when she died. Claire Reisberg never married. The infant's father never came forward, was never identified. Was Joseph P. Herbert, Junior, the father of her unborn child? Is that why she died? Is that why Regina Cole died? To protect your inheritance?"

"No," Vincent Herbert said. Slowly, his eyes came up to meet Barent's. His breath came faster. His head reared up and his nostrils flared and a terrible light seemed to burn in his eyes. "No," he said, "that's not why she died."

Barent nodded, almost to himself. Moran sat with a faint smile on his face. Kurtz sat unmoving, feeling as if the faintest sound or movement on his part would break the spell. Barent said, "Then what did your sister, your seven year old sister, see that caused Harold Van Gelden to burn the memory out of her brain? Of course, there are other explanations. For instance, you must have known Claire Reisberg, too. You visited your brother frequently, twice a month, we were told. Somewhere along the line, you must have met his nurse. Did your sister Eleanor stumble upon you and Claire Reisberg in a back bedroom, making love? Or did she see you kill her?" Barent smiled thinly. "By the way, your family chauffeur at the time, a man named Jason Lester? He's still alive. He's given us a statement that he transported Claire Reisberg's dead body." Not exactly true, Barent thought, but it would do for the moment. "The body was found at the Van Gelden Institute, and so, if what Mister Lester told us is correct, then she must have been strangled somewhere else.

"Unfortunately, Mister Lester is very old. He was unable to tell us anything more than that. Miss Herbert, you'll remember, dreamed that she saw old wooden doors and old wooden windows. This is an old house. The doors are made out of wood. The windows are modern, but what did the windows look like sixty years ago? Where was Claire Reisberg killed? Was it here? We don't know." Barent raised a brow and smiled at Vincent Herbert. "But I'll bet you do."

Slowly, saying not a word, Vincent Herbert rose to his feet and staggered from the room. Moran took a step forward, as if to go after him. Barent shook his head and Moran stopped. He shrugged and resumed his seat. Eleanor Herbert gave a deep, slow sigh, and sipped her tea. The expression on her face was thoughtful, almost serene, but her hand, as she raised the teacup to her lips, was trembling.

Chapter 34

By 11:00 AM the next morning, Kurtz had already been operating for an hour. Luckily, it was a routine case, an inguinal hernia in a healthy, fifty-year old male—since Kurtz more than once found his mind wandering, his fingers cutting and sewing more by instinct than design. His thoughts kept returning to the events of the night before. After their agonizing interview with Eleanor and Vincent Herbert, the ride back to the city had been nearly silent.

Eleanor Herbert had been calm. She had thanked them politely for their efforts. She had refused to believe that her brother might be responsible for the deaths of either Claire Reisberg or Regina Cole. "My brother is a gentle, considerate man," she had said. "He wouldn't hurt a fly. I've lived with him for a very long time. I know him. You don't." Her voice had been calm but had brooked no argument. "You will admit, I am sure, that your evidence is entirely circumstantial."

"Considerably less circumstantial than your evidence against Doctor Adler," Kurtz said.

"This is true," Eleanor Herbert said, unruffled. "It's also irrelevant." She fixed Barent with a sharp eye. "Is this all that you've discovered?"

Barent hesitated. There was no way to determine if the loan that Stardust Realty had made to the Herbert Development Corporation had ever been repaid. The two companies had merged in 1937. Herbert Development had merged with and bought out numerous competitors over the years, and still Herbert Development survived, an institution, a colossus. What this all might mean to their case, and why Mark Woodson had felt it important enough to hide, they had not yet found out, and Barent did not feel it wise to mention any of this to Eleanor Herbert.

"Yes," he had said.

Eleanor nodded her head in patrician gratitude. "Then thank you," she said, and once again, sipped her tea. Her eyes were remote. They had clearly been dismissed.

"Tie," Kurtz said. The nurse handed him a piece of chromic. He placed it around a vessel that was too big to cauterize and knotted it down. Adler snipped off the ends without having to be asked.

Adler was looking better. The furor over Gina Cole's death was finally beginning to dissipate. Most people, when they thought of these things at all, assumed that Eleanor Herbert was a batty old woman, which, all things considered, was not too far from the truth.

"Give me a cough, Mister Laskin," Kurtz said loudly.

The patient cleared his throat and coughed, which he was able to do since he was awake, his anesthetic a spinal. The wound quivered but did not bulge. Good. A nice, solid repair. Kurtz picked up a staple gun and stitched the edges of the incision together. "Put on a dressing, will you, Steve?"

"Sure," Adler said.

Vincent Herbert was almost ninety years old. They could arrest him but it would constitute little more than harassment. As Eleanor Herbert had said, all the evidence was circumstantial. The charges would never stick, not regarding Claire Reisberg, and certainly not regarding Regina Cole. Kurtz shook his head. Forget it. Any punishment that Vincent Herbert was going to receive would have to come from God and the retribution of his sister.

It was almost noon. Kurtz grabbed a turkey sandwich in the hospital cafeteria and took it with him to the office. Mrs. Schapiro looked up as he walked in. She was typing something and had the phone tucked under her chin at the same time. She looked harassed. "There's somebody waiting to see you," she said. "He said it was important. Also personal." Mrs. Schapiro looked at Kurtz speculatively and shrugged. "I let him into your office."

Kurtz stopped. His unknown assailant was still on the loose. He didn't want strangers running around his office. "Who is it?"

"He gave his name as Jerome Herbert."

Kurtz thought about that for a moment. "Thin guy? Blonde hair? Blue eyes? Three piece suit?"

"He said it was important," she repeated.

"Okay. Thanks." Kurtz walked back to the office, peered inside. Jerome Herbert was indeed sitting in the chair across from Kurtz' desk, reading a paperback book. "Hello," Kurtz said.

"Sorry to have come unannounced." Jerome Herbert lacked his usual air of languid self-satisfaction. His lips were set, his expression grim. "I wanted to talk to you."

"You don't mind if I eat?" Kurtz did not wait for a reply. He set his sandwich out on the desk and popped the top on a can of root beer. "So. What can I do for you?"

Jerome Herbert did not answer right away. He placed his book into the side pocket of his jacket and stared at the desk in front of him while Kurtz took a bite out of his sandwich. Finally, Herbert said, "My aunt likes you."

Kurtz inclined his head. "I like her, too," he said cautiously.

"Eleanor has always been my favorite relative. She was upset by what you told her last night." He gave a tired grin. "Very upset."

"I don't blame her."

"She told me all about it," Jerome Herbert said. "It's quite a story. I've heard of Joseph Herbert, Junior, of course. He's a part of the family legend. He died young. There's a certain tragic glamour in dying young, don't you think? All that unfulfilled potential. Such a handsome man. Such a shame." He shook his head. "I never heard the story of Claire Reisberg, of course, nor Veronica Nye. Nothing glamorous in any of that. Does Gina Cole's family know?"

"About the relationship? No. Or at least I don't think so. There's only her father. It's possible that Gina or Mark Woodson may have told him but it seems likely he would have mentioned it to the police if they had."

"But he will be?" Jerome Herbert seemed quite interested in the answer to this question. Kurtz wondered exactly why.

"I suppose so," he said.

Jerome Herbert made a sad, clucking sound between his teeth. "Would you like to know a secret?" he asked.

Kurtz looked at him.

"I knew Gina Cole," Jerome Herbert said.

Kurtz stared at him. "You did?"

"Uh-huh. I did." Jerome Herbert gave Kurtz a prim, satisfied smile.

"And?"

"And what? Did I kill her?" He shook his head. "No. Do I know who killed her? I might. I'm not really sure. Do I know why she was killed? Again, I might." He rose to his feet. "Tell your friend the Detective. I'll be in later on today to give him a statement." He grinned faintly and added, "With my lawyer."

Kurtz tried to speak and found his mouth full. Hastily, he swallowed. "Why have you told me this? Why didn't you go to the police, right away?"

Jerome Herbert rubbed the bridge of his nose. He shook his head. He looked suddenly unhappy. "Oh, I don't know. I suppose I had to get used to the idea. Ease my way into it. There are things that you don't know, things that my family wouldn't want me to speak about." He walked to the door, hesitated. "I don't like what they did to Eleanor," he said. "She always was my favorite relative." He grinned again, faintly and without the slightest bit of mirth. "But then, I already told you that." He walked out.

Kurtz found himself suddenly with no appetite. He put down the sandwich and shoved it to one side of the desk. He thought about telling Mrs. Schapiro to cancel his appointments for the afternoon but then reconsidered. It wouldn't be fair. Some of the patients no doubt had had to take time off from work or arrange for baby sitting. He owed it to them to do his job.

He rose to his feet and peered out the window. A couple of hundred people were walking by on the street below, a couple of hundred people who had never heard of Richard Kurtz and couldn't have cared less about his problems. There was something reassuring in that. Jerome Herbert came out the front of the building, crossed the street and turned the corner.

Kurtz drew a breath of fresh air, then another. Then he saw the phone sitting on his desk and suddenly almost laughed. He picked it up and dialed Barent's number.

Three hours later, Kurtz had seen his last patient, dictated his last chart. He poked his nose into David Chao's office. "You done yet?" Kurtz asked.

"Soon. One more to go."

Kurtz nodded. "See you in the morning."

Mrs. Schapiro had already gone home. The waiting room was quiet. Kurtz closed the door behind him and walked down the stairs to the street. A yellow Nissan Sentra drove past him and stopped. The window rolled down. A gun pointed at Kurtz' midsection. The man holding the gun appeared to be about thirty. He was white and had a brown beard. "Get in," he said.

Kurtz hesitated.

"Don't try it," the man said. His tone of voice was level and pleasant. "Get in or I'll kill you."

Kurtz got in.

"So what have you found?" Barent asked.

Moran dropped a sheaf of papers on the desk. "Not much. For tax purposes, a corporation is as much a legal entity as a human being. We would need a search warrant and a court order even to look at their books. Forget it."

It was pretty much as Barent figured. Barent had a theory, a theory based on the fact that Mark Woodson had found the loan agreement between Herbert Development and Stardust Realty of sufficient importance to steal, and upon the related fact that some person or persons unknown had found Mark Woodson's actions sufficiently disquieting to have murdered him.

"Don't the members of the Board have to be registered with the SEC?" Barent asked.

"They do if it's a public corporation. Not if it's private."

"Oh, yeah." Barent glumly nodded. "I forgot."

"Stardust Realty ceased to exist in 1937. There's no way to tell if they ever got their money back from Herbert Development."

Moran, unaccountably, looked happy. Moran often looked happy just as their situation began to look its worst. The fact that a case had reached an apparent dead end always seemed to confirm his opinions on the perverse nature of fate and mankind. Barent, whose attitude toward frustration was more conventional, sucked in a lungful of smoke and blew it across the desk, where it drifted around Moran's head. "There's one thing we can check on," Barent said.

"Oh?"

"The deed on the Herbert place. A deed is public domain."

Moran looked at him, sipped from his cup of coffee and took a bite out of a jelly doughnut. "So?"

"If the price of the loan was Herbert Development, then the mansion might have been part of the package."

"You think the Herberts don't own the place? That makes no sense at all.

They've lived there for a hundred years."

Barent thought about it. "I'm probably wrong," he conceded. Then he smiled. "Find out."

Moran grimaced, leaned back in his chair, and took another bite out of his doughnut. Strawberry jelly oozed out of the doughnut and spattered on the desk. Moran frowned at it. Barent found himself smiling. Moran gave him a hurt look.

At that moment, the phone on Barent's desk rang. Barent stared at it, then shrugged and picked it up. He listened for a moment, puffed his breath out in a long, amazed sigh, said, "Uh-huh," once or twice, then said, "Okay. Sure." He gently put the phone down in its cradle and smiled.

"Something?" Moran asked.

"Jerome Herbert just left Kurtz' office. He says he has information about who killed Gina Cole. He'll come in later to give us a statement."

Moran whistled. "Kurtz," he said. "Gotta hand it to the guy."

Barent looked at him, gave a small frown and smoked his cigarette.

By five o'clock, Jerome Herbert and his lawyer had still not arrived. Barent was tired of waiting. He picked up the phone. "Let's find him," he said.

Two hours later, it was apparent that Jerome Herbert could not be found. Neither, as it turned out, could Kurtz.

Chapter 35

The mob, or Kurtz' nameless assailant, or whoever was behind this, did not seem to think very highly of Richard Kurtz. They didn't tie him up. They didn't even bother to search him. And there were only two of the bad guys, the driver and the man with the gun. The man with the gun was about five foot ten, around thirty or so, wearing a black suit with a restrained blue and red tie. He looked like an undertaker. He also looked bored.

Good, Kurtz thought, let him be bored.

"You guys got names?" Kurtz asked.

The driver ignored him. The gunman shook his head. The gun never wavered from the center of Kurtz' chest. The gun, Kurtz noted, was a Ruger 9-millimeter with a blue matte finish.

"You want to tell me where we're going?"

"It doesn't matter," the gunman said. "You won't be leaving."

Somehow, Kurtz had suspected as much.

"Maybe you could humor me. Satisfy my curiosity while I wait for the inevitable."

The gunman gave him a doubtful look. "You're a cool one, aren't you?"

Kurtz shrugged.

"The cool ones sometimes get ideas," the gunman said. "Don't get ideas. You'll live a little longer."

It occurred to Kurtz that his situation might be improved somewhat if the bad guys continued to hold a low opinion of his abilities. He drew a deep breath, swallowed, said in a trembling voice, "You've got the wrong guy. I swear it. I didn't do anything."

The gunman only looked at him, gave a sad smile and shook his head.

Kurtz didn't ask any more questions and the gunman volunteered no answers. They drove uptown along the West Side Highway and when they got to the George Washington Bridge, they crossed over into New Jersey. They went through miles of suburbs and then the terrain grew hilly and the houses became scarce and a little while later they were passing fences and green fields and cows. The sun began to set. Altogether, they drove for over two hours.

Finally, they turned onto a two lane paved road, which wound steadily upward around a wooded hill. They passed the lights of small contemporary homes with decks and hot tubs and a few minutes later pulled up into a carport with a redwood canopy covering a blue Honda Accord. The Honda was empty.

The car stopped. The gunman stretched his back and yawned. After the first few miles he had seemed to take Kurtz' presence for granted, evidently deciding that a cowering Kurtz did not pose a significant threat. This had suited Kurtz just fine. Kurtz reached forward and grabbed the gunman's wrist with his left hand. "Fuck!" the gunman yelled. He tried to jerk his hand back. His finger squeezed the trigger. The gun went off, firing two shots. Kurtz had figured this would happen and even through the kevlar of the bulletproof vest, it hurt. Kurtz grunted but kept hold of the gunman's wrist and pulled the gunman toward him. With the palm of his right hand, Kurtz struck the gunman on the bridge of the nose. He could hear cartilage crunch. The gunman screamed. Kurtz hit him again in the same spot and the gunman screamed again, louder this time, then grew limp as fragments of bone penetrated the base of his brain. The whole thing had taken less than three seconds. Kurtz picked up the gun and pointed it at the driver, who was fumbling wide-eyed at his jacket. "No, no, no, no," Kurtz said. "Behave yourself."

The driver stared at him. Kurtz met his stare and grinned. "Now," Kurtz said, "what's this all about?"

The driver opened his mouth but seemed to have difficulty getting the words out. He cleared his throat and tried again. "Marty said to wait for you. He said sooner or later you'd be coming out, probably around five, maybe six o'clock. He said to pick you up and bring you along."

"Marty. Marty Burnett?"

"Yeah," the driver said.

"And what else did Marty Burnett tell you?"

"He said that Herbert had a loose mouth." The driver gave him a sideways glance and hesitated. "He said to grab him and then grab you."

"Jerome Herbert."

The driver nodded. "Yeah."

"So you already have Jerome Herbert?"

The driver looked down at the floor of the car and gave an aggrieved grunt.

"We're in a carport," Kurtz said. "Where is the house?"

"Up the hill. A couple of hundred yards."

"How many people are up there?"

"I don't know."

Kurtz found himself suddenly unamused. He delicately placed the barrel of the gun against the driver's forehead. "How many do you *think* are up there?"

The driver gulped. "Maybe five."

"Does that include Jerome Herbert or doesn't it?"

"No. Five of us."

Long odds, but maybe he could surprise them. Presumably, the rest of the bad guys hadn't heard the gun go off. Kurtz figured that was probably a safe bet, since the doors and windows of the car were all closed and nobody had yet come out to disturb them. Though if Kurtz and his abductors didn't show up soon, the rest of the gang would no doubt get suspicious.

"Burnett works for the Herberts," Kurtz said. "Why would Marty Burnett kidnap Jerome Herbert?"

"I don't know," the driver said. "I just do what I'm told."

Kurtz looked at him. He was young, probably in his early twenties. He looked scared.

Kurtz unclipped his cell phone from his belt and dialed 911. Nothing. He shook his head, not surprised. There were a lot of dead zones out in the country.

"You got a CB in here?"

"What's a CB?" the driver said.

"Never mind," Kurtz said. He shook his head regretfully. He really would have liked to have been able to call for some help. It occurred to him that they could back the car up, turn around and hit the road. Find a phone some place. Put in that phone call to the local cops or the FBI. Unfortunately, by the time he had done that and come back, Jerome Herbert might well be dead—if he wasn't dead already.

Five to one, maybe more. Kurtz sighed. "Get out of the car," he said. "On my side. Slide over."

Slowly, making no sudden movements, the driver slid across to the right side of the car, opened the front door, and got out. Kurtz followed him. "Raise your arms over your head and turn around," Kurtz said. The driver did what he was told and Kurtz hit him on the top of the head with the gun. With a soft hiss of escaping air, the driver slumped to the ground. Kurtz put the gun in his belt and quickly went through the driver's clothes. There was a Dan Wesson .38 in a shoulder holster and a Swiss army knife in his jacket pocket. Kurtz slipped the knife in his own pocket and the .38 under his belt. He took the car keys and opened the trunk of the car, where he found two folding shovels and a hundred feet of climbing rope. He tied the drivers hands and feet together, made sure he was still breathing, dumped his limp body in the trunk of the car and closed the lid.

Railroad ties arranged into steps led up and around the side of the hill. Kurtz ignored the steps. Burnett might have thought to post a man at the top. Instead, he went into the woods about twenty feet from the stairway and climbed up the hill, flitting from tree to tree. There was a full moon, for which Kurtz was grateful. The woods were thick. The trees, mostly old oaks, towered high over his head.

Less than five minutes brought him to a level area where the steps let out into a small lawn, which led to a cedar A-frame with two levels of decking, one on the ground and another encircling the second floor. A hot tub was sunk into the ground level deck. The A-frame was tall and narrow, three stories high. Kurtz had seen the layout before. The kitchen, family room and maybe one bedroom would be on the first floor, a couple of smaller bedrooms on each of the upper floors. The house was built into the hill. The upper deck was twenty feet above the ground in the front but only six or seven feet up near the back. Kurtz could jump it easily if he wanted to. There were two sliding glass doors on the upper deck, presumably leading into the bedrooms on either side of the house.

The whole front of the house appeared to be windows, all of which looked down across a wooded valley and at a line of mountains, probably the Poconos, on the horizon. No way that only five men could cover all possible approaches, Kurtz reflected, not with all that glass, but judging from the fact that they hadn't left a man posted at the top of the stairway, it seemed unlikely that they were concerned.

The sides of the house on the ground floor had only two small windows, presumably because there was nothing to look at from the sides but trees. The last tree was only about ten feet away from the house. Kurtz stayed in the tree line as long as he could, scurried across the few feet of lawn on his stomach, rose to his feet under the window and peeked inside. Jerome Herbert lay on a bed, all alone, his hands and feet tied together and a piece of duct tape across his mouth. His chest rose and fell slowly. His hair was tousled, his shoulders slumped. Gingerly, Kurtz tried the window. It was locked. Too bad.

He pressed his ear to the glass. He could hear voices coming from somewhere inside the house but the words were inaudible.

He scurried along the side and around the corner to the back, then through the tree line. From twenty feet up the hill, he was above the roof of the house, with a moonlit view of both sides. Nobody was outside. He climbed back down, reached up and, as quietly as he could, pulled himself onto the deck. He lay there on his stomach for a few moments, his nose only inches from the cedar planking.

Still on his stomach, he crawled around to one side of the house. The sliding glass door, as he had figured it would, opened onto a small bedroom. The lights were off, the bedroom empty. He put his ear against the glass. Nothing. Hopefully, all the occupants were downstairs. He grasped the edge of the door and pushed. It didn't move. Peering inside, Kurtz could see that the door was locked by a steel cylinder set into the bottom frame.

He could break the glass and get in that way. The floor of the room was covered with carpet. It might muffle the sound. He seriously considered it. Time was passing. Maybe Burnett was holding Herbert for ransom. If he was planning on killing him, there was no reason that Kurtz could see to wait. But even if they were all down on the main floor, they might hear the sound of breaking glass and five against one—maybe more—without the advantage of surprise was not good odds.

Kurtz worked his way around to the other side of the house. Another locked glass door, another empty bedroom. Kurtz was beginning to get desperate. He had just about decided to break the glass and take his chances when he heard voices. Kurtz stayed on his stomach. The light in the bedroom turned on. Two people, a man and a woman, came in and closed the door. The man was about thirty, well built, dressed in jeans and a tee shirt. The woman was younger, black-haired and very pretty. They closed the door. The man said something to the woman, reached out and ran his hand over her breasts while the woman smiled, closed her eyes and arched her back. Then the man kissed her, ran both hands up under her shirt and pulled the shirt off over her head. She wasn't wearing a bra. She stood there for a moment, letting him look at her breasts, then they both undressed. The man sat on the edge of the bed and the woman knelt on the floor between his legs. Her head bobbed up and down in his lap for a minute or so while the man caressed her hair, a soft smile on his face. Finally, he pulled her head up, kissed her on the mouth and lay back on the bed. She climbed on top of him and they began to move together.

Great. His own little dirty movie.

The woman's mouth was open. She moaned.

Kurtz frowned, then he smiled. The woman was moaning pretty loudly.

He scurried back across the deck to the other bedroom. Through the glass, he could see that the inner door to the room was closed. Good. He took the Swiss army knife out of his pocket, scored a deep circular line in the glass near the lock. He hoped the woman was still making noise. He took off his jacket, wrapped his fist in a sleeve and punched the middle of the circle. The glass came out in a single piece and fell to the carpet with hardly a sound. Kurtz reached in, grasped the cylinder and raised it. The door slid open. Kurtz stepped in and put his ear to the wall. The woman's moaning had stopped. Kurtz thought about it. The bad guys were split up. Maybe this improved the odds. Maybe it made them worse. He decided that he didn't like the idea of having the enemy behind him as well in front. He would wait. About ten minutes later, he could hear a door open down the hall. The woman said something that Kurtz could not make out and the man laughed and their voices vanished down the stairs.

Kurtz crept forward, opened the door a crack. The hall was empty. Trying not to make a sound, Kurtz put one foot in front of another and tiptoed to the top of the stairs. He could hear voices and laughter and the clink of ice cubes and music playing. Even bad guys like to party.

A lot would depend on the interior layout. If the stairwell opened out near the back of the house, then he had a chance of getting down without being seen. If it opened onto the living room or the den or wherever Burnett and his men were holed up, then he would have to reconsider his options.

There was a landing halfway down, where the stairway took a right turn. Kurtz crept down to the landing and peered around the corner. The stairs ended in a hallway. On one side of the hallway was the kitchen, on the other, the den. At right angles to the hallway was another, smaller hallway which led to the bedroom where Jerome Herbert was tied up. Kurtz crept under the guardrail, held onto the edge of the landing with his fingers and hung over the side. His toes were a few inches from the floor. He let go, landed soundlessly on the carpet and crouched under the stairwell for a moment. The voices continued from the end of the hallway, unalarmed. Kurtz could make out a word here and there. He took the .38 out of his belt and held it in his left fist, then, crouching low, he took two quick steps into the opposite corridor, grasped the doorknob with his right hand and turned it. He stepped into the room, closed the door behind him and locked it.

Herbert saw him. He raised his head off the pillow, made a gasping sound behind the tape covering his mouth and began to struggle. "Hold still," Kurtz said. "This is going to sting." He pulled the tape off Herbert's mouth. Herbert groaned. "Sorry," Kurtz said. He opened the Swiss army knife and cut the cords binding Herbert's hands and feet. The cords were tight. Herbert's fingers were blue. Herbert sat up, hissed softly between his teeth. His face was ashen and he was shivering. "I feel sick," he said. "I think I'm going to throw up."

"Take a few deep breaths. We're not out of this yet." Kurtz took a quick look around the room. The night table was bare. "No phone?"

"No. There's only one phone; it's in the den."

"Too bad," Kurtz said. "The local police would look awfully good right now."

For the first time, Herbert seemed to actually see Kurtz. "Where did you come from, anyway?"

"They grabbed me when I left the office."

"So? Why aren't you tied up, too?"

"It's a long story. I'll tell it to you later. Right now, let's get going."

Herbert nodded, rose to his feet, tottered for a moment and then collapsed onto the bed. He groaned. "My legs don't work. I was tied up too long."

"Rub them," Kurtz said. "Get the circulation back."

Gingerly, Herbert reached down and rubbed his toes. He grimaced. "It hurts."

"Keep rubbing. In the meantime, tell me what's going on here."

Herbert shook his head, looking bitter. "Burnett is not a dummy. He knew that I was sick of it. I suppose he was ordered to get rid of me or watch the game go up in smoke."

Kurtz looked at him. "Tell me about the game," he said.

"Briefly?" Herbert sighed. "Herbert Development has been owned by the mob for nearly seventy years. My grandfather was not much of an executive. It was 1937. The country was in a Depression. Prohibition was over and nobody wanted to pay money for bathtub gin. He sold out. He didn't have much choice, since he was in hock up to his eyeballs." Herbert grinned bitterly. "The corporation puts up the money. We invest most of it and ship the rest to the Cayman Islands or wherever. There are a dozen different dummy corporations and charitable foundations. And who owns them?" Herbert shrugged. "I don't know."

Kurtz shook his head. "Corporations have every right to invest their money overseas. What's the big secret?"

Herbert snorted. "The secret is where the money comes from. It starts out as heroin and prostitution and loan-sharking and extortion and anything else you can think of. Herbert Development is one giant money-laundering scheme."

"Oh," Kurtz said.

"Right," Herbert said glumly. He rubbed his hands together and groaned. "My fingers are numb, too."

"Wriggle them. Hurry up. We've got to get out of here."

"I'm trying, damn it," Herbert said. He clenched and unclenched his fists, groaning.

Kurtz watched him impatiently. Sooner or later, Burnett and his boys were going to get tired of partying and decide to do whatever it was they had come up here to do. Kurtz wanted to be long gone by the time that happened. Herbert tried again to stand, gave a stifled moan and sat back down on the bed. "A few more minutes," he said.

"I don't get it," Kurtz said. "After a whole lifetime, just like that, you decide that you've had enough. Why?"

"I told you why, back at your office. Eleanor, and Gina Cole. Gina Cole is why."

Kurtz looked at him. "Tell me about Gina Cole."

Chapter 36

"No," Lenore said. "He's not here. He's usually home by now." She was silent for a moment, then she grudgingly admitted, "I'm worried."

So was Barent, but he didn't want to say so. "I understand," he said. "I wish I could tell you more. Let us know if he shows up. Otherwise, we'll keep you posted."

Calls to Mrs. Schapiro and to David Chao both proved little help. David could pinpoint the time when Kurtz had left the office but that was all.

"At what time did Herbert walk out?" Barent asked Mrs. Schapiro.

"About one thirty," she said grimly.

Barent glanced at the clock. It was now almost eight. Plenty of time for Jerome Herbert and Richard Kurtz to vanish. Jerome Herbert might be worth kidnapping and holding for ransom. But Kurtz?

"What are you going to do?" Mrs. Schapiro asked.

What a mess. They had already put out an all points but beyond that, he hadn't a clue. Kurtz, and Jerome Herbert, could be anywhere. He glanced again at the clock, watched the second hand ticking away.

Anywhere at all.

"Wait," he said.

"We had an affair."

"Who did? You and Gina Cole?"

Herbert gave a tired little laugh. "She was involved with a man named Mark Woodson. Gina's mother had died a few years before. Her father was retiring and selling the house. She and Woodson were helping him pack the place up. They were rummaging through a trunk in the attic and they came across some papers that Gina's great-grandmother had left, letters from Joseph P. Herbert, Junior to Gina's great-grandmother, and some other stuff about the corporate finances back in the thirties. God knows why the old lady saved them. God knows how she even got them—stole them, I suppose. Maybe she had some notion of putting in a claim against the estate. Maybe she was the sentimental sort. Anyway, Woodson figured out that Gina was old Joe Junior's great grand-daughter. He tried to blackmail us. Gina didn't like blackmail. She told Woodson to take a hike but she was intrigued. Suddenly, she had a bunch of relatives she didn't know existed. She wanted to meet us." Sadly, Herbert shook his head. "She called and made an appointment with my father and myself. Dad was suspicious of her at first. I mean, after sixty years, what was the purpose of all this? He figured she was just a phony but she wasn't like that at all. She didn't want anything from us at all, just to meet us, just to talk." Herbert shook his head sadly. "She was so innocent, so sweet. I fell in love with her."

"Gina and I had a date the night after the hospital dinner. We spent the night at my apartment. Gina left in the morning. I never saw her again."

"Why didn't you go to the police?"

Herbert made a rude noise and gave Kurtz a look that said he should have known better. "Herberts don't go to the police," he said. "Too much chance they might get interested in the wrong crimes. Besides, we have our own way of dealing with things."

"Things? Like Mark Woodson?"

Herbert shrugged. "Woodson had evidently done some digging. He didn't have a lot of proof but his suspicions regarding the corporation were essentially correct. He was threatening to expose the organization. I'm not surprised he wound up dead."

"But naturally you don't know a thing about it."

"No," Herbert said. "And frankly, I don't give a shit."

Neither, frankly, did Kurtz, now that he thought about it. Not at the moment, anyway. He glanced at his watch. "Can you walk yet?"

Herbert rubbed his toes and grimaced. "A few more minutes."

Kurtz looked longingly at the window and sighed. "Why didn't you tell your aunt about Regina Cole?" he asked.

"We would have. I was planning on surprising her. Dad and I had talked about bringing Gina to the next family dinner, but then she vanished."

"How did your father react when she turned up dead?"

Herbert looked at him keenly. "He seemed distraught. Why? Do you think he did it?"

"I don't know. Do you?"

Herbert just looked at him. Kurtz said nothing. After a moment, Herbert looked away and gave a little shrug. "The thought had crossed my mind," he admitted. He shrugged again. "I doubt it. My father is a businessman. I can't see him as a murderer."

Murderers, or so Barent had often said, came in all shapes and sizes. The fact that Jerome Herbert didn't think his father had done it showed a touching familial loyalty but meant absolutely nothing. Kurtz said, "A man who is willing to have his oldest son killed in order to keep a family secret wouldn't think too much about murdering Gina Cole and Mark Woodson."

Herbert grimaced. "You mean me? I doubt that my father knows anything about it."

"Doesn't Burnett work for your father?"

Herbert made a faint, disparaging sound. "It might be more accurate to say that my father works for Burnett. The Herberts, let me point out, are not exactly the tycoons that we appear to be. We're employees—well paid employees, but employees just the same. A part of the front, that's all. Gina had no interest in the family finances and she wasn't trying to blackmail anybody.

"Woodson was a different story. Woodson was threatening to blow the whole scam wide open. I'm not surprised that they whacked Mark Woodson." Herbert shook his head sadly, then flexed his feet and took a few small steps. He smiled. "Let's get going."

About time. The window opened outward. It should be just big enough for Kurtz to scramble through. He removed the inner screen, set it on the floor and cranked the glass open.

Just then, the doorknob rattled. Herbert stared at it.

The doorknob rattled again. Outside the room, somebody said something that might have been a curse. Kurtz couldn't make out the words but the tone was definitely annoyed.

Kurtz boosted Herbert up to the window. "Climb through," he said. "Run for the trees."

A loud thump came from the door. The wood around the lock suddenly splintered. Kurtz scrambled up to the window ledge just as the door opened. Two men, both of them large, both of them carrying guns, rushed in.

There was no time to be careful. Kurtz let himself fall out the window. He landed heavily on his left shoulder and rolled over onto his back. His shoulder throbbed but he ignored it and pulled the Ruger from his pocket. A hand poked out the window, holding a gun. A head followed. The head was bearded and looked angry. The head saw Kurtz lying on the ground and the hand holding the gun came down. Kurtz shot him. The man's left eye exploded in a mist of blood and his head thudded against the window jamb, then flopped back to the floor inside. Kurtz scrambled to his feet and ran a zig-zag for the woods.

Two men charged toward him from around the front of the house. They didn't stop to negotiate and neither did Kurtz. Both of them began shooting. Kurtz dived for the tree line, felt a sharp pain along his calf, turned to his left and scrambled up the hill, trying to keep trees between himself and Burnett's men.

The bad guys couldn't see him but that didn't stop them from peppering the woods with bullets. A loud whine buzzed past Kurtz' ear and in front of him, a dried branch flew off a tree with a shower of splinters. It was hard to see where he was going, even with the moonlight. Ahead of him, a large oak tree had fallen, the trunk lying at an acute angle to the ground, its empty branches making a lacy pattern against the starlit sky. The base of the tree was covered with dried brown leaves, making a dark crevasse. Kurtz crawled under the trunk and quickly covered himself with leaves. Then he waited. His lower leg throbbed. A warm trickle ran down his pants and into his sock but it didn't seem to be too bad. He ignored it.

Burnett's men were city boys. They were no doubt pretty good at tracking a target down a concrete sidewalk but a forest—particularly a forest at night—was a different story entirely. Kurtz had grown up on a farm and spent his childhood roaming through woods much like these. Now that he himself wasn't making any noise, he could hear his pursuers quite clearly. Two of them were stumbling through the woods off to his left and another was behind him and to the right. He had already killed one of them. He wondered how Herbert was doing. If Herbert was smart he would hole up somewhere and wait it out. The two men to his left were getting further away. The one to his right was coming closer.

Kurtz pondered his options. He could hope to evade pursuit, lay low until his pursuers wandered off and then hit the road. A reasonable plan. The only problem was that he didn't know where Herbert might be and he doubted the younger man's ability to keep himself out of Burnett's clutches. Burnett and his men were probably not too good in the woods but then neither was Herbert and Burnett had a lot more men. Kurtz didn't doubt that a few phone calls had already been made. Burnett probably had reinforcements coming right now.

Besides, Kurtz wasn't the laying low type.

Leaves crunched underfoot, no more than a few feet from his head. A few seconds later, Kurtz could see a short, skinny guy with slicked back hair and a moustache stumbling by, carrying a gun in his fist. He passed not more than two feet from where Kurtz was hiding. Kurtz smiled, brought his own gun around and aimed it.

"I've got a gun pointed at your crotch," Kurtz said quietly. The little man froze.

"Good," Kurtz said. "Now, I wouldn't want you to get any funny ideas because then I would have to shoot you. You ever see a man who's been shot in the crotch? A lot of delicate structures in that part of the body. You know what I mean?"

"Don't shoot," the little man said.

"Then drop the gun and keep your mouth shut."

The little man did as he was told. Kurtz rose to his feet and touched his gun to the back of the man's head. Kurtz could feel him shiver. "Turn around slowly," Kurtz said. "Face the tree." Kurtz stayed behind him while he turned, keeping the gun against the back of his head. "Get down on your knees."

"What are you going to do?" The man's voice was terrified.

"Just do it," Kurtz said. "Otherwise I'll shoot you right now."

Trembling, the little man sank down to his knees, his head only inches from the fallen tree trunk. Kurtz transferred his gun to his left hand, reached out with his right hand, grabbed the man by the hair, slammed his forehead into the tree trunk and watched impassively as he slumped to the ground. Kurtz removed the man's belt and jacket, tied his legs with the belt, wrapped the jacket tightly around his upper body and rolled him under the trunk.

"Sweet dreams," Kurtz said.

Neophytes and city boys always went by the paths. Paths, after all, were there to be walked on. If you wanted to stay hidden in a forest, you stayed off the paths. A small path led away from the clearing. Burnett's men thought of themselves as the hunters, not the hunted. They had no desire to stay hidden. A few minutes later, Kurtz could hear them. He smiled. They were whispering, walking as quietly as they knew how but that was still pretty loud. Kurtz went off the trail and into the woods, circling. Five minutes later, he was crouching behind a bramble. A minute or so later, two men walked by. One of them was the big guy who had been having sex with the pretty woman in the upstairs bedroom. The other was smaller, a plump guy with thinning black hair. Both men carried guns, their eyes darting from side to side. Kurtz grinned to himself. It was dark out and they didn't know where to look. As soon as they passed Kurtz' hiding place, he stepped out behind them onto the path and said, "Peek-a-boo."

They stopped.

"Drop the guns and raise your hands."

They both stood still, hesitating.

"Don't think too long," Kurtz said. "I've already killed two of you guys today. A couple more wouldn't trouble me." His voice grew hard. "Now drop the guns."

They looked at each other and some wordless communication seemed to take place. They dropped the guns and raised their hands.

They were both young. They both had sharp eyes and tight expressions and neither of them looked particularly scared. "How many more of you are there?" Kurtz asked.

Both of them stared at him. Neither of them answered. Kurtz grinned. "I saw you making it with your girlfriend," he said. "Good looking woman. Is she out here, too?"

The man on the left frowned. "Fuck you," he said.

Kurtz made a clucking sound between his teeth. "Let's not get confused. I'm the one with the gun." He pointed it at the plump one. "Well?"

The big one turned his head to the side and spat. "You start shooting, Marty and the rest will come running."

Kurtz smiled ferociously. "That doesn't bother me. I know my way around the woods. You guys are clowns." He extended his arm until the gun was pointing at the fat man's head. "You have till three."

The plump one didn't look too happy. A fine sheen of sweat was beading on his forehead. "Wait," he said. "Don't shoot." He swallowed.

Lover boy gave him a disgusted look and shook his head.

The plump one ignored him. "There are seven of us, including the women."

"How many women?"

"Two."

"Are they out here, also?"

"No. They're back at the house."

So Burnett was the only one left to worry about. Kurtz liked that. "Okay," he said. "Turn around."

The two men looked at each other. "What are you going to do?" the plump one asked.

Kurtz sighed. "I'm not going to kill you unless you make me. Now shut up and do it."

They both turned around. Kurtz stepped up toward them and hit them both in the head with the Dan Wesson .38, the Ruger being a little light for the purpose. They both slumped to the ground and again, Kurtz tied them up with their own jackets and belts. They probably could work themselves free after a while, which worried Kurtz a bit. He knew that it would have been safer to have simply shot them, or better yet, to have slit their throats with the Swiss army knife, thus avoiding unnecessary noise, but Kurtz also knew that he couldn't do it.

From far in the distance, he heard shouting, then gunshots. Kurtz shut his eyes for a moment, ran down the path. His leg, where the bullet had passed through it, throbbed but otherwise seemed fine. The shouting grew louder. He plunged through a thicket, ran between the boles of trees, then up a little rise. No more than twenty feet away, he could see a large man, outlined in the moonlight, holding a gun. Lying on the ground at the big man's feet was a body. The big man nudged the body with a toe. It didn't move.

"Drop it!" Kurtz cried.

Burnett looked up at him. His teeth flashed white. He calmly put another bullet in the body, then dived for the cover of a tree. Kurtz began shooting. His first bullet went wide but the second hit Burnett in the leg and Burnett fell.

Burnett still had his hand on his gun but he was lying on the ground, the gun pointed down and to the side. Kurtz' gun was pointed at Burnett's chest. "Throw away the gun or I'll kill you," Kurtz said.

He could see Burnett hesitate. Kurtz almost hoped he would try it. He would have loved to kill Marty Burnett at that moment, fill him full of holes, watch his body jerk and shudder with every shot, watch the light go out of his eyes. But Burnett didn't give him the chance. With a flick of his wrist, he tossed away the gun.

Kurtz walked toward him, keeping his gun on Burnett's chest. The body was Jerome Herbert. Kurtz knelt down and put a hand on his carotid. A trickle of blood ran down the corner of Herbert's mouth. His eyes were open and staring. He was dead.

"Get up," Kurtz said.

"I can't," Burnett said. "You shot me."

The upper part of Burnett's pants was dark with blood. The bullet had gone through the fleshy part of his thigh. There was a lot of blood but Kurtz didn't think the wound should be incapacitating, not unless the bullet had broken a bone. "Bullshit," Kurtz said. "Get up or I'll kill you right now."

Burnett looked at him and decided that Kurtz meant it. Wordlessly, he pulled himself to his feet. "I underestimated you," he said. He looked annoyed. He did not appear to be worried.

"Start walking," Kurtz said. "Down the trail."

Burnett did as he was told. He limped a little but went at a steady pace. "Where to?" he asked.

"Straight ahead," Kurtz said. "Just follow the trail."

New Jersey was not exactly the forest primeval. Sooner or later they would come to a road or maybe a house in the woods. They walked for about twenty minutes before Kurtz saw a small log cabin in a clearing. There was a car parked in front of the cabin and lights danced in the windows. "Hey, in there!" Kurtz yelled.

A moment later, a man wearing coveralls appeared on the porch of the house, carrying a shotgun in the crook of his arm. He looked like he knew how to use it. "Can I help you boys?" he asked.

"Would you be so kind as to call the police?" Kurtz asked.

The man with the shotgun looked at him, considering. "I believe I might do that," he said.

Chapter 37

Marty Burnett lounged casually against the side of a swing set while they waited for the cops to arrive, apparently ignoring Kurtz. Kurtz kept the gun centered on Burnett's chest. Neither of the two men said anything and Burnett made no move to escape. The man with the shotgun stayed inside the house, which Kurtz thought prudent of him and which he appreciated, not wanting to be distracted. The police showed up within twenty minutes and ordered Kurtz to drop his gun. Kurtz did so. Burnett at this point put a wounded expression on his face and tried to claim that he had been kidnapped by a madman. Kurtz told his version of the story. The police decided to take both of them into custody.

They escorted them to a local Emergency Room first, where Kurtz and Burnett both had their wounds bandaged. Kurtz proved to have only a shallow laceration in the calf but it hurt and Kurtz was feeling a post adrenaline let-down. His head ached even worse than his leg. He wanted to go to bed and sleep for about twenty hours.

Burnett's wound was more serious than Kurtz'. The ER doc recommended keeping him overnight. Burnett was escorted upstairs under police guard. They took Kurtz to the station house.

Lew Barent arrived two hours later, along with Harry Moran and Lenore Brinkman. Lenore searched his face anxiously, then gave him a fierce hug and sat very close as Kurtz told them what had happened. Barent sat frowning the whole time. While they were talking, a pale man with a harassed expression, wearing a rumpled raincoat and a dark business with a tie, arrived at the station house. He announced himself as David Kravitz, Marty Burnett's lawyer. He glowered at Kurtz as he walked past.

"What's going to happen now?" Kurtz asked.

"Nothing," Barent said. The local police had already located the two women in the A-frame, along with the dead bodies and the four men Kurtz had tied up. The victims had been carted off to the morgue and the others had been kept away from each other. They had all refused to talk without a lawyer. "They'll make bail and you won't see them again until the trial. Don't worry about it."

Kurtz frowned. "It's my word against theirs', and there are six of them."

"The bullets that killed Jerome Herbert presumably came from Burnett's gun. His prints will be all over it. I don't think you need to worry." Barent grinned. "That is, if you're telling us the truth."

Kurtz gave him a hurt look.

"It's too bad about Herbert," Barent said.

"Yeah. I tried to save him."

Moran puffed up his cheeks and glanced at the heavens.

"Let's get out of here," Barent said.

Kurtz had only one case scheduled for the next day, luckily not until the afternoon, a sigmoid colectomy. He received a call from Adler at four-thirty in the morning, informing him that the prospective patient was having chest pains. Kurtz glanced at the clock and groaned. Lenore barely stirred. "Cancel the case," Kurtz said. "Have cardiology see him."

"Right," Adler said.

Adler. Kurtz shook his head. Despite everything, Adler was still officially a suspect in the murder of Regina Cole. Kurtz made a disgusted sound, rolled over and went back to sleep. It was nearly ten before he woke up again. Lenore had already left for work. Kurtz got up, scrambled a few eggs with some bacon and read the newspaper. An hour later, he was feeling restless. He decided to go for a run but found once he started that he didn't feel like running. He didn't even feel like walking. He decided to return to the apartment and take a nap. He woke up again a little after three. He was thinking about getting up and taking a shower, when the phone rang. It was Barent. He sounded pleased. "Some new information came in a little while ago," he said. "I'm going back up to Rye to see Eleanor Herbert. You want to come along?"

"Sure," Kurtz said.

"Then meet me at the station in an hour."

Eleanor Herbert was drinking sherry when they arrived. She looked grim. Not surprising, Kurtz thought. Her nephew had just been murdered and the whole rotten edifice that was Herbert Development was about to come tumbling down around her ears. The Justice Department had already been called in. A federal judge had been awakened the night before and had signed the necessary papers. Herbert Development was going to be invaded by the righteous hordes of the FBI and the IRS. Even if the corporation somehow avoided being seized and sold off piecemeal, the assets and business of Herbert Development would be tied up for years.

"You usually drink tea," Barent said.

Eleanor fixed him with a beady eye. "I'm not in the mood for tea this evening. I'm in the mood for sherry. Would you like some?"

"No, thank you," Barent said.

Eleanor shrugged. "Now then, you said that you needed to speak to me. I assume it's about Jerry."

"No," Barent said. "This isn't about your Jerry. It's about you. We know that Herbert Development has been a scam for over sixty years. We know that your father lost his money during the Depression and sold out. We thought at first that you and your brother were a part of it, that this place, this mansion belonged to the mob. I still have no reason to assume differently, except that we pulled the deed from the public records. Herbert Development doesn't own this place. Neither does Vincent. You do. It belongs to you."

"That is correct," Eleanor said, and sipped her sherry.

"Then I have to ask you," Barent said, "what is your relationship to Herbert Development?"

Eleanor Herbert, a mob boss? The secret owner, the criminal mastermind behind Herbert Development? Eleanor Herbert did not look like a criminal mastermind, Kurtz thought. She looked like a little old lady, a depressed little old lady.

"I have no relationship at all to Herbert Development," Eleanor Herbert said. "None whatsoever. I know about the corporation, of course. My father sold out his shares back in the 1930's. My brother used to work for the new owners, and now my nephew performs the same role. Exactly what that role may be, I don't know, and I don't want to know."

"And who are these owners?" Barent asked.

"I have no idea," Eleanor Herbert said, and serenely sipped her sherry. "The Herbert fortune, as you know it, does not exist." She grinned. "Which does not imply that there is no fortune. There is—the Renson fortune. My fortune. My husband was a wealthy man. When he died, this place was mortgaged to the hilt. I paid off the mortgage on condition that ownership transfer to me."

She smiled. "This is why I knew that my brother Vincent could not have killed Regina Cole. The motive that you assumed him to have was ridiculous. Regina Cole could not have made a claim on Joseph, Junior's estate. Joseph's inheritance, what there was of it, had long since been squandered away."

"Money," Kurtz said.

They all looked at him.

It was obvious, Kurtz thought. He felt a grin spreading across his face. All so obvious. "Tell me," Kurtz said, "do you have a will."

Eleanor Herbert seemed to find the question absurd. "Of course I have a will."

"So Marty,"—Barent smiled at him—"tell me, Marty. What would you do for money?"

Burnett gave him an annoyed look, a look that said Barent was wasting his time. Otherwise, he said nothing.

"We know you killed Jerome Herbert," Barent went on. "A man who considers it a part of his job to kill one man would probably not find it too hard to kill another." Barent grinned at the glowing tip of his cigarette. "Or a woman."

Burnett puffed up his cheeks and sadly shook his head.

Barent, who had conducted many such interviews over the years, was not discouraged. Burnett, despite his air of disinterest, was as attentive as a dog on point. "Now, jail is not a very nice place to be, I'm sure you know that. But there's jail and then there's jail. Frankly, Marty, I'm interested in only one thing here, and that's murder. I don't care about Herbert Development. I don't care about money laundering or loan-sharking or prostitution or gambling. I care about murder. We've got you for one. The question is, do we have you for two, or even three?"

"People die all the time," Burnett said. He idly inspected the tips of his fingers, frowned at a small hangnail. "Who am I supposed to have killed?"

"A young woman," Barent said. "A young woman named Regina Cole, and a man named Mark Woodson."

"Ah…" Burnett nodded.

Barent broke into a smile. "You recognize the names?"

"They were in the papers."

"This is so, and as I'm sure you can imagine, I want the person or persons who killed Regina Cole. That's my interest here. My only interest."

Burnett looked at him. "Tell me more," he said.

Barent smiled even wider. "I think you'll like it."

She was tough, Barent had to give her that. She sat in the chair and kept her head high.

Her lawyer, a tall dignified man named Gerald Conley, did most of the talking. "This is absurd," he said. "You have no evidence whatsoever against my client."

"Well," Barent said, "there is this phone bill." He handed Conley a slip of paper. Conley turned it back and forth in his fingers as if it were printed in hieroglyphics.

"March twentieth," Barent said, "and again on the twenty-second. And the twenty-third."

"So?"

"They're phone calls from the Donaldson home in Westchester to Martin Burnett's apartment in Manhattan."

"So what? Anybody could have made them."

"Really? Are you saying that Mr. Donaldson made the calls?"

Conley, evidently realizing that he was saying no such thing, frowned at the phone bill. "I am not obligated to speculate about who might have made these phone calls or the subject of any conversations that may have taken place. Speculation, as you well know, is not admissible in court."

Barent smiled at him. "Marty Burnett says that Mrs. Donaldson called him. He was very specific about that. He said that she offered him five million dollars to kill Regina Cole."

Allison, sitting in her chair, sniffed in disdain. Conley gave her a worried look.

"He said that the money was to be payable on the death of Eleanor Herbert. He said that Mrs. Donaldson was expecting to inherit nearly a hundred million dollars at that time. Do you want to know why Mrs. Donaldson was willing to pay five million dollars to have Regina Cole killed?"

Conley looked at his client and frowned. "No," he said. "I have no interest whatsoever in anything Mr. Burnett has to say. Mr. Burnett is under arrest for the murder of Jerome Herbert. His testimony could hardly be regarded as credible."

Barent ignored him. "He said that Eleanor Herbert's will divides everything she has among her nieces and nephews. The will reads exactly that way, except that she exempts her nephew Ronnie, figuring he's a priest and the Catholic Church has enough money. Aside from that, she didn't specify which nieces and nephews. Eleanor Herbert loves children, you see, and she's devoted to her family. She didn't want to play favorites, and maybe she suspected all along that a few distaff members might turn up, knowing what the men in her family were like. Anyway, if any of these nieces or nephews would happen to die before Eleanor Herbert, then their share of the estate is to be divided equally among their natural heirs. Lena Nye was, we think, the daughter of Joseph P. Herbert, Junior, which made her Eleanor Herbert's niece. Her only living descendant was Regina Cole, which would have entitled her to a third of Eleanor Herbert's estate once the old lady passed away. Interesting, no?"

Despite himself, Conley did look interested. He glanced at his client and frowned very slightly. "Marty Burnett told you this?"

"He did, and Eleanor Herbert confirms it, the part about the will, anyway."

"Conjecture," Conley stated. "Mr. Burnett is trying to put the blame on a convenient suspect. Why Allison? Why not Garrison? Or even Jerome? They would have had a similar motive."

"They might have, but only if they knew what was in the will. Eleanor Herbert is attached to her family, you see. When she went to have a will drawn up, she gave the business to Gordon Donaldson, which should have made it confidential on old Gordon's part but, hey, people tell their wives all sorts of things."

Garrison Herbert claimed to know nothing of the contents of his aunt's will, though he could have been lying. Barent didn't think so. Garrison had been as down as any man Barent had ever seen. "My whole life," Garrison had said. "Do you know what that's like? My whole life, living a lie, pretending to be a wealthy man, to have power and influence and respect, and the whole time, we were puppets, dancing a little jig at the end of a string." He raised a sad face to Barent. "But I was making it come true. My father had no interest in the business. Why should he? It wasn't his business. He was paid to keep his mouth shut and go through the motions, but I love the business. I really love it. I decided way back in the beginning that I was going to become what I appeared to be, and I had almost made it. I'm good at what I do. I'm very good. Under me, Herbert Development has become almost a legitimate corporation. Why take all that money, do nothing with it and ship it off to the Bahamas? I use it to build things. I make a profit. The owners appreciate that. I'm well paid. You could even say I'm rich."

"But not wealthy, influential and powerful," Barent said.

Garrison shook his head tiredly. "No, I'm not wealthy, influential or powerful. I have a nice house and a nice car and a nice pension and a couple of million in the bank. I could have made a better deal with a different company—a much better deal. Do you know what Michael Eisner makes? Paul Allen? Sumner Redstone? *Real* top executives? Hell, I eat lunch with those guys. They've got nothing on me. Nothing. But I couldn't leave. Burnett would have killed me. The fact is, I'm a hostage. I've been selected to pay for the sins of my grandfather and Jerry, if he lived, would have had to pay after me. That's why he drank so much. Jerry was the crown prince, the heir-apparent to nothing."

Garrison gave a resigned shrug. "I always knew Eleanor had the real money in the family but what will that do for me? It's not money that I care about. The money is just a way of keeping score. It's what you can do with the money that counts. No matter how much money I inherit, I'll still be stuck in Herbert Development, a bug on a pin."

Barent felt sorry for Garrison Herbert, which wouldn't save him from going to jail.

Nor, Barent thought with satisfaction, his sister.

"If that was all we had," Barent said to Conley, "you might be right. It's his word against hers, and Marty Burnett is not looking too credible, right now." Barent smiled thinly, a look that Betty always said made him look like a shark. "But there's also this." Barent pulled a small plastic box out of his pocket and placed it on the table next to Conley.

Conley looked down at the box but made no move to pick it up. "What is this?" he asked.

"It's a tape," Barent said.

For the first time, Allison stirred in her seat. She looked at Barent and frowned.

"A tape," Conley said.

"Yep. Burnett never conducted important business on the phone. He met Allison for lunch on four separate occasions. You can hide a tape recorder in a pocket." Barent chuckled. "Four conversations, four tapes. We have all the evidence we need."

Allison opened her mouth to say something but before she could speak, Conley held up a hand. "Unless you can play us these mythical tapes, this conversation is going nowhere."

Barent nodded. "I can play them," he said. And he did.

After that, it was easy. Conley, listening to Allison's voice calmly offering five million dollars for the murder of Regina Cole, appeared to visibly wilt. Allison remained impassive. When the tape was finished, she sighed. "Well, I guess that's that."

"Shut up, Allison," Conley said. "Don't make it worse."

"Shut up yourself." Allison looked at him coldly. Then she looked at Barent with eyes that almost glowed. "Do you know what it was like, growing up a Herbert, knowing that we used to be people that counted for something, people who commanded influence and respect, knowing that we were living a lie? When Gordon married me, he thought he was marrying wealth. Stupid me, I didn't enlighten him." Allison shrugged. "Gordon is not a very good lawyer. He's a handsome man. He's charming, good in bed, a good father, but he doesn't make a lot of money.

"And who the hell was Regina Cole, anyway? The great-granddaughter of a playboy and a whore. What did she ever do to deserve a hundred million dollars? That money belongs to the Herberts—the *real* Herberts, the ones who suffered for it. Regina Cole," Allison said with dignity, "didn't pay her dues."

Chapter 38

But who was Herbert Development?

"You know who they are," Kurtz said. "The mob. Mickey Nolan, guys like that."

"The mob." Barent looked at him pityingly. "The mob is a million different people in a thousand different cities and towns. Cocaine and prostitution and loan sharking are the merest tip of the iceberg. The mob is also illicit arms shipments to Syria and Iran. The mob is campaign contributions slipped into politicians' back pockets. The mob is hotels and banks and foundries and internet development companies. Mickey Nolan is just a crook. The guys at the bottom of this have had sixty years to keep their hands clean. Their grandfathers might have been crooks. Now they're institutions." Barent shrugged.

Institutions. Dead is dead, either way. Kurtz hoped that Jerome Herbert, wherever he was, appreciated the difference.

Barent, however, did not seem worried. "Thankfully," he said, "racketeering is not my job. Let the feds worry about Herbert Development."

A reasonable attitude for a man in Barent's position, Kurtz thought. The criminal enterprise that was Herbert Development was somebody else's problem. Good luck to them.

But help in the case against Herbert Development came in an unexpected form. The next evening, Kurtz' phone rang. It was Barent. "Eleanor Herbert would like to see us again," he said. "You up for it?"

"This is getting a little tedious. Why doesn't she ever come to see you?"

"Because she's rich, and because she's old. You want us to haul her in?"

"No," Kurtz said.

"Then be here in an hour."

"Right," Kurtz said, and hung up the phone.

"Again?" Lenore asked.

Kurtz shrugged. "I'll try not to be too late."

Lenore smiled knowingly, shook her head and kissed him.

An hour later, Kurtz walked into Barent's office. Harry Moran was sitting in his accustomed chair. A middle-aged man wearing a blue suit with a vest sat in the chair opposite. He had black, curly hair and a disapproving expression on his face.

"Richard Kurtz," Barent said. "John Haines. Mr. Haines is an attorney with the Justice Department."

John Haines frowned at Kurtz. "I don't see why we're bringing along somebody who has no official relationship to the case."

Barent looked at Kurtz and rolled his eyes. "Because we feel like it, that's why."

Haines sniffed.

A few minutes later they were on their way. Moran drove, with Barent next to him on the front seat. Haines and Kurtz sat in the back. The drive was awkward. Haines avoided looking at Kurtz. He seemed preoccupied, evidently the officious sort. Kurtz laid his head back against the seat and closed his eyes. He had almost succeeded in falling asleep by the time the car pulled to a halt at the front door of the Herbert estate. Kurtz yawned and followed the others out. It was dark and misty, a cloudy evening turning into a murky night. Kurtz thought it would probably rain. Very appropriate, he thought. He felt like Holmes running over the moors, pursuing the hound of the Baskervilles.

Eleanor and Vincent Herbert were both sitting in the drawing room when little group walked in. Vincent appeared despondent. His cheeks were sunken. He stared at the carpet and barely acknowledged their presence. Eleanor sat in a chair next to a fire, glass of sherry at her side, looking much as she had the other night, somber and grim. "Thank you for coming," she said. She glanced at Haines. "You are from the Justice Department?"

"Yes," Haines said.

"Good. My brother has something to tell you."

Despite her words, Vincent did not look ready to tell them. For nearly a minute, he continued to stare into space. Finally, Eleanor cleared her throat, at which Vincent blinked his eyes, gave a shrug and looked up at them. "I might as well," he said. "It's going to come out now anyway. After sixty years, I have nothing left to hide."

He sighed and his head sank down once again to his chest. "Your suppositions regarding Claire Reisberg were incorrect," he said. "I didn't kill her." A flicker of a smile crossed his lips. "But I did know her. I knew her quite well.

"The Van Gelden Institute was a convalescent home for the very wealthy. My father, in fact, helped to fund the place. It was, of course, not the only such establishment. There were at that time, and today there still are, perhaps a dozen similar institutions scattered throughout the country. The Betty Ford Clinic is one. The Institute for Living in Hartford is another. But Van Gelden was unique both in his attention to detail and in the range of services that he provided. If your Uncle Albert couldn't keep his hands off little boys, why the Van Gelden Institute was just the place for his recovery. If your grandmother passed out drunk by the middle of the afternoon, then Van Gelden could offer you help. If your eldest son had a liking for a snort of cocaine or two, then Van Gelden had a bed for him. All very proper and discreet. All very expensive."

Herbert smiled at them. "The rich are used to their comforts. The windows at the Institute had bars on them but the rooms were bright and airy. The food was the best that money could buy and there was wine with every meal, for those patients, at least, for whom wine would not interact poorly with their medication. The Institute had a swimming pool and a tennis court and even a nine hole golf course. The Institute catered to every one of their clients' needs. All of their needs, properly, privately and discreetly." He stopped and raised an eyebrow.

"Don't tell me," Barent said.

Herbert chuckled morosely. "Officially, Claire Reisberg was a nurse at the Van Gelden Institute but she never attended a nursing school and the nature of her responsibilities had nothing to do with nursing, unless your definition of the word is very broad, indeed. She and Veronica Nye were originally dancers at a speakeasy in New York, a business venture of my father's and one of his associates, a Mister Owney Madden." Vincent stopped and looked at them. "You've heard of Owney Madden?"

"We've heard of him," said Barent.

Vincent nodded. "Neither Claire Reisberg nor Veronica Nye were very talented dancers. But it served Owney Madden's purpose to have pretty girls on his payroll. The two women were more rivals than friends. My brother, at various times, was involved with both of them, separately and occasionally, together. My brother could afford his little pleasures, you see.

"Claire Reisberg was introduced to Van Gelden by my brother. Van Gelden found her qualifications acceptable and he offered her employment. She was beautiful and totally uninhibited and would do anything for money. She, along with a small coterie of similarly minded young ladies, serviced the needs of the male clientele, and for all I know, the female as well." Herbert hung his head and sighed.

Kurtz, who could not imagine where all this was leading but who was fascinated by the journey, waited patiently for Herbert to go on. Finally, the old man sighed again and said, "Harold Van Gelden was a remarkable man, an entrepreneur in the truest sense. He was totally unscrupulous but he gave good value for his money. Van Gelden was a legitimate psychotherapist, though his methods were unorthodox even for his own time and would be considered outright malpractice today. My brother was not his only patient in this family. Nor was my sister."

Herbert looked at Eleanor, who met his eyes with cool dispassion. Herbert said, "Van Gelden had a unique theory regarding the nature of psychiatric illness. He claimed a remarkable success rate."

Kurtz spoke up for the first time. "Deprivation therapy," he said.

"You've heard of it." Herbert smiled without warmth. "I shouldn't be surprised. Yes, deprivation therapy. Aversion therapy might be a better term. I understand that there was such a therapy, many years ago. It shared many characteristics with Van Gelden's. I don't know which therapy came first." He shrugged. "Not that it matters. But there was a positive side to the therapy as well as a negative, a reward as well as a punishment."

"Claire Reisberg," Kurtz said. Barent looked at him questioningly, then he seemed to understand. He nodded.

"Yes," Vincent Herbert said. "Claire Reisberg was the reward. Can you imagine what it meant for a young man of that era to be uninterested in women?" Herbert looked at each of them gravely. Nobody said a word. Moran frowned down at the carpet. Haines looked embarrassed. "Homosexuality is hardly accepted even today as a viable lifestyle but in that day and age it was regarded as bestial and unnatural. You could be deprived of your civil rights for harboring such feelings and confined to jail for acting upon them. I unfortunately, did harbor such feelings, though I only rarely acted upon them. I realized when I was only a very young boy that I had no desire for women, not for their bodies, at any rate. The thought of carnal intercourse with a woman, quite frankly, disgusted me. I experimented a few times with like-minded boys at school but I found the results unsatisfactory. I could not understand my feelings. I despised my urges and I came to despise myself.

"And so Harold Van Gelden and his psychological theories. Picture the scenario: I am in the arms of a Hercules, rutting, ecstatic, almost swooning with lust. Van Gelden pushes the plunger on a syringe of insulin and I find myself growing dizzy, then violently nauseous. I find my lust transformed almost instantly into an urge to throw up on my Hercules' hairy chest. For a moment, I black out. Perhaps I suffer a seizure. I find these experiences, on the whole, to be unpleasant. I begin to associate the Hercules with, uh, what is the term? Negative sensory impulses? Either way, I lose consciousness, and when I wake up, there is Claire Reisberg, naked by my side, soothing me, caressing me. She brings me back to life, you see. Once or twice, I even had an orgasm."

Herbert looked at them all. He raised an eyebrow. "Do you understand what I'm saying? It would be too much to say that the experience made me desire women instead of men. It did, however, make any sort of sexual activity seem not worth the risk. I became, for a time, impotent, which my poor father must have regarded as a step in the right direction. In later years, I married, and though my wife and I never had what I would regard as a 'normal' relationship, I was at least able to satisfy my marital duties. My wife eventually sought consolation in a series of affairs. I did not blame her for them.

"Van Gelden regarded me as a qualified success. Claire Reisberg, on the other hand, came to see me as an avenue to easy riches. God knows what she must have been thinking. She was a prostitute, but I suppose that ordinary prostitution, while it might have led to a scandal for someone in my social position, could at least have been dismissed with the easy notion that 'boys-will-be-boys.' I was something else." Herbert grinned again without amusement. "She came to see my father and threatened blackmail. My father was not impressed. He ordered the servants to confine her to an upstairs bedroom and called Van Gelden. Van Gelden came at once. He was shocked by his employee's behavior. He was mortified. He begged the opportunity to make amends. My father granted his wish. Van Gelden and my father went upstairs together and Van Gelden strangled her. It was as simple as that. They brought me along to witness, of course. It was a part of my therapy." He gave them a cold smile and fell silent.

Kurtz, Barent, Haines and Moran all stared at him. Only Eleanor Herbert seemed unaffected by her brother's story. She sat impassively in her chair, frowning out the window.

"But not quite as simple as that." Herbert winced. He closed his eyes and tiredly rubbed his forehead. "Eleanor, you see, was supposed to be in bed. She wasn't. She was eight years old at the time and mischievous. Her room connected through an inner hallway with the bedroom where Claire Reisberg was confined. She heard the commotion and came outside to look. She saw everything. She saw my father, impassively watching. She saw me, looking on in horror as Van Gelden choked her. She saw Lester, the chauffeur, wrap the body in a carpet and transport it down the back stairway.

"And then my father saw Eleanor, standing there in the corner of the room, tiny and shivering and afraid. My father was perhaps not the most intelligent of men. He associated himself with the most corrupt elements of our society in a vain attempt to promote the fortunes of his corporation, attempts which were, in the end, woefully unsuccessful. He was, nevertheless, not a man who hesitated at difficult decisions. He knew immediately what had to be done." He smiled at them. "And that is all."

There was a long moment of silence. Finally, Barent broke it. "Why are you telling us this now?" he asked.

"Why not?" Vincent Herbert said simply. "My brother died soon after Harold Van Gelden murdered Claire Reisberg, by his own hand…perhaps because Claire Reisberg was no longer there to comfort him. Who knows? My father's business deteriorated with the end of prohibition and he had neither the wit nor the foresight to adjust to changing times. He died a few years after. I inherited only debts." He shrugged. "The money was gone but I was offered a position in the new regime. They needed a Herbert to lend legitimacy to the operation. I accepted. I felt that I had no choice. Neither my education nor my inclination had prepared me to earn a living.

"My sister was drugged and tortured in order to obliterate the memory of what she had witnessed, and now my grandson has been murdered because of the mistakes that I made, as well as Regina Cole, the innocent niece who I did not even know that I had. No." He shook his head. "Sixty years is long enough. I am willing to testify. I am eager to testify." He nodded at Haines. "Call in the federal agents, the FBI, the Department of Justice. I will do whatever you ask."

Chapter 39

It was nearly ten o'clock by the time they returned to the precinct. Kurtz was surprised to see Lenore sitting in a chair in the waiting room, paging through a magazine, but he felt his heart beat a little faster, his step feel a little lighter, at the sight of her.

"What are you doing here?" he asked.

She looked up at him and smiled. "I got tired of waiting. I took a cab over. Was it bad?"

"You could say that. Vincent Herbert had quite a story for us. Van Gelden killed Claire Reisberg because she tried to blackmail Joseph P. Herbert. She was threatening to reveal that Vincent is a homosexual. Eleanor happened to walk in on them."

Lenore grimaced. "I see," she said quietly.

Kurtz yawned. He felt his shoulders slump, suddenly feeling the weight of all he had gone through in the last twenty-four hours.

"Did you stop for dinner?" Lenore asked.

"No, we wanted to get back." He grinned wanly. "We brought along a guy named Haines, a lawyer with the Justice Department. Herbert is willing to spill the goods on Herbert Development. Haines and Lew were both in a hurry."

"Would you like to go someplace?"

He thought about it, decided that he didn't have the energy. "I'd just as soon go home," he said. "I'm tired.

Lenore nodded. "Come on, then." They walked out, holding hands. The earlier clouds had passed by and the night was clear. The air smelled fresh. Kurtz gulped it down gratefully, deep into his lungs.

"How about if I drive?" Lenore said.

"Sure. That would be nice."

He sank back into the seat and closed his eyes. The ride home passed in a daze. Every time he closed his eyes, he would see Jerome Herbert's body lying in the woods, his lifeless eyes open and staring. He would see Marty Burnett looking at him calmly, without pity and without regrets. He would imagine Harold Van Gelden strangling Claire Reisberg while Eleanor Herbert looked on, eight years old and afraid.

Kurtz felt a sudden cold shiver pass through him and he zipped his jacket a little tighter.

Lenore's hands were sure on the wheel, her fingers long and graceful. Her blonde hair was held back by a hair band and fell to her shoulders. Kurtz reached out his hand and caressed her hair where it draped over the back of her neck. Lenore smiled. "Don't distract me," she said.

"Sorry." He closed his eyes. Five minutes later they pulled into the garage underneath the building. Lenore parked in Kurtz' reserved spot and turned off the engine. The sudden silence seemed strange. Kurtz yawned as they got out of the car.

A man stepped out from the shadow of a cement pillar. He was smiling and carrying a gun.

"Hi, folks," the man said. "I've been waiting for you."

"Oh, shit," Kurtz muttered. Kurtz recognized him…well built, a brush hair cut. He had paralyzed Kurtz with a taser before kicking him in the head.

The man made a tsk-tsk sound. "I told you I'd be back," he said.

"What do you want this time?" Kurtz said. What a dumb question. He felt ridiculous even asking.

The guy was young and good-looking, broad shoulders, narrow waist. He walked toward them, smiling. He carried the gun as if he knew how to use it. The gun was steady and pointed at Kurtz' head. "Revenge," he said.

Kurtz was almost too tired to feel fear but not too tired to appreciate absurdity. "For what?" he asked. "What did I ever do to you?"

"Simple. You killed my girlfriend."

Offhand, aside from a few hoods, Kurtz could not remember killing anybody lately, certainly no women. "I kill so many people. Refresh my memory."

The man gave a wolfish grin. "Kimberly Morgan. Remember now?"

The jumper. Kurtz stared at him. "Kimberly Morgan killed herself because her boyfriend flew off to California with another woman. Was that you?"

The guy's hand tightened on the gun. His lips thinned. "It was a dumb thing to do. We had an argument. I would have made it up to her, but thanks to you, I never got the chance."

Kurtz was standing between two cars with no place to run. Lenore was in front of the car, the gunman only a few feet away. The garage was otherwise deserted. A row of fluorescent lights in the ceiling cast a cool glow. The garage smelled of oil and gasoline and dust.

"She died from a fatty embolus," Kurtz said. "That sometimes happens with broken femurs. It was unavoidable."

The man snorted. "Baloney. You botched the surgery. That's why she died." He grinned again.

"This time there's a witness," Kurtz said. He nodded his chin at Lenore. "You plan on killing both of us?"

"Why not? You killed my woman. Why shouldn't I kill yours?"

There was the sudden sound of locks snicking into place. The lights in Kurtz' car blinked on. The gunman's eyes snapped to the side. The gun wavered. It was all the opening Kurtz was going to get. He charged. The gun arced smoothly back toward Kurtz. His only hope was that the bastard would miss but it wasn't much of a hope. Kurtz was still three feet away and already staring down the round, black barrel of the gun. The gunman's lips were pulling back into a smile, his trigger finger tightening, when Lenore kicked him. He said, "fuck!" The gun went off. Kurtz felt a wash of heat graze his cheek, then he was on top of the bastard. He heard somebody screaming, realized it was himself and didn't care. He punched the guy in the jaw and felt the jaw break, then grabbed the hand holding the gun and shattered the elbow over his knee. A scream ripped from the gunman's throat and the gun dropped to the floor. Then the gunman was on his back on the floor of the garage and Kurtz was sitting on top of him, punching his head from side to side.

"Richard."

He heard Lenore's voice, vaguely and far away.

"Richard, stop!"

It was almost like sex, raw and savage and deeply satisfying. He loved it. He felt a cheekbone break under his fists and he hit him again, the blood spraying.

There was an explosion. Kurtz blinked and looked up. Lenore was holding the gun, pointing it at the ceiling. Kurt looked down at the misshapen face, the bloody lips and swollen eyes. Abruptly, he rose to his feet.

"Are you alright?" Lenore whispered.

"Yes," Kurtz said shortly. He felt, suddenly and unaccountably, nauseated. "What happened?"

"I had the car keys in my hand." She gave a crooked smile. "I pressed the automatic door opener. I figured it might distract him."

"Well, you figured right."

Lenore grinned wanly. "I guess I should call the cops."

"That's a good idea," Kurtz said. "Why don't you do that?"

His name, Barent said, was Franklin West. He had served time in the Marines, and later had gone into government service. The FBI files were curiously reticent on exactly which branch of the service. What was entirely clear, however, was the psychiatric profile. Franklin West had been allowed to gracefully retire, under threat of summary discharge. In a service that valued discretion, Franklin West was a loaded gun waiting to go off. "They've washed their hands of him," Barent said. "Confidentially, they weren't surprised. The guy is nuts."

"Tell me about it," said Kurtz.

The money came from Chicago and San Diego. It came from Philadelphia and Tallahassee and Palm Beach. It came from Pittsburgh and Seattle and Las Vegas and a dozen other cities across America. It arrived dirty and it left clean, turned into condo developments and shopping malls and skyscrapers.

The story surrounding Herbert Development, an epic spanning four generations and seventy five years, was a sensation. The names mentioned in connection with the scandal soon included two current Senators and a former Vice-President of the United States. Everybody doubted that these men would spend time in jail but their political careers were, a jaded public hoped, at an end.

Eleanor Herbert continued to live in the big house in Rye and Charles continued to serve her. If she ever forgave her brother, nobody knew of it, and none were inclined to ask.

In consideration of his age and his willingness to cooperate, Vincent Herbert was sentenced only to a period of probation. He lived for another year and died peacefully in his sleep.

David Kravitz, Martin Burnett's lawyer, spent a spirited session with Ted Weiss, the Assistant District Attorney, and a couple of bland-faced representatives of the Justice Department. After five hours, they left the room. All of the men were smiling.

Martin Burnett was given limited immunity in return for his testimony against Allison Herbert. Burnett had guaranteed three of his men a cut of the five million that Allison had promised him. Since preserving the sanctity of Allison's inheritance did not exactly fall under the rubric of "Company Business," the agreement that they reached was entirely private. They waited for Regina Cole to emerge from Jerome Herbert's apartment, abducted her at gunpoint, strangled her in the backseat of a 1999 Lincoln Town Car and then dumped the body.

Allison was given twenty years to life. Her husband divorced her, moved to Miami with their children and opened up a law practice, at which he did moderately well.

Garrison Herbert was not involved in the murder of Mark Woodson, the order for which had come from somewhere much higher up in the organization, how high up, even Burnett was uncertain. The reason, however, was quite clear: only with the death of Mark Woodson could the ownership and true business of Herbert Development be kept secret. Burnett testified to this in a calm and level voice, without the slightest evidence of regret or remorse.

Though murder was not one of his crimes, Garrison Herbert was not held blameless for the sins of the corporation. Forty-eight hours after his indictment, Garrison Herbert went home at the end of the day and blew his brains out with a hunting rifle.

Martin Burnett served two years in a maximum security prison and then entered the witness protection program. He was found shot to death less than a year later in his apartment in Boise, Idaho, where he worked as a private security guard. His hands and feet were bound with duct tape. There were two bullet holes in his head, one in the left temple and one under his chin. Martin Burnett's killer was never found.

After the murder of Jerome Herbert and the arrest of Franklin West, Kurtz moped around the house for a few days, unhappy. His image of himself, as a man always in control, of his own mind if not of the events that surrounded him, had been dealt a severe blow.

Three incidents cheered him up. The first involved Adler, who was now entirely cleared of suspicion in the death of Regina Cole. Adler came up to Kurtz in the hospital and thanked him, then said, "It's ridiculous. Women I don't even know are calling me. Now that they don't have to worry that I'll strangle them, it's like I'm a celebrity."

Kurtz snorted. "Fifteen minutes of fame. Enjoy them while it lasts."

Adler rubbed his hands together happily. "You bet I will." He smiled at Kurtz. "Thanks again," he said.

"Don't mention it," said Kurtz.

The second incident involved Eleanor Herbert. He received a call from her at his office. "I'm sorry not to have come to you in person," she said, "but I find at the moment that I cannot bear the thought of leaving this place, of coping with the noise and the crowds—not now. I sit here in the silence and I listen to the voices of the past, or I try to. I try to remember. Sometimes, late at night when it is very quiet, it seems to me that I almost can."

"That's alright," Kurtz said gently. "I understand."

She said nothing for a long moment. Then she said, "I wanted to thank you. Without you, I might never have known the truth, and my family might have remained cursed for another ten generations."

Was the truth really so much better than the lies that the Herberts had lived? Eleanor seemed to think it was, and Kurtz was glad of that. Eleanor Herbert deserved whatever solace the truth or her family could give her.

"Goodbye, Doctor," Eleanor Herbert said. "And thank you, again."

"Goodbye," he said.

The third incident involved Lenore's mother, of all people. "Don't worry so much," she chided him. "Bad people, they do something that maybe they shouldn't be so proud of, this doesn't bother them. Good people, they worry about it, but what can they do? It's over. You did the best you could. So you're not perfect. Nobody is. Cheer up."

"You mean," Kurtz said, "because I'm worried, this proves that I'm a good person, and so therefore I should stop worrying?"

She nodded. "Exactly," she said.

Somehow, this reasoning seemed a bit circular. Kurtz scratched his head. He looked at Lenore, smiling serenely, and at her mother, who was grinning triumphantly. "Why not," he finally said. "Why not?"

Printed in the United States
131435LV00004B/151-243/P

9 781930 008120